THE WASHINGTON STRATAGEM

THE
WASHINGTON
STRATAGEM

A YAEL AZOULAY NOVEL

ADAM LEBOR

BOURBON
STREET
BOOKS

An Imprint of HarperCollinsPublishers
www.harpercollins.com

HarperCollins books may be purchased for educational, business, or sales promotional use. For information please e-mail the Special Markets Department at SPsales@harpercollins.com.

FIRST EDITION

Designed by Pat Flanagan

Library of Congress Cataloging-in-Publication Data has been applied for.

ISBN 978-0-06-233001-7

14 15 16 17 18   OV/RRD   10 9 8 7 6 5 4 3 2 1

For my brother, Jason LeBor

With the hammer she smote Sisera,
she smote off his head

THE SONG OF DEBORAH
which recounts the story of Yael, Judges 5:26

PROLOGUE

Astara, Iran-Azerbaijan border

Ramzan Hilawi forced himself not to stare at the gray metal door.

It was tall, narrow, and pockmarked with rust. It creaked when it opened and hung suspended in its frame for a few seconds before it closed, tantalizing those waiting to walk through it. At 7:00 a.m. the queue already reached back to the end of the customs shed. The walls of the building were khaki colored, the floor rough concrete, dotted with the husks of pumpkin and sunflower seeds. Three large signs each showed a packet of cigarettes, a mobile phone, and a camera, all struck through with red lines. The damp air smelled of sweat and tobacco. The crowd was subdued, anxiety hanging over them like a fog.

Hilawi glanced through the window, set high in the wall so passersby could not see inside. There was no heating and he shivered in his shirt and thin denim jacket. A baby cried, an old man coughed, the phlegm bouncing and rattling in his chest. Hilawi did not look around. His face was set in the expression of studied blankness adopted instinctively by those waiting to leave the Islamic Republic of Iran. A tattered poster, its colors bleached from the sun, advertised Iran Air's fleet of Boeing 727s. Hilawi imagined himself on an airplane, speeding through the atmosphere over mountains and seas, border guards and customs controls.

The door creaked and swung open again, then slammed shut. Hilawi had an almost overwhelming urge to sprint forward, barge the travelers in front of him out of the way, shove the border guards and customs officials to the side, and leap through the doorway into Azerbaijan. He might even make it, although it would be a very brief visit before he was bundled back to Iran. And it would certainly be his last.

Instead he flicked through his passport, stopping at the page with his personal details and his photograph. Black hair, brown eyes, a neatly trimmed moustache; regular, even features. A pleasant, but forgettable, face. His name was Ramzan Hilawi. He breathed slowly and regularly through his nose. Ramzan. Hilawi.

If questioned, he would be polite but not meek, courteous but not cowed. He had every right to cross the border here, indeed anywhere he chose. He was a postgraduate engineering student, traveling to visit his aunt in Baku. His rucksack held three T-shirts, socks, underwear, a Farsi-language newsmagazine, a bottle of water, an acrylic sweater, a packet of dried figs, and a bottle of perfume, a gift. He was born in Tabriz, Iran, in 1980. Tabriz. 1980. His widowed mother worked part-time as a secretary at a state publishing house. His father was dead, killed in the Iran–Iraq War. He was the son of a martyr and so should be treated with respect. This part, at least, was true. There was nothing different about this trip, he told himself. His passport was filled with Iranian exit stamps and Azerbaijani entrance ones. The fear was an unpleasant but familiar companion.

The baby was crying louder now, a stuttering howl, ignoring its mother's anxious attempts to calm it. A slim man stepped out of a side room. His eyes were a startling shade of blue-gray, his skin the color of cappuccino. He was bald with a carefully trimmed salt-and-pepper beard. He wore a gray suit jacket with a pale thin stripe and a white collarless shirt with no tie. It was illegal to sell neckties in Iran, although wearing one was permitted. But the regime's ultra-loyalists would not even put on a shirt with a collar. The man looked the crowd up and down, effortlessly processing the scene. There was only one Iranian agency whose plain-clothes officials could wander unhindered at an international border. Conversations stopped. The waiting travelers became intensely interested in their feet. The man walked over to the young mother. Her face turned fearful and she held on tightly to her baby. The man in the gray jacket smiled, patted her baby on the head, handed her a tangerine, and ushered her forward, to the head of the queue.

The customs officials waved her on. As she stepped through the narrow door, Hilawi could see the taxi across the dusty square, parked outside the Hotel Caspian. The car was a Soviet-era relic, a red Lada covered in a film of fine brown dirt. Its windows were greasy, the side door was dented, and the front and rear bumpers were missing: standard-issue local transportation. The driver was unfamiliar, but security demanded that they use a different person every time Hilawi crossed over. This one was a heavyset man with short gray hair. He sat on the hood, smoking and cracking sunflower seeds. He seemed to be staring at Hilawi. He cracked another sunflower seed with his teeth, and spat the husk on the ground. A half smile flitted across his lips. Then Hilawi saw the sign—a wire coat hanger was jammed into the radio aerial socket in the shape of a letter *L*. The door clanged shut again.

The queue crept forward. Hilawi was now third in line. A couple in their early twenties stood in front of him. Neither wore a ring but they kept glancing at each other, their eyes alive with excitement. It was difficult and dangerous for young unmarried lovers to be alone together in Iran. But Azerbaijan wore its Islam lightly—very lightly—and had no such restrictions. Their destination, Hilawi guessed, was the Hotel Caspian across the square, where rooms were available for the afternoon.

An elderly man with silver hair carrying a string bag waited at the head of the queue. He handed his passport to the Iranian border guard. The guard was skinny, in his early twenties, a wisp of a beard on his chin. He barely filled his camouflage uniform, but his stern expression showed that he was determined to properly discharge his duties as a protector of the Islamic Republic's frontier. He carefully looked at the photograph, back at the elderly man, checking his features, decided he posed no threat, and waved him through.

The young couple stepped forward. The hairs rose on the back of Hilawi's neck. He forced himself to not look around. His mobile telephone was loose in his trouser pocket. Hiding in plain sight, they called it. Everyone carries a mobile; it would be strange if you did not, they had told him at the safe house in Tehran. There was no reason for the border guards to take out the SIM card and examine it. None at all.

Hilawi felt the eyes of the man in the gray jacket on him. Not hostile, but certainly interested. Hilawi's heart sped up again. Acid rose up the back of his throat. This was not a place to spark the *interest* of the authorities. He closed his eyes for a second and steadied himself. The phone felt hot and heavy against his leg. The border guard looked through the passport of the young man and handed it back. He examined the young woman's documents with considerably more interest, looking down at the photograph, up at her, and back at the photograph, as if imagining how she would look without her hijab, possibly without other items of clothing. Her companion, waiting next to her, began to get angry.

The man in the suit jacket walked over. He wore fine black leather gloves. He waved his right hand impatiently, ushering the young couple forward, as though brushing away a fly. The border guard instantly handed their passports back. The young couple walked forward into Azerbaijan, their relief almost tangible.

Hilawi forced himself to think about the Lada. The Lada, just a few yards away, over there, through the rusting door. He had never sat in that particular car, but had traveled in hundreds like it. All he needed to do was imagine the car and he would soon be sitting inside, he told himself. He could almost smell the cigarette-reek of the interior, hear the creaking seat, feel the hard springs pushing into the flesh of his legs and backside when he sat down. What delicious discomfort, what sweet relief it would be. He could even visualize what would happen next. The driver would throw that day's newspaper onto the backseat; the months-old pine air-freshener and blue glass talisman against the evil eye dangling from the mirror would rock back and forth as the car lurched away from the uneven sidewalk, down the potholed road.

What Hilawi would not think about was the state of his brother's body after his remains had been returned to their mother from Evin Prison, in Tehran. Hilawi wondered instead about his contact. They were due to meet in Baku, the capital of Azerbaijan. Hilawi had been promised a suite in one of the new five-star hotels, overlooking the Caspian Sea. Last night, at the briefing, Hilawi had seen a photograph of his contact. She would fly from New York to meet him. She looked very pretty in the picture and he kept sneaking glances at it during the briefing.

Then he had done something very stupid. He liked her so much that when nobody was looking he had taken a photograph of her photograph with his mobile phone. Hilawi swallowed, trying to moisten his dry mouth. He had meant to delete the file when he awoke this morning, long before he arrived at Astara, but had forgotten. As soon as he crossed the border he would erase her picture.

Hilawi's turn was next. His heart thumped so loudly he was sure it was audible. He handed his passport to the border guard. The guard barely glanced at it and gave it to the man in the gray jacket. He looked at Hilawi, taking in his face, his clothes, his bag, then examined his passport.

His manner was thoughtful, almost delicate. He stood so close Hilawi could smell his breath, a sweet mix of fruit and peppermints.

"Wait here please," he said to Hilawi. He walked away, into the room at the back of the customs hall.

A snake writhed inside Hilawi's stomach. His skin prickled with a cold, clammy sweat.

Two minutes passed, then three and another five. The queue behind him was growing restless. Why did they have to be delayed because of this troublemaker? The sentiment was unvoiced, but it hung in the air. *A spy—arrest him!* Hilawi felt the walls of the customhouse close in on him. His legs wobbled. He thought he might faint.

The man in the gray jacket finally reappeared, talking on his mobile telephone. He looked at Hilawi and nodded.

Hilawi's fear suddenly vanished, to be replaced by a dull resignation. He would not shout or make a spectacle of himself. He would go with dignity. He looked at the door. It had not closed properly behind the young couple. It rocked back and forth, just an inch or two.

"Here is your passport, Mr. Hilawi," said the man in the gray jacket. "Enjoy your visit to Azerbaijan."

He handed Hilawi his passport back and held out his arm. Hilawi shook his hand. His grip was strong and firm. The leather glove was soft and cool against Hilawi's skin.

Hilawi walked forward. His hand was shaking and he struggled to open the rusty door. It sprang open and Hilawi stepped through.

Azerbaijan.

The smell of coffee, exhaust fumes, grilled meat. The

sound of Turkish techno music. Women with their heads uncovered. The sun hard and bright against a turquoise sky.

Hilawi wanted to dance. Instead he walked a few yards to the Azerbaijani border post, which operated out of an old bus. He handed in his passport. The border guard glanced at the first couple of pages and stamped it immediately. The customs officers sat on an aluminum table nearby, smoking and drinking coffee. He looked at them but they ignored him.

Hilawi stepped away and stood still for a moment, breathing in the dusty air. He placed his hand on his chest, his palm tingling, hot and wet with sweat. His heart slowed down. Hilawi looked at the Lada driver and began to walk across the square.

The Lada driver put his newspaper down and nodded at Hilawi. He cracked and spat out a final seed and opened the door. Hilawi smiled with pleasure, the relief still coursing through him as he clambered into the car. The Lada was just as he had imagined. The springs poked the underside of his thighs. The inside smelled of tobacco and the last remnants of a fading air-freshener. There was even a newspaper on the backseat, that day's issue of *Respublika*, an Azeri daily.

The driver put the car in gear and it lurched forward, bumping down the road. Hilawi sat back, picked up the newspaper, and scanned the headlines. Astara sped by, a blur of dun-colored buildings, hooting cars, children selling sweets and chewing gum. He read for a while but the letters began to shimmer and a roaring sound filled his ears.

Hilawi blinked several times and tried to focus.

The world spun and turned black.

PART 1

WASHINGTON, DC, AND NEW YORK

1

Yael Azoulay walked briskly across the Prometheus Group's lobby to the welcome desk, kitten heels clicking on the polished floor.

Tall vases of fresh orchids stood at either end of a long, curved slab of black granite, scenting the air with their heavy fragrance. A Gaggia coffee machine hissed and gurgled in the corner, wisps of steam curling around its burnished steel fittings. Yael was the only visitor. The receptionist, a sleek, well-preserved brunette in her midfifties, looked up from her computer screen. She regarded Yael with indignation, as though she was disturbing the sanctity of a cathedral.

Yael paused for a moment, and glanced swiftly at her watch before she spoke. "Please pass my apologies to Mr. Clairborne," she said, her voice polite and regretful, the hint of annoyance barely detectable.

The receptionist's face fell for a moment before she quickly fixed her professional smile in place. In all her fifteen years at the company nobody had ever walked away from an appointment with the chairman and CEO of the Prometheus Group. And it would be on her head.

"Ma'am, I can only apologize again. Mr. Clairborne certainly knows you are here and is expecting you," she said, her voice emollient. She reached for the telephone. "Can I offer you a coffee, some water?"

"Thank you, but I have just received an urgent e-mail. I have to travel back to New York immediately. We'll try again, next time," said Yael as she started walking toward the door.

It was now 11:27 a.m. Her appointment had been for 11:00 a.m. She had arrived twenty minutes early. After reading that day's editions of the *Washington Post*, the *Daily Beast*, and Gawker.com, it was time to put her iPad away and throw a grenade into the mix. Yael looked back to see the receptionist speaking on the telephone, her body hunched, her voice low and urgent.

Yael had almost reached the entrance when she heard someone call her name. She turned around to see a young woman striding quickly across the foyer toward her. Her blond hair was gathered into a tight bun and her bleached teeth gleamed under the artificial lighting.

"I'm *so* sorry for keeping you waiting; it's been such a crazy morning," she exclaimed. "Welcome to the Prometheus Group, Ms. Azoulay. I'm Samantha, Mr. Clairborne's executive personal assistant. Mr. Clairborne is *really* looking forward to meeting you. Please let me know if I can do anything to make your experience here more comfortable or productive. Mr. Clairborne is ready for you now."

Yael shook Samantha's hand. It was cool and dry, her grip firm but not aggressive. She sensed Samantha instantly assessing the cut, season, and cost of her clothes. Samantha wore a fitted black Dior jacket with a cream trim and a matching skirt that showed off her shapely figure and Manolo Blahnik shoes. Yael had seen the Dior outfit in last month's *Vogue*. She knew the shoes were Manolo Blahniks, because she had looked longingly at an identical pair in a shop window, but reluctantly decided that the $700 they cost would better be invested in her savings account, even though she had no idea what she was saving up for.

Yael let the empty words wash over her. Fareed Hussein's many requests over the last few months for a meeting with Clarence Clairborne had been studiously ignored. One had even been leaked to the *Daily Beast*. "UN Secretary-General Pleads for Prometheus Face Time. Again," the headline had read. As a last resort the SG had personally called an acquaintance who sat on the Prometheus board, asking him to intervene. Such a personal plea was a major admission of weakness, which indicated that Hussein's position, and office, counted for little. Clairborne had softened, barely. He still refused to meet the SG, but had grudgingly agreed to see Yael for fifteen minutes. The website had run another story this morning on the SG. "Fareed Hussein Denies Claims of Ill-Health, Aims to Serve Full Term." The article, which Yael had read on the train from New York, was an especially skillful construct. Most of the piece was taken up with speculation about Hussein looking increasingly tired, reports that he was suffering from blackouts, and two quotes from unnamed "Western diplomatic sources" expressing concern about his apparent ill-health. The denial, from Hussein's spokesman, was buried at the bottom.

Yael suddenly felt dowdy in her Zara black trouser suit and white fitted shirt, both bought two summers ago. A loose button fell off her cuff and rolled across the floor. She reached down to pick it up and a jagged pain shot down her left side. She breathed in sharply and stood up. The button rolled away.

Samantha instantly leapt forward. Yael used the moment to quickly check that the small blue enamel UN brooch pinned on the lapel of her jacket was securely in place.

Samantha bounced back and handed the errant button to Yael. "Are you OK?" she asked. Her voice was full of concern but a triumphant half smile played on her lips.

"Thank you, I'm fine. Too much tennis," said Yael, briskly.

The pain in her side faded but Yael's unease grew. Clairborne had a legion of former cabinet members and corporate heavy hitters on his board, the best lawyers in the United States, and a virtually unlimited pot of money to keep them all loyal.

She had a single sheet of photocopied paper.

In Washington terms, the Prometheus Group was a curious hybrid. Its headquarters took up much of a block on K Street, the only address that counted when it came to the capital's legion of lobbyists. The Prometheus Group was a lobbying firm, like its neighbors. It was renowned for its excellent connections to the Pentagon and the United States' numerous intelligence agencies. But it was also a private equity company, specializing in asset management in the Middle East, Asia, and the developing world. Its new security division, providing corporate security and intelligence, was open only to select clients who were guaranteed anonymity. Their names were the subject of much fevered speculation in DC's clubs and bars.

Prometheus claimed to have strong firewalls between its divisions to prevent messy conflicts of interest. But few believed the claims, especially in a town where so many had made fortunes from blurring the lines. Either way, the group's shares had more than doubled in value over the last two years. Two investigative bloggers had tried to dig deeper into the company's wealth and its military and intelligence connections, but their stories had not been followed up by the mainstream media. One of the bloggers was quickly outed, apparently, as a pedophile and had closed his site. The other was now working for Prometheus's corporate liaison department.

Despite the flowers, the newspapers, and the coffee machine, the lobby was less welcoming than it seemed. The ceiling was studded with small black half domes, which concealed wide-angle CCTV cameras. A thick wall of reinforced glass ran across the front of the lobby. The only way in and out was through a circular steel-and-glass cubicle in the middle of the glass wall. For the cubicle doors to open, the doormen had to manually punch a code into a keypad. A heavy wooden door, at the back of the area, controlled access to the suites of offices. The doormen, both of whom had the build and posture of former soldiers, wore blue suits, white shirts, and navy ties emblazoned with "PG." Two heavily built men, dressed in the same outfit, sat on the leather sofas at each end of the foyer. All had copies of the *Washington Post* on their laps. The four men seemed to be waiting for someone, but they did not pick up or read their newspapers.

One wall was covered with photographs of board mem-

bers: two vice presidents, three former secretaries of state—
one dating back to the Kissinger era—an equal number
of former national security advisers, and at least a dozen
former congressmen and senior diplomats, including two
former US ambassadors to the United Nations. The latest
addition to the board of the Prometheus Group was Eugene
Packard, a hugely popular television evangelist.

Yael walked back across the lobby with Samantha. They
stood by the wooden door, which was firmly closed. Yael
watched with interest as Samantha rested her right palm on
a small monitor mounted on the wall. There was a keypad
above. The monitor lit up; Samantha covered the pad with
her left hand and punched in a six-figure code. The keypad
beeped once. Samantha then placed her right thumb in the
center of the screen. It beeped again, the main door opened,
and they rode the elevator together. It stopped at the twelfth
floor but the door did not open. Samantha inserted a special
key, embossed with the PG logo, into a narrow slot on the
side of the cabin. The door slid aside, and they stepped into
an anteroom. A slim Southeast Asian lady in her sixties,
elegantly dressed in a green business suit, sat at her desk in
front of a computer monitor, wearing a headset and microphone. She smiled at the two women and buzzed Clairborne, informing him that his visitor had arrived. The door
to his office swung open.

"Ms. Az-ou-*lay*," exclaimed Clairborne, stretching out
the syllables of her surname in his Alabama accent as he
bounded forward to greet her. "Thank you so much for
making the time to visit with us today."

Everything about Clarence Homer Lincoln Clairborne

III was big. His shoulders, a reminder of his time as a line-backer on the University of Alabama football team; his hands, the flesh of which swelled around his wedding and college rings; his hair, a stiff helmet of red and gray, held in place by gel and spray; his face, burned mahogany on the deck of his oceangoing yacht and the golf course; his hand-tailored suit with its roomy, two-button jacket and deep lapels that could not conceal the epic swell of his stomach. Even his voice was big, booming across his office as he greeted Yael.

Clairborne ushered her to a corner, where two leather armchairs stood, identical to those in the reception area. A small side table stood between them, a jug of water and a large cigar box standing on it, its lid embossed with a large "PG."

Yael sat down, the polished leather squeaking underneath. Her pulse quickened; her senses were on full alert as she scoped her surroundings, totally focused now. The parquet wooden floor was covered with an enormous single Persian rug, the walls wood paneled, while an old-fashioned desk with a rectangle of green leather on the writing surface took up most of one corner. Two photographs in silver frames, of a young woman and a teenage boy who looked like a youthful version of Clairborne, stood on its right-hand corner. The lighting was muted and the air smelled faintly of cigar smoke and fresh coffee. The most important signifier in any Washington office, Yael knew, was the occupant's power wall. Company foyers showcased an array of formal portraits of the board members, while the CEO's office usually had more relaxed shots, showing him glad-handing, eating, and drinking with the great and good. There was a hierarchy to decode: a snatched picture at an event with a DC rainmaker was lower on the totem pole than a common table at a charity dinner. Best of all was something *à deux*: just the two guys, enjoying themselves and shooting the breeze.

Yael had expected to see an array of casual pictures of Clairborne with the numerous VIPs whose official portraits filled the reception area. Instead there were just four photographs, separately displayed and all roughly the size of a sheet of printer paper—small by Washington standards. Three showed Clairborne playing golf with the last three former presidents. In each Clairborne had his arm around the president's shoulders. The fourth, mounted away from the others, showed Clairborne shaking hands with Eugene Packard, the television evangelist. The chairman of the Prometheus Group, Yael understood, was subtler than he first appeared.

Yael declined his offer of coffee or tea and placed her mobile telephone on the side table between the chairs. She sensed him watching her, like a lion scoping a nearby zebra, and quickly deciding that this young woman from an organization he despised posed no threat. He had marked his territory. Now it was her turn. A blue light at the bottom of her phone blinked repeatedly.

"Please switch off the microphones and cameras, Mr. Clairborne."

Clairborne looked at the phone, and back at her. "This room is swept twice a day, Ms. Azoulay."

Yael nodded. "It's not intruders' mikes that I'm worried about."

Clairborne smiled, amused. "You have to watch your back in this town, Ms. Azoulay. You never know what might end up on YouTube."

Yael sat back and said nothing. The silence stretched out. Clairborne gave her a long look, as though reassessing his initial judgment. He stood up, walked over to the telephone on his desk, and punched a series of numbers into the keypad. The blue light on Yael's phone went out, replaced by a green one.

"Thank you," said Yael, as Clairborne returned and sat down.

"You know the rules," replied Clairborne, gesturing at her phone.

Yael nodded. She slid out her mobile's battery and SIM card and laid the pieces of the telephone on the table. "So do you."

Clairborne did the same. He offered Yael a glass of water. She nodded and he poured them both one. He emptied the glass in one draft and looked at her. "What can I do for you?" he asked, his voice now cool and businesslike.

Yael explained what she wanted, slowly and in detail. Clairborne watched her as she spoke, his wide, doughy face impassive.

She had prepared for this meeting for a week. Her briefing notes were an inch thick. They included a detailed history of the Prometheus Group, biographies of its key personnel and directors, and flowcharts showing Prometheus's reach into each US government department and the firm's contact official there. There were multiple lines in and out of the major departments, including Commerce, Treasury, Labor, Justice, Transportation, the Federal Reserve, and the Immigration and Naturalization Service, and fewer connections into smaller departments such as Food Safety. The Pentagon had four separate pages, one each for army, navy, air force, and procurement. Yael had read the notes several times in New York, and again on the train that morning. She had been briefed verbally on Prometheus's connections to the United States' intelligence agencies, by her UN colleague Quentin Braithwaite, a former British army officer. Prometheus, Braithwaite had explained, was especially well connected to a new US government covert agency that operated off the books. Braithwaite had forbidden Yael from taking any notes at his briefing. Nor was she to discuss or mention this new agency on the telephone or in any electronic communications, no matter how well encrypted.

Clairborne was silent for several seconds. "Ms. Azoulay, I really have no idea what you are talking about."

Yael took a sip of her water before she spoke. "Maybe I wasn't clear enough. The Iranian regime is under sanctions. It is illegal for American firms to do business with Iran, whether directly or through foreign-based subsidiaries. It is especially illegal for American firms to do business with the Revolutionary Guard, which as you surely know, has been designated a terrorist organization."

Clairborne shrugged, his eyebrows raised, his hands open and forward in the universal declaration of innocence. "Indeed it has. But I have no idea why you are sitting here telling me that. I am sorry, Ms. Azoulay, that you seem to have had a wasted trip. If there is anything else we can help you with, anything at all . . ."

"You should know, Mr. Clairborne," said Yael, holding his gaze, "that President Freshwater is taking a strong personal interest in this matter."

Renee Freshwater, the first female president of the United States, had been in office for three years. As the most liberal Democrat to ever hold office, her election had provoked fury among Republicans. She had started her career in the State Department, where she had been one of the most outspoken advocates for intervention during the genocide in Rwanda in 1994. She had risen up the ranks to serve as the United States ambassador to the United Nations, from where she had been appointed secretary of state. Once in office, Freshwater had twisted Congress's arm to force through reforms on labor law, immigration, and banking regulation, enraging Wall Street. But it was her decision to sign up the United States to the International Criminal Court that had sent her conservative opponents into a frenzy. Based in The Hague, the Dutch seat of government, the court had been set up in the wake of the genocides in Rwanda and Bosnia, with the aim of preventing future mass slaughters. Freshwater had now agreed to the theoretical possibility that American citizens could be extradited to The Hague for war crimes or crimes against humanity. This, her opponents had pledged, would never happen. The Republicans declared all-out war on her administration, aided behind the scenes by numerous right-wing Democrats who wanted Freshwater out, to be replaced by one of their own.

President Freshwater's husband, Eric, had been killed in a skiing accident, the full circumstances of which remained unclear, while on holiday in Aspen last year. The investigation, which was still ongoing, had not come up with a concrete explanation of why his bindings had suddenly failed, or why he had suddenly skied away from his family and gone off-piste. Many had expected Freshwater to resign. Instead she had renewed her onslaught on the corporate world with ever-increasing vigor, targeting military subcontractors and the outsourcing of intelligence to the commercial sector, especially focusing on the Prometheus Group. But Freshwater's political honeymoon was long over, the sympathy engendered by the death of her husband evaporated. Her most recent bill, which would have brought all outsourced security functions—whether field operations or desk analysis—back under government control, had been thoroughly wrecked by Congress in a rare bipartisan filibuster. Freshwater's plans for intervention in Syria were also quickly derailed.

Clairborne sat back, completely unfazed by the mention of the president's name. "So what? Renee Dead-in-the-Water can bring another bill to Congress." He brushed some imaginary fluff from his trousers. "Under whose authority are you here today, Ms. Azoulay?" he asked, the last trace of Southern bonhomie now gone.

"I represent Fareed Hussein, the secretary-general of the United Nations."

Clairborne laughed. "How is Fareed? I just read that he's not doing too well at the moment."

"He's fine. What matters to you is that he is mandated

by the P5, the permanent five members of the Security Council. Including the United States, whose government has contracts with Prometheus worth one point two billion and which shares his concerns."

Clairborne's smile faded. He extracted a cigar from the box on his desk. He examined the tube of tobacco, probing it for firmness, before holding it up in front of him. "Well now, Ms. Azoulay. Why don't you let me think about this. I will consult my board of directors and get back to you, just as soon as I can."

"No," said Yael.

Clairborne looked puzzled, as though he had never heard the word before. "Pardon?" He leaned forward as he spoke, his face set, his shoulders seeming to swell around him as he stared at Yael.

"You heard me, Mr. Clairborne. This ends today. Now. You cut your connection with Tehran."

She watched Clairborne carefully. Yael read people: She knew the meaning of every eye movement, curl of the mouth, touch of the tongue to the teeth, dilated vein under the skin, subtle intake of breath or exhalation, tiny flicker of emotion across a face—the microsigns that to everyone else were imperceptible. She knew when someone was dissembling, when they were telling the truth, and even when they were perhaps subconsciously trying to tell the truth, albeit buried under a carapace of lies. Behind his belligerent exterior, Clairborne also had his ghosts. She remembered her briefing notes: "Despite his success, Clairborne remains insecure, haunted by the memory of his father, Stockwell, whose business empire collapsed almost overnight after he bounced a check. Stockwell had been running a pyramid scheme. He was arrested and sent to prison for fraud. His son visited him once and was profoundly traumatized by the experience. Stockwell later died in prison and his name is never mentioned."

"And what if I refuse your . . . request?" asked Clairborne, turning the cigar over and over between his fingers.

Clairborne was playing for time, a classic ploy. The side of his mouth twitched twice, while a vein on the right side of his temple pulsed fast. She could feel him thinking, his mind racing as he asked himself, *How the hell did they find out . . . ?*

Yael said, "You should also know that the Department of Justice, the District of Columbia state attorney, and the FBI regard the Prometheus Group as an object of interest."

"Is that a threat?"

Yael shook her head. "Of course not. Merely a statement of fact."

"Ms. Azoulay, as I said, I will get back to you when I have considered your request. You have made a number of accusations here, very serious accusations, and I will need to consult my lawyers and other board members. . . ."

"Mr. Clairborne, I am not accusing you of anything. I am merely bringing to you a request for your assistance with a sensitive matter that is of interest to a number of parties."

Clairborne lumbered to his feet. "Thank you for your time, Ms. Azoulay. I will be in touch when I have some news for you."

Time to strike, Yael thought. Her heart was thumping, but she was pleased to see her hand was steady.

"Please sit down, Mr. Clairborne," she said.

Clairborne stared at her, his expression a mix of puzzlement and hostility.

Yael gestured at the armchair. He sat back down. Clairborne's nickname was "the Bull." Now she would be the matador. She opened her leather folio and slid the sheet of paper across the table.

Clairborne glanced at the paper quickly, then again, more slowly. He placed the paper on his lap and stared into space for several seconds, patting his hair, as if to check each strand was still in place before standing up and walking over to the photograph of Eugene Packard. He looked at the television evangelist for a full minute before returning to his seat. Clairborne sat down, closed his eyes, and gently rocked back and forth, the fingers of each hand resting on his temples as he silently and fluently mouthed the familiar words of prayer.

"Where did you get this?" he eventually asked.

"Keep it," said Yael. "We have plenty of copies. Give it to your lawyer. You may need one soon. Once it is all over the Internet."

Clairborne leaned back and suddenly laughed out loud, a deep rolling sound that came from inside his belly. "Are you shitting me? Do you want a job here, Ms. Azoulay?"

Yael shook her head. "No thanks. Your answer, please."

The smile vanished from Clairborne's face as quickly as it had appeared. Underneath the joshing, he was unused to losing—especially in his own office.

Clairborne slapped the arm of the leather chair. The noise sounded like a pistol shot. "This is blackmail. You have no right to come in here, to my office, to blackmail and threaten me."

Yael stood her ground, now certain of her instincts. "Mr. Clairborne. I am not blackmailing you. I have made a request of you. Now I am merely showing you a piece of evidence that may assist you in making the right decision."

She paused. Stockwell. "Decisions have consequences, Mr. Clairborne. A single bad move and the whole edifice can come crashing down. Bankruptcy. Prison."

Clairborne stared at her, his eyes glacial, his body rigid with anger. "I think it's time you left."

Yael pushed harder. Angry people made mistakes. "It's not me that you have to worry about. The president has got you by the balls, Mr. Clairborne. She is going to shut you down. You could be looking at ten to fifteen. I don't think your VIP friends will be coming to visit you in jail."

Clairborne's fingers turned white as he gripped his armchair. He reared up, his nostrils flaring. "The president can go fuck herself. Which nowadays is her only option. We . . . ," he said, suddenly stopping in midsentence.

He sat back down, closed his eyes for a few moments, and slowed his breathing. "Nice work, Ms. Azoulay."

Yael watched him slide the end of the cigar into the cutter, suddenly the very picture of self-control.

"Are you familiar with the word *krysha*?" he asked.

"It's Russian for *roof*." The word was also mafia slang for protection, she knew.

Clairborne pressed down on the edge of the cutter. The blade slid through the packed tobacco. The end tumbled off like the head of an aristocrat guillotined in revolutionary Paris.

Yael watched the stub roll to the edge of the desk.

"Tornado season is coming soon, Ms. Azoulay," said Clairborne. He flicked the stub into the nearby trash can. "Check your krysha."

2

Najwa al-Sameera carefully picked up a half-full cup of cold coffee from the edge of Sami Boustani's desk and placed it on a nearby filing cabinet; cleared a space among the piles of yellowing press releases, reports, drafts of future reports, and reports about reports; shifted the glossy UN magazines extolling the virtues of sustainability and conservation and the pile of used notebooks aside; dropped the last third of a stale iced doughnut in the trash can; and finally perched herself on the desk's edge.

She considered the scene in front of her. The last time Najwa had seen the UN correspondent for the *New York Times*, he was dressed in his typical uniform of baggy jeans and untucked long-sleeved shirt worn over a T-shirt, his black curly hair was long and unkempt, and he needed a shave. As usual, he looked like a scruffy graduate student who had wandered into a seminar after a long night on the town. It was a successful guise; over the years Sami's casual attire and apparently disorganized manner had deceived numerous UN officials and diplomats from around the world into giving away far more information than they had intended. But today he was wearing a pressed white shirt, a cream linen sports jacket, and blue chinos. His hair had been neatly styled and he was clean shaven.

Najwa tilted her head to one side before she spoke. "He looks like Sami Boustani. He types like Sami Boustani. He is sitting in Sami Boustani's desk," she said, her voice puzzled. "But where is Sami Boustani and who is this male model . . . ?"

Sami muttered a greeting but did not turn away from his screen. "I'm busy, Najwa."

She flicked through a clutch of receipts lying by his keyboard. "Busy shopping. Armani AX. Banana Republic. Bloomingdale's. Are you in love?"

Sami smiled and carried on typing. "What can I do for you, Najwa?"

"You could tell me what story you are working on, its news value, who your sources are, the basis on which they are talking to you, and their contact details. Then call them all up and tell them to talk to me as well," she replied, her toned legs swinging back and forth in her trademark black patent-leather boots.

Sami laughed. "I could, but I won't. But I will give you a heads-up an hour before it goes online. Maybe even a copy, if you promise not to run it before me."

"Of course, *habibi*. As if I would ever do such a thing." Najwa tried to make herself more comfortable in the small space she had managed to clear. "How do you survive in here? My offer is still open. And we have someone come in and clean our office every day," she said as she looked around the room, shaking her head. She sniffed the air and crinkled her nose. "Is something burning in here?"

"The new halogen lamp, I think," said Sami.

As if on cue, the bulb began to crackle and flicker. The United Nations bureau of the *New York Times* was barely ten feet by ten. The walls, recently repainted white, had already turned gray. The damp patch on the new white plastic ceiling tiles was larger than ever. The electric cable, which the maintenance team had repeatedly promised to secure, poked through the gap and was covered with condensation. A small window in the corner looked out on the building's airshaft. The newspaper had a standing request in for a new office, but it was a point of pride for the UN's building managers to give the major Western media, especially those that probed hardest for scandal and corruption, the smallest and most uncomfortable places possible. There was even talk that the *Washington Post* and the *Financial Times* might be forced to share an office. Newspapers and television stations from the developing world, such as Al Jazeera, were a different matter.

Sami stood up and switched the ceiling light off. The room descended into gloom. He shook his head. "Thanks, Najwa, but I told you, my editors would never allow me to share space with another news organization."

"Even though we work together so nicely?"

Najwa turned, stifled a yawn, and stretched languorously like a cat in the sun, her skintight blue cashmere sweater highlighting the curve of her substantial chest. Najwa was a niece of the king of Morocco, spoke five languages fluently, had degrees from Oxford and Yale, and had caused a minor scandal across the Arab world by modeling swimwear for a Parisian designer. The United Nations correspondent for

Al Jazeera had thick black hair, doe-like brown eyes, full lips, clear olive skin, and no compunction whatsoever about using her looks to get the contacts or information she needed.

After a year as neighbors and occasional colleagues, Sami knew every one of Najwa's weapons for disarming uncooperative males. Almost every male reporter among the two hundred or so correspondents accredited to the UN had invited her for lunch, together with a good number of females. Najwa usually said yes, then filleted her hosts of their insight, insider information, and usually a good number of contacts as well. Occasionally she progressed to a one-off dinner. But that was it.

Sami and Najwa had settled into an easy camaraderie, with an undercurrent of rivalry, punctuated by sporadic moments of bickering and flirtation. They both knew that Najwa's languorous sexuality had the ability to unsettle him. Sami made sure not to turn and watch the brief show, to keep focused on his computer screen.

Najwa's star was rising at Al Jazeera, the most popular independent television channel in the Arab and developing world. Her investigation of women's rights—or the lack of them—in Saudi Arabia had got her banned for life from the kingdom, and a deluge of death threats on Facebook and Twitter from Sunni extremists. But it was her recent documentary, coscripted with Sami, that had firmly established her reputation as one of the most influential new media voices.

"How is your girlfriend, Sami?" she asked.

Sami blinked, a slight flush on his cheeks. "She is not my girlfriend."

"Whatever. How many dates have you had?"

"Two," said Sami, his voice terse as his typing sped up.

Najwa smiled. "Two. That's good. She must like you."

"I hope so. How is your fiancé?" asked Sami, brightly.

"As handsome and successful as ever. He is due here later this month. I will introduce you when he arrives. I'm sure you will like him. We will all have dinner together," Najwa replied, easily parrying Sami's riposte.

"That would be fun," said Sami, doubtfully. Najwa's fiancé was always about to arrive but so far had never been seen inside the building, or, as far as he knew, anywhere else in New York. "What was his name again?"

Najwa ignored the question. "So when is your next date?"

Sami smiled. "Tomorrow."

Najwa looked thoughtful. "Third date. The big one. Where are you going?"

"To her place."

"No wonder you are looking so good." Najwa shook her head, regretfully. "It's not a good idea, habibi. I will introduce you to my cousin."

"So you keep saying. But I am fine, thanks."

Najwa stood up, trailing a cloud of Chanel No. 5. She rested her hand on Sami's shoulder. "She is *haram*, forbidden, Sami."

Sami ran his hand through his hair. "Why?"

"Where shall I start?" Najwa paused. "Firstly, because she is an . . . Israeli. And you are an Arab. A Palestinian. Haram for both of you."

Sami stiffened, his dark eyes glinting with annoyance. "We are consenting adults and American citizens."

"Passports are not the point."

"So what is?"

"She is a *source*. She works for the UN. Habibi, you cannot mix business and pleasure. What happens if you get a story about her? Will you warn her? Tone it down? Spike it?"

"I didn't spike the story about her and the coltan conspiracy. And we included her in our documentary," said Sami defensively.

Dying for Coltan: How the UN Was Almost Hijacked exposed an attempt by the KZX Corporation, a German multinational, and the Bonnet Group, a powerful French industrial firm, to take control of the world's coltan supplies. The mineral, mined in Congo in near slave-labor conditions, often by children, was vital for the production of mobile telephones and computers. The film, based in part on Sami's reporting in the *New York Times*, revealed how senior Bonnet and KZX officials had conspired in Africa together with rogue UN officials and executives of Efrat Global Solutions, an Israeli firm that ran one of the world's largest private armies. KZX and the Bonnet Group had agreed to sponsor the UN's first joint corporate development zone in Goma, a border city in eastern Congo. The pilot project had been hailed by Fareed Hussein, and many others, as the model for a new era of cooperation between the UN and the corporate world.

But the real plan, exposed by Sami, was for Efrat Global Solutions to start a regional war, by pitting Hutus against

Tutsis in a rerun of the 1994 Rwanda genocide. UN peace-keepers would then be deployed across eastern Congo to sta-bilize and take control of the region. KZX and the Bonnet Group then would expand the Goma Development Zone under the flag of the United Nations, with the protection of UN peacekeepers, to everywhere that coltan was mined.

UN peacekeepers, known as Blue Helmets, were oper-ating in fifteen conflict zones around the world. They were deployed under resolutions passed by the Security Council, whose decisions have the force of international law. The UN could not stop countries going to war. But it could help keep the peace once the fighting was over, by moni-toring the ceasefire line and helping to stabilize the situa-tion. The Blue Helmets were more armed observers than a proper fighting force. Often that was all that was needed. Blue Helmets had been deployed on the Golan Heights, be-tween Israel and Syria, for example, since the end of the Yom Kippur War in 1973. The Golan Heights mission was counted as a success: until Syria collapsed into civil war, its border with Israel remained peaceful.

But that peacekeeping model had been designed for the Cold War era, of stable nation-states and a rough equilib-rium of power between the United States and the former Soviet Union. Its limitations were made clear in the Yu-goslav wars of the early 1990s and the Rwandan genocide of 1994. The federal state of Yugoslavia collapsed into its constituent parts: war erupted in Slovenia, Croatia, Bos-nia, Kosovo, and Macedonia. Peacekeepers were dispatched to ensure the safety and passage of aid convoys. But when paramilitaries blocked the road, or plundered the supplies, the Blue Helmets often stood by and did nothing. There was no mechanism for dealing with the rise of what academics called "non-state actors," such as warlords, local militias, or quasi-statelets. The UN's neutrality was judged more important than ensuring the arrival of the aid or even saving lives. This policy had a tragic human cost. In spring 1994, Canadian peacekeepers deployed in Rwanda were forbidden from raiding the weapons caches of the Hutu militia that was preparing for the genocide. Over the next few months, eight hundred thousand people were slaughtered. In July 1995, Srebrenica, a UN-declared "safe haven" in eastern Bosnia, was captured by the Bosnian Serb army. Dutch peacekeepers stood by as Bosnian Serb troops took away over eight thousand Muslim men and boys. The prisoners were all killed.

The ghosts of Rwanda and Srebrenica, of families cut down by machetes, of rows of men and boys standing in a field in Bosnia with their hands tied behind their backs as the guns were reloaded, still haunted the organization. In response, peacekeeping had evolved. Peacekeepers in Africa were now equipped with proper weaponry and attack helicopters, and were provided with up-to-the-minute intelligence from Western spy agencies. They shot back. KZX and the Bonnet Group had planned to exploit the new, more muscular policy for their own ends to take control of swathes of territory where coltan was, or could be, mined. It was a brilliant attempt at what Sami and Najwa had dubbed "Resource Capture." *Dying for Coltan* had premiered at the Sundance Film Festival, garnering great critical acclaim. It had been short-listed for several prizes. Several of the protagonists, named in the documentary, were now serving prison sentences, but many more remained free. Some had even been promoted. The role of Yael Azoulay in the affair remained unclear and a source of frustration for Najwa, who knew that there was much more to investigate.

"Yes, we included Yael. In a bit part," said Najwa. "We both know she should have been center stage. And she was still pissed with you that she was mentioned at all. Then you moped about for days until she made nice again. And what if she feeds you some disinformation? A well-placed article in the *New York Times* can serve all sorts of purposes. Had you thought of that?"

Sami sighed. "Najwa, what do you want?"

"Cancel your date."

Sami looked indignant. "Why? Because she is a source?"

"Because you need to see what arrived in our post this morning."

They call her the "Magician," their laughter tinged with envy. She slips easily past the sweating tourists, the housewives laden with fruit and vegetables from the Carmel Market, the bleary-eyed hipsters blinking in the white sunlight.

This is her final exercise before she graduates. Her instructors have told her she is the best in the class, perhaps the best they have ever trained.

The watchers have her in a box. The paunchy middle-aged man in denim shorts and a blue T-shirt in front of her, pretending to window shop; the young woman wearing a tank top and jeans behind her, drinking a can of Coca-Cola; and across the road the gray-haired man holding a newspaper and walking toward the bus stop.

She senses their eyes upon her, feels them observing her. They all are smart, brave, and quick-witted, which is why they have been chosen to serve their country. But what she has is something extra: a sixth sense. She can see inside people's heads, read their body language like an open book, predict what their next move will be.

Yael waited until her New York–bound train was a few minutes outside Baltimore, the first stop after Washington, DC. There were two of them. A tall man, almost bald apart from a few strands of greasy gray hair, was sitting nearby, pretending to read the sports section of the *Washington Post*. His colleague, shorter with broad shoulders, was hiding behind a copy of *Bloomberg Businessweek* at the other end of the carriage. They had both exits covered. She watched them watching her. Perhaps she should have brought Joe-Don with her. An extra pair of hands, especially those large, calloused ones belonging to her bodyguard, could prove extremely useful in situations like this. But she wanted to prove to Joe-Don—and herself—that she could spot, and deal with, surveillance on her own. Especially after Geneva.

The carriage was barely half-full and the seat next to the bald man was empty. Yael walked over and sat down next to him. He carried on reading his newspaper, his scalp shining under the carriage lights.

"Baltimore's a great town," she said. The city's outer suburbs rushed by, a jumble of warehouses, housing projects, and freeways.

He ignored her, shifting in his seat as though trying to get more comfortable.

"Have you ever been there?" Yael asked.

The bald man did not answer. He continued reading.

"I asked you something," she said, her voice curious.

"No. I have not been to Baltimore," he said, irritated. This was not how his script was supposed to play out.

"I really think you would like it," said Yael, enjoying his unease.

"Please leave me in peace, miss, to read my newspaper."

The air smells of the city: the salt tang of the sea, Turkish coffee scented with cardamom, the falafels frying at the stand on the corner.

A siren howls as a police car roars down the middle of the road. Heads turn.

She makes her move.

She watches the team from her sanctuary: their disbelief, their anger that they have lost her.

She smiles to herself. She is the best in her class.

She is invincible.

Yael reached inside her pocket and took out her smartphone. She held the phone in one hand and gently pulled the page of the newspaper down. The bald man's mouth twisted with anger until he saw the screen. It showed his face, pin sharp. Yael swiped her finger across the image. A second photograph appeared, of him lurking on the concourse at Union Station.

"I have some nice shots of your friend over there as well," said Yael, gesturing at the other end of the carriage. "Would you like to see them?"

The bald man scowled and said nothing.

The conductor's voice sounded through the carriage, "Next stop, Baltimore, next stop, Baltimore."

"Your stop," said Yael.

"And what if I don't want to go to Baltimore," the tall man asked, his breath sour with stale coffee.

Yael tapped her mobile phone. "The UN Twitter feed has two million followers."

He stood up. The train lurched and Yael fell against him for several seconds.

"Sorry," she said, not sounding very sorry at all, as she righted herself and stepped away.

The train slowed as it pulled into Baltimore Station. The man reached for his bag and raincoat.

"Don't forget your friend," said Yael, brightly.

"Fuck you," said the tall man as he walked over to his companion, and they exited. Yael waved at the two men as they stood on the platform at Baltimore, watching as the train pulled out of the station.

Buoyed by her victory, she walked through the carriage to the adjoining restaurant car, bought a hot tea and a bar of dark chocolate, and returned to her seat. Yael placed the tea in the cupholder in the fold-down tray in front of her and emptied two creams and a packet of sugar into the drink. She looked down at the left cuff of her jacket and picked out the loose thread still hanging where the button had been. That was so embarrassing. And how could Samantha afford Dior and Manolo Blahniks on a PA's salary? Clearly, it was time to ask Fareed for a wardrobe allowance. She took a long drink of the tea. Surely the world's superpowers would want her to be properly power dressed?

Yael sat back and let the tension drain out of her. Her left shoulder was throbbing again, fueled by the vibrations of the train. She slipped her hand inside her blouse and traced the edge of the small circular scar with her thumb. The hard flesh was puckered and knotted. She pressed down on the scar. Jagged pinpricks of pain shot out in all directions. She winced and closed her eyes for several seconds, thinking through the events of the day so far.

Yael had enjoyed a minor triumph, getting rid of the two men following her. But this assignment made her uneasy, she admitted to herself. She had never operated on a mission whose target was based in the United States. She had faced down killers from Kabul to Kinshasa, brokered deals with warlords and militiamen across the world's conflict zones. But Clairborne exuded a different kind of menace, the absolute confidence of those who ran the secret fifty-first state of the most powerful country in the world: the military-intelligence industrial complex. The warlords' fiefdoms were small, usually extending to the next village or checkpoint. Clairborne's reach, she knew, stretched around the world, and certainly to her home in Manhattan.

She sat up, opened her eyes, unwrapped the dark chocolate, and broke off a segment. Clairborne's threat had been quite open, which meant he felt confident. This was a game of poker, with extremely high stakes. Clairborne might accede to her request or he might refuse. They both knew that, if Yael followed up on her implied threat to release the information she had about the Prometheus Group's connections with Tehran, there would be blowback for both her and the United Nations. After reading the *Daily Beast* story about Hussein's health, which had immediately been picked up by the media around the world, she realized that her roof, indeed that of the whole United Nations, might be less able to resist one of Clairborne's tornadoes than she had believed.

The media reports about the SG's blackouts were a mystery. Fareed Hussein had certainly never fainted near Yael, nor had he ever seemed to be about to pass out. He was overweight, a legacy of the endless rounds of diplomatic lunches and dinners, but otherwise in good shape for a man in his early seventies. His eyes still shone with the true believer's evangelical zeal, his shoulders were upright, and his skin glowed with its usual mahogany sheen. After he had passed Yael the file on the Prometheus Group at their briefing, he had hugged her. She could still smell his coconut hair lotion.

In fact, Hussein was if anything newly energized by the planning for the upcoming Istanbul Summit. Today was Monday. The summit was due to start a week from Thursday, in ten days' time. It would be the crowning glory of the SG's career: the world's most ambitious peace conference yet, dedicated to sorting out the bloody chaos in Syria, the perpetual instability in Egypt, and the running sore of the Israel-Palestine conflict. The presidents of all the major powers had agreed to attend and to twist the arms of their client states as hard as they could to reach an agreement on the three interlinked conflicts—thanks in part to the many days Yael had spent negotiating with the P5's UN missions and foreign ministries, making it clear that the rise of radical Islam threatened all of their interests.

She sat deep in thought, as the train trundled on to Philadelphia. When she actually looked back over the planning for the summit, however, there had been several unexplained cancellations at surprisingly short notice. Hussein had not turned up for important meetings, claiming scheduling conflicts or an immediate crisis that needed his attention. His place had been taken by the deputy SG, an American diplomat named Caroline Masters. Hussein had also missed the receptions celebrating several countries' national days, including that of his homeland, India. That had triggered fevered gossip across the Secretariat Building and the nearby diplomatic missions. So was there something going on? Perhaps the SG really was ill, but was exceptionally skilled at disguising it. That she could understand.

The UN's New York headquarters was a cross between the court of the Borgias and the last days of the Roman Empire. Part of her relished the challenge of operating across thirty-eight floors of intrigue, conspiracy, backbiting, and betrayal. Another part longed for normality. Especially when she thought of her friend Olivia de Souza. Olivia had met a horrible death, pushed off a balcony on the thirty-eighth floor that looked out over the UN headquarters' airshaft. Mahesh Kapoor, who had served for years as Fareed Hussein's chief of staff, was now serving a life sentence for Olivia's murder. Somehow, Yael's personal history with Kapoor had stayed out of the media coverage. But there was no guarantee whatsoever that it would not leak in the future.

The happy laughter of a young boy interrupted her reverie. Yael watched a man in his thirties walk down the center of the carriage, holding the hand of his son. The man was tall, dark haired, and quite handsome, the boy wide-eyed with excitement to be traveling on a train with his daddy. They sat down nearby and she could hear the father listing all the exciting things they would do in New York together. The boy saw her watching, smiled, and waved, his fingers sticky with the candy bar he was eating. A father, a child, a simple family trip. The boy was about five, she estimated. She counted five years backward. Five years ago, this month, in fact. She could still smell the antiseptic and the starch on the nurses' uniforms.

Yael smiled back at the boy, her face belying the feelings surging up inside her. There was no point fighting them. She closed her eyes, let the emotions wash over her, and then carefully put them away in the box in her head that she opened rarely, but which had lately seemed to be frequently bursting open of its own accord.

Yael looked out the window, at the fields and distant buildings as the train sped toward Philadelphia. She wiped her eyes and put her phone back in her bag, her hand shaking only slightly.

3

The office of the secretary-general of the United Nations never failed to impress visitors. It extended across the entire width of the thirty-eighth floor of the Secretariat Building, and along most of its length. The front windows, facing out over First Avenue and the east mid-forties, showcased a densely packed grid of skyscrapers and soaring apartment buildings. On a clear day you could see all the way through the city, down East Forty-First Street to Twelfth Avenue and the Hudson River. The back windows looked over the East River, the shoreline of Queens, and its giant billboard advertising Pepsi-Cola, while the side view took in First Avenue all the way up to the Queensboro Bridge.

The Secretariat Building was built in the early 1950s. The thirty-nine-story modernist skyscraper was the centerpiece of an eighteen-acre complex that was physically in the United States, but legally in international territory. The UN had its own security service and fire department, and issued its own stamps. The NYPD and the FBI had no jurisdiction there, although criminals were usually handed over to the local law enforcement agencies because the UN had no court or prison. The complex also included the General Assembly building, where member states gathered, a conference building, and a library named for Dag Hammarskjöld, the second UN secretary-general.

There were several grades of hospitality in the SG's suite. Those out of favor were not offered any kind of chair and were left to stand. Everyday visitors were seated in front of the giant black desk, made from environmentally certified Brazilian hardwood, on a chair just a couple of inches lower than the SG's own. More prized guests shared space with the SG on his sofa at the side of the office. The most valued confidants and VIPs were invited to the leather armchairs in the corner, a cozy nook with its own small table. The walls of the suite were covered with numerous photographs of Hussein shaking hands with current and former presidents and prime ministers, mainly of the P5, plus a legion of pop stars and Hollywood actors. Hussein was notorious for his love of glamour and celebrities. They were usually happy to reciprocate.

The SG led Yael to the corner space and gestured for her to sit down. The nook felt surprisingly cozy. The lighting was soft, matching the dusk outside as the sun slowly set over the city. The coffee machine wheezed and sighed, scenting the room with the SG's special blend of Ethiopian fair-trade arabica beans. A white china teapot stood next to a plate covered with a small mountain of muffins and cookies. Yael smiled with surprise and pleasure when she saw who was already sitting there.

Quentin Braithwaite stood up to greet Yael. She quickly glanced sideways at the SG. He had already sat down, absorbed in his papers. She mouthed the word "Baku" to Braithwaite as though asking a question. Braithwaite shook his head, almost imperceptibly.

The SG put his papers down and poured drinks: coffee for himself and Braithwaite, and tea for Yael. Hussein had recently commissioned a special blend for her, a mix of strong Assam and Kenyan, which he kept in a large jar labeled "Builder's Brew." Yael was more amused than touched by the SG's newfound solicitousness. Hussein rarely did anything without calculating the cost-benefit ratio to his own position at the UN.

Yael thanked the SG, taking in his appearance and demeanor as he poured her drink. He seemed in perfect health and as charming and attentive as ever, as indeed he had been since Yael's return to work. But she remained wary of the SG and had promised herself not to get too close to him. Hussein had already shown that he would dump her like an empty soda can if need be. Yet despite—perhaps because of—their tangled history, Hussein still aroused powerful emotions in her. Part of her wanted to slam him against the wall. Yael knew that Hussein knew far more than he had admitted about the death of the person she had loved most in the world, which was one reason why she had returned to work at the UN. Yet something about Fareed Hussein still drew her to him. The SG's voice, deep and sonorous, was curiously comforting. His hand, resting on her arm as he guided her across his office, had felt warm and dry. She was annoyed to realize that, even now, the other part of her still sought his praise and approval.

The SG put his folder down, a signal that the meeting was beginning.

"I know you and Quentin are old allies, Yael," said Hussein, his voice only slightly barbed. "So you will be pleased to hear that Quentin is now on secondment to this office as special envoy for the Istanbul Summit, which is why he is joining us now."

Yael sipped her tea. She made sure not to let her surprise—and relief—show as she digested this news. Colonel Quentin Braithwaite was a tall, sturdy Englishman with red hair, striking blue eyes, a splash of freckles over a ruddy outdoors complexion, and a taste for tweed jackets with leather elbow patches. He was a jocular and genuinely engaging companion. Braithwaite was the unacknowledged leader of the UN's interventionist faction, a firm believer that the best way to persuade errant warlords to cooperate was a brisk salvo from the guns of an attack helicopter. Fareed Hussein took a very different view. The two men were not allies. The previous year Braithwaite had caused fury on the thirty-eighth floor when he had ripped off the epaulettes of a Dutch peacekeeper for cowardice—until it turned out that the Dutch soldier had been part of a human-trafficking ring that reached from Congo to Europe. Almost alone among her UN peers, Braithwaite had stood by Yael during the coltan scandal. He had been appointed to oversee the commission of inquiry, which was moving at a glacial pace, thanks to Fareed's maneuverings behind the scenes. But Braithwaite too was a deft operator. His recent appointment as special envoy for the Istanbul Summit made him the most senior UN official dealing with the gathering, other than the SG and Caroline Masters, Hussein's deputy. This was good news indeed, Yael thought. Although not for Fareed; someone—the Brits, she guessed—must have twisted the SG's arm behind the scenes to get Braithwaite this position.

Hussein looked at Yael. "So, Washington. How did it go?"

Yael opened her folder and took out her notes. "Clarence Clairborne is not our friend," she said, her voice wry, before giving a brisk account of her meeting with the chairman and CEO of the Prometheus Group.

"And President Freshwater? Did you mention her?" asked Hussein.

Yael nodded. "I did. Clairborne almost spat when I said her name. Called her 'President Dead-in-the-Water.'"

"He might be right," said Braithwaite.

Yael remembered Clairborne's crude dismissal of President Freshwater, that she could go "fuck herself." And the way he had started a sentence with "we" before suddenly stopping himself from saying any more. That part, she decided, she would keep to herself for now and share with Braithwaite later.

Yael sat back. Her shoulder was pulsing again. She closed her eyes for a moment, once again seeing Clairborne rigid with anger, gripping the armchair so hard his fingers had turned white. She opened her eyes to see the large photograph of Lucy Tremlett, a willowy blond English actress, still in the center of the facing wall. Hussein had appointed Tremlett an ambassador for UNICEF, the UN's children's fund. The photograph showed him standing with his arm around her at a refugee camp in

Darfur, surrounded by barefoot African children, who were smiling with excitement. "Fareed, thanks for everything," Tremlett had scrawled on the print in her big, loopy handwriting. "We are doing so much good." *But were they?* Yael asked herself, her mind drifting away. *Were they really?*

The SG's voice cut into her reverie. "Yael, are you with us?"

Yael sat up straight and focused herself. "Sorry. Yes, of course."

"Did you show Clairborne the paper?" asked Braithwaite.

Yael nodded. "Yes. I did. He was furious. But he wouldn't back down, even when I said it might soon appear on the Internet. He threatened me; then he threw me out. On the surface he seems very confident."

"So the trip was a waste of your time," said Hussein.

Yael shook her head. "No. It was not. I learned something very valuable."

"What?" demanded the SG.

"He was scared."

Hussein nodded. "Of course. He is scared of going to prison. His father died in prison."

Yael shook her head. "It was more than that. After I showed him the paper, he sat for at least a minute, praying to himself. As though he was caught up in something that was out of his control."

"He is," said Braithwaite, reaching inside his briefcase. He pulled out two plain manila cardboard folders and handed one to the SG and one to Yael. "Read this."

I t's not her," said Sami, his shoulders hunched, his voice tight.

Najwa rested her hand on his arm, but kindly, no longer the vamp of the Levant. "Sami, habibi, it is."

The Al Jazeera bureau was just a few yards away from Sami's dank cubbyhole, but it seemed like a different world. The bright light of a spring Manhattan morning poured in through the floor-to-ceiling windows. One wall was covered with four giant television screens. They showed feeds from Al Jazeera Arabic service, Al Jazeera English, and the new Al Jazeera America service, while the fourth had the BBC World News channel playing. The furniture was sleek and modern, polished chrome and black leather, and the computers state-of-the-art with wafer-thin LED monitors. The walls were decorated with framed black-and-white stills from the recent uprisings that had convulsed the Arab world. A jumble of plaques, metallic statuettes, and slabs of engraved plastic, Najwa's awards for her reports and documentaries, covered most of one shelf.

Sami and Najwa sat at her desk, watching the film playing on her computer monitor. A tray on the side table was piled high with pastries and fruit. Sami's coffee was untouched. He had taken a single bite out of a chocolate muffin, but it had turned to dry crumbs in his mouth when the video started playing. Najwa's producer, a taciturn but talented Spaniard named Maria, sat next to them, also watching, happy to let her star reporter run the show.

Sami leaned back, staring at the ceiling, shaking his

head slowly, conflicting emotions churning inside him. "But how . . . what . . . ?" he stuttered, for once at a loss for words.

"We have checked the footage, Sami. It's real, the raw CCTV feed, not spliced or enhanced. It's a hotel but we don't know which one yet."

Sami nodded. He reached forward and pressed the play button again.

The video clip started with a rear view of a slim woman walking down a long, narrow corridor. The walls were light brown, the carpet darker and patterned. She wore a wrap-around raincoat and a fashionable military-style cap. She carried herself with poise and confidence on long, slim legs. There was no sound and the footage was clear and steady.

Two stone-faced security guards stood outside the door of room 3017. A room service waiter walked down toward her, pushing a large trolley covered with used plates and glasses. The footage was sharp enough to see the name on his badge: "Miguel." He mouthed something to the woman and smiled at her reply. She carried on toward 3017. The security guards instantly moved in front of her, blocking her path. They spoke and the woman presented her ID. The camera zoomed in on a driver's license in the name of Sha-ron Mantello. She raised her arms and the taller security guard rapidly frisked her. She opened her bag. One of the security guards took out a heavy, old-fashioned mobile tele-phone. There was some discussion; then the woman took the mobile telephone back and placed it in her bag. The guards opened the door. The camera view flipped around to show the woman's face.

Sami pressed the pause button. "She doesn't wear glasses."

"She does there," replied Najwa. She passed him a print-out. "We photoshopped the glasses out. There is no point arguing. It's your girlfriend."

Sami picked up the sheet of paper and glanced at it. "I really wish you would stop calling her that," he said, exhaling loudly.

Najwa pressed the pause button again. The film showed the woman talking to the security guards, presumably trying to persuade them to let her into the room. One of the guards opened the door and she walked in. The door closed and the film stopped.

"That's it," said Najwa.

Sami sat back. "OK. So what is the SG's special envoy doing in a hotel, presumably pretending to be an escort, using a fake ID to get into a room that has two security guards outside? And who sent the DVD?"

Najwa shrugged. "We don't know. It arrived hand-delivered, in a plain brown envelope. Marked for my attention. This was the only file on the disc."

"The metadata?" asked Sami.

"Nothing."

"No date, time, and make of camera? It should be embedded in the video file."

Najwa ran the cursor over the video file's properties. Every field was empty. "Stripped out. But a note came with the disc."

She handed a sheet of folded paper to Sami. There were two words, "More follows." The phrase dated back to the era when news stories were typed up over several sheets of copy paper. "More follows" indicated that the article ran onto another sheet. The letter *r* was malformed, missing its horizontal spar.

Sami nodded and stared back at the screen. "Run the clip again, please."

The screen filled with the woman walking down the corridor. Sami stared, then pressed the pause button after a few seconds. The picture froze. He scratched his head. "I know where that is. I need to call my news desk. Is this another joint production?"

Sami reached for the play button to watch the end of the clip.

Najwa grabbed his hand before he could press down. "That depends," she said, gripping his wrist.

"On what?"

Najwa smiled sweetly. "You."

Sami looked wary. "You have the video file. I don't."

"But you have information about someone we are both very interested in. Information that you have not shared, habibi."

"I told you everything that I could confirm. It's all in our program."

Najwa closed the video window on her screen. She looked at Sami, still holding his wrist. "Everything you could confirm. And the rest?"

"There is nothing else," he said indignantly.

Najwa released his hand. "OK."

She picked up the telephone on her desk. "I'll see you later," she said to Sami, turning away. Najwa dialed the switchboard. "Can I speak to the *Washington Post* bureau, please?"

Sami instantly leaned forward and pressed the button on the handset cradle.

Najwa looked at him expectantly, still holding the handset. "Yes?"

Sami said, "There is more."

"For me?"

"Yes, Najwa. For you."

Najwa put the telephone back down. "We can get the story on the eight o'clock news tonight. I will give you the clip, exclusively, for the *Times* website. But Sami . . ."

"What?"

"We go in hard this time. No more protecting her because you are dating her . . ."

"Let's get to work," said Sami, before Najwa could finish her sentence, already hating himself.

Thirty floors above the Al Jazeera office, Yael leaned forward and put Braithwaite's folder down on the coffee table. The information the folder contained, while shocking, did not surprise her, especially after Clairborne's performance. Suddenly a wave of tiredness hit her. The sun had set, blanketing the UN headquarters in darkness. She had got up at dawn to catch an early train to Washington, DC; confronted one of the most powerful men in America; been threatened, followed; spent another four hours getting back to the UN; and now this. She watched a police helicopter sweep by, its searchlight cutting through the dusk as it followed the path of the river, flying so close that its blades rattled the office windows.

Yael briefly squeezed her eyes closed, only half-listening as Hussein outlined the implications of the information in Braithwaite's dossier for the UN, and by implication, for the SG's career. Who was this man, the eighth secretary-general of the United Nations? A refugee turned multimillionaire; a self-proclaimed champion of the poor and downtrodden who adored luxury and celebrities; a fighter for peace who had stopped the UN intervening in so many wars. What did he want? What drove him?

Yael knew the facts of the SG's biography so well she could recite them on demand. Born in Delhi in 1940, Fareed Hussein was the son of a Muslim father and Hindu mother. His father, Ahmad, had owned a private bank. The Husseins were a mainstay of the city's business and social elite, with a wide network of friends and business partners among Hindus and Muslims, Sikhs and Jains, Parsis and Jews. The family door was always open, and their home full of visitors dropping by for tea and often staying on for dinner. Hussein and his younger brother Omar were privately educated in a school modeled on Eton, the training ground for Britain's ruling class, just outside the city. Even now, the SG still used the idioms and slang of the 1940s Raj, an affectation that he carefully, and secretly, cultivated by regularly reading P. G. Wodehouse novels.

Hussein's comfortable world vanished in the violence of partition in August 1947. Families of mixed religious and ethnic heritage, like his, were often the first targets of extremists from both sides. The Husseins fled to Zurich, Switzerland, where Ahmad had business contacts who helped him obtain residence permits for everyone. Fearing the worst, Ahmad had already sent most of the family's money out of India. But the bank was gone. So was their house in Delhi, their summer home in the mountains, all their wordly goods, apart from the contents of their suitcases. Worst of all, they lost Omar. He disappeared in the chaos at Delhi Station and was never heard from again. There was a photograph of Omar on Hussein's desk: a skinny, bright-eyed boy, six years old, with a winning smile. Next to it was a framed half of a postcard of the Taj Mahal that had been torn in two. Even at the age of seven Fareed Hussein had already sensed the coming cataclysm. He had bought the postcard, solemnly torn it into two, and handed one half to Omar on the terrace of their Delhi villa one Sunday morning. The brothers had pledged to keep their halves for life if they were separated.

From Zurich, Hussein and his parents had eventually moved to London, where he studied at the London School of Economics. He worked as an investment banker in Frankfurt and New York, before joining the UN in the early 1990s as finance director of the UN Refugee Agency. His appointment had come out of the blue, as he had no experience with any humanitarian, public policy, or development organizations. But his opponents soon learned that his faux-aristocratic mannerisms hid a ruthless, silken operator. Hussein swiftly moved from finance to the far more glamorous and influential field of policy-making and began his steady ascent up the UN ladder. By the early 1990s he was assistant secretary-general in the Department of Political Affairs. The DPA was the most powerful UN department. It decided everything from which country's cuisine would be featured in the week's menu at the staff canteen, to the agenda of the Security Council meeting—which meant the DPA helped shape the superpowers' response in a crisis. Most DPA officials dealt with a particular region of the world. But Hussein carved out a global role for himself, and quickly made a name as an intermediary between Britain, France, and the United States on one side and Russia and China on the other. Hussein soon became known across the organization for being an arch-conciliator. His prime concern always seemed to be keeping the P5 happy by avoiding anything that might run counter to their aims.

After the Department of Peacekeeping split off from the DPA in 1992, there were fears that the peacekeepers, newly emboldened by their own mini-empire, might take a more robust approach, open fire when threatened or obstructed, and prioritize saving lives over the UN's fabled neutrality. Which is why the P5 ensured that Hussein, who had no military or peacekeeping experience, was appointed head of the new DPKO. Yugoslavia was ablaze and the Hutu *genocidaires* were already planning their mass slaughter of Tutsis in Rwanda, but Hussein's primary concern, publicly at least, was to ensure that the neutrality of the UN, which he liked to describe as "sacred," was not violated. Hussein made much of his personal history, and often referred to his own experience as a refugee in his speeches and articles. Several chapters of his memoir, *My Journey for Peace*, were devoted to the buildup to the partition of India, the explosion of violence, and the family's subsequent life as refugees.

Hussein had written movingly from the perspective of a young boy who sees his safe, secure world slowly starting to crumble around him.

Yael had worked for Fareed Hussein throughout her UN career. It was a relationship, she knew, underpinned by a kind of mutual exploitation. She used him, and the UN, to try and save lives wherever she could. Hussein used Yael as his secret conscience. Behind the scenes, Hussein had been happy for Yael to, if not violate, at least bend the concept of neutrality, as long as nothing could be traced back to his office. Indeed, that was one of the reasons her job existed: to broker the covert deals that kept the wheels of superpower diplomacy turning, and to ensure that the balance sheets of multinational corporations stayed healthy. Yael knew she operated in a gray area of compromises and trade-offs, sometimes sordid ones. Warlords walked free; crimes went unpunished. But lives were saved and wars averted. Overall, her moral account had stayed in the black.

Hussein had been her patron and protector, at least until Yael had been sent to Goma, in eastern Congo. There her task was to negotiate a deal with Jean-Pierre Hakizimani, a Hutu Rwandan warlord wanted by the International Criminal Court for genocide. Hakizimani, a former minister of health, had once been marked out as one of the new generation of African leaders. But after his wife and three daughters were killed in a car bomb, blamed on Tutsi extremists, Hakizimani became the ideologue and propaganda genius behind the Rwandan genocide. His theory of "Hutu Power" demanded the complete extermination of the Tutsis. Every day, for hour after hour, he had broadcast on Radio Milles Collines, exhorting his Hutu compatriots to squash, kill, and stamp on the "cockroaches," meaning the Tutsis. His instructions had been diligently followed.

Yael was to offer him a shorter sentence, in a comfortable prison in Paris, in exchange for surrendering and dismantling his militia. Almost two decades after the genocide, the Hutu militias had regrouped in eastern Congo. Under Hakizimani's command they were launching raids into Rwanda and threatening to destabilize the whole region. Yael found the assignment repulsive, but she could not refuse. That was her job. She knew how to handle killers. It was a little late for her to start getting squeamish. The only difference this time had been the numbers involved. But Yael also had more personal reasons for wanting to meet the man dubbed "the Goebbels of Africa."

Yael glanced at the SG's desk. Next to the picture of Omar was one of a pretty young Indian woman—Rina Hussein in her graduation gown. Rina was a human rights activist. She and her father had not spoken for years. Rina had recently caused an international incident at the UN headquarters in Geneva. Rina and her comrades had pelted UN officials, Lucy Tremlett, and her rock-star boyfriend at a press conference with the yellow sludge from which coltan is extracted. Yael knew that the SG had pulled strings with the Swiss authorities to get Rina and her group released. Rina probably suspected as much, and it only seemed to fuel her rage against her father, whom she had recently denounced on Twitter as an "accomplice to genocide."

Yael brought herself back to the room. The SG, she realized, was still talking. She listened patiently as he finished his exegesis on the file he had just read and Yael's meeting in DC that morning, outlining what he called the "potentially catastrophic consequences" if the UN took on the Prometheus Group.

Braithwaite picked up his folder. "I beg to differ, Fareed. We need to go public with this. It's dynamite."

"Indeed it is, Quentin. Which is why it stays inside this room, at least for now," said Hussein. He turned to Yael and gave her a questioning look.

"I go with Quentin. Just leave a printout in the pressroom early one morning. Nothing can be traced back to us." A vision of Sami picking up Braithwaite's dossier flicked through her mind. She could almost see the excitement on his face. Perhaps she would leave it there herself, she thought with a trace of a smile.

Hussein shook his head. "Not now. Not yet."

Yael and Braithwaite looked at each other, then reluctantly nodded. The SG, it was understood, had the last word.

Yael leaned forward as she spoke. "Fareed, can I ask you something?"

"Of course."

"Forgive me for bringing this up. But you will have seen the story on the *Daily Beast* today. Is it true? Are you suffering from blackouts?"

"No. I am not," he said indignantly. "I'm fine."

Yael watched Hussein carefully as he spoke. There were no microsigns of dissimulation. He was telling the truth. "Then who is leaking these stories about you?"

"Clairborne?" asked Braithwaite. "You have plenty of enemies in DC."

Hussein's energy seemed to leak away. His shoulders slumped and he suddenly looked weary. "Not just in DC," he said. "In this house."

4

Yael checked the dinner table once more, making tiny adjustments to the two place settings, the wine and water glasses, which made no discernable difference whatsoever. The knives, forks, and spoons sparkled; the glasses gleamed; the candlesticks shone. It was a rare outing for her grandmother's best silver cutlery.

The SG had given Yael the day off after her trip to see Clairborne. She had slept in late, then spent Tuesday shopping and preparing dinner. She had told Sami to come over at around 7:30 p.m. The dinner was ready—all she had to do was heat it up—and the champagne and wine were chilling in the fridge. It was the first time in months she had cooked: she usually existed on the food served in the surprisingly good UN canteen, room service while on mission, or takeout.

She finally stopped fiddling with the table and looked around her apartment, which was as clean and tidy as she had ever seen it. It was a decent-sized one bedroom in a stately building that had been constructed in the 1930s on the corner of Riverside Drive and West Eighty-First Street. The walls were thick, the ceilings high, the bedroom had an en suite bathroom with pipes that rattled and groaned when she ran the shower or the tub, and the large windows looked out over the Hudson River. The building's elegant black-and-white marble foyer looked like something from a Hollywood film set. Each time she came home she half-expected to see Fred Astaire tap-dancing his way across the floor. She had moved in over a decade ago and the apartment was part of her family history. Her grandmother, Eva Weiss, had fled Budapest at the end of the Second World War and bought the place for perhaps a hundredth of what it was worth now. She had left the apartment to Yael, together with instructions to look after her art deco furniture, find a husband, and start a family. Yael rested her hand on the back of one of the mahogany dining chairs. The table and chairs were still in good shape, she thought, smiling to herself. The rest, well . . .

Yael was thirty-six years old. Born in New York to an American mother and Israeli father, she had grown up on the Upper West Side, six blocks from where she lived now. She was the middle child of three: her brother David was seven years older, her sister, Noa, three years younger. Yael's parents had owned and ran a company called Aleph Research that supplied business and corporate intelligence to companies, individuals, and governments. Aleph kept a low profile, was not even listed in the telephone directory, and did not look for business. But it had a sterling reputation for discretion and accuracy and was never short of work. Some clients wanted the broad-brush approach, such as a report on potential future wars in the developing world and their likely impact on commodity prices. Others wanted something much more precise, such as the level of security and controls on Mexico's border with the United States. Yael's father and several "freelance researchers," most of whom seemed to be Israelis, brought in the information. Her mother, Barbara, was a former journalist. She compiled the information, wrote and edited the reports, and ran the business side. Yael had spent some of her school holidays at the midtown office as a child, helping with the filing. Despite Yael's repeated questions, her father had never properly explained how he gathered the information. She eventually realized that he had been part of the Israeli intelligence establishment—perhaps still was—and was using his former contacts and colleagues.

As a young girl Yael had been close to her mother, especially as her father was traveling so much on company business. But as she grew into an exceptionally pretty young woman, her relationship with her mother changed. Her parents' marriage began to collapse. Her father seemed to be continually on the road. Whenever he came home, there were arguments. Some were about the firm: the kind of clients her father was bringing in and the research they asked for. Other fights were domestic. Yael's mother resented having to raise three children on her own. Yael felt that her mother saw her as a rival for her husband's affection. In response, Barbara poured all her attention onto Noa and David, which made Yael distance herself further from her mother. So Yael went to her father for affection and reassurance, which he readily gave and which further alienated her mother, in a self-perpetuating spiral. Yael was too young to understand this, her mother too angry at the end of her marriage to try and fix her relationship with her older daughter. Yael's parents divorced in 1991 when she was fourteen. She went to live in Tel Aviv with her father. At the age of sixteen they moved to London for two years, before she returned to Israel and began her military service.

Yael had started her UN career, after graduating with a master's degree in international relations from Columbia University, as an administrative officer in the Department of Peacekeeping Operations (DPKO). She was responsible for ensuring that the reports and briefings were written in correct, grammatical English and that they were distributed on time to the relevant committees. Yael was a polyglot: fluent in Arabic, Hebrew, French, and Spanish, with a decent command of Hungarian. Her job was far more demanding than it sounded. The UN had six official languages, and a legion of zealous, protective interpreters; Yael soon learned to find her way through both the thickets of bureaucracy and the jungle of competing egos. The reports were also a matter of life or death, because the DPKO sent armed troops into harm's way in the world's conflict zones, where they fought and sometimes died. Quentin Braithwaite, then on reassignment from the British Ministry of Defense, had quickly noticed Yael's skill at defusing both office crises and the perpetual power struggle with the rival Department of Political Affairs, which distracted staff and sapped their energy. Braithwaite had brought Yael into the operations room, the command center for the peacekeeping missions. There she proved ice-cool under extreme pressure. He then started sending Yael out into the field. Even her detractors, jealous of her rapid rise, admitted that Yael showed a rare ability to guide opposing sides to the conclusion she wanted, while persuading the protagonists that such a result was anyway in their best interest.

Fareed Hussein had noticed Yael's skill set while she was on mission in Afghanistan. There she had negotiated a deal between US troops and the Taliban. American soldiers, disguised as locals, would guard the Taliban's opium fields, in exchange for the Taliban guaranteeing the safety of a new gas pipeline from central Asia. Hussein soon made her his protégé, which instantly brought her far more enemies than allies. Hussein gave her increasingly challenging assignments and she had thrived. Her UN ID card said she was political adviser to the UN High Commissioner for Refugees. Her actual job, as the SG's special negotiator, did not officially exist. She had brokered ceasefires from Gaza to Darfur; negotiated the release of hostages in Baghdad and Algeria; set the terms for corporations wishing to invest in the developing world. The men—they were nearly always men—with whom she dealt looked askance at Yael when she first walked into the room. But if she spoke for Fareed Hussein, she spoke for the P5. On a good day, she was the most powerful woman on the planet. But she still woke up alone every morning.

She walked over to the sideboard. A clutch of framed photographs stood on the surface. The largest, in solid silver, showed David, standing by his UN Jeep on the outskirts of Vukovar during the Croatian War in the winter of 1993, soon after he started working for the UN High Commissioner for Refugees. David had been a good-looking young man: tall, broad shouldered, with wavy black hair and green eyes. The sight of her brother still made Yael's stomach lurch. David had been killed in April 1994 in Kigali, at the start of the genocide in Rwanda. Despite their desperate, repeated calls for help to the UN peacekeepers stationed nearby, David and eight other UN workers were hacked to death by a mob wielding machetes. An internal report had exonerated the UN, including Fareed Hussein, then the head of the Peacekeeping Department. Instead it blamed communications breakdowns, uncertainty over the peacekeepers' mandate, and interference from the P5 and the Security Council. Yael was sixteen and living with her father in London when David was killed. She had been left utterly bereft by her brother's death.

Yael believed the UN report was a whitewash. She would never give up her quest to find out why her brother had died, and who was responsible. Hussein had brushed off her attempts to find out more, especially when she asked him about his movements for the day of the killings. She had discovered that Hussein's schedule from that week had mysteriously gone missing from the UN archives. There seemed to be no written records of his meetings and telephone calls. Yael knew from the look in Hussein's eyes and the way his body stiffened when pressed, that he knew more, perhaps much more, than he had so far revealed. He had given Yael the photograph of her brother after the coltan-KZX-Bonnet scandal, when Yael was reinstated to her job. She had been uncertain whether to accept the gift, but eventually took it home.

Yael picked up the photograph and stared at her brother and his UN vehicle. Was it just a present from the SG, she wondered, or something more, perhaps even a symbol of atonement? She picked up a ring sitting on top of a small, painted ceramic dish. It was a wide band of white gold that David had bought in the Jaffa flea market. He had let her wear the ring on "loan," as he said with a smile, but they both knew the loan was open-ended. Yael stared at the Arabic calligraphy that flowed around the ring, a declaration of love from a husband to his wife. She placed it on the second finger of her right hand. Twenty years on from his death, the ache inside her, the longing to see her brother, had barely faded.

Another photograph showed Yael's sister, Noa, surrounded by eight children. Noa had married a yeshiva student while on a visit to Israel and was now blissfully living in a settlement outside Jerusalem. The two sisters were divided by thousands of miles and very different politics. But Noa, Yael knew, had always been there for her and always would be. Her sister had both hands on the shoulders of one young boy, the tallest in the group. Noa was pushing him forward, as though showcasing him.

Yael turned away and paced around the room. She could not believe how nervous she felt. Not because of the two men who had been following her. This was a different kind of nervousness to that which she had felt at the Prometheus Group: the kind she had not felt since she was a teenager, about to go out on her first date with Eli Harrari, the school heartthrob. He had taken her to the cinema, to see *Thelma and Louise*. They had held hands and she had cried at the end. They went to a café on Dizengoff Street afterward, to eat ice cream, and then down to Tel Aviv beach to watch the waves. Eli Harrari. Her first love. They were together for almost five years, had trained together, lived together in a crummy one-room apartment in south Tel Aviv.

She had thought about marrying him. Until the day when she knew she would resign and return to the United States. She had tried to persuade him to come with her. Eli had laughed in her face. "You should be proud, not ashamed, of what you have done," he had said. They were the elite, chosen to serve their country. A country at war, with enemies who did not stick to any kind of rules. This was a rough neighborhood, not a cricket match. "He was a child," she had replied. Fourteen years old. Eli had shrugged. It was *regrettable*—that was the word he had used—but they needed to move on, not focus on the casualties. The casualties. Sometimes she woke at dawn, scared that she too had become one.

Yael had built a wall around herself. She could never discuss the real nature of her work, and certainly not with another UN member of staff. At first she had been invited to her colleagues' birthdays and celebrations and parties, but as her career progressed she found such occasions increasingly awkward. Everyone was intrigued about what she actually did. The Secretariat Building was a hothouse of gossip and intrigue. They wanted details. Yael didn't want to lie and she didn't want to stonewall. So in the end it seemed easier just to refuse the invitations, which dried up anyway. She became used to being alone, or meeting her needs through dead-end flings. But now, she realized, she did not want to grab brief solace in a tent on a mountain in Afghanistan, or even a suite booked for the afternoon in a five-star hotel in Manhattan. She did not want to be alone anymore. She wanted to trust someone.

She walked into her bedroom and checked herself again in the mirror. Her shoulder-length auburn hair was gathered up in a ponytail. She wore a black dress, fitted but not too tight, with a scoop neck that showcased her slim figure, a single strand of her grandmother's pearls, and black sandals. A light, clear lip gloss accentuated her wide, sensual mouth; a subtle application of mascara highlighted her green eyes. She grimaced at herself in a parody of a smile and moved her face nearer the mirror, turning from side to side. The lines around her eyes and mouth seemed slightly deeper. She looked closer. Shadows, she told herself, a trick of the light.

Satisfied, more or less, with what she saw, she walked out and picked up the ice bucket holding the white wine. She poured some into a glass, lifted it to her mouth, then put it back down. She could wait, and she would wait. She checked the food again. Her signature dish of *maqluba*—a spicy mix of chicken, rice, and vegetables—was cooked and keeping warm in the oven under a lid to stop it drying out; the salads were in their bowls in the fridge, covered with plastic wrap and ready to go. She took the bottle of champagne out of the freezer, checked it was cold enough, and placed it in the fridge door. *Maqluba* meant "upside down" in Arabic, and the flipping of the pot over a serving plate to display the dish the right side up was always a moment of great theater.

She grabbed a packet of Marlboro Lights on the sideboard. She usually only smoked on missions abroad. Cigarettes were a useful icebreaker, before negotiations began. She lit one, took a drag, then immediately stubbed it out. She lit the candles, blew them out, then lit them again. This was ridiculous, she told herself. She was behaving like a teenager. She walked over to the door and picked up a clutch of envelopes she had placed on the small standing table. The doorman had handed Yael her mail the previous evening and she had not bothered to check them. A heavy cream envelope was stamped with the frank of the Israel mission to the UN. She opened it: an invitation to a dinner for the visiting Israeli foreign minister in two weeks. It was the latest in a recent surge of invitations to receptions, cocktails, dinners. Why now?

When Yael had first started working for the UN, the Israelis had deluged her with invitations. But she had deliberately stayed away from the mission on Second Avenue, didn't even know anyone who worked there. Eventually, the invitations stopped. There must a reason for this latest charm offensive, she thought, and put the dinner invitation to one side as she leafed through the rest of the mail. A white envelope had been hand-delivered. Her name was written on the front, and there was no return address.

She was about to open the envelope when her telephone rang. The screen displayed "Unknown number."

Yael put the envelope down and pressed the green button. "Who is this?"

"Hi, this is Manuel Garcia. I am calling from the Al Jazeera UN bureau. We would like to get your comments on some footage we have that appears to show—"

"How did you get this number?"

"Is this Yael Azoulay?" Garcia asked.

She hung up.

She walked over to the picture window and stared at the Hudson River, unsettled now. The lights glimmered in the apartment blocks on the other side, shimmering in the dark water. What footage? *And where was he?* She lay down on her bed and looked resolutely at the ceiling, determined not to look at her watch. And no, she would not call. He knew where she was; he had a mobile telephone and her number. Perhaps he had been delayed. Perhaps there had been a flood or a fire in the subway.

Her mobile phone beeped again. She grabbed the phone. A text message declared, "Bon Appetit :-)" The message was from Isis Franklin, an American woman in her midforties who was head of public diplomacy at the US mission to the UN. Yael and Isis had met in Kandahar five years earlier while Yael was on mission. Yael was then a frequent visitor to Afghanistan. Isis was working for USAID, the American government aid organization, organizing literacy programs for young Afghan women. The expatriate bubble in Afghanistan was almost as macho and sexist as the country itself: a world of soldiers and spies, mercenaries and military contractors, "fixers" and the dubious hangers-on that were attracted to every war zone. Yael had dubbed them the "Oakleys," after the brand of wraparound sunglasses the men inevitably wore. The two women had naturally gravitated to each other. They spent time together, hanging out in the UN compound, chatting, because there was nowhere else for them to go in the evenings. The television room was usually full of soldiers watching soccer games or action films. A social trip into town was out of the question. The pressure-cooker world of Afghan expatriate life—the stress, danger, and isolation—accelerated their friendship. After a while, Yael and Isis became close. After Kandahar the two women lost touch, but now that Isis was in New York, she and Yael quickly fired up their friendship again. Perhaps because she worked for the State Department, rather than the UN, Isis did not try and manipulate Yael or extract information to use for her personal advantage. Instead they talked about their families, men, relationships, and their lack of them. Yael had started to confide in Isis, at least about personal issues. She had told her about her date tonight. Isis's eyes had lit up with excitement at the prospect of what she called an "in-house" romance. Yael thought about calling her, but it was too embarrassing to admit he had not arrived yet. Instead she typed a quick thanks and sent it. She and Isis were due to have lunch soon anyway to dissect the evening, although Yael was starting to suspect that it would be a very short conversation.

She looked at her watch again, promising herself it was the last time. It was 8:00 p.m. He was half an hour late, and not a word of apology. She walked into the lounge, sat down, and switched on the television news, pensive now. She went through the local channels first—there were no floods or fires on the subway—then checked CNN, Fox News, and the BBC. Manuel Garcia had unsettled her. Her number was restricted. Apart from UN colleagues, and Isis, only Sami had it. How had Al Jazeera got it?

Yael changed channels to Al Jazeera. The screen showed a scene of carnage in Afghanistan. The blackened wreckage of a car was scattered across the dirt road: melted, burnt lumps of metal, shreds of upholstery, a section of steering wheel. Three twisted, charred figures lay by a nearby drainage ditch.

Najwa's voice said, "Afghan officials have reacted with fury to the refusal of US authorities to investigate after a car traveling to the UN compound in Kandahar was hit in a drone strike in January this year. Four civilians were killed, all members of the same family, including a two-year-old boy. The boy, Babur Hamid, was taken to a US military hospital with severe burns but never regained consciousness and died the next day. Thus far, no US official has been called to account for any civilian deaths caused by drone strikes. The Afghan president has demanded to see the so-called Black File, the classified record of all drone strikes, including operational planning and debriefings. A US government spokesman expressed regret at the loss of life, but said he was unable to comment on matters of national security."

Najwa continued talking. "Coming up next . . . a Millennium mystery. What is Yael Azoulay, the secret envoy for the United Nations, doing in a New York hotel apparently posing as an escort? Stay with us, after the break."

Yael sat transfixed, all thought of her dinner date gone. She walked over to the ice bucket, poured herself a large glass of white wine, and sat down again in front of the television. A series of advertisements—investments in Qatar, Rolex watches, holidays in Oman—dragged on.

Eventually the program returned to the studio.

The video footage showed a slim woman wearing a cap

and wraparound raincoat walking down a hotel corridor. The film stopped. The camera angle switched around.

Yael's face filled the screen.

Clarence Clairborne sat back, screwed his eyes closed, and breathed deeply. He tried to remember his private prayer session with Eugene Packard early that morning and the strength it had given him, but all he could think of was his Emmy, and her, what was the word . . . *partner.*

The two of them, together. Waking up together. Going to sleep together. The things they did at night before they went to sleep. He shook his head to make the visions go away and opened his eyes. He looked at the telephone on his desk, dreading what he knew was about to come. What was the matter with him? He was a confidant of presidents, an A-list DC power broker, a regular on the *Forbes* rich list.

Clairborne held out his fingers. They trembled slightly. Was he nervous because of the call he was going to make, or because of his visitor yesterday? How much did they really know?

He willed himself to pick up the handset. It slid out from his palm and landed with a crash on the wooden edge of his desk. He placed it back in the holder and took a fresh monogrammed handkerchief from the pile in the drawer of his desk. He first wiped his forehead, then his meaty palms, one after the other, sat back, and closed his eyes.

He is lying on his bunk at Da Nang Air Base, an envelope in his hand. The air is thick and humid, heavy with the stink of fuel, the roar of airplanes and helicopters landing and taking off. The tinny sound of the Everly Brothers leaks from a radio nearby.

It is 1971 and he is twenty-one years old, an accomplished veteran of combat patrols, and already a lieutenant, popular and respected for the cares with which he treats his men's lives. The letter had arrived that morning—he was to receive a Silver Star for bravery while rescuing his sergeant under heavy fire. The medal means nothing to him. He signed up at the age of seventeen, lying about his age. A childhood spent hunting with his father had given him an easy familiarity with weapons and he proved a natural soldier. He won several awards for marksmanship and trained as a sniper.

A messenger arrives. A visitor is waiting for him in the office of Colonel Hewson, his commanding officer. He shrugs, gets up, brushes himself down, and walks across the base.

The visitor, a tall, rangy American with a midwestern accent, dressed in civilian clothes, introduces himself as Mr. Smith. Colonel Hewson leaves. Mr. Smith chats with him for a while, subtly drawing out his feelings about the war. He quickly guesses that "Mr. Smith" is from the CIA. Clairborne is a soldier, with a grunt's natural suspicion of spies, but Mr. Smith was easy to talk to and nobody had ever asked him what he thought about being in battle, taking life, and seeing men die around him. Before he realizes what he is saying, he admits that he feels hidebound by the rules of war and the Geneva conventions. America would never win in Vietnam with one hand tied behind its back, he declares. Then he stops talking, fearful that he has said too much.

Mr. Smith smiles. The two men talk some more, now about Alabama, sports, and music. After a few minutes Colonel Hewson returns. He looks at Mr. Smith, who nods. Clairborne has a choice, said Colonel Hewson. He was a much-valued officer and could stay under his command, or he could go with Mr. Smith.

He does not hesitate. He shake hands with Colonel Hewson, packs his bag, and says good-bye to his comrades. An hour later he and Mr. Smith are in a helicopter, flying along the Vietnamese coastline, before crossing over the border to Laos. They land in a training camp run by the CIA's Special Activities Division. Clairborne is recruited into the Phoenix program, a black-operations campaign designed to decapitate the North Vietnamese Communist leadership—by any means necessary.

After weeks of training, he is sent on a solo mission into territory controlled by the North Vietnamese Army. He is ordered to return with the documents of an enemy officer of at least a captain's rank. He brings back the documents of a colonel, the edges brown with the man's dried blood.

Clairborne brought himself back to the present. He wiped his hand once more with his handkerchief and checked the time. It was 7:30 p.m. in DC, which meant it was 4:30 p.m. in San Francisco. Today she only taught for a half day and came home after lunch. He looked at the two photographs on the corner of his desk, one of each of his children. A tall, well-built boy with sandy hair and a freckled grin, holding a soccer ball, stared out from the silver frame. Clarence Clairborne IV. A liquor cabinet left unlocked at a teenage birthday party. A life stopped short at the age of sixteen at the bottom of the family swimming pool. The pool had been filled in and bricked over. Clairborne's wife had never recovered from what they called "the accident." She spent her days in a haze of gin and tranquilizers, her rictus grin pulled ever tighter after each bout of plastic surgery. Despite his time in Southeast Asia, Clairborne had never believed in what he called that "karma BS." But every time he looked at the picture of his son, a memory flashed into his mind: his finger tightening on the trigger, a teenage Vietcong soldier spinning backward, the crimson spreading slowly over his uniform. At least the VC soldier had died quickly, in battle. The others, the prisoners they had taken, had not been so lucky. Those images he forced from his mind.

Clairborne stared at the other photograph, of a plump, pretty teenager, smiling uncertainly at the camera. Daddy's girl.

He picked up the telephone and dialed.

A female voice answered. He felt the familiar sense of being flustered, trapped, of being dropped into a world he did not understand, no matter how hard he tried. He glanced again at the photograph of his son.

"This is Clarence Clairborne," he said, scrunching the handkerchief in his palm. "Can I speak to Emmeline, please?"

"Hello, Mr. Clairborne. This is Abby. Please wait a moment."

He heard her put the phone down and walk across the room. He could visualize the scene: the kitchen of the apartment on Sanchez Street, the sun shining in through the wide bay windows, Emmeline asking who it was, Abby telling her, Emmeline's face set in stone.

"I'm so sorry, Mr. Clairborne, she can't talk to you right now."

"Can't or won't?" said Clairborne, his agitation barely under control.

"Either. Both. I'm sorry, Mr. Clairborne."

Clairborne felt his world sliding out from under him. Abby's friendly manner made it worse because he could not even be angry with her. "Abby . . . ," said Clairborne, his voice calm now.

"Yes, Mr. Clairborne?"

"What can I do?" he asked gently, pleading.

"Wait, Mr. Clairborne. Just wait."

The line went dead.

He stared at the handset as though it could somehow calm the torment inside him.

How had his life taken these turns? He believed in God, freedom, and the fight against tyranny, and he had proved it, every day, for five years, even when the politicians had turned on him and his comrades. Operation Phoenix had been closed down in 1972 after a series of Congressional hearings in which it was described as a "depersonalized murder program." Clairborne then spent the next two years training fighters from the Hmong, welding the Laotian hill tribesmen into an anti-Communist army. Clairborne and his Hmong soldiers raided Vietcong bases and disrupted the Ho Chi Minh trail, the main supply route from North to South Vietnam. But when the United States finally left Vietnam in 1975, it also abandoned its proxy militia. Hundreds of thousands of Hmong fled Laos and the vengeful Communists to live in squalid refugee camps in Thailand. Clairborne had combed the camps for his men and their families. He had personally brought more than three hundred Hmong to the United States and arranged for them to be naturalized, including Mahina, the sister of his closest comrade, who now sat on the other side of his mahogany office door.

But now he was working with the Iranians. A country that hated and despised the United States. A people that called his homeland "the Great Satan." A regime that wanted to wipe Israel off the map and finish what Hitler had started. His wife's cousin had been one of the fifty-two Americans held hostage in the embassy in Tehran for 444 days. He had returned home a broken man. No matter how many times the others talked him through the plan, Clairborne still had doubts. He had sinned. He had killed; he had destroyed the livelihoods of his rivals, driven at least one to suicide. He had fornicated and drank alcohol. But throughout he had remained a patriot. He was still a patriot, he told himself. It might look like he was turning on his country, abandoning the values that had sustained him all his life. And yes, sometimes he woke up in the middle of the night, sweating with fear, scrabbling for the prayer card that Eugene Packard had personally written out and dedicated to him. But all this was ultimately for the *good* of America. It would make the United States, once again, the greatest and most powerful country in the world.

Clairborne remained at his desk, his head in his hands again, letting the emotions course through him. He picked up the photographs of his children and stared at them for several minutes. He kissed each one and put them back in their place. You can't fight the pain, Eugene Packard had told him, and if we suffer it is because of God's plan, which only he knows. Clairborne found some comfort in Packard's words, but there were other comforts as well.

Clairborne reached for a glass and a crystal decanter on a small bar cart by his desk. The bourbon inside was specially blended for him by a boutique distillery he owned in Alabama. He poured himself a generous measure and swallowed a quarter of the glass. It brought him no pleasure. Instead of the familiar sweet-sour warmth, the bourbon tasted sweet and sickly. He put the drink down, and opened his planner.

The visitor was arriving Thursday. He was a crack shot and they were going duck hunting. Clairborne was no coward, neither in business nor in combat. He had seen men die around him, built up his firm from nothing. Despite his emotional turmoil he even managed to keep fairly composed when trying to talk to his daughter. But there was something especially unnerving about this man and the look in his eyes, one blue, the other brown. Especially when he had a gun in his hand.

5

Yael knelt down and put her backpack on the ground as quietly as she could. She took out two plastic containers and a bottle of Poland Spring water with a paper napkin tied around the neck and placed them near the sleeping man's shoulder. The larger box contained a portion of chicken and rice and a plastic fork, the smaller one a good-sized helping of fresh fruit salad and a plastic spoon. A yellow Post-it note, on top of the bigger box, said, "Bon Appetit—a neighbor." The homeless man was a recent fixture at the Soldiers' and Sailors' Memorial Monument. Yael had often seen him there on her early-morning runs, standing by the bicycle path, watching the sun rise over Riverside Park and the Hudson River. He was young, in his midtwenties, brawny and healthy looking, and she often wondered how he had come to be living in a park.

The memorial stood on the edge of Riverside Drive, by West Eighty-Ninth Street. It was an imposing but little-visited architectural gem, built to commemorate the soldiers and sailors who fell in the American Civil War. Twelve Corinthian columns were arranged on a raised, circular base, topped with a marble roof decorated with eagles. The memorial stood in the center of a small plaza, surrounded by low walls that looked over the Hudson River. A series of stepped terraces and walkways led down to Riverside Park. Despite the hum of traffic running by on the Henry Hudson Parkway, the memorial was a place of grace and tranquility.

It was barely 6:00 a.m. and the cream stone glowed softly in the early-morning light. The homeless man was ensconced in a corner of the lower level, curled up in an army-surplus sleeping bag on top of several sheets of thick cardboard, his breathing deep and regular. A camping stove, a jar of coffee, and several empty sandwich wrappers lay nearby. He stirred as Yael stood up but did not waken. She smiled ruefully to herself as she walked away. It was not exactly what she had planned for the dinner she had cooked, but at least some of it would go to feed somebody.

She walked briskly down to the path that ran alongside the river and began her warm-up, touching her toes and bending frontward, backward, and sideways. A silver-haired man in his seventies wearing a Ralph Lauren jogging suit trotted by, nodding to her in greeting, another of the dawn regulars. The Hudson shimmered black and silver as the city awoke, the first rays of sunlight cutting through the overcast sky. Riverside Park, a long strip of green that ran from Seventy-Second Street to 158th Street, was one of Yael's favorite places in Manhattan. On free days she sometimes cycled from one end to the other and back again. She had been thinking about inviting Sami on a bike ride next weekend—if the dinner date had gone well.

Yael ran hard and fast as her feet hit the ground, rapidly overtaking the elderly man, hoping that the physical exertion would burn away the hurt, even if only for a few minutes. How could she be such a complete idiot? A woman blessed with a near-paranormal power to read body language, sense others' emotions and desires, predict with chilling accuracy what they would do, could not see that the only reason Sami Boustani was interested in her was for the information she had.

Yael kept a steady pace until she passed the clay tennis courts at Ninety-Sixth Street, her legs pumping, her breathing deep and regular. There she sped up and sprinted another ten blocks or so. The morning breeze smelled fresh and clean, carrying a hint of the Atlantic Ocean. She took it deep into her lungs, as if it would somehow cleanse her. She slowed down at 119th Street at the next set of tennis courts, wiped the sweat from her forehead, and slowly got her breath back. Her heart was racing and her legs were aching, protesting at her unusually fast pace, as if to say you are thirty-six now, not twenty-six, and it's time you took note. Usually, she ignored that inner voice. But today she listened, and she stood by the river for several minutes, watching the colors of the water change from dark gray to green and blue as the city started a new day.

The man in the sleeping bag waited for a few seconds after Yael had left before he opened his eyes. He sat up, smiling as he saw the boxes of food, but stayed focused on his task. He took out his mobile phone from under his makeshift pillow. The text message was already written. He pressed the send button, then quickly took out a camera with a telephoto lens from inside his sleeping bag. He followed Yael down to the path that ran through Riverside Park.

Of course, the Sami thing would never have worked out anyway, she told herself. There were two large elephants in the room, both of which she had willfully ignored. The first was that Sami was a journalist, and journalists, she had learned long ago, were usually not to be given any kind of access to her private life. It was not that they were bad or immoral people. It was just that they seemed driven by an inner mania to tell the world things that really were sometimes better kept secret. But Yael really had believed that she could trust Sami. Before the coltan scandal had broken, she had shared various nuggets of information with him over the last year or so about other stories. At first Yael had wondered if he wanted to see her because he liked her, or because she knew something useful. Both, she soon realized. That was OK, people were complicated; they had mixed motives. Sami had respected her confidences, never once even hinting to his colleagues and rivals that she was a source.

But then he had burned her for the first time. Last year, Sami had somehow got hold of a memorandum Yael had written to the SG, outlining her disgust at the deal she was brokering with Hakizimani. The Hutu warlord, she had written, should be in prison. Instead he would escape justice for "tawdry reasons of realpolitik and commercial interests."

Which was completely true. The memorandum had been encrypted, but Sami, she had later learned, had received a clear copy. She still did not know for sure who had sent it. Sami had written the story; Fareed Hussein had blamed Yael for the leak, ignored her denials, and sacked her. Her life had been turned inside out.

Eventually, Yael had rationalized Sami's article. Or maybe she had persuaded herself to rationalize it. Sami was a reporter. Her memo was a major story and he had to use it. In a way she had been using him as well for a while, sending him in certain directions to cover other stories that she wanted to see in print, usually to do with human rights abuses that the SG and P5 were ignoring for political reasons. There was another explanation, one that she did not like to think about. Perhaps, subconsciously, she was attracted to Sami because part of her thought it would never work—which meant she could never get deeply involved and so never get hurt. But that was too depressing to contemplate. After Yael returned to work, she and Sami had spent some time together—a dinner or two, an exhibition at the Museum of Modern Art—but nothing physical had happened. Their growing mutual attraction was obvious, but Yael did not want a quick fling, nor did she want to jump into anything too quickly, especially with someone who worked in the same building, in case it all went wrong. She thought Sami had understood, that he wanted the same thing and was enjoying the slow buildup. She had certainly been expecting to move to a more intimate connection last night.

This, in a way, made his betrayal all the more shocking. Yael could still see him on her television screen, sitting next to Najwa, nodding knowledgeably and discussing her—her job, her *life*—as though she were just another story, which clearly, for him, she was. The other elephant was perhaps even bigger: she was an Israeli and he was a Palestinian. So far, on their coffees and lunches, they had both skirted around this, with an implicit agreement that the topic was best avoided, at least for now. Yael did not care what religion or nationality Sami—or anyone else—was. She spoke Arabic almost as well as Hebrew and felt quite at home in Levantine culture, with its clamorous family gatherings full of vivacious relatives and piles of delicious spicy food. The Palestinians too deserved their own state, she strongly believed. But it would take more than a plate of hummus to bridge the gap between her and Sami. There was no way that he would still want to see her if he found out who she used to work for, and her involvement in the fate of that frightened teenage boy at the Gaza border. Unless, perhaps, she was completely honest, told Sami herself, and explained why she had left Israel and returned to the United States. It was all entirely academic now. And probably for the best. Still something welled up inside her, something she knew she could never outrun, no matter how fast she sprinted.

Yael turned away from the river and walked into the park for a couple of minutes, picking her way through the trees along a narrow muddy path. The sound of traffic faded away, replaced by the trilling and cooing of birds. The sun had broken through now. The leaves, still wet with morning dew, sparkled in the light. She sat on a heavy branch that had fallen to the ground and leaned back against a tree.

Two sparrows landed nearby, chirping happily before they suddenly took off in unison, soaring upward, into the trees.

*S*he is lying on her back, on a narrow metal bed, naked apart from a green hospital smock. The room is white, spotless. The doctor is a woman in her forties, with a kind face.

The IV needle slips easily into her arm. She feels the speculum slide inside her, the metal cold against her skin.

*Y*ael closed her eyes, held her head in her hands, and let the tears flow.

*T*he gray Post-it note was tiny, barely the size of a stamp. Sami might have missed it if it hadn't been stuck to the handle of the door to his office. He peeled it off and read the handwritten message: "Your dinner is on the table." He checked the door again, carefully, in case there were any more mini missives. He felt excited and guilty— very guilty. Excited, because he had finally made the front page above the fold, with a story across six columns. "UN Envoy in Mystery Visit to Millennium Hotel" was that day's lead—and the newspaper had an exclusive on Najwa's CCTV footage, which was now the most-watched film in the history of the newspaper's website. Sami's editors were ecstatic.

His telephone had been ringing nonstop all morning. Jonathan Beaufort, the veteran UN correspondent for the *Times* of London had called him at 6:00 a.m. to try and get more details. Beaufort, the doyen of the UN press corps, was Sami's greatest rival. He had covered the organization for more than twenty years, had seen several SGs come and go, and had an unrivalled network of contacts. Beaufort was usually a day or so ahead of the rest of the press pack, except for Sami. It was already one o'clock in the afternoon in London, and Beaufort's editors were demanding a follow-up. Sami had eventually agreed to meet him today in the Delegates Dining Room for lunch. The DDR, as it was known, was Sami's favorite restaurant in the New York headquarters, renowned for the quality of its gossip and intrigue as much as for its food and spectacular views over the East River.

Guilty, because he knew he had hurt someone who cared about him. Someone smart, beautiful, and brave, who seemed—to his amazement—to be attracted to him. Sami had barely slept that night and not only because of the telephone calls from his relatives scattered across the Arab world who had been thrilled to see him on Al Jazeera. He turned the sequence of events over and over in his head, wondering if he had made the right move in choosing his career over his personal life. And not for the first time. He had burned her, again, and knew that this time there would be no going back. But nobody had forced him to, and so now he would have to live with the consequences.

Sami was thirty-five years old. He had joined the Gray Lady as a trainee a decade ago, fresh from Columbia University's postgraduate journalism program. His parents were incredulous when he'd managed to win a job at the country's most important newspaper with no personal connections or bribes. Even now, when he offered his thick white business card, embossed with his name and title of "United Nations Correspondent," he still felt the same frisson as on his first day. This was his third staff position, after covering Congress in Washington, DC, and a brief stint at Parliament in London. He had enjoyed London but was still mystified by the Brits. Their love of understatement and the passive conditional, and their inability to say anything directly made them impossible to decode. How did so many of them manage to do so well in New York? There were no such communication problems at the UN. The Secretariat was a hive of diplomatic maneuvering, insider information, and international intrigue, handily located a twenty-minute walk from his apartment.

Sami's contacts usually either worked for the UN itself, or one of the dozens of diplomatic missions nearby. Often there was no need to even leave the building because all the information needed for an article could be gleaned in its bars, cafés, and long, narrow corridors. The main question when dealing with contacts and sources was not so much the information they had, but the basis on which it could be reported. Sami was not naive enough to think that diplomats and UN officials told him things because of their commitment to freedom of information. His sources almost always had an agenda. There were four levels of attribution. On the record, meaning the source could be named, was usually the least useful. Nobody, apart from official department spokesmen and women, wanted to be reported as having any views or opinions on anything, and even official spokespeople were careful to be as anodyne as possible. If the conversation was going well, he pushed for a "UN official with knowledge of the issue," which narrowed the field but was still sufficiently anonymous. If that didn't work, Sami could usually persuade the source to be a "UN official," which, he argued, was adequate camouflage, as around sixty thousand people worked for the UN across the world. Otherwise, he settled for "deep background," which meant the information could be used but not attributed to anyone. Whatever their basis, the conversations were still worth having and all added nuance and texture to Sami's understanding. The really sharp operators knew how to play the system backward and kill a story. When Sami heard the words "I am going to tell you this but you cannot use it," he stopped the conversation—because to carry on would prevent him using that information if he heard it from another source.

Despite its repeated impotence, most recently in Syria, the UN was still the center of international negotiations, and the SG the world's most influential diplomat, especially during times of crisis. Decisions made by the Security Council had the force of international law. Every one of the 192 member states expended much time and energy trying to find out what those decisions might involve. Information, not money, was the building's most valuable currency. It could be—and was—bought and sold, traded and swapped. The mere sight of two diplomats from hostile countries attending the same reception could trigger speculative cables back to foreign ministries, pontificating about a potential reconciliation.

The very geography of the UN complex lent itself to

intrigue. Those who wanted to be seen talking together gathered in the Delegates Lounge, a long, wide space on the ground floor of the General Assembly building, with floor-to-ceiling windows that looked out onto First Avenue. A small raised bar at the far end, up a flight of stairs, offered a little more privacy. Away from the see-and-be-seen places were several obscure cafés and coffee bars in the bowels of the buildings. Each floor of the Secretariat Building had a small maintenance balcony that looked out over the building's inner airshaft, reached by a door from the main corridor. Until recently, these had also been popular places for confidential assignations. However, the murder of Olivia de Souza had reduced their appeal. Any invitation to meet on a balcony immediately prompted morbid quips about writing wills or buying a parachute.

Almost everybody wanted to talk to the *New York Times*, and most of his sources were just a few minutes' walk or an elevator ride away from the door of his office in the press complex in the Secretariat Building. Some contacts wanted to be wined and dined in nearby gourmet restaurants; others enjoyed a conspiratorial huddle on a little-known back staircase. He had once felt someone slide a folded piece of paper into his jacket pocket in a crowded elevator. It was an expenses claim from the assistant secretary-general for public affairs: $39,000 for a trip to the UN headquarters in Geneva with his research assistant. The resulting story had set off a firestorm and promises of reform. Six weeks later the man had been promoted to department head, taking his "assistant" with him.

Sami opened the door, and the smell of warm, stale food

hit him. His desk was covered in a mess of yellow rice, sultanas, and pieces of chicken. His computer monitor was streaked with thick white yogurt, slivers of cucumber, and shreds of fresh mint that had congealed in a puddle underneath. His chair was covered with a soft brown mess. He quickly stepped toward it and sniffed, relieved to discover that the dark slop dripping onto the floor was the remains of a chocolate mousse. An empty bottle of Taittinger champagne had rolled into one corner, a bottle of Cloudy Bay sauvignon blanc into another.

Sami picked his way through a pool of liquid on the floor that stank of alcohol. At first, his keyboard, at least, seemed to have escaped. But when he looked closer, it was dripping. He picked it up and tipped it sideways. A thin trickle of white wine ran out onto the floor.

The door opened and Najwa appeared. She was about to speak until she took in the scene in front of her.

"She said she was going to make maqluba," said Sami, his voice wry as he tilted the dripping keyboard.

Najwa could not stop laughing. "And she did. *Wallah*. She is really pissed at you."

Sami put the keyboard down, the wine still seeping from the corner. He looked for somewhere to sit in the chaos, but gave up. "I wonder why."

Najwa walked over to his desk and poked about in the mess. She extracted a small strip of brown bark and sniffed it. "Fresh cinnamon. You missed a great meal."

"I didn't miss anything. It's here. All over the office." He shook his head, as though trying to convince himself. "It's better like this. It would never work."

Najwa dropped the cinnamon in the trash can. "No. It would not. It's very simple. You are a reporter. It's your job to report. You cannot date your sources or the people you write about. If you don't like it, then get another job."

"I don't want another job. I'm good at this one," said Sami, as he traced a pattern in the yellow puddle of wine on his desk.

"Yes, you are. So let's clear this mess up."

6

Yael swerved as the man's fist flew at her.

She parried the blow with her right hand, smacking his knuckles away with an open palm, and countered with a fast left hook. He jumped away from her punch.

She jabbed again with her left and then again with her right, her palm stinging from the impact. He blocked her; she dodged and punched. Her vision narrowed, her breathing rasped in her throat, and the sweat flew from her head like a fine spray.

The pounding bass of Eminem's "Rap God" filled the space, his voice raw and angry, the thumping beat pumping up the flow of her adrenaline. All thoughts of wrecked dates, doomed romances, and meals cooked but uneaten were gone, burned away in the fierce concentration of the fight. Her body was on fire, her focus total, her eyes locked not on her opponent's face, but his upper chest, whose muscles signaled the movement his arms were about to make.

The gym was large and well equipped, reserved for residents of her apartment block. Rows of television screens hung suspended from the ceiling. A giant air conditioner rattled and hummed. Much of the space was taken up with lines of running, rowing, and cycling machines. There was a rack of weights in one corner, exercise balls in another, and a couple of benches. The floor of one corner was covered with blue exercise mats, now slippery with their sweat.

She came back with a right hook, twisting her body around for extra power. His right arm flew up, blocked her arm just above her wrist. She winced from the impact. In the second that Yael was exposed, he jumped forward, bear-hugged her under her arms, and lifted her up.

Yael had practiced Krav Maga—Hebrew for *contact combat*—for more than twenty years. Invented in the 1930s by Imre Lichtenfeld, a Hungarian Jewish boxer, as a means for Jews to defend themselves against Fascist attacks, Krav Maga was soon adopted by the Israeli army and numerous other military and law enforcement agencies. It is fast, effective, and dirty—at least compared to the formalities and etiquette of karate and kung fu. Most techniques consist of three or four moves: block, counterattack, disable the attacker, and leave the danger zone—all as quickly as possible. But the essence of Krav Maga, born out of the Holocaust, could be summed up in one word: *fight*. Yael practiced every day for at least half an hour, followed by half an hour of yoga. Yoga kept her flexible, calm, and centered. Krav Maga kept her alive.

Yael leaned back and drove her thumbs forward, straight at his eyes. There was no defense against this move. The body instantly dropped back, the reflex to save eyesight hardwired into the human brain.

He let her go.

Eminem faded away as the track ended.

They stepped apart and bumped fists, panting as the sweat poured off them.

"Feel better now?" asked Joe-Don Pabst as he handed Yael a pint bottle of Poland Spring mineral water and a towel.

She wiped her face with the towel and quickly emptied the bottle. Her heart was racing; her muscles ached; her arms, wrists, and palms were red with the impact of smacking away Joe-Don's punches.

She looked at the clock on the wall—it was nine o'clock in the morning. Her half-hour private session was over. Someone was already knocking at the door.

Yael smiled. "Yes. Much."

You did what?" asked Joe-Don forty-five minutes later, his voice disbelieving, his fork suspended in midair over a plate of eggs and bacon.

Yael briskly explained, for the second time, the fate of most of the dinner she had cooked for her and Sami.

"When did you go?"

"This morning, around dawn. I couldn't sleep. I also gave some of the food to a homeless guy but I still feel kind of guilty. It was a terrible waste," said Yael.

The waitress appeared and placed three plates in front of Yael. The first held a large tortilla, still steaming from the pan, the second was filled with brown lima beans, and the third held a tomato and onion salad.

Joe-Don looked at the food. "Are you going to eat all of that?"

Yael nodded. "You can help me," she said, slicing off a chunk of the tortilla and offering it to Joe-Don.

He shook his head. "It's all yours."

They were sitting in La Caridad on the corner of Broadway and West Seventy-Eighth Street, a few blocks from Yael's apartment. Apart from an elderly Cuban man in one corner, nursing a cup of coffee and reading that day's edition of *El Diario la Prensa*, a Spanish-language daily newspaper, the restaurant was almost deserted. The early-morning crowd had gone home and it was too early for lunch. One of the last Chinese Cuban diners in New York, and still a mainstay of the Upper West Side, La Caridad was Yael's regular breakfast spot.

Yael sprinkled chili sauce over the beans and tortilla, speared a forkful of beans, and raised it to her mouth. "Sure you don't want some?" she asked. Clean, showered, dressed in fresh clothes, she was suddenly ravenous. A run, her sparring with Joe-Don, then half an hour of yoga while Joe-Don went for a walk in Riverside Park had triggered a ferocious appetite. The food revived her quickly. She smiled, half-laughed at a memory from last night—at least, she thought, she had gone down fighting.

"What's so funny?' asked Joe-Don.

"I called Al Jazeera after the story went out. I asked for Sami, said I had some new information for him. He was still in the studio. They put me through. I said, 'Hello, this is Sharon Mantello. I hear you have some footage of me.'"

Joe-Don laughed. "And he said?"

"Nothing. I changed my accent but he knew it was me. I could sense it. I asked him if he burned all his sources. Then I hung up."

She looked out the window. An old man was slowly making his way across Broadway with the aid of a Zimmer frame. A young mother was pushing a twin baby carriage around the corner, down Seventy-Eighth Street. A policeman with an impressive paunch was chatting with the owner of a stall, half a block long, selling secondhand books. An everyday spring morning on the Upper West Side. If she thought hard enough, she could still see her father, mother, sister, Noa, and brother, David, all walking through the door here for their Saturday-morning brunch treat.

Yael's mobile telephone suddenly trilled and vibrated. She checked the incoming number: a 510 area code—Berkeley, California. She looked at the telephone for a couple of seconds as it gently shook.

Joe-Don glanced at the screen. "It's your mom. Take it."

Yael chewed her lip, unable to decide. After her parents divorced, Barbara had gone to live in San Francisco. David's death, and the brutal manner of his slaying, triggered a nervous breakdown. Barbara eventually recovered, and in the process discovered, or realized, that she preferred women to men. She had moved in with her former therapist, and they now lived in Berkeley, where they owned an antiques shop. Yael was not estranged from her mother, but relations had been cool at best, usually confined to a telephone call every couple of months. Yael still felt that Barbara had abandoned her for David and Noa and that she unfairly blamed Yael for getting divorced. In return, Barbara had never forgiven her daughter for going to live with her father. It was a poor choice, thought Yael, for she had ended up with neither parent in her life. Recently, though, her mother had been in touch more often. They had started to e-mail each other more frequently. A couple of weeks earlier, on the twentieth anniversary of David's death, Barbara had called Yael. She knew Yael would be thinking about her brother that day, she said, as Yael had been. Barbara said that she was planning a trip to New York soon. Yael had invited her to come and stay with her. Yael watched the phone trill, then let the call go to voice mail.

Yael turned back to Joe-Don. "I will call her later."

"Will you?" he asked, his voice disbelieving. "You should make up. It's been long enough."

"I will. I promise. Now let's get back to work. Who filmed me, and how did Najwa and Sami get hold of the footage?" she asked, her voice rising in annoyance.

Joe-Don frowned. "I don't get it. Our hacker friend disabled the hotel's CCTV system. The security manager agreed to an outage of twenty minutes. I called in a lot of favors to set that up. The hotel system was definitely down. And we timed everything to the minute."

"Someone hacked into the hotel's CCTV system and set up their own feed. That's a quite elaborate operation. And now my cover is blown for good," Yael said, stabbing at her tortilla with her fork.

"You knew that would happen sooner or later. I'm amazed it lasted this long, in the digital age. And you made a lot of enemies over the coltan scandal. It would help if we could get hold of a copy of the video. Then we could try and trace it back to the source," said Joe-Don. He looked at Yael, a hopeful smile playing on his craggy face.

Her body stiffened, the tines of her fork scraping across

the plate. "*No*. No, no, and no. I don't want to talk to him. I don't want to see him, hear about him, or be in the same building as him."

"Who said you have to talk to him? Just get the DVD."

"What if they e-mailed it? Or used Dropbox?"

"They didn't. My guy in the UN mailroom told me. It was a DVD. He saw Najwa open the envelope."

Yael put her fork down. "I'll think about it."

Joe-Don put his hand on hers, his callous fingers rough against the skin of her hand. "I'm sorry. I let you down."

Yael squeezed his palm. "Never."

Joe-Don Pabst, a twenty-year veteran of the UN's Department of Safety and Security, was Yael's bodyguard. A taciturn US Special Forces veteran in his late fifties, Pabst had sloping shoulders and the physique of a boxer who, despite an outer layer that had softened with age, was still hard muscle at the core. Born in Minnesota, he had thick steel-gray hair that was cut close, and a pink, fleshy face. His almost simian build belied a subtle, nuanced intelligence and a sense for danger that had made him a legend at the UN. He had served in almost every war and crisis zone where the UN had a presence. His small blue eyes exuded the steady wariness of those who had seen combat and its human cost, as they continually scanned their surrounds, seeking and processing information about potential threats.

Joe-Don passed her that day's *New York Times*, with Sami's story on the front page.

"I've read it and watched the film. Several times. The video shows me walking down the corridor, then through the door of the room, then it stops. I guess that's all they have. There's nothing about Hakizimani or what actually happened."

"For now. It could still be coming."

Yael scowled. "Really?"

"Absolutely. There shouldn't be any sound or video from inside the room. We swept it cleaner than the Oval Office. But even if there isn't, we may still have a problem. They have footage of you going in, so they presumably have footage of you leaving. And also of Hakizimani being wheeled out in a body bag."

Yael nodded. "Plus, they will have filmed you and Miguel rushing down the corridor to save me. How is Miguel, by the way?"

"Miguel sends his regards. He is fine."

"*Mmmm*, isn't he?"

"I thought you were heartbroken about your dinner date."

"That was this morning."

Joe-Don looked at his watch. "It's ten twenty-two."

"Don't worry. He's too young for me."

Joe-Don and Yael had worked together since she had been chosen by Fareed Hussein for her special role. He had saved her life when insurgents tried to kidnap her in Baghdad and Kandahar. He still walked with a slight limp from the bullet he had taken in his right leg when they were caught in a Gaza gunfight between Hamas and Fatah militants. Joe-Don was utterly uninterested in office politics. His blunt manner had made him numerous enemies, including Fareed Hussein. Back in 2003, Joe-Don had written a long memo to Hussein, then under-secretary-general of the Department for Political Affairs, outlining the security flaws at the UN headquarters in Baghdad. The report detailed how the building, which was extremely exposed, needed zigzagged approach roads with properly manned checkpoints, blast walls, and shatterproof glass. Hussein had never replied to the memo. A year later a suicide bomber had driven a truck laden with high explosives into the building, killing twenty-three people. Joe-Don had been fired for "dereliction of duty." Soon afterward, his memo was published in the *New York Times*. A discreet reminder from the US ambassador to the UN that the United States paid 25 percent of the UN budget saw him reinstated. Joe-Don had unfettered access to every UN mission and office around the world and a network of other contacts that could get him into almost any building he wanted.

"There's more," said Joe-Don. "Read page twenty-seven."

Yael turned to the business news section.

GERMAN PROSECUTORS DROP CHARGES AGAINST KZX EXECUTIVES

Decision Opens Path for NYSE Flotation

By SIMON DAVIDSON

BERLIN—German authorities have closed down a criminal investigation into the chief executive officer, finance director, and chairman of the KZX Corporation, the world's largest media conglomerate, in relation to the company's activities in eastern Congo. Although a planned merger with the Bonnet Group, a French industrial conglomerate, is on hold for now, a company official, who requested anonymity as he was not authorized to speak to journalists, said the path was clear for KZX's flotation on the New York Stock Exchange.

The closure of the German probe will be also welcomed by charities and educational institutions enriched by KZX's philanthropy. All three senior KZX executives are expected to attend the gala opening of the new Columbia University School for International Development in New York, endowed by the company, later this month, said Reinhardt Daintner, the company's chief of public affairs. "KZX is entering a new era of social responsibility. We are looking forward to proving our commitment to forging a new partnership between the corporate world and its partners in sustainable development."

Mr. Daintner refused to comment on recent rumors that KZX is engaged in discussions with the Prometheus Group, a powerful lobbying and asset management firm based in Washington, DC.

Yael put the newspaper down. "They got away with it."

"Did you expect any different?"

"Of course not. But it would be nice to be proved wrong once," said Yael as she carved herself another chunk of tortilla.

"At least you managed to stop them going through with their plan. You can be proud of that for your whole life. You helped to save thousands of lives."

"*We* did. . . . I couldn't have done it without you."

Joe-Don smiled, a barely noticeable widening of his mouth. "Whatever."

"And now KZX is in bed with Prometheus."

Joe-Don nodded and sipped his coffee. "Daintner flies into DC tonight. He is having dinner with Clairborne in the private dining room at the Prometheus headquarters. Speaking of which . . ."

Yael did not bother asking Joe-Don how he knew about Daintner. His network of contacts was unrivalled, from beat cops and spies to congressmen and ambassadors. She thought for several seconds before she answered. "Clairborne got the message. He was pretty pissed. Then he threw me out of his office."

"Did the lapel mike work?"

Yael took out her mobile phone. "Perfectly. And the microbattery."

She handed the mobile telephone to Joe-Don. The waitress appeared to fill up his coffee cup. He waited until she had left, then held the phone to his ear and played the sound clip.

"The president can go fuck herself. Which nowadays is her only option. We . . ." he recited. Joe-Don played the clip for a second time, through to the end. "We what? And who is we, apart from Clairborne?"

"I don't know. He stopped himself from finishing the sentence. He was very angry."

"I would be angry too if someone turned up in my office and ordered me to stop doing business with the Iranian Revolutionary Guard. He will be wondering what else you know, how you are getting this information, and how to stop it."

"He can't go to war with the CIA and MI6."

"No. But he has plenty of powerful friends, in DC and in London. And he can go to war with you. We are outnumbered. Why don't you take a vacation for a week, or a month or three?"

"I could, I guess. Or maybe I should get a job somewhere else." Yael looked thoughtful, remembering her grandmother's instructions. "I have a useful skill set. That might not be so bad. I could have a normal life."

"Yes," said Joe-Don, giving her a sharp look, "if you really wanted one. Meanwhile, you are famous and not just on Al Jazeera. Your Twitter hashtag is trending."

"What Twitter hashtag?"

"YaelUNagent."

Yael smiled. "How many mentions?"

"As of nine thirty-five this morning, six thousand seven hundred and seventy-five."

"It will pass. In thirty-six hours nobody will care. So now what? How am I going to handle the other reporters?"

"Stonewall. Get Henrik Schneidermann to deal with the questions. He is the SG's spokesman. And what does the SG have to say about all this? Is he going to burn you again, like the last time Sami wrote about you?"

"I don't think so. Fareed called me early this morning."

"And?"

"He seemed quite amused. Said the UN had never looked so exciting and glamorous. He must have seen the UN's Twitter feed. We are meeting in a couple of hours."

"Watch yourself. Fareed Hussein has one overriding interest."

"I know. Fareed Hussein."

Yael reached into her pocket. "Here. I brought you something else." She handed a BlackBerry to Joe-Don, together with the battery. "I scanned it. There are no more mikes or power supplies, and the GPS is disabled."

"Whose phone is it?" he asked, turning the phone over in his hands.

"One of the guys that followed me on the train. I lifted it just before he got off at Baltimore. I told you that you didn't need to come. It was a good exercise for me. I spotted the cars and picked up the foot team," she said, feeling pleased with herself.

"Are you sure you made everyone?"

Yael drank some more of her tea. The caffeine and sugar buzz gave her added confidence. "Absolutely. Two cars while I was in the taxi and a single team of two in the station."

Joe-Don pulled out his mobile telephone and showed her a photograph of a tall, balding man standing in the concourse of Union Station. "Is the guy?" he asked.

Yael nodded. "That's the one. How did you get . . . ?" Realization dawned.

"You were good. But not good enough."

Yael poked his arm, playfully, but with an edge. "I wish you would stop shadowing me."

"I'll stop when you realize I'm there."

"So who is he?"

"Colin Duncan. Ex-cop, DC vice squad. There was a

scandal about him and a teenage hooker. She killed herself. Nothing was ever proven but he left the force and joined Prometheus's security department." Joe-Don slid the phone into his pocket. "My tech guy will strip it clean. Mr. Duncan won't need it anymore."

"Why not?"

"I got a call from a friend of mine in the DC police this morning. They found him floating facedown in the Potomac."

7

Yael walked into Fareed Hussein's office to see Caroline Masters behind his desk, sitting in his chair. The deputy SG stood up and greeted her with a hug, a broad grin, and an air kiss on each cheek. Masters smelled of Shalimar perfume and face powder, a trace of which she left on Yael's right cheek. Yael resisted the urge to wipe her skin clean.

Masters picked up a file from the desk and walked across the room, to the corner where Yael had sat on Monday with the SG and Braithwaite. She gestured for Yael to join her there.

Yael followed her and sat down. She was puzzled and perturbed. Masters was not usually the hugging type. And what was she doing here, anyway?

"Where's Fareed?" Yael asked. "We had an appointment, now, at one o'clock."

Masters leaned forward, her face creased in concern. "Fareed isn't feeling well. He sends his apologies. There is no need to worry. He is resting. He has fully briefed me on this meeting."

Yael watched Masters closely as she replied. "I saw him yesterday. And I spoke to Fareed this morning. He had just finished a tennis game. He sounded fine."

The warmth in Masters's voice dropped by a notch. "As I said, Yael, Fareed sends his apologies. He is OK now, but he just had a blackout during his lunch. He is at home, with his doctors. He is exhausted." She waved her right hand around the room. "The maintenance department is fixing the heating in my office, so I thought it would be easier to meet in here. Would you like some coffee or tea?"

Yael nodded, processing both the news about the SG and its delivery. The hand waving was an unsubtle marking of territory. Masters was trying to keep her voice light and casual, but Yael sensed the brittleness underneath, her powerful hunger for ownership of the space. "Tea, please. Shall I help?" she asked, glancing at the kettle and coffee machine in the corner.

Masters looked puzzled for a moment until she realized that Yael was expecting them to make their own drinks, as Fareed often did. Masters shook her head and buzzed through to Hussein's secretary. "Grace, can we have some tea for Yael and coffee for me, please."

Masters's BlackBerry beeped to announce the arrival of a message. She picked up the phone and looked at the screen. "Will you excuse me for a moment, Yael, I have to deal with this."

Yael nodded and checked out the familiar surroundings while Masters rapidly tapped the tiny keyboard. At first the SG's office seemed the same as ever, but the scene nagged at her. Something was different. More than one thing, Yael soon realized. The photograph of Rina was no longer on the SG's desk. Nor was the picture of his brother Omar. The framed half postcard of the Taj Mahal was gone. A frame of dust on the opposite wall marked the space where the photograph of Lucy Tremlett used to hang. Yael looked again at the coffee machine in the corner of the room. Even that corner looked different, she realized. Hussein drank his coffee thick and black. The jar of his special blend of Ethiopian beans had vanished. So had Yael's jar of "Builder's Brew."

Masters was making a very bold power play, a declaration of war in all but name. She must feel very certain of her ground, thought Yael. When Hussein heard about her takeover of his office, he would surely try to sideline her, then slowly ease her out of the organization. Assuming, that is, that he was in a position to do so. But what if he was not? What if he really was ill? Hussein said he was not suffering from blackouts. Masters said he was. Somebody was lying. Yael's money was on Masters.

Yael and Caroline Masters had known each other since their graduate student days at Columbia University. They had been friendly, although not close. At fifty-two, Masters was sixteen years older than Yael. She had worked as a journalist in Bosnia, Kosovo, and Central America, then for a human rights organization in Latin America, before returning to college as a mature student. Yael remembered her as outspoken and idealistic, a liberal interventionist, but one who believed that change had to come from within the system. After graduating with a doctorate in humanitarian law, Masters had joined the State Department.

Her career progression had been steady—she served as cultural attaché in Bogotá and political second secretary in Delhi before rising to first secretary in Berlin three years ago. This was an important post. The first secretary was responsible for analyzing and advising on German and European politics, so Masters had considerable influence over the ambassador, an elderly State Department veteran about to retire. Masters had also spent three months on a placement at the KZX Corporation, working in their newly formed Office for Social Responsibility. In every posting, Masters had been accompanied by Didier, her French partner of two decades. Didier described himself as a human rights activist but never worked for any well-known organizations and seemed to have no source of income. He and Masters had never married, or even been engaged. Masters had once told Yael, while they were both students at Columbia, that she did not care about the lack of a ring on her finger, and that what mattered was mutual commitment, not bits of jewelry. Yael did not tell Masters that Didier had asked her out for coffee at least six times, undaunted by her repeated refusals, but she sensed that Masters already knew this.

Masters had been appointed deputy SG six months earlier. It was a surprise, both because of her comparative lack of UN experience and because she was an American. The post was seen as a comfortable sinecure, usually given to a woman from the developing world to demonstrate the UN's commitment to diversity and women's rights. Hussein, Yael knew, was not happy about Masters's arrival, but there was nothing he could do and anyway they both believed he had little to worry about. The deputy SG had little input into policy-making, and no deputy SG had ever made the jump to the office on the thirty-eighth floor. Until now, it seemed.

The drinks arrived, brought in by Grace Olewanda, a statuesque Congolese woman dressed in a green and gold traditional African outfit. Grace's disapproval of the interloper on her territory was almost tangible.

Masters thanked Grace and poured herself a coffee. Yael eyed Masters's folder on the table and poured three times more milk into her tea than usual.

"As you can imagine, Yael, there have been several high-level discussions about how to proceed after the news coverage yesterday and today." Masters fidgeted in her chair and brushed her bob of blond hair away from her face several times as she spoke.

Yael shrugged, picking up the signals of Masters's unease. "I spoke to Fareed—he seemed fine about it. We have been here before. It will all blow over in a day or so."

Masters's BlackBerry beeped again. She looked at the screen. "It seems Fareed is on sick leave as of today. The doctors are worried about his blackouts. They have prescribed complete rest for at least two weeks. You are the first to know, so please keep it to yourself," she said, her voice tight now.

Yael sipped her tea. "And the Istanbul Summit? It's Wednesday today. The summit opens next Thursday, in eight days. The presidents and the delegations start arriving on the Monday. Nobody knows more about the planning than Fareed."

Masters stiffened. "The preparations will continue. With or without Fareed. As you know, I have been closely involved since the idea was first conceptualized."

Yael sat up straight, on full alert now. Masters had attended several meetings in place of Fareed but had not been closely involved in the planning or agenda. Now Fareed was out of the picture—for whatever reasons—and Masters was taking over. "Why are we here, Caroline?"

"To discuss your future."

"Go on," said Yael, her eye still on Masters's folder.

The sniper is a Bedouin, thin and dark. He looks through the telescopic sight. He prepares to take the shot, his movements fluid but precise.

She places her hand on his rifle barrel and gently eases it downward. The sniper tenses, his expression angry, and turns to his commanding officer. The lieutenant is young, barely in his twenties, but this is a young people's army; compulsory national service starts at eighteen.

The lieutenant looks at her. He is nervous, jittery. There will be little credit for him if she succeeds. If she does not, he will take the blame. But these are his orders, to obey her. He hands her the wire clippers.

She thanks him and holds his gaze, her green eyes almost hypnotic.

"Five minutes," he says.

"Fifteen," she replies.

"Ten."

She nods and walks out.

Masters continued talking. "The . . . events at the Millennium Hotel, and subsequently in Geneva, took place while you were suspended from the UN. In addition, it is no secret that many of us have long been doubtful about the usefulness of your work for Fareed. The Goma Development Zone fiasco is a prime example. With the help of the corporate world, the UN could have brought stability and ended the world's longest-running humanitarian disaster."

Yael almost spat out her tea. "How? With the help of Jean-Pierre Hakizimani? He helped kill eight hundred thousand people. Most of them by hand. Including my brother. And he was planning another mass slaughter. With the help of some senior people in this house."

Masters looked grave as she spoke. "With hindsight, yes, it was a mistake to involve Hakizimani. It had never been our intention to let killers completely escape justice. But this is the real world, Yael. Sometimes we have to shake hands with the devil, for the greater good. You, more than most people, know that." She paused. "Yael, we are all so very sorry for your loss. I cannot imagine how painful it must be, especially when your personal life and your work responsibilities become mixed up. Some wounds don't heal, even after twenty years."

Yael sat up straight, on full alert now, damping down her anger. Masters was provoking her, implying that Yael was not thinking straight, because of the murder of her brother. She would not respond. But she would remember this moment, that Masters had used David, and his death, as part of an office powerplay.

Yael put her cup down. "What now?"

Masters needlessly rearranged the papers on the table. "While I recognize your contribution to the planning of the Istanbul Summit, clearly, you can have no further involvement of any kind in such a high-profile event."

Yael's voice was calm. "Without me, there would be no Istanbul Summit. It took months of work to get the P5 ambassadors into the same room, let alone agree on an agenda."

"That is my decision and it is final."

Yael sat back and regarded Masters. She had aged well. She wore a blue Donna Karan fitted jacket and knee-length skirt—Yael had the same outfit in black in her wardrobe—and a cream silk blouse with a simple gold necklace. The overall effect was elegant but feminine. The pretty, determined journalist was now a handsome career woman, with well-defined features, intelligent blue eyes, and the remnants of a tan from a winter skiing trip to Switzerland. Only the two deep lines running from her nose to her mouth and the crinkled skin around her eyes hinted at her age. Masters had once been close to President Freshwater, who had spoken of her as a protégé, a potential secretary of state.

"You were the first one in, weren't you?" asked Yael.

Masters looked puzzled. "To where?"

"Srebrenica, after it fell. I was only a teenager but remember reading your article in the *Washington Post*. 'A Harvest of Corpses.' That was the headline. That kind of reporting stays with you. And you wrote an op-ed as well. A blistering attack on the UN and on Fareed Hussein. 'A place without shame,' you said. And now you are running it."

Masters looked down, away from Yael's gaze. Her hand shook slightly as she put her papers down. "That was the past. We are here to talk about your future. There are three options."

Yael sensed ambivalence, even a hint of guilt. A picture of Clairborne, furious, slapping the arm of his chair, flashed into her mind. Provoking him had been fruitful. Normally Yael would not use the tactic she was about to, but Masters had broken the rules by bringing in David. So she too would go for the jugular.

"Let's do that, Caroline, but before we start—guess who I saw on the subway last week?"

After a month in Berlin, Didier had suddenly dumped Masters and set up home with a Danish anticapitalist protestor twenty years his junior. Soon after that, Masters was seen in the company of Reinhardt Daintner, the charismatic head of communications for KZX. The US embassy began to organize more receptions for businesspeople. There was less talk of democracy and human rights in the developing world, and more of the need for "market-based solutions." Masters and Daintner became a fixture at the city's power soirees. The whispers that Masters was running her own version of US foreign policy became ever louder. Some even said that Daintner was running the show, manipulating Masters to further the interests of KZX.

But in the perpetual internal State Department struggle between idealism and commercial interests, Masters had powerful allies who, like her, wanted a closer relationship with global corporations, especially American ones. After Didier left, Masters threw herself into her work. She wrote a paper, now famous in UN and government circles, that argued for a new partnership between development agencies and international corporations, with the UN leading the way.

Fareed Hussein had been ambivalent about Masters and her paper. He still thought of himself as an old-school idealist who believed that money and the UN's moral obligations should not mix. But he sensed that the mood was changing in Washington, DC, in favor of a greater role for corporations within the UN—and Washington paid 25 percent of the UN budget. He was also instinctively opposed to any new ideas from subordinates unless he could somehow claim credit for them, which in this case was not possible. However, Hussein had not risen to the thirty-eighth floor without a keen sense for the changing zeitgeist. As Masters's paper was increasingly cited and quoted, especially in meetings with US officials, the SG began to shift his position. Yael and many others believed that Masters's theories had provided the intellectual underpinning of the KZX–Bonnet Group plan for the Goma Development Zone. However, as a highly skilled political operator, Masters had managed to keep her name from being publicly associated with the scandal. Thus even though the Goma Development Zone had gone horribly wrong, Masters had emerged with her reputation more or less intact.

Those inside the UN who were less enthusiastic about big business had dubbed Masters's proposals "aid wash," a mechanism for companies to launder their reputations through the UN. Nonetheless, Masters's paper had been enthusiastically received by the State Department. Masters had moved to New York two years ago, tasked with setting up the new Corporate Liaison Department of USAID, the American government development agency, working out of the US mission to the UN. After six months, once that was up and running, she joined the UN's Department of Political Affairs as an assistant secretary-general. Didier had also moved to New York and they briefly reunited—until he obtained a fast-tracked green card and returned to his Danish girlfriend.

Masters shrugged. "Is this relevant?"

Yael smiled, ignoring the question. "Didier. He's married now, to Renate. You remember her, the Danish woman? They have a child on the way. They are living in Red Hook. He seemed very happy. He said he had tried to call you but no luck so far. He gave me his number. Would you like it?"

It was a half truth. Yael had not seen Didier on the subway, but the rest was true. Nor did Yael have Didier's telephone number, but she knew she would not need it.

"Sure. Thanks." Masters's face froze for several seconds before she tried to recover her composure. She reached for her coffee cup, her hand still unsteady. "Actually, no. I don't want . . . need it."

"Oh, I'm sorry. I thought you knew. You aren't in touch anymore?" asked Yael, her voice full of concern.

"No. We are not." Masters's eyes shone with anger and not just because of the news about Didier. She knew exactly what Yael was doing. She had fallen straight into the trap and humiliated herself.

Yael stopped smiling. "Is that what this is all about, Caroline?"

"All what?"

"Aid wash. KZX. Your love affair with big business. This is your revenge, isn't it?"

Masters stared at Yael, her coffee cup in her hand. She placed the cup down carefully on the table, as though worried it might spontaneously shatter from the force of her emotions.

"You, Fareed, Braithwaite," Masters almost hissed, her chest rising and falling, her eyes blazing, her voice tight. "You are all dinosaurs. Countries, borders, nation-states— it's all over. *You don't get it.* The only people who understand global governance are the corporations. KZX has a bigger turnover than the GDP of twenty-three countries. *That* is the future." She closed her eyes for a few seconds and shivered.

Yael watched Masters with fascination. It had indeed been a useful lesson. "Maybe. But my future? Three options, you said."

Masters opened her eyes, calm now. "The first is to follow the opinion of those in this house who feel that you should be sacked, immediately, stripped of your immunity, and handed over to the law enforcement agencies that wish to interview you."

"Fareed has confirmed my UN status," Yael replied. The anger was rising inside her again, but she would not show any emotion, especially not to Masters.

"In writing?"

"Of course not. But he gave me his word."

"Fareed's word may not be enough."

"Meaning?"

"I told you. Fareed is on sick leave. He may not be well enough to confirm your conversation."

Yael watched Masters carefully as she spoke. For a split second the deputy SG's eyes had looked at the door. *Bingo,* thought Yael. *Subconsciously, she wants to escape. She is not comfortable with this. I can work with that.*

Masters continued talking. "And there is this." Masters opened the folder on the corner table and took out two photographs. Underneath the pictures, Yael saw, was a pile of e-mails, addressed to Fareed Hussein. Amid the jumble of upside-down text, she saw the word "Prometheus."

Masters continued talking as she handed Yael the first photograph. "There are new developments, with serious implications. The NYPD and the police in Geneva have both launched murder investigations. The NYPD is investigating the death of Jean-Pierre Hakizimani, seen here, on the floor of room 3017 at the Millennium Hotel."

Yael looked at the picture. The color balance was washed out, as though the printer had been running out of ink. But it was definitely Hakizimani, staring at her with lifeless eyes, his body barely covered by the hotel bathrobe he had been wearing when she had jabbed him for the second time with her stun gun, disguised as a mobile phone. She had not intended to kill him—or thought she had not—but there was no point in denying her actions.

Yael gave the photograph back to Masters, saying nothing. That was one of the first lessons her instructors had taught her: watch, listen, and don't speak unless you have something to say. Let the other person fill in the silence, especially if they, like Masters, were unsure of themselves.

Masters passed Yael the second photograph. "The other investigation has been launched by the Swiss police."

Yael looked at the image. It showed a bald man with pronounced ears floating facedown in Lake Geneva. Yael willed herself not to touch the small circle of scar tissue on her left shoulder. She smiled to herself at the irony of her

situation. She had spent much of her career presenting photographs and other evidence to warlords, killers, and corrupt businessmen to get the result she wanted. Now she was
on the receiving end.

"A murder investigation is a very serious matter, Yael,"
said Masters. "Especially one in Geneva. It is crucial that we
maintain good relations there."

"The second option?" asked Yael, picking up her tea.
She dipped her little finger into the drink. It was barely
tepid now.

"You will depart gracefully, as you wish to explore new
opportunities outside the UN. We would recognize your
decade of loyal service with a year's pay and a guarantee of
lifetime legal immunity, subject of course to you signing a
confidentiality agreement."

Yael leaned forward as if to ask a question, and dropped
her cup onto the table. It shattered, splashing tea all over
Masters.

She apologized profusely. Masters's face twisted in anger
for a second, before resuming its professional mask. Yael
grabbed some napkins and made to pat Masters's leg dry.
The deputy SG shook her head, got up, and walked over to
the small kitchenette, her back to Yael. A puddle of brown
liquid crept toward Masters's folder.

T*he heat hits her like a wall as she walks into no-man's-land.
Even the wind is hot—yellow with sand, heavy with the
stench of sewage. Nothing moves, except the waves breaking gently
on the beach nearby. She feels the watchers staring at her from both
sides of the border, their eyes boring into her.*

The boy is standing on a patch of scrubland, wearing a blue windbreaker and jeans. His jacket bulges unnaturally. He is short, perhaps thirteen or fourteen, leaning forward as though weighed down. He looks strangely calm, almost serene.

He smiles as she approaches.

She greets the boy in Arabic. He returns her greeting.

She crouches down next to him, so their heads are the same height. He tells her of the money that has been promised to his family, of the paradise that awaits. She nods, listening carefully, smiling at him, making careful eye contact. She sees that he is mentally handicapped. He speaks with the phrases, and articulates the thoughts of a much younger child.

The boy's face suddenly turns fearful as though only now does he realize what he is about to do. He tenses and turns pale, the fingers of his right hand tightening.

She slips her hand around his, her voice soothing.

Yael had a few seconds at most. Masters's back was still turned. She opened the folder, grabbed the e-mail printouts, slipped them into her purse, and closed the folder.

Masters returned, her skirt still damp. "Let us continue," she said, suspecting nothing.

Part of Yael wanted to jump at Masters's offer. Twelve months' salary, combined with her savings, would be enough to live on for several years. Especially because she owned her apartment. But she would decide her fate herself, not be disposed of at the convenience of career bureaucrats like Masters. And if she left, she would never find out the truth about David's death. "I don't want to resign. Why can't I just have my job back?"

Masters looked at Yael. "I have already explained. There are two ongoing murder investigations into your activities. Returning to work in your former position is out of the question until they are resolved."

"You know as well as I do that you can make all of this go away with a couple of telephone calls."

Masters smiled. "You overestimate my influence. And in any case, the UN is committed to transparency in legal proceedings, Yael, *especially* where its staff members are concerned."

Yael shrugged. "Sack me if you want. Hand me over to the NYPD. Send me to Switzerland to face trial. I won't resign." She paused. "But I might give some interviews."

Yael knew that there was no chance of her either being arrested or extradited. She knew far too much about the UN's inner workings, and too many of the P5's innermost secrets, to be surrendered to an outside law enforcement agency. Masters couldn't sack her because of the publicity that would follow. The whole organization would look guilty, as though it had something to hide. The UN press corps would have a feeding frenzy. So what next?

Yael sat back and sipped her tea. Masters's offer was coming, she was sure.

"There may be a third option," said Masters. "Although I doubt it will appeal."

"Please let me be the judge of that. What is it?"

"The Trusteeship Council."

Yael almost laughed out loud. It was a beautiful maneuver. Masters clearly wanted her out of the picture, but in a way that would not raise questions.

Sidelining her was, from Masters's perspective, the best alternative. The Trusteeship Council would certainly do that. The council was the UN's graveyard, a final stop for those whose careers had come to an end. It had been set up in 1945 to oversee the transition from colonial rule to independence for territories such as Italian Somaliland. It had suspended operations in 1994, but met very occasionally to read and consider reports on its former fiefdoms. If Yael accepted the Trusteeship Council position, she would still be tied to the UN, where they could keep an eye on her, but completely marginalized. Or so Masters clearly believed.

Her mobile telephone rings. The boy jumps at the sound. She gives him the phone.

The boy listens to his mother's voice and starts to cry. Something falls from his right hand, suspended by a wire. She catches it.

The boy leans against her, choking and stuttering, her shoulder sodden with his snot and tears. She reaches into her back pocket.

An army Jeep roars up, its blue-and-white flag fluttering in the wind, and stops fifty yards away.

There are three passengers. A bomb-disposal expert emerges, lumbering toward her in full body armor and fishbowl helmet, like a khaki astronaut.

She signals to him, a thumbs-up. The bomb-disposal expert lurches forward until he is standing in front of her. He holds his hand out.

She drops the detonator in his palm.

Yael looked out the window, over the East River. The sky was darkening, thick gray clouds gathering. A storm was brewing. And she had to be in a distant part of the city in less than two hours. Masters thought she had outmaneuvered her. Let her believe that, because for the moment at least, both of their interests coincided. Masters wanted her trapped inside the UN. And she had to stay, for David, for herself, and even, she thought to her surprise, for Fareed. This was the only option.

"The Trusteeship Council sounds great. I will take it."

8

Henrik Schneidermann knelt forward and spat out the last morsels of his lunch. The shreds of beef and vegetables landed on the back of the toilet and slid down into the water, leaving a trail of slime on the cistern. He sat up, breathing hard, and wiped away the skein of saliva hanging from his mouth, counting how many times he had retched. This was the sixth bout, so hopefully he was done now. He had reached for the button to flush the toilet when his stomach convulsed again. He bent over as a gobbet of liquid shot out of his mouth; then he coughed, and groaned softly. But the vomit was clear now, just saliva and stomach juices.

Schneidermann waited, still on his knees, for a minute. The churning in his guts slowed, then stopped. He sat up, wiped the sheen of cold sweat from his forehead, closed the lid, and pressed the flush button. The built-in electric motor swiftly and silently sucked away the detritus. He was done. There was nothing left.

He turned sideways and leaned against the wall of the UN's executive bathroom, his eyes closed, his shirt damp on his skin, his heart racing. The Italian tiles felt cool against his back. The room was peaceful, the only sound that of water flowing through the pipes and the distant hum of an air conditioner. Perhaps he could just stay here for the afternoon. He looked at his watch. It was 3:40 p.m. Another twenty minutes until his weekly mauling began. Today, after the Al Jazeera and the *New York Times* stories about Yael, it would be especially tough. Unless he revealed what he had recently learned, which would trigger a different kind of uproar. He smiled to himself. Maybe he would tell all. But not at the press conference, just to one select journalist, and carefully. Schneidermann had closed his eyes and begun to drift away when he heard a sharp knocking on the door.

"Henrik, are you OK? You have been in there for ages. Shall I call someone?" asked a husky female voice.

He swallowed, his mouth still sour with the taste of vomit. "I'm fine," he said, trying to sound more convinced than he felt. "Just something I ate at lunchtime didn't agree with me. I will be out in a minute."

Roxana Voiculescu was Schneidermann's ferociously ambitious Romanian deputy. "Are you sure? I can take the four o'clock if you like," she replied, barely able to keep the hope out of her voice.

Schneidermann opened his eyes. "I said I am fine. I will call you if I need you," he said, his voice stronger now. "Have you finished the press bio of Caroline Masters?"

"It's on your desk."

"Thanks. I will see you in a couple of minutes."

Her footsteps faded away. He stood up and opened the cubicle door, for a moment feeling unsteady on his feet.

He stepped outside to the sink, rinsed his mouth, rested his palms on the edge of the basin, and stared at himself in the mirror. A Belgian man of medium height, in his late thirties, stared back at him: pale, podgy with rounded shoulders and washed-out blue eyes. His shirt was crumpled, his straw-blond hair thinner than ever. He gently pushed his right index finger into the soft flesh under his chin. The jowls sagged around it. Unlike many male UN officials, the spokesman for the UN secretary-general was smart enough, and blessed with enough self-awareness, to know that he was quite resistible to women. Even Roxana had stopped flirting with him after her first week, after he had rebuffed every eager smile and flick of her silky black hair.

Schneidermann had started work as UN spokesman the previous year. The job of a journalist covering the UN he had then believed, was not to hunt for scandals, corruption, and mismanagement, but to spread the word about the UN's achievements and good work so that it could enjoy more success and save even more lives. He had certainly taken this approach himself. Schneidermann had been part of the UN press corps, as a correspondent for an obscure news agency in Paris, which covered health and development issues. Most of his stories consisted of rewriting press releases from the World Health Organization and other allied UN agencies about their latest successes in combating gruesome parasitical diseases. His plan as spokesman had been to accentuate the positive. Sure, there were plenty of freeloaders and timeservers. But there was also a solid core of UN peacekeepers and aid workers who were daily risking their lives in conflict and disaster zones around the world. Just recently, tens of thousands of terrified civilians had taken refuge in the UN base in South Sudan, where they had been protected by UN troops. Schneidermann wanted to get these stories out, emphasize the human-interest angle, and try and change the way the press corps viewed the organization.

It didn't work. Nothing had prepared him for the savagery of his first briefing as spokesman: the ceaseless, relentless questioning, the refusal to take anything he said at face value, the deep-rooted cynicism underpinned by a collective assumption that everyone in the building was there to either line their pockets, build their own empires, or preferably both. The correspondents treated him with a mix of disdain and mockery. Once he had got over the shock, he did not blame them. His job, he soon discovered, was not to provide information to the two hundred or so journalists accredited to the New York headquarters, but to stonewall, obfuscate, and divert their inquiries.

The pattern was set and simple: every weekday afternoon Schneidermann shared the news the senior management wanted to be made public at a briefing long dubbed the "four o'clock follies." The journalists descended on his bland offerings like a pack of ravenous hyenas, ignoring the information he imparted and launching a barrage of questions about the latest corruption scandal or the UN's inability to act when one of its members was slaughtering its own citizens. Schneidermann replied with expressions of regret about the massacres and promises of yet more inquiries into the fate of missing monies. And then a fresh wave of stories would appear in the international media, again portraying the UN as a secretive, unresponsive organization with something to hide. The bosses' news-management strategy was a disaster, he soon realized.

Schneidermann had asked for a meeting with Caroline Masters, who as deputy SG was in charge of the Department of Public Information. He had been granted eight minutes, during which he explained his concerns and argued for a more open, responsive information policy. Masters had listened politely. The following week Schneidermann was sent on a three-day course on "maximizing interpersonal skills." Roxana Voiculescu held the press briefings, deftly batting away the press corps' questions with wit and verve. The resultant coverage was as critical as ever, but the whisper now was that Schneidermann had lost his fire. Roxana's star was rising and his, he knew, was fading.

As his disillusionment grew, Schneidermann—who was privy to much high-level gossip—found himself idly wondering if he could set up a kind of information exchange, rather like the New York Stock Exchange, where facts, rumors, and predictions could be monetized and traded like any other commodity. He was certain that the problematic part would be the technicalities of running the operation, rather than a shortage of material.

Today's press conference would likely be his last, he believed. Masters had briefed him about the topics about an hour and a half ago, in Fareed's office. He turned on the cold tap and cupped his hands under the cool water, splashing his face and neck. The water revived him and gave him courage as he thought of his instructions for the briefing. There were four main topics: Fareed Hussein's medical condition, Caroline Masters, Yael Azoulay, and the Istanbul Summit. Schneidermann did not for a moment believe that there was anything wrong with the SG's health. Nor did he believe that Yael Azoulay had willingly chosen to give up her position as the SG's secret envoy to run the Trusteeship Council. Masters had sidelined her because she was an ally of Fareed. The housecleaning had started and he knew his turn was coming soon. Masters had already dropped several hints about the need for a new head of communications for the Universal Postal Union, one of the most obscure UN agencies, which was headquartered in Bern, Switzerland. At least there he might be able to keep his lunch down, he thought, although he had no intention of taking the job.

A few months ago he had, as instructed, tried to destroy Yael's reputation. He had believed Masters when she told him that Yael was implicated in the murder of Olivia de Souza, Fareed Hussein's secretary, and was connected to the KZX-Bonnet scandal.

Schneidermann knew better now. It was thanks to Yael that Olivia's killer had been caught—and that the UN had not provided the cover for another genocide in Africa. He stood up straight. He patted down his unruly hair, fixed his tie, and smoothed his jacket. Despite Masters's explicit instructions to trash Yael, he would not make the same mistake today.

The last time Yael had seen the man known as Cyrus Jones in person was little more than a month ago in Istanbul. Now, just as her anonymous correspondent had promised, Jones was back, standing inside the front cabin of the four o'clock ferry from Staten Island, one of many passengers watching the Manhattan skyline as the ship headed toward Battery Park.

Yael was sitting behind him, about twenty yards away to the right. She was breaking all the rules by following him. Jones was a killer, one with a very personal grudge against her. She was alone, with no backup. No matter how skillful her tradecraft, she could not change her face, which Jones knew. Joe-Don, Fareed Hussein, Quentin Braithwaite, all thought she was ensconced in her new office in the UN building, mastering the intricacies of the Trusteeship Council. She had disabled the GPS in her mobile phone so she could not be tracked. But she was not scared, or even nervous.

Instead, she was locked on, totally focused as the adrenaline coursed through her. Feel the space, its borders, its atmosphere and feel the target, his movements, his behavior, his thought patterns, her instructors had told her. Use your instincts and trust them. So far, they had served her well. Her senses had gone into a familiar turbo-drive. The air was thick, charged with electricity. She could hear a conversation on the other side of the cabin, taste the Atlantic on the wind. She felt coiled, energized, as though the whole side of her body facing Jones was a giant sensor, picking up his slightest movements, thoughts, intentions.

But Jones too was a trained operative. If she could sense him, perhaps he could sense her. Yael had her hair tucked under a black woolen hat, which was covered in turn by the fake fur hood of her gray-green anorak. She wore a pair of tinted glasses, and held a pen in her hand as she pretended to do the crossword in that day's *New York Times*, which was resting on her right knee. From the side, it was almost impossible to see her face. Yael knew that Jones might still recognize her if he saw her up close, but she had no intention of allowing that to happen.

The weather had changed for the worse since her morning run. The Manhattan shoreline was wreathed in a gray mist under a sky the color of lead. The ferry was half-empty, apart from a few intrepid tourists and Staten Islanders heading into town. Rain dripped from their coats and rolled-up umbrellas, forming puddles of grimy water on the floor. The boat's central cabin was flanked by two wide, enclosed corridors on either side. Rows of hard green plastic chairs ran parallel with the corridors' large windows. Yael sat on the end of a row against the back wall. Here she could look in three directions at once and nobody could approach her from behind. Two young women near Yael were discussing the merits of the new economic adviser at the mayor's office, where they worked. She was eavesdropping, enjoying the innocent gossip, when her mobile quietly vibrated inside her coat pocket.

Keeping one eye on Jones, she took out the phone. Yael smiled as she read the SMS message:

Hey—no word from U saw Sami on AJ—guess dinner was canceled ☹ How about that lunch? X Isis.

The idea of some girl time suddenly seemed immensely appealing. Yael's thumb hovered for a second over the tiny keyboard before she slipped the mobile back inside her coat pocket. Instead, she pretended to do the crossword and continued watching Jones.

He was standing quite still, as though in a kind of trance. Jones was slim, of medium height, dressed in jeans and a black single-breasted raincoat. At first glance he looked the same as he had on the Istanbul waterfront: the broad, pale face dotted with freckles, thin lips, short dark-blond hair, the red and purple birthmark that ran down the left side of his neck from his ear to his collar. But his soul patch was gone—his face thinner now, his features sharper—as were his Oakley wraparound sunglasses, unneeded in the fading winter light.

Yael took out her phone and angled it toward Jones. The phone had been specially modified; its zoom lens had been increased by a factor of six, with diamond-sharp resolution, and the high-definition video shot ninety frames a second of near-broadcast quality, certainly good enough to withstand close examination on a full-sized computer monitor. The phone had also been fitted with extra software that allowed her to surreptitiously download content from other phones up to fifteen yards away via an encrypted Bluetooth connection. She pressed a button on the right-hand side, and Jones's sideways profile filled the screen. A small menu at the top showed the mobile telephones within range of her Bluetooth connection. One phone showed among the list as having high-level encryption. This one, she guessed, was his. She tried to connect and download his data. The telephone did not yield. Yael shut down the connection, wary of alerting him that she was trying to break in.

In the summer, tourists would be surrounding Jones, snapping pictures of the Manhattan shoreline. But today the seats, not the panorama, were coveted. The light was fading and the wind growing stronger. Waves slapped at the vessel's side, sending tremors through the hull. Yael resisted the temptation to take out the hand-delivered letter she had received yesterday, now folded in half in an envelope in her jacket pocket, and read it again. The typewritten missive had proved accurate. Jones was here, on the ferry, just as promised. She had come prepared. She tucked her legs under the seat, feeling the reassuring weight against her right ankle.

The only problem was that after five cups of strong tea that day, she urgently needed to pee. That would mean leaving Jones, but the pressure was building. Perhaps she should have brought Joe-Don after all, to cover for her during trips to the washroom. A cabin window was open and Yael shivered as a gust of cold, damp air hit her. The bumpy ride, as the ship rose up and down with the waves, was not helping. She squirmed on her seat. It didn't work. She had to use the restroom. The waves were higher now and water was splashing onto the corridor. A loose door swung back and forth in the wind, banging against a heavy, rusty chain. One of the young women sitting near Yael stood up, walked over to the window, and closed it. The boat lurched and she slipped on the wet floor, but managed to right herself in time.

Jones, however, seemed completely unperturbed as he rode the rise and fall of the waves. Then he suddenly turned around, scanning the passenger deck. Yael instantly dropped her head, absorbed in the *New York Times* crossword. She could see, out of the corner of her eyes, that he was walking toward the stairs to the lower deck. She was about to stand up and follow him when a plump woman in her early thirties sat down next to her.

One day," her instructor tells her, "you will be on a mission, maybe in a foreign country. You will meet someone you know—by pure chance, in a hotel, an elevator, or an airport. The world is much smaller than we think. They will say your name. You may be far from home, in danger, so happy to see a friendly face."

"And what do I do?" she asks.

"You learn to lie. Or you die."

They had harvested her life and given her a list of people, places, and times. College friends gathering in a café, former army comrades having a reunion, even her childhood sweetheart on his way home from work.

She had appeared as instructed, made sure she was seen at each place. None of her friends knew she was coming; all were pleased to see her—at first.

She passed every test: shrugged off their greetings, stayed stone-faced at their protestations, walked away from their pleas. Most were puzzled; a couple became angry. Several believed her, and apologized for their mistake, for bothering her. The power of it thrilled and terrified her.

Her instructors are pleased. She has done very well, and the exercise is over. She is free for the rest of the day. She calls her favorite cousin, Sarah, and arranges to meet at a café on Dizengoff Street.

Yael?" the woman sitting down next to her asked.

Yael said nothing.

The woman peered around and stared into Yael's face. "I thought it was you," she said delightedly, her Bronx accent cutting through the rumble of the boat's motors. "What are you doing here?"

9

The buzz of conversation in the pressroom faded away as Henrik Schneidermann walked in, flanked by Roxana Voiculescu holding the printouts of the day's briefing notes. Many of the UN press corps were genuine journalists, but their numbers were leavened with a good number of spies whose reports were much appreciated by their bosses but certainly never published. Several correspondents, Schneidermann knew, reported both for their declared media and to their national intelligence service. Some "correspondents" had never written a news story, nor would they know how to, because they were not journalists but relatives of diplomats at the various missions to the UN who wanted an easy way to get a US visa.

Usually, a few dozen journalists at most turned up for Schneidermann's weekly briefings. A good turnout was around one hundred. Today, there were more than double that. It seemed to Schneidermann that every accredited reporter was here, rows of them, staring at him as though he were about to announce the second coming. The UN rumor mill had been working overtime during the last couple of days: Yael Azoulay was about to be stripped of her legal immunity and arrested in connection with the death of Jean-Pierre Hakizimani; the Swiss authorities had demanded her extradition because she'd drowned someone, possibly an American, in Lake Geneva; Fareed Hussein was in the hospital after suffering a heart attack; the Istanbul Summit was about to be canceled; Caroline Masters had organized a coup.

The back of the room and the sides were filled with television crews: Schneidermann counted familiar faces from the BBC, CNN, Al Jazeera, Reuters, Russia Today, and Associated Press, as well teams from Japan, Brazil, Pakistan, India, and South Africa. A platoon of microphones, their thick tangle of black cables trailing onto the floor, stood on the long wooden desk in front of his lectern. The camera operators fussed over their headphones, checked their sound readings, and peered through their viewfinders, while their correspondents subtly jostled each other, trying to ensure that they had a better position than the competition. Najwa al-Sameera and her crew were in pole position, at the front of the room on the right-hand side.

Sami Boustani, Schneidermann saw, was in his customary place, leaning on the wall toward the back of the room, looking strangely preoccupied. Sami rarely asked questions at the press briefing. He had no taste for grandstanding, and also did not want to reveal even a hint of his interests for fear of alerting the competition to a potential story. Instead he usually arranged to see Schneidermann privately.

The UN spokesman stood at his lectern, its beige wood emblazoned with the UN emblem, against a backdrop of dark blue fabric. His slim, angular microphone pointed upward on a metal rod. Roxana walked down the rows of chairs, handing out that day's printed briefing: a one-page biography of Caroline Masters and the usual summaries of resolutions passed by the UN's numerous committees.

Schneidermann leaned forward. He felt calm and in control. Even his stomach had stopped growling. He tapped the microphone and the last murmurs faded away. Dozens of expectant faces looked back at him as he began to speak.

"As many of you know, the secretary-general has not been well lately. The SG is now on sick leave. Some of his responsibilities will be divided up between the under-secretaries-general, the department heads. But the main burden of his workload will be assumed by Caroline Masters, the deputy secretary-general. The regrettable cause of Ms. Masters's promotion notwithstanding, the UN management board is pleased to confirm her appointment as acting secretary-general."

The journalists looked at each other, nodding. It had been worth turning up today. Caroline Masters was a major story. The print reporters started scribbling, the radio journalists checked their sound levels, peering at the readings on the dials. Some of the television correspondents anxiously looked at their cameramen, fearful that their crews might be missing Schneidermann's announcement. Najwa had no such worries. She leaned against the wall, holding her mobile telephone. The instant Schneidermann had finished his sentence she pressed the "tweet this" button on her phone screen. Najwa had already written the short message announcing Masters's appointment and had just needed Schneidermann's confirmation.

A tall, languid Englishman, wearing creased jeans, a black turtleneck sweater, and a brown corduroy jacket immediately stood up.

Schneidermann nodded in acknowledgment. "Yes, Jonathan," he asked.

Beaufort intentionally paused for several seconds, combing his blond hair back with his fingers as the tension rose in the room. He looked puzzled as he spoke. "Henrik, if the SG is sick, then why was he playing tennis this morning?"

Schneidermann smiled, his voice confident and friendly. "I have no information on the SG's sporting activity this morning, or any other morning. His daily routine, before he comes to work, is his own affair—"

Beaufort interrupted, his voice indignant. "The SG is the world's most important diplomat. His health is a matter of legitimate public interest. His health is everyone's affair—"

Schneidermann jumped in. "Jonathan, if you would *please* let me finish my sentence. Of course his health is a matter of public interest. And I have told you. He is now on sick leave. But the precise details of his medical condition are a matter for his doctors. I am sure you understand, Jonathan, that those details should remain confidential. Even though he is a public figure, as a human being he deserves the same privileges as any patient."

Beaufort looked puzzled. Where was the Schneidermann of old, brusque and irritable? When had he learned to bat back press inquiries so smoothly, making the questioner seem ill-mannered and intrusive? He switched topics. "Who decided that Caroline Masters should take over the

SG's role? What kind of consultation has there been on this, and how long do you expect her to fill the position?"

Schneidermann had an almost overwhelming urge to reply, *Caroline Masters's appointment is a complete mystery to me. I don't believe that Fareed is really sick, I am still trying to work out how she got the job, and I am sure that nothing good will come of this.* Instead he said: "As Fareed's deputy, Caroline was the obvious candidate. All the members of the Security Council were in agreement."

Beaufort looked doubtful. "Even the Iranians?"

Iran had just started a two-year term as one of ten nonpermanent members of the Security Council. Schneidermann nodded. "As I said, all fifteen members of the Security Council were in agreement, both the P5 and the nonpermanent members. Thank you, Jonathan, and now, I am sure some of your colleagues have questions."

"Why has Yael Azoulay been demoted?" demanded Najwa. "Is it because of our report and the article in the *New York Times* today?"

Schneidermann leaned forward, a pleasant smile on his lips. "Najwa, let me assure you and your colleagues that Ms. Azoulay has not been demoted. She has been *promoted*. She now holds the rank of assistant secretary-general, which as you all know, is only one level below that of department head. There is no mystery about this. It is all there, in print, on the briefing note you have been handed by Roxana."

Najwa looked down at the sheet of paper and snorted derisively. "Assistant secretary-general in charge of the Trusteeship Council, which has met precisely three times this century."

Every eye in the room was on Schneidermann's duel with Najwa. He swallowed, then rallied. "Many of the problems the world faces nowadays, from Syria to Somalia, relate back to the dissolution of the former colonial empires. We think Yael's unique skill set will prove immensely beneficial."

She snapped back, "Like posing as a hooker under a false name in the Millennium Hotel?"

Schneidermann looked puzzled. "Meaning?"

Najwa said, "I hope you watch Al Jazeera. You certainly read the *New York Times*. You saw Sami's piece."

"I did. And I saw your report, Najwa."

"Great. So what is the UN's response?"

Schneidermann had been expecting this of course, either from Sami or Najwa. He had discussed with Caroline Masters how to respond to Najwa's report and Sami's article about Yael. Masters had instructed him to say that Yael's private life was her own affair, meaning: hang her out to dry. When Schneidermann had argued strongly against this because it would be an unfair smear, Masters had looked him in the eye and reminded him that there was no evidence that Yael was on official UN business at the hotel, which was in fact true. Schneidermann had tried a different tack. Such an answer, he said, would trigger questions as to why, if there were such questions over Yael's judgment and personal life, she had been promoted to assistant secretary-general. But Masters had dismissed his concerns, and he understood why. The press corps would sense that the UN was distancing itself from Yael, and so pursue her and the hotel story with even greater vigor. Eventually the pressure on Yael would become unbearable, her position untenable, and Masters could force her to resign. And by then, if Yael did go public with her knowledge of the UN's secret deals and maneuvers, her revelations would be dismissed as the fantasies of an embittered ex-employee.

Schneidermann kept his face composed. "All I can say at this stage is that we are seeking further information."

Najwa stared at him, her voice indignant. "We are also seeking further information, Henrik. Who was inside the room? Was this official UN business? If so, can we have some details please? If not, then what was Yael Azoulay doing there? Why were there two security guards outside the door? Who were these security guards and who did they work for?"

"We are seeking further information," Schneidermann repeated beatifically. "You can quote me. That's it on that subject."

Najwa rolled her eyes and sat down.

"Any other questions? The Economic and Social Council meeting this afternoon looks like it could be especially interesting. . . ." He looked around with a practiced air of faux expectation. The only UN council meeting that ever produced any news was the Security Council, which was not meeting today.

Murat Yilmaz stood up and raised his hand. Yilmaz, the correspondent for Anadolu, the Turkish state news agency, was a gray-haired, portly man in his late fifties, with deep lines around his brown eyes. Courteous and friendly, a bon vivant who took full advantage of New York's restaurants, Yilmaz had been posted to the UN for over a decade. Like his homeland, Yilmaz cultivated good relations with all sides, including the Americans, Saudis, Iranians, and Israelis. Schneidermann was certain that if he was not an actual spy, he was feeding information to the Milli İstihbarat Teşkilatı, the Turkish intelligence service.

"Thank you, Henrik. Regrettably, I must pass on your kind offer," he said in his rich baritone, provoking gentle laughter, "but I would like to ask about the forthcoming Istanbul Summit. As you know, the UN, the P5, and of course Turkey itself have invested enormous time, effort, and resources. Fareed Hussein has said that a successful summit will be his legacy to the organization. How will this be affected by the appointment of Caroline Masters?"

Schneidermann nodded. "As you can see from the biography which my colleague Roxana has distributed, Acting SG Masters has herself been closely involved with the planning for the summit. She has been fully briefed by SG Hussein. We do not anticipate any delays or difficulties."

"So everything is going ahead as planned? The summit will open in eight days, next Thursday? It will still deal with Israel-Palestine, Syria, and Egypt? President Freshwater will attend, together with the presidents of Russia, China, France, and the British prime minister?"

"Yes, Murat, absolutely. And your own honored president as well. We should have more details for you in the next few days."

Yilmaz finished scribbling his notes and sat back down.

Schneidermann allowed himself to relax a little. The SG's health, Yael Azoulay, the summit, and Masters's appointment were covered. A few more questions followed on

Iran, Syria, and a new World Health Organization program to eliminate polio before the journalists began to file out of the room, volubly complaining that they had learned almost nothing about why Masters had been appointed or the latest developments in the Yael Azoulay saga.

Schneidermann felt quite pleased with himself, especially when he saw Roxana's irritation at how well the press briefing had gone. Even she would have to report to Caroline Masters that it had been a bravura performance. He had deflected the difficult questions while being generous with information that was already in the public domain, thus confirming him in every UN correspondent's mind as a typical functionary, which today at least had been his intention.

As Sami walked out, he returned Schneidermann's nod of greeting. The UN spokesman's mobile rang. He looked at the screen and saw it was the acting SG's office. He did not want to speak to Caroline Masters now. He ignored the call, took out an old, obsolete Nokia phone, and quickly tapped out a message. A second later Sami's mobile telephone beeped that an SMS had arrived.

A dozen blocks north of the Secretariat Building, just off East Fifty-Fourth Street, Fareed Hussein sat at his desk in his home office, his coffee cooling in front of him. Number 3 Sutton Place, the official residence of the secretary-general, was a five-story, fourteen-thousand-square-foot house built in 1921 for Anne Morgan, the daughter of J. P. Morgan, and later donated to the United Nations. Its centerpiece was a heavy dark wooden staircase that curved around the spine of the house, as though the mansion had been transplanted from the countryside to the Upper East Side. Hussein's office on the third floor was decorated in a similar style to the other rooms: tasteful but bland, with the faux elegance of a five-star hotel. The walls were pale yellow, the floor polished hardwood. A small painting hung in the center of each wall: two of thorough-bred racehorses, two of New England in the autumn. The window looked over a small playground and the East River.

Hussein picked up the book on the top of the pile. As usual, the cracked spine fell open at page 162.

That day, August 15, 1947, is seared forever onto my memory. We left home early, around seven o'clock in the morning, nervous and excited, our bags packed and stowed in the trunk. Our parents told us it was just for a couple of weeks, until the situation calmed down again. Perhaps they even believed that. But we would never return to live in newly independent India.

The drive to the train station from our house usu-ally took about fifteen minutes, but my parents had allowed for an hour. I was sitting on the backseat of our Morris Oxford with Omar and my mother. My father was in the front, next to Anwar, our driver.

We had gone about a mile or so when we heard the shouting. Anwar told us all to close the windows and check that the doors were locked. The mob sur-rounded us a few moments later. Anwar tried to re-verse, but the crush of people was too thick. They were banging on the roof, screaming and howling like banshees, rocking the car back and forth. The rear windscreen cracked. They ripped the mirrors off.

Anwar said he would go out and try and calm them. My father protested, said we should wait, that the crowd would disperse and help would come.

Anwar smiled and opened the door. He stepped onto the road, his hands in the air to show he was not carrying a weapon. He began to speak. I can still see his lips moving through the car window. For a moment there was calm. Then the mob surged forward, as one. They punched, kicked, spat upon Anwar. He stumbled and fell. I could see dozens of legs, all swinging back and forth.

I pulled Omar toward me and covered his eyes. The seat turned warm and wet underneath us. My father was praying; my mother was crying. Anwar lay there, unmoving, a pool of crimson forming around his head.

The mob swirled around our car again. I remember how blue the sky was, a pale, light color, dotted with clouds of purest white. As blue as the flag, with the white emblem in the center, that fluttered from the hood of the car that was slowly driving toward us.

Hussein stopped reading and flicked through to the front of his memoir. He looked at the dedication: "In Memory of Anwar Hindi, 1915–1947," and put the book down.

Hussein walked over to the window. The sky was overcast and the breeze was cold, blowing in from the East River. He watched a garbage scow chug upriver, toward

Spanish Harlem and the Bronx, looked southward, toward the UN complex, then glanced at his watch: just after four o'clock. Schneidermann would be giving his press briefing. He would miss their chats. The Belgian was finding his feet, and had some increasingly good ideas about policies and how to better the UN's press coverage. He had been thinking of promoting him, making Schneidermann a special adviser. But that was not going to happen, at least not for a while. What was the phrase that had been so popular in the 1960s? "Today is the first day of the rest of your life." Today was Wednesday. It was hard to believe that just two days ago he had been sitting in his office with Yael and Braithwaite, discussing the Istanbul Summit and the Prometheus Group.

He was not suffering from blackouts. He had been getting ill, but from stress, his nerves stretched like violin strings, waiting for the next hint from Caroline Masters that he should miss a meeting, suddenly be unavailable. The threat was never spelled out, but then it didn't need to be. A brief e-mail to Masters from a new hire in the UN's archives, cc'd to Hussein, was enough. A file from the Department of Peacekeeping records, about eastern Bosnia in early July 1995, believed to have gone missing soon after the Srebrenica massacre, had just been relocated. Hussein knew it had gone missing because he had personally removed it from the archives. It was locked in his office safe, on the other side of the room. As far as he knew, there were no copies. So where had this one come from? Those papers, he knew, could destroy not just his career but also his reputation. There would be no charitable foundation once he retired, no library, no invitation to join the "Elders," the team of gray-haired former statesmen, diplomats, and businessmen that jetted around the world, trying to do good. And all because he had followed his instructions. Just as he had always done, even as a child.

Hussein closed his eyes for a moment and rested his head against the window, overwhelmed by the memories.

The car is an American army surplus Jeep. A large blue and white UN emblem is painted on each door; two small UN flags flutter above the headlights. The crowd falls silent as the car draws nearer, wary of officialdom, worried now about what they have just done.

A short, wiry Indian man steps out of the car. He carries no weapons and wears civilian clothes. He checks Anwar's body, shakes his head, and walks over to the Hussein family car.

One of the leaders of the mob stands in front of him, a bloody stave in his hand. "Muslim or Hindu?" he demands.

The man looks up at him. "I work for the United Nations. We are neutral."

The mob leader looks at the Jeep, then back at the UN official, frowning in puzzlement. "Muslim or Hindu?" he asks again.

"Neutral," says the UN official, calmly. "The UN does not take sides. It is neutral."

The mob leader stands aside. The UN official walks over to the Hussein family's car and quickly ushers them into his Jeep.

Hussein lifted his head, turned, and looked at the photographs on his desk. His wife, Zeinab, looking glamorous at a reception for President Freshwater. Zeinab had been away for months. She said she was ashamed to show her face after the *New York Times* had reported that she had shares in a firm linked to the coltan scandal. Hussein had not tried very hard to persuade her to return. They had grown apart years before but stayed together for the sake of Hussein's career. His daughter, Rina, in her graduation dress. Rina would not speak to him, kept denouncing him on Twitter to her 11,678 followers. He walked over and picked up the half postcard of the Taj Mahal. If he thought hard enough, he could still feel Omar's tiny fingers entwined with his, hear his cry of fear as his hand was pulled away and he vanished into the chaos at Delhi Station. The guilt still gnawed at him, was especially bad on days like these. Why had they gotten on the train? He should have stayed, stayed to search for Omar. He could still see his father shouting, his mother almost hysterical. Hussein stared down at his fingers, the fingers that had failed to hold on to his little brother. He clenched his hand, digging his nails into his palms until his knuckles turned white.

There was a new photograph on his desk. This one he usually kept in his drawer at his UN office but at home there were no constraints. The picture had been taken earlier that year. It showed Hussein and Yael at a refugee camp in Jordan, after he had inaugurated a new UN education program. She wore combat trousers and a long-sleeved T-shirt, her hair covered under a head scarf as she crouched down, talking to a Syrian boy from Aleppo. She was one of the bravest and most talented people he had ever worked with. Despite their tangled, difficult history, in some ways they were a perfect match. Yael did not talk to her father. He did not talk to his daughter. They both filled part of the void in each other's lives, he liked to think. Yael had only failed on one mission. He had asked her to make contact with Rina and try and fix his broken relationship with his daughter. The two women had met several times and enjoyed each other's company. Until Yael had mentioned Rina's father. Rina had walked out of the restaurant and never spoke to Yael again.

And Yael was right about Prometheus. The material Braithwaite had shown them yesterday, detailing the full extent of the links between the Prometheus Group and Iranian intelligence, was explosive. Up on the thirty-eighth floor, he had hesitated. There were subtle calculations to be made about such a move and its consequences. The view from Sutton Place, on sick leave for a nonexistent illness, however, was much clearer. Once the full Prometheus–Iran connection was public knowledge, Masters's UN career would be over. So would all this nonsense about a role for corporations. He might even be able to persuade the Justice Department to look into criminal charges.

Hussein's plan was simple enough. He just needed to make sure there were none of his fingerprints on it. He opened the drawer of his desk, took out a file of papers, and flicked through the sheets. He smiled. Everything was ready.

She is five minutes early, sitting down at a table reading Haaretz, *when her telephone buzzes. She takes the call, lis-*

tens, does not protest at the intrusion, argue with her new orders, for there is no point.

Sarah arrives and greets her, smiling with pleasure.

Yael's face is blank. She says, "Who are you?"

"What a question. I am your cousin. We just spoke on the phone. What's wrong?"

"I don't know you. You are bothering me. That's what wrong."

"Is this some kind of joke? Because it's not very funny." Sarah reaches inside her bag and takes out a book, the new Amos Oz novel. "Here, you asked for this."

Yael looks her in the eye. "I said, I don't know you." She pushes the book back across the table, ignoring the anguish tearing at her inside. "And I don't want your book."

Sarah's open, trusting face twists in pain. She reaches for Yael's hand. Yael instantly pulls it away. She sits back, her arms crossed, her eyes cold.

"Why are you doing this?" asks Sarah, her voice cracking.

Yael returns to her newspaper.

Sarah stands up and walks away, tearful now.

She watches Sarah go, willing herself not to cry.

The ferry sounded its foghorn, a deep lowing that carried far over the water. The mournful sound matched Yael's mood. The encounter on the boat had broken her concentration. The demons had gleefully marched back in, feeling quite at home. What a trail of destruction she left in her wake, she thought: dead bodies, wrecked relationships, stillborn love affairs, ruptured family connections. Her relationship with Sarah had never properly recovered. Yael had called her a couple of days later, to invite her for a coffee. Sarah had not answered her calls. Eventually, Yael had gone to her apartment, claiming complete ignorance of their previous encounter. Sarah had eventually agreed to meet her, but despite Yael's best efforts they never regained the closeness they had enjoyed before.

And now Yael could add Miranda Napolitano to her list. The two women had worked together a decade or so ago, when Yael first joined the UN, and soon became friends. Miranda had been the PA to the head of peacekeeping. Bronx born and bred, Miranda had been taking night classes in international affairs at college when she had become pregnant. Under pressure from her Italian family, she had married her boyfriend and resigned. Although she and Yael had promised to stay in touch, they had eventually lost contact.

Miranda had proved surprisingly persistent when she sat down, or perhaps Yael was losing her touch. Miranda had explained that she was now a housewife, still married to her boyfriend, living on Staten Island. Miranda simply did not believe that Yael did not recognize her. Yael's mask began to slip. She had ached to tell Miranda that she was right, to talk about old times and bring her up to date on the latest office gossip. Then Cyrus Jones had reappeared. Yael's inner wavering evaporated. Her mask slid back into place. Miranda eventually gave up, annoyed and disbelieving, and went to sit somewhere else.

Yael watched Manhattan slide closer into view. The radio masts on the skyscrapers' roofs blinked orange and their windows were a honeycomb of light in the gloomy dusk. The mist was thick now, trailing around the buildings, ghostly tendrils floating through the canyons of Wall Street onto the surface of water the color of gunmetal. Yael looked for the newly built Freedom Tower, which had replaced the Twin Towers destroyed on 9/11. A memory flashed into her mind: her fifteenth birthday lunch at the Windows on the World restaurant in the old World Trade Center with her brother David. He had told her he was gay. The news had not surprised her. She had long wondered why he never brought a girl home. She turned David's ring around on her finger.

Apart from Joe-Don, there were no men in her life. Except, of course, for Cyrus Jones, she mused, with a glimmer of a smile. The waves were rougher now, foaming white on their crests, slamming hard against the sides of the hull. Yael could feel the engines straining to keep the ship on a straight path as the ferry slowed, beginning to maneuver itself into the harbor. She thought briefly of Sami, his intelligent brown eyes, his wild curly hair and almost touching naïveté with women, or at least with her. Then she remembered his appearance with Najwa on Al Jazeera. Not so naive, after all.

She watched a giant cargo ship sail by, its long deck piled high with shipping containers. The wind blew the cabin window open again, and it smashed back and forth against the handrail. She shifted in her seat, trying to get comfortable. The pressure in her bladder was near irresistible now. She had to go to the toilet. It should be OK. She and Jones were on a boat. He couldn't go anywhere else and they were not due to arrive at South Ferry for another ten minutes. There was a restroom near her seat, but within Jones's peripheral vision. Yael stood up, turned around, walked along the deck away from the prow, and down the stairs to the ladies' restroom.

She was washing her hands in the basin, her purse next to the tap, when the door opened behind her. She looked up into the mirror.

"Hello, Yael," he said.

The restroom was narrow, barely eight feet wide. As Jones said the first syllable of Yael's name she was already twisting in midair.

By the time he finished the second syllable she crashed face-first into him, slamming him backward into the rear wall.

Jones's shot went wide and hit the mirror. It shattered, showering the washbasin with slivers of broken glass.

Yael instantly grabbed the barrel of his gun with her left hand. She slammed the pistol against his chest, trapping the weapon under her forearm, using her bodyweight to pin him hard against the wall.

The room shrank around her, as the adrenaline pumped and her sixth sense went into overdrive. She knew how Jones would counterattack before he knew himself.

Jones tried to twist out from under her, his left hand balling into a fist as it flew at her face.

Yael dodged the blow, turned at the hip, and slammed her right fist into his groin again and again. Buttressed against the wall, Jones had nowhere to go. He grunted and turned white.

The heavily scratched silencer on Jones's pistol added a good five inches to the barrel. That was a disadvantage for him. It made the gun more difficult to use against an opponent versed in close-quarter fighting, and it gave Yael extra leverage as she held on.

Jones tried to squirm away from her. She kept her grip on the barrel, pushing his gun arm so hard against his ribs that she could feel them pressing against her fingers. But then she moved her hips out to bring her body weight into another punch to his groin.

Jones felt the lessening of pressure on his chest. He drove his left fist into her left shoulder, his middle knuckle extended, twisting around to dig into her scar as though he had been precisely briefed on her weakest point. She gasped as the pain shot down her left side. She willed herself to ignore it and shifted back to push the gun harder against him.

Yael brought her right knee up fast, toward his groin. Jones blocked her with his thigh and raised his left hand again, his fingers extended now, jabbing at her eyes.

Yael jerked away, taking the blow on the side of her face. Jones's fingers slid down her cheeks, scraping her skin. She yanked the gun sharply upward. Trapped inside the trigger guard, Jones's right index finger snapped. He yelped in pain and slammed his fist down toward Yael's nose.

She dodged sideways, feeling the hammer blow on her collarbone as she swept his legs from under him. The gun flew away, sliding back and forth across the restroom floor as the ferry was buffeted by the waves. They scrabbled trying to reach it. Yael slipped and went down hard. Jones landed between her legs and jumped on top of her, grabbing her throat with both hands, ignoring the pain in his broken finger, driving his thumbs into her windpipe.

Yael coughed and jerked her head sharply to the left, trapping the fingers of his right hand between her throat and her collarbone. The move distracted Jones and bought her a precious second. She yanked Jones's thumbs down and away from her neck. She pushed her back up into the bridge position, taking his weight on her knees and thighs, raising his body above hers. Held up by her hips, Jones flailed uselessly, too high for his blows to connect.

Yael clenched her left fist and slammed it into his right side, using the momentum to flip him sideways and underneath her. Now she was on top. But Jones was also trained in close-quarter combat. He tried the same maneuver, pushing his hips up to try and flip her over.

Yael was too fast for him. She punched him in the face with her left hand, lifted his head and slammed it against the floor, rolled backward over her left shoulder, and jumped up, hands up in front of her face, ready for a counterattack. There was none.

Jones lay supine and dazed for several seconds. He tried to slide toward the gun.

A brown mist descended over Yael's vision. She kicked Jones in his side.

Her breath turned thick in her throat.

Something fell away inside her.

Jones lay still.

She raised her foot over his head.

The brown mist darkened.

Jones groaned, a thin trickle of blood dripping from his nose. His eyes opened.

Yael's vision widened out. The mist receded.

She dropped her foot, controlled her breathing to center herself. She quickly stepped around him and picked up the gun. It was a .22 Beretta, she noted with interest. The same caliber and make that had fired a bullet through her shoulder on the shore of Lake Geneva.

The weapon felt slippery in her hand.

She pulled the trigger.

The gun made a muffled pop.

The bullet hit the floor a foot away from the right side of Jones's head.

He stared at her, his face contorted in a mix of fear and fury. "We are coming for you, Yael. If not me, then someone else. And we won't stop. Ever."

She thought quickly. There was a powerful argument for killing Jones. He knew her face, where she worked, and could easily find out where she lived. And this was personal. Any man who had thought he was going on a dinner date in a romantic restaurant overlooking Istanbul only to end up in a basement owned by the Syrian affiliate of al-Qaeda, with footage of the ordeal freely available on the Internet, had good reason to want revenge. Yael had killed before: Hakizimani in the Millennium Hotel and her attacker on Lake Geneva. But Hakizimani's death had been an accident, perhaps. The fight on Lake Geneva had been a fight for her life. She had no doubt that her opponent would have killed her. Jones was different. He could have shot her as soon as he walked into the washroom, yet for whatever reason, he had not. To kill him now would be cold-blooded murder. In addition, the South Ferry terminal had CCTV. Her DNA and fingerprints were all over this room. Her UN immunity would not extend to a third corpse in her wake. In fact, that would give Masters the perfect excuse to turn her over to the NYPD. And Jones surely had valuable information.

"Sit up," she ordered.

Jones struggled to raise himself, panting as he moved, his face pale and damp.

"Whom were you meeting on Staten Island?" Yael asked.

He laughed, coughed, spat out a tooth. "Your boyfriend. Oh, I forgot, you don't believe in boyfriends."

"Try again," she said, ignoring his provocation. She aimed at Jones's leg, her hand steady.

Jones stared at her. "You won't shoot me," he said, his voice confident.

"Maybe not on purpose. But it's hard to hold a gun straight in a storm." Yael moved the gun slightly to the left. As if on cue, the ferry juddered and lurched. She fired again. The bullet hit the wall six inches from the left side of his head. Jones tried to control himself but he was trembling. "Phone," said Yael.

Jones spat on the floor again, blood and saliva hanging from his mouth. "Come and get it."

"Do you want to walk out of here? Or leave in an ambulance?" Yael fired again. The ship slowed for a moment. The bullet slammed into the floor, inches from Jones's knee.

Jones reached into his pocket and took out his phone.

"Slide it over to me."

Jones pushed the telephone across the floor. Yael picked it up.

"Take it. You will never get in."

Yael pocketed the phone. "How much is Clarence Clairborne paying you?"

Jones hesitated before he spoke. Yael saw something flicker in his eyes. He blinked once and his body stiffened slightly. "Who?"

"Your boss. Clarence Clairborne, the CEO of the Prometheus Group."

"Never heard of him."

Yael knew he was lying. Keeping Jones covered with the Beretta, she took out a plastic restraint from her purse and dropped it on Jones's stomach. "Cuff your ankles together."

She could feel the fury radiating from him. His birthmark, now purple, seemed to pulse.

Yael stood with the gun still trained on him. "Seven rounds in a Beretta clip. That's four down and three to go. Do you want another one?"

He picked up the white plastic strip, fastened it around his ankles, and pulled the restrainer until it reached its limit.

"Good," said Yael. "Now pull it tighter." His eyes flitted from the gun to her face and back again. She sensed him calculating range and distance. "Try it, Cyrus. You have to stand, jump, and take me down, all with your legs tied together. I just have to squeeze this little trigger."

She stepped back and put her left hand inside her purse again, still covering Jones with the Beretta. She retrieved a pair of handcuffs and placed them on his chest. "Put your hands in front of you. Cuff yourself to the water pipe."

Jones placed the handcuff on his right hand, as instructed, then looped the handcuffs around the water pipe that ran along the lower wall to the washbasin before closing it around his left wrist.

Yael knelt down next to him. His skin was wet with sweat. His cheeks were covered with blond stubble. He seemed boyish, almost vulnerable, until she remembered the body in the water off the Istanbul shoreline, the neat row of teeth marks in the dead man's shoulder.

She ran the silencer slowly down the side of Jones's head. She felt his body stiffen under its touch. "Your friend Clarence Clairborne."

Jones stared straight ahead, his body rigid, as though willing himself not to give anything away. "I told you. I have never met him."

Yael twisted the silencer into his temple. "What is he planning in Istanbul?"

He winced. "I don't know what you are talking about."

The ferry sounded its foghorn again. She glanced quickly at her watch. The ship was about to dock. It was possible that Jones had never met him, but he certainly knew who Clairborne was. His body language had confirmed that. There was no time now to continue this conversation.

Yael stood up. She took her phone from her pocket, turned on the camera, pointed it at herself, and started filming. "My name is Yael Azoulay. I work for the United Nations," she said. She turned the lens toward Jones. "This man calls himself Cyrus Jones. He works for a black-ops department of the US government known as the DoD, the Department of Deniable. He is somehow connected to the Prometheus Group, which is trading illegally with Iran and the Revolutionary Guard. Cyrus Jones tried to kill me today, on this boat, the Staten Island Ferry."

She zoomed in on Jones's face so that it filled the screen. "He or his friends may try again. This film will be uploaded to a secure server. If anything happens to me, it will be posted on YouTube. Remember, Cyrus Jones. Clarence Clairborne. The Prometheus Group. The DoD."

Yael pressed stop and put her phone away. She unscrewed the silencer from the Beretta and placed the gun and the silencer in her purse.

Jones watched her intently. She saw hope flare in his eyes, believing that now she was effectively unarmed.

Yael bent down, lifted her jeans, and took out the Baby Glock 26 from her ankle holster. She placed the muzzle of the gun in Jones's right ear. "Don't move, Cyrus, and don't get any ideas. Just listen. Nod if you understand me."

Jones did as she said.

"If you, or any of your friends, come near me again, I will kill you." She pushed the gun against his ear. "Got that?"

Jones nodded.

Yael slipped the Glock into her pocket and stood over the washbasin. She checked herself in the remains of the mirror, quickly washed her face, pulled out some antiseptic cream from her purse, rubbed it into the scratch on her cheek, straightened her hair, and walked out.

Sami Boustani sat back on his sofa and opened a bottle of Brooklyn Lager. The lumpy cushion began to slide out from under him. He pulled himself up and the sharp end of a spring poked through the faux-tweed upholstery, jabbing his thigh. He put his beer down and pushed the cushion back into place. This time it stayed put. He ignored the metal prong that still poked his leg and shifted back and forth, trying to get comfortable. After several attempts he gave up, took a long swallow from the bottle, leaned back, and closed his eyes.

It was nine o'clock at night. He had barely eaten that day and the beer went straight to his head. He enjoyed its sharp, bitter taste, but the alcohol did not lift his mood. It only increased his sense of gloom. He had spent most of the morning cleaning up his office. It was too embarrassing to ask Yuri, the taciturn building manager, for a cleaner. Najwa had helped, and had proved surprisingly swift and efficient. The wine-sodden keyboard was wrecked. But his computer monitor, once wiped clean, still worked. Yael had not destroyed his hard drive, and his laptop had remained at home.

At least he was spared the need to explain Yael's origins to his mother and sister, he thought. The Boustanis were Christian Palestinians who had arrived in the United States twenty years ago from Gaza. They had settled in Manhattan, where Sami's father, Hamza, had relatives. Hamza died seven years later, struck down by lung cancer after a lifetime of heavy smoking. Sami's mother, Maryam, was still alive, living in Brooklyn with Sami's sister, Leila, and her husband and five children. The pressure on Sami to settle down was steady and growing. He was not especially experienced with women, and had yet to master the ruthless, complicated rules of the New York dating game. Yael's interest in him was a source of wonder, and lately he had found himself planning imaginary dialogues with his mother and his sister about her. He had even thought about inviting Yael for dinner at Leila's restaurant in Brooklyn. He smiled as he imagined the resulting frenzy of speculation and questions, his nieces and nephews bringing endless trays of appetizers as an excuse to check her out. "The good news," he would tell them, "is that she speaks Arabic." Her father was born in Baghdad. The bad news was that she was an Israeli. Or an American Israeli. Or maybe he wouldn't need to mention that part until they had met her and fallen in love with her. As he was starting to. His smile faded. That discussion, of course, was now entirely academic.

He did not imagine that she would ever speak to him again. He certainly would not, if their roles were reversed. It was one thing to be stood up on a date, quite another to have your most sensitive work exposed on an international television channel—and by the person you had cooked dinner for that same evening. But what options did he have? Either he was a journalist, committed to investigating the UN, or he was not. Najwa was right. Reporters cannot date their sources. The media interest in Yael had not abated after the resolution of the KZX–Bonnet Group scandal. In fact the story seemed to be taking on a new life, swirling around the long narrow corridors of the Secretariat Building, filling newspaper pages and television screens. Sami had to be part of that. So he told himself. Again. He had a choice: Love or career? Career or love? Every choice exacted a price. The price of his choice was Yael.

Sami raised the beer bottle to his mouth again, hesitated, then put it down without drinking. Najwa had invited him to a documentary film festival in Tribeca that evening. She wanted them to meet the director, to persuade him to show their film. But Sami was in no mood for schmoozing. He glanced down at that day's *New York Times*, which lay on the coffee table in front of him. He picked the newspaper up, removed the front page with his name in bold type, crushed it into a ball, and threw it across the room, before sinking back onto the sofa.

Sami's apartment was a dark and cramped one bedroom, in the basement of a brownstone on Ninth Street, in the East Village. The cream walls had faded to light brown, streaked with darker shades. The floor was covered with an orange acrylic carpet, the pipes thumped and pounded, and the erratic hot water in the bathroom ran brown as often as clear. The furniture dated from the 1980s, but its dilapidated condition displaced any notions of retro chic. The bedroom had a twin bed. Even though Sami had lived there for more than two years he still had not properly unpacked. He told himself that was because it was temporary accommodation, that he would eventually find somewhere more suitable for a *New York Times* reporter. But at a mere $1,500 a month, the apartment, which belonged to his uncle, was incredibly cheap for Manhattan. A recent brief glance at a couple of rental websites had made Sami realize that, despite the gloomy décor and old-fashioned furniture, he was not moving anywhere, at least for the moment.

That, and the prospect of romance, had finally inspired him to tidy up the place. The boxes of books, papers, and long-forgotten research materials were neatly arranged in the corner. The kitchen was clean and tidy, the counters gleaming, the linoleum floor swept and mopped down. He had even bought a vase, which now stood on the kitchen table holding a bunch of daffodils. He walked over to the kitchen, took out one of the flowers, and sniffed it. It smelled stale. The stalk wilted in his hand.

Sami dropped the flower in the trash can and opened the fridge door. The beer had suddenly made him ravenously hungry. There was a bottle of ketchup, a pot of hummus, and a block of yellow processed cheese inside. He found some pita bread in the bread bin, so dried out it almost snapped under his fingers. He squirted some ketchup onto the plate, added the bread, cheese, and hummus and took the food through to the sitting room. He put the plate down on the coffee table, picked up his laptop from the sofa, and placed it on the sideboard before he started eating.

The hummus was ringed by a dark brown crust. He sniffed it, dipped his finger in, and tasted the beige paste. It was on the edge of turning sour but still edible, just. The cheese was cracked and fissured with age. The pita bread was spotted with mold on the edge. He broke that section off, put it aside, and dipped the remainder into the hummus, before switching on the television to the CNN early-evening news. The screen showed a photograph of Caroline Masters.

The anchor, a young Chinese woman, was interviewing Roger Richardson, the UN correspondent for CNN, in the network's mini-studio in the Secretariat Building. Richardson, a tall, middle-aged man with a dry sense of humor, was a veteran of the UN press corps, posted there almost as long as Jonathan Beaufort.

"The UN is back in the news, Roger, tell us why," asked the anchor.

"That's right, Amy, it certainly is. We have a new secretary-general, or rather acting secretary-general, Caroline Masters. She is the first American to hold the post," said Richardson, before giving a brief resume of Masters's career.

"How sick is Fareed Hussein?"

Richardson looked puzzled. "It's curious. As far as I understand, from multiple sources, he was playing tennis this morning. And then this afternoon we were told that he was on sick leave. Maybe the game was too much for him. But you must remember, Amy, that Fareed Hussein is over seventy years old, and has been under a lot of stress organizing the Istanbul Summit."

"Remind us what that is, Roger," said Amy, as an image of the historic Turkish city filled the screen, before it switched back to the CNN UN studio.

"It's the most ambitious diplomatic project in history. The aim is to negotiate final peace agreements for Israel-Palestine, Syria, and Egypt. All the superpowers will be there, next Thursday, just eight days from now."

"But is Istanbul safe? We've seen two bombings in the last couple of weeks, both of which targeted the tourist heartlands: one in the covered bazaar and another just outside the Blue Mosque. Are these bombs a prelude to an attack on the summit? Tell us about the recent arrests, Roger."

The screen showed pictures of three men, all in their early twenties, dark skinned, unshaven, staring at the camera.

"The Turkish authorities say they have broken up a Kurdish terrorist ring, a new grouping called the Kurdish People's Liberation Army, which planned to attack the summit. The Kurds strongly deny any connection. They and the democratic opposition say the bombs were planted by government agents, to give the Turkish authorities an excuse to crack down on dissent and detain anyone they want before the summit opens. It's impossible to know, but we do know that there have been many arrests."

"What does the UN have to say about the crackdown, Roger?"

Richardson smiled knowingly. "Not very much, Amy. Fareed Hussein has expressed his 'concern' but that's about all. Both he and the Turkish government know that preparations are so far advanced that it would take something very serious to delay or derail the summit."

Amy nodded. "And one person won't be attending," she continued, as Yael's face filled the screen.

Richardson shook his head. "No, sadly for Yael Azoulay, it looks like her brilliant career has hit a wall. The UN's top behind-the-scenes negotiator has a new job. A non-job, some might say—not coincidentally, I think, after the release of some curious video footage of her dressed very alluringly in a prime downtown New York hotel." The screen showed a few seconds of the footage of Yael in the hotel corridor, before he outlined the role of the Trusteeship Council.

"The Millennium Hotel seems a much more exciting assignment. What exactly was she doing there, Roger?"

"We are working on that," said Richardson, a smile on his face.

The program moved on to the row in Congress about President Freshwater's latest attempt to return intelligence gathering to national agencies, in the process breaking the contracts signed with private military contractors for more than $50 billion. Sami watched for a while, but his mind was not really on the story. Instead he was remembering his conversation with Henrik Schneidermann after the press conference earlier that day. Sami often met the UN spokesman in private, usually in his office, or sometimes in the Delegates Lounge, the bar and open space on the ground floor of the Secretariat Building, or in the Delegates Dining Room. This time Schneidermann had summoned him to McLaughlin's, a dark Irish bar on the corner of Second Avenue and Forty-Seventh Street, at six o'clock in the evening. They had met in a private room at the back. The excessive precautions seemed over the top to Sami, until Schneidermann explained why he had wanted to meet.

Sami pondered how he would use this information. It was potentially the start of an investigation that was bigger than anything he had reported so far—if the Iranian connection was true. Schneidermann had promised to provide evidence, in the form of incriminating e-mails, but only on the strict condition that he did not share it with anyone—especially not with Najwa. Schneidermann and Najwa had fallen out after she, against Sami's advice, had run a story on a quiet news day claiming that Schneidermann would be the next casualty of the KZX-Bonnet scandal and Roxana Voiculescu was being groomed to succeed him. The story had an element of truth—it did appear Schneidermann was being sidelined—but he was unlikely to be sacked.

Sami had told Najwa there was no sense alienating Schneidermann with a report of such little interest to the wider public. Sami knew he was right, even though his judgment was shaky when Roxana was involved. He still cringed inside at the memory of the "non-date," as he had dubbed their first and only meeting. After weeks of hints, suggestions, and, eventually, near demands from Roxana that he take her out for a drink, he had eventually spent part of an evening buying her expensive cocktails at a hipster bar before stealing confidential UN documents out of her handbag. Eventually Sami had agreed, reluctantly, to Schneidermann's terms, after Schneidermann promised he would produce the e-mails in the next twenty-four hours. They had a tentative plan to meet for breakfast tomorrow morning at a bar near the UN building. Schneidermann had promised to call if he was not coming.

Sami drained the last mouthful from the bottle of lager and wiped out the tub of hummus. The brown crust fell away and landed in the pot. Sami pushed the tub away and was cutting himself another wedge of cheese when the doorbell rang.

11

Beaker Kormandy held up the mobile phone under the light of an antique Anglepoise lamp and turned it back and forth in his hand.

"A BlackBerry," he said, intrigued, as though he was an archaeologist who had accidentally stumbled on the remains of a long-forgotten civilization. The phone's screen glinted under the glare of the bulb. "It belongs to . . . ?"

"The owner," said Yael, her voice deadpan.

"Who is?"

"Me."

Beaker looked doubtful. "Last time I saw you, you had a souped-up iPhone. BlackBerrys are for corporate executives and government officials. You working for the man now? Or the government?"

Yael shook her head. "No. Still striving for universal peace and harmony at the UN."

"Inside or outside the building?"

Yael smiled. "Both."

Beaker turned the lamp toward Yael. "What happened to your face? It's all scratched up."

She touched her left cheek and shrugged. "I slipped in the shower. I'm fine. Don't worry about it."

Beaker's face showed he did not believe her, but he did not press the matter. "The battery?"

Yael handed it to Beaker. "Here. I checked. There are no other power sources. Nothing hidden away inside to secretly transmit when you think it's powered down."

Beaker nodded. "Good." He connected a power cord to the BlackBerry. The screen wobbled for a moment, then went dark again. "What do you want me to do?"

Yael picked up a half-eaten Hershey bar that was lying on the worktable. "Crack it open," she said as she broke off a piece. "I can't get in."

"What's the matter? Did you forget your password?"

"Something like that."

He tapped the screen of the BlackBerry. "Is this legal?"

Yael laughed. "Is this?" she said, gesturing at the table where they sat.

It was covered with circuit boards, tangles of multicolored wiring, keyboards, track pads, hard drives, and pieces of tablet computers and mobile telephones in various states of dismemberment. Lines of computer code ran across two large monitors, while a third showed a screensaver of the Chain Bridge in Budapest, arching gracefully over the Danube at night. A nest of black and gray cables snaked back across the room to half a dozen hard drives in standing cases. A pizza box sat on one corner, spotted with grease from the two slices inside.

Beaker and Yael were childhood friends. Their grandmothers were both Hungarian and had gone to school together in Budapest. Both survived the wartime ghetto to flee Hungary at the end of the Second World War and settle in New York with what remained of their families. Beaker and Yael had grown up together, their families spending Sunday afternoons in a make-believe Mittel-Europa, sitting on Biedermeier furniture, eating open sandwiches topped with a sliver of salami, followed by Dobos torte, a seven-layered buttercream cake topped with crunchy caramel, listening to Mozart piano sonatas, watching the adults down glasses of chilled *pálinka*, fruit brandy, when the memories and the longing for home became too much to bear.

Beaker was a scientific prodigy, another of the Hungarian geniuses who had brought the world numerous innovations, including the carburetor, telephone exchange, nuclear weapons, vitamin C, and the ballpoint pen. He had graduated from Harvard at the age of twenty, moved back to Budapest for a while, set up several IT companies that still provided him with a tidy income, and then returned to New York with his girlfriend, Lysette, a green-eyed blonde nurse in her late twenties. Beaker was one of the world's most accomplished computer hackers. Corporations and government departments hired him to break into their networks, reveal the holes in their security, and close them up. But Yael knew that Beaker also did "off the books" jobs, for free, for activists and NGOs that he wanted to help.

Yael handed a chunk of chocolate to Beaker. "Please."

"Thanks." He ate the chocolate as he tried a different power lead and pressed the buttons on the BlackBerry keyboard. Nothing happened. The room was silent apart from the whir of the computer hard drives.

Yael walked across the room to look out the window while Beaker worked. He and Lysette lived in a large four-room apartment on 162nd Street in Washington Heights, overlooking the Hudson River. This part of Manhattan had not yet been gentrified, and apartments were large and cheap. Yael was about eighty blocks north of her building on Riverside and Eighty-First. The view here was just as engaging as hers, perhaps even more so. The Hudson was a wide black ribbon, shimmering under the lights of the George Washington Bridge, sixteen blocks north. A police launch roared downriver, its spotlight cutting through the night, as though racing the cars that whizzed along the Henry Hudson Parkway, following the course of the river.

The door opened and Lysette walked in, carrying a tray with a two-liter bottle of Coca-Cola and two glasses. She smiled at Yael as she put the tray down, a terse movement of her lips while her eyes remained cold. *Relax*, Yael wanted to say. *You really have nothing to worry about.* Yael and Beaker had always enjoyed each other's company and years ago had gone out on a few dates. Beaker had wanted to take things further, but Yael could not imagine him as a lover. Eventually she persuaded him that they were better off as friends. Lysette handed the Coca-Cola to Beaker.

"Thanks, *édesem*, sweetheart," said Beaker. She moved to sit down with them.

Beaker shook his head. "It's probably best if you miss this."

Lysette glared at him, nodded perfunctorily at Yael, and walked out.

Sami walked quickly to the front door and peered through the spy-hole. Two men stood outside on the stoop. One wore a black overcoat, the other a brown one. The man in the black coat leaned forward and pressed the doorbell again.

Sami opened it.

"Mr. Boustani?" asked the man in the black overcoat.

"Who are you?"

"INS."

Sami was suddenly alert, his beer-induced lethargy evaporating. What did the Immigration and Naturalization Service want with him at ten o'clock at night? He switched on the outdoor light. The man in the black overcoat was slim, of medium height, with straw-blond hair, his collar raised against the rain. His companion was six inches shorter, stocky, with the flushed jowls and veined nose of a heavy drinker. They started to walk into the apartment.

Sami held up his hand. "Hey, hey, ID please."

The man in the black coat flashed an open wallet, showing a badge, for a few seconds, then folded it closed. His face was scratched and bruised.

"Is this is a raid? Are you arresting me?" asked Sami.

"No," he eventually said, as though suggesting this was a distinct possibility in the future.

"Then let me see both of your IDs, properly, please."

The men reluctantly handed their IDs over to Sami. He looked carefully at both and memorized their names: Wayne Taylor in the black coat and Robert Williams in the brown.

He handed the IDs back. "I am an American citizen. What do you want?"

"A *naturalized* American citizen, I believe, Mr. Boustani," said Taylor. "We would like to talk to you. Can we come in? Or do you want to do this on the doorstep?"

Sami stared hard at him. "Do you have a warrant?"

"No. But we could come back with one if you like. Then we might stay around a little longer than we planned to tonight."

"Give me a moment, please," said Sami.

Sami closed the door and went back inside. He walked into the bathroom, put the shower onto the coldest setting, and stuck his head under the water for half a minute, before vigorously toweling himself dry. Shivering but wide awake now, he walked into the lounge. He stayed in the room for a minute, returned to the door, and opened it.

The two men followed him in. He did not offer them coffee or anything else, but gestured at them to sit down while he cleared away the remains of his supper. Taylor reached inside his pocket, his movements slow and careful. Sami saw that his right index finger was bandaged. A birthmark ran down the left side of his neck.

"What do you want to talk about?"

Taylor dropped a photograph onto the table. "Her."

The door shook in the frame as Lysette closed it hard. "I'm sorry," said Yael. "I don't want to make life difficult for you."

Beaker shrugged. "Don't worry. She's Hungarian. You know, difficult, passionate, irrational. Not straightforward, like you. We will make it up later." He gestured at the sideboard. "Pass me that laptop please," he said, pointing at an ancient-looking IBM ThinkPad, as he cleared a space in front of him.

Yael handed him the computer. It was black and very heavy.

Beaker sensed her curiosity as he put the laptop on the table. "The shell is antique. The technology inside is not. Plus, it's air gapped. That means it has never been connected to the Internet and cannot connect to the Internet, so nobody can hack into it. But it does have three sandboxes inside, what we call safe zones on the hard drive, where we can play with the code on your BlackBerry."

He fired up the laptop and connected it to the third monitor. It whizzed and whirred and the screen lit up. A terminal window, where program commands could be entered, opened. Beaker tapped out a line of letters and numbers. A second line instantly appeared underneath. He connected the BlackBerry to the IBM. A new window flashed up on the monitor. Fresh lines of code flew across the screen, glowing softly in the semidark apartment.

Beaker smiled, his eyes narrowing, a hunter on the trail of his prey. "Well, *pimp . . . my . . . ride*," he said.

Yael leaned forward. "What is it?"

"Shredbox. NSA standard. Government issue only. It takes a file, chops it into dozens of sections, encrypts each one, and sends it off via a relay of proxy servers around the world to a secure server where the pieces are reassembled."

"I know. I've got it on my other phone."

"How did you get it?"

"A friend gave it to me."

"Lucky you, having friends like that. I've wanted to get my hands on this for a while. It's theoretically unbreakable."

Yael smiled. "Theoretically. Especially in your case."

Beaker nodded to himself, now totally absorbed in his task. Yael sat down on the sofa, watching him work. Bald, broad shouldered, hunched over the table, wearing a loose linen shirt, Beaker looked like a medieval monk transported to the twenty-first century. The light from the lamp reflected off his shiny scalp as his stubby fingers moved nimbly across the keyboard.

Beaker's words echoed in Yael's head, her thoughts bouncing around like a pinball. Not irrational. Perhaps not even passionate. But straightforward. Did she want to be straightforward? She didn't think so. She wanted to be passionate. A picture flashed into her mind, of Beaker and his girlfriend, their limbs tangled together under a quilt, laughing. She brushed it aside. Another image appeared, as if autogenerated: a dinner table, set for two, the candles alight, the wine chilling in an ice bucket, the thin, iridescent layer forming on the food as it congealed. That too Yael forced from her head. God, she was so sick of eating on her own. At least she'd had company at breakfast this morning. La Caridad too triggered a fresh surge of memories, of family brunches and dinners after excursions downtown or to the beach in New Jersey.

Yael had not spoken to her father for more than a decade. She had thought he would be proud of her when she started her first job at the UN. For all their rows and arguments, Yael's parents had brought her, Noa, and David up to have an intelligent, informed interest about the world. But her father was not proud. He was furious. She could still hear him yelling that he had lost his son to the UN and now he had to sacrifice his daughter as well? Yael had regularly called and e-mailed, keeping her father up to date with her news, to reassure him that she was quite safe. But the more she flourished at the UN, the more her father withdrew.

A few days before her vetting for top-level security clearance, he'd called her. He was in New York unexpectedly on business, he explained, and wanted to take her for dinner. She was glad to accept, but he spent the evening trying to persuade her to resign. She was hurt and puzzled, especially as things were going so well for her. He invoked David's memory, which annoyed her because she knew, as much as she had ever known anything, that her brother would approve of her choice of career. Yael's father claimed to be worried about her safety, but at that early stage she only occasionally went on field missions, and then always as a part of a team with high-level security. Yael knew her father was lying about why he wanted her to resign. There was something else flowing underneath his anger: a nervousness, even fear. The evening ended badly.

Soon after, on her twenty-sixth birthday, Yael received her security clearance. The process had proved surprisingly slow, compared to her colleagues. She had undergone an extra interview, at which she had been asked numerous detailed questions about her precise relationship with her father. That same day he had called her from Tel Aviv to wish her happy birthday. At least that was the pretext. His voice on the telephone had sounded even tenser than when they'd had dinner together. Yael knew his actual agenda: to try, again, to persuade her to resign. She cut the call short, citing the pressure of work, and promised to call him back. After hanging up she had sat for a while, thinking, wondering why her father was so stressed about her job. She typed his name into the peacekeeping department's highly classified database. The database received information from all the P5's intelligence services. What she had read still haunted her. She had sat, staring into space, for an hour afterward. Her database search was noticed. Soon after, Yael was called in by the UN security department and ordered to report any contact with her father. Yael had not spoken to him since.

Yael's mobile telephone rang. She looked at the screen. A 510 area code. She pulled her legs up underneath her, made herself comfortable, and took the call.

Taylor stared at Sami. "OK, wiseass. Let's stop fucking around."

Sami nodded. "Yes. Let's. It's a federal offense to impersonate a government official. Why don't I call the cops and let them sort this out," he said, reaching for his mobile telephone.

Taylor leaned back and looked at Sami with interest, as though this was a novel plan of action that could prove mutually beneficial. "Good idea. Let's see what they have to say. It's also a federal offense to lie on your immigration forms. One that can result in being stripped of citizenship, deportation, and/or imprisonment. As can being a known associate of terrorists."

Sami's hand remained suspended in midair, still holding his phone. He sat very still for several seconds, his mind racing. "Meaning?"

"Let's talk about your girlfriend," said Taylor.

Yael closed her eyes and sank back into the sofa, pleased that her mother had called again. Sitting in Beaker's apartment, hearing her mother's voice, had brought back some welcome childhood memories of shared Sunday-afternoon family parties—and a sudden craving for Dobos torte. She and Barbara had spoken for almost twenty minutes, their longest conversation for several years. Her mother had been worried and unusually maternal. She had seen Yael on Al Jazeera the previous evening and fired a battery of questions about what was going on in Yael's life and whether she was safe. Yael had reassured her that everything was fine, that she was OK. Barbara had been somewhat reassured, Yael could sense, but not completely. She was happy that Yael was at Beaker's, although Yael did not tell her why she was there. Yael and her mother had agreed that Barbara would definitely come to New York soon. There were some things that they needed to talk about, Barbara said. Important things, not to be discussed on the telephone. Suddenly Yael felt shaky and exhausted. The adrenaline had worn off and her body ached from the fight with Jones. Tiredness rolled over her in waves. She felt as if she could curl up and sleep for a week. Except she could not, she needed to stay awake. She traced the circle of scar tissue on the front of her left shoulder through her sweater.

She pressed it hard, almost digging her nails into the carapace of ridged skin. Needles of pain shot out. She slid her hand around to the back of her shoulder. Another circle of scar tissue, slightly higher than the one in front, poking through the soft wool. She thought often about the sheer randomness of being shot. If the gunman's hand had moved a millimeter or two in one direction, or if he had slipped, he would have missed. A millimeter or two in another direction, the gun held at another angle, and the bullet would have taken her in the throat, in which case she would not be sitting here.

Beaker put the BlackBerry down, his eyes gleaming in triumph. "We have a visitor."

Yael jerked to attention, scanning the room, her hand instantly reaching for the Baby Glock she had strapped back on her ankle.

Beaker watched her with interest. "Not here." He tapped the BlackBerry. "Here."

Yael sat up, and let her hand fall away. "Meaning?"

"There are two ways into Shredbox. You tap the user's Internet connection while it's sending the packets out. Or you use spyware to listen to the phone's SIM card as it transmits the information."

She stood up, walked over to Beaker's worktable, and poured herself a glass of Coca-Cola. The sugar rush helped, and she was suddenly ravenously hungry. "May I?" Yael asked. There was no Dobos torte, but she reached for a slice of pizza.

Beaker put the BlackBerry down on the table. "Help yourself. I found the spyware. Someone has been tapping this phone."

"Who?"

Beaker shrugged. "Impossible to say. Someone with access to this type of technology. A government or government agency. Or a private company working for them."

"Can you find out what the phone transmitted?"

"I can try."

Yael waited for a moment, her mouth full of pizza. It was cold, greasy, and completely delicious. "Good. Please do." She ate one slice, and then a second.

The IBM flickered. Lines of characters appeared, flying back and forth across the terminal windows as they filled the screen.

Beaker said, "We're in."

The IBM beeped repeatedly, as though excited that the encryption had been cracked. Beaker watched the screen for a while. He reached for the bottle of Coca-Cola and took a long swig. "Were you followed when you came here?" he asked, deadly serious now.

"Why?"

Beaker reached over to the pizza box. Finding it empty, he cracked some more chocolate off the Hershey bar. "Well, *drágám,* darling. You turn up at night, out of the blue, with a scratched face, looking exhausted, carrying an encrypted BlackBerry loaded with Shredbox. The BlackBerry has been compromised with a fancy piece of spyware and you have a pistol strapped to your ankle. All of which is fine. But it would be good to know that nobody came with you."

Yael shook her head. "South Ferry to 168th is about a forty-minute subway ride on the one. I spent three hours getting here, including a lengthy ride up and down the escalators on every floor of Macy's, half an hour crisscrossing the subways at Times Square, and a walk across Central Park. So, no, I don't think I was followed."

Beaker nodded. "I hope not. Take a look at this."

Sami sat down with the two men, watching them carefully, fully alert now. He knew this was bullshit. The INS did not operate like this. They either called people in for an interview or raided premises where illegal immigrants were living. This was not an interview, nor was it a raid.

The photograph now lying on his coffee table erased any doubts. He could call the police. But that would not solve anything. These two, or others even worse, would soon be back. It was better to find out as much as he could about who they were and what they wanted, so he knew with whom he was dealing. Sami looked out the corner of his eye at his laptop, open in the corner of the room.

The man with the birthmark tapped the photograph. "What do you know about her?" he demanded.

Sami picked up the photograph and looked at it for several moments. He put it down, looked up at the ceiling, and thought for several moments before he replied. "She's a good cook."

12

Henrik Schneidermann strode down First Avenue, confident and full of vim, as he deftly weaved a path through the crowds of early-morning commuters. It was 7:45 a.m. on Thursday and the sun was bright in a turquoise sky dotted by white wisps of cloud, as though it had been washed clean by the squalls of the previous evening. The smell of coffee and cooking bacon drifted out from a diner on the corner of East Fifty-Fourth Street. He stopped to let an elderly lady dressed in a navy-blue designer jacket and matching skirt pass by. She was leading a tiny pug on a leash with one hand and holding a Starbucks cup with the other, and smiled as she thanked him. Taxis hooted; gusts of steam rose from the sidewalk grill. The air crackled with energy and opportunity. He would miss these Manhattan mornings.

His meeting with Fareed Hussein had dispelled any lingering doubts about his planned course of action. The SG had called him at 6:30 a.m. In normal times he and the SG often met early in the morning at his residence to talk through the day's news agenda. From there they sometimes rode to the office together in the SG's limousine, which still gave Schneidermann a childish thrill. But there had been no limousine rides since the SG had gone on sick leave, and Schneidermann doubted they would resume any time soon, especially after their conversation today.

Schneidermann had almost let Hussein's call go to voice mail because he did not recognize the number. The SG, it seemed, was no longer using his UN-issued telephone, but he remained in the four-story townhouse and had invited him to come over for breakfast. Schneidermann had hesitated because of his breakfast date with Sami Boustani at 8:30 a.m. But he had accepted. He had not seen his boss since Caroline Masters had moved into Hussein's office. It was clear to Schneidermann that Masters had indeed organized a coup, and he knew his days were numbered. Roxana Voiculescu now appeared in his office on unnecessary errands almost every hour, barely able to contain her excitement as she assessed the furniture and fittings, far less subtly than she supposed.

Schneidermann's curiosity was piqued when the SG requested he use the rear tradesman's entrance of the townhouse, rather than the front door where the NYPD maintained a twenty-four-hour watch. The SG had skated over Schneidermann's questions about his health, stonewalling with claims of specialist appointments and waiting time for test results. Schneidermann had watched him carefully during their meeting. His hand did not shake when he poured the coffee or when he proffered a plate of pastries. His eyes were clear, his sentences lucid, his posture upright. They talked cordially about the plans for the Istanbul Summit during their brief breakfast and Hussein's regret that he was no longer involved in its organization.

Both knew that the house was bugged by all of the P5's intelligence services and probably several others. Hussein had suggested a walk in the garden. He was as fit and composed as ever as they walked back and forth across the manicured lawn. There Hussein gave Schneidermann a slim blue folder. He'd leafed through the contents and immediately understood the reason for his summons. As he slipped the folder into his briefcase, Hussein wished him an enjoyable breakfast with Sami Boustani. The message was clear. Schneidermann smiled as he imagined Sami's reaction when he gave him the folder. Its contents were explosive—and further proof of what Schneidermann already knew.

Schneidermann stopped at the corner of East Fifty-Second Street, waiting for the lights to change, his briefcase in his hand. He planned to walk the ten blocks or so to McLaughlin's. He wanted to think through his breakfast with the SG. How did Fareed know that he was having breakfast with the *New York Times* correspondent? The same way that he knew so much about what was happening in the Secretariat Building. It was impossible to serve as secretary-general of the UN without having finely tuned political antennae, and Fareed had an uncanny ability to read the runes, calibrate and recalibrate policies as necessary, depending on the flow of power among the P5. Information was power and Hussein was a survivor. He had survived the KZX-Bonnet scandal, even though the UN had almost been hijacked under his leadership and his wife, Zeinab, had been exposed by Sami Boustani as a major shareholder in a Congolese firm that would have reaped enormous profits from the planned UN–corporate development zone. So the question was, why had the SG seemingly surrendered this time without a fight, and allowed this nonsense about blackouts, when he was clearly in perfect health?

Schneidermann had of course heard the whispers that Hussein had been compromised for decades. They led back to the darkest days of the UN: the Rwandan genocide in spring 1994 and the capture of Srebrenica the following summer, when Hussein had served as head of the Department of Peacekeeping and had forbidden the UN troops to intervene, claiming they had no mandate to do so. Most UN insiders believed a few battalions of peacekeepers could have stopped the Rwandan massacres within a few days had there been sufficient will to deploy them, either in the Secretariat or among the P5. Mbaye Diagne, a brave Senegalese peacekeeper, had saved hundreds of lives on his own by physically preventing the Hutu militiamen from killing their planned victims. A UN commission of inquiry had later found that Hussein had acted correctly in his interpretation. Schneidermann truly believed that the UN's disastrous response—or lack of one—to the Rwandan genocide could not be blamed in large part on Hussein. It was the result of an outmoded and dysfunctional organization, one designed for another era, which had proved completely inadequate for the challenges of the postwar world.

The catastrophe at Srebrenica, however, remained a mystery. Schneidermann knew that Hussein was haunted by his actions, or lack of them, during the summer of 1995, a year on from the slaughter in Rwanda. A small city in eastern Bosnia, Srebrenica had been besieged by the Bosnian Serbs for three years but was supposedly protected by a battalion of Dutch UN troops. UN military observers had warned for days that the Bosnian Serbs were preparing to attack the enclave. When the onslaught came, the UN troops stood by. The promised air strikes never materialized.

There were rumors that the UN had done a deal with the Bosnian Serbs: *We will let you take Srebrenica in exchange for signing up for a peace deal to end the war.* If there had been such a deal, it had gone horribly wrong. The Bosnian Serbs marched in, and the peacekeepers watched as eight thousand Bosnian Muslim men and boys were led away and slaughtered. The Dutch troops even forced three hundred Muslims out of their compound, where the terrified civilians had taken refuge. A second UN commission of inquiry had again exonerated Hussein, arguing that the troop's mandate did not provide for an armed response. But the whispers about Hussein's culpability still swirled around the building. One claim in particular horrified Schneidermann. But that was in the past. The information in this folder was incendiary and a very dangerous power play by Hussein, for once it was released it could never be recalled. The blowback might see Hussein back in his office within days, or bring him down for good.

Deep in his thoughts, Schneidermann barely noticed when something bumped into his left side. He stopped and looked around. A man had slipped on the sidewalk, banging into Schneidermann as he went down. He looked Middle Eastern, with sallow skin and a neatly trimmed salt-and-pepper beard. He looked at Schneidermann, his hand outstretched as he scrabbled to get up.

Schneidermann instinctively reached down to help.

"I am sorry. Thank you so much," said the man, grasping Schneidermann's hand. "Excuse me for the inconvenience. It's never a good idea to rush with new shoes and their slippery soles."

Schneidermann nodded, wondering about the man's accent, but barely registering the incident. "It's no problem. You are welcome. Take care."

The man thanked him again and walked off. Keeping a tight hold on his briefcase, Schneidermann watched him disappear into the crowd, wondering why the man was wearing black leather gloves on such a warm spring day.

Sami Boustani put down that day's edition of the *New York Times* and looked around the back room of McLaughlin's. It was dark, musty, and smelled of stale beer. Last night's dirty glasses were piled up on the long wooden bar. The dark brown walls were still stained with nicotine, even though smoking had been banned in Manhattan bars for more than a decade. This was his second visit to McLaughlin's in the last twenty-four hours. It had a ramshackle charm for an early-evening drink but would not have been his ideal choice for a breakfast meeting. Sami was the only customer. There were no staff in sight. Did they even serve breakfast here? The place was open and Schneidermann had suggested it, so it must serve something. He checked his watch. It was now 8:50 a.m. Where was he? Schneidermann was usually punctual for their meetings. If he was going to be late, because of some developing crisis at the UN, he always called or sent a text message. He had promised to call or text if he could not make it. Sami checked his mobile once more: no messages. He called Schneidermann's mobile for the third time, but it went straight to voice mail. Sami had already left two messages. There was no point leaving another.

The waitress, a skinny woman in her early twenties with black spiky hair, appeared out of a side door near the bar.

"Hi. Ready to order?" she asked.

"Can I see a menu?"

She stifled a yawn. "Eggs, oatmeal, or corned beef hash."

"Oatmeal. And juice and coffee please."

The waitress left and Sami returned to his newspaper, scanning a story out of Washington, DC. A right-wing Republican, known for his ties to the Pentagon, was demanding that the United States withdraw from the Istanbul Summit, saying it would only benefit America's enemies. President Freshwater had condemned the call but the new secretary of defense, Harlen Delacroix, said he shared some of the Republican senator's concerns. Delacroix was a Southern Democrat, appointed by Freshwater as a sop to her party's right wing. He was best known for trying to pilot a bill through Congress that would have reduced the United States' contribution to the UN budget by 90 percent. Delacroix had only been in office for two weeks, so it was early to be staking out his own position. Either Freshwater was weakening or Delacroix had powerful backers, or, most likely, both.

Sami put the newspaper down. He couldn't really concentrate on Washington's version of Kremlinology at the moment. He felt unsettled, perhaps, he admitted to himself, even scared. At first he had stonewalled his visitors, saying he knew no more about Yael than was public knowledge: she carried out sensitive assignments for the SG and was now sidelined, running the Trusteeship Council.

The man with the birthmark had told him to try harder. When Sami continued stonewalling, he had produced another set of photographs. Now Sami reached into the inside pocket of his jacket and took out an envelope. He stared at the prints for the countless time that morning. There were six shots—of Sami, his mother and sister on their trip to Gaza the previous summer to see their relatives. The men had left, assuring Sami that they would be back in a day or two.

He looked up as the door swung open. At last, he thought, until he saw who walked in. What was she doing here? It was barely nine o'clock and his day was going from bad to worse. Sami quickly gathered the photographs together, placed them back in the envelope, and slipped it back into his jacket pocket.

Najwa sat down opposite Sami. He felt even more nervous now, nervous and guilty.

The waitress walked over with Sami's coffee and looked at Najwa. "I'll have the corned beef hash and coffee," Najwa said, ignoring Sami.

Sami was about to speak when Najwa turned to him. "Don't worry. He is not coming."

The offices of the Trusteeship Council were situated at the end of a long, poorly lit corridor on the third floor of a little-used annex of the General Assembly Building, near the Dag Hammarskjöld Memorial Library. The bemused security guards had spent twenty minutes looking for the keys to open the doors. There were two rooms: one around fifteen feet by twelve, with a small window, and a smaller windowless space.

An old-fashioned metal desk stood in the center of each space, on top of which sat an electronic typewriter and a rotary telephone.

Yael picked up the handset of the telephone in the larger room and held it to her ear. Silence. She checked her mobile telephone. There was no signal from any of the UN Wi-Fi networks. There was barely any mobile network signal. One bar of the network reception indicator showed on her phone, as did the telltale blue light.

Yael had, in theory, a staff of two—Lucy Chen, her personal assistant, and Jindal Patel, her political adviser. She had never heard of either, let alone met them, and had googled their names the previous evening. Chen, the daughter of the Chinese deputy chief of mission, was moonlighting at a Chinese technology company, whose New York office was conveniently located on East Forty-Third Street. Patel, the daughter of the press attaché at the Indian mission, was an intern at *Glamour* magazine.

The air in the room was musty. The single, narrow window was coated in grime so thick that the glass was almost opaque. A large green patch of mold reached from the floor halfway up the wall. The window resisted Yael's first attempts to open it, but she finally yanked it loose. It looked out onto an inner courtyard, whose rough concrete walls were covered with wide aluminum pipes. The roar of air conditioners filled the office, and a small cloud of dust floated over Yael. She quickly closed the window, coughing, when there was a knock on the door. She opened it to see Quentin Braithwaite standing there.

"Good morning," he said wryly, raising his eyebrows.

"Is it?" asked Yael, brushing the dust off her clothes. "Come in, please. Welcome to the Trusteeship Council."

Braithwaite walked briskly inside, taking in his surroundings. "Congratulations."

"For what?"

"For being still alive. And of course, on your promotion. I had no idea this part of the building even existed. You have two rooms. That's a step up." He looked out the window. "Don't think much of the view, though."

Braithwaite's smile faded and his voice was tight. "Yael, we need to talk. . . ."

Before he could finish his sentence Yael put her forefinger over her lips and traced a series of letters in the thick coating of dust on the desk—"NOT HERE—DHP IN 15"—before wiping the words away.

The Englishman nodded in understanding and left.

Before Yael met up with Braithwaite in a place where they could talk, she had something even more urgent on her agenda.

She opened the drafts folder on her smartphone, checked again that the connection was encrypted, selected an e-mail with several attachments, and scanned through them, carefully reading each PDF. She put the phone down, her face thoughtful as she considered her course of action. There would be no turning back, she knew. She ran her forefinger down the mold on the wall. It came away green.

She reached for her phone again and pressed "send."

W̲ho is not coming?" asked Sami.

"Your breakfast date."

"How do you know?"

"*A'raf*. I know." Najwa stared at Sami. "You seem distracted. What's up?"

Sami looked at her while he considered his response. *What's up*, part of him wanted to say, *is that some very nasty people, apparently attached to an arm of the US government, are demanding that I betray someone I still care about, very much, even though there is no chance of fixing that relationship. And if I don't, my family and I might be taking a one-way trip back to Gaza. Where they had been following me on my last trip and taking photographs. And, they know about my teenage cousin who disappeared after being taken into Israeli custody.* That's what was up. Meanwhile, where was Schneidermann?

"Najwa, why are you here?" he asked.

"Why do you think? I am having breakfast."

The waitress arrived with their orders.

"And here it is," said Najwa, slipping her fork into the glistening pile of potatoes, pink with shreds of corned beef. "This is delicious. Really, the best in town. Would you like to try some?" she asked, sliding the plate across the table.

"No thanks, I'm fine with the oatmeal." The smell of food was making his appetite return. Sami raised his spoon and was about to dip in when Najwa's hand snapped around his wrist.

"I am not angry with you, Sami. Really, I am not. I am just . . ." She looked up at the grubby ceiling, as though searching for inspiration. "Disappointed. Yes, that is the word. I am disappointed."

"Why?" asked Sami, his voice innocent. "We were great together on the program." When Sami had checked his

Twitter feed this morning, he saw Najwa had been tweet-
ing about the Tribeca film festival until 3:00 a.m. It didn't
show. She was perfectly turned out. She wore a black cashmere turtleneck sweater and skillfully applied light makeup
that accentuated her full mouth and black eyes, eyes that
were now staring at him, with none of their usual friendly
flirtatiousness.

Najwa stared at him. "Yes, we were. I was glad to invite
you. But that was Tuesday night. Now it's Thursday morning. I am not on your breakfast program, am I? It's fine if
you want to go your own way. Really. We don't have to
cooperate. But don't sneak about behind my back."

Najwa's grip tightened and her black eyes glittered. "Be
a man, and tell me yourself. Because I won't run after you,
or anyone else, Sami. Ever."

Sami's resolve melted away inside him. Ambassadors
returned his calls, State Department officials met him for
lunch, think tanks invited him to sit on panels to discuss
important international policy issues. Only Najwa could
make him feel like he was six years old, caught with his
hand in the cookie jar.

"By the way," she continued, her voice lighter now, "I
saw Jonathan Beaufort at the film festival. He invited me for
dinner, again. I think I will say yes, this time."

Sami looked at her, alarmed. "Don't do that. Please."

"Why not?" demanded Najwa, her grip on his wrist easing by a fraction.

It was time to surrender, he knew.

"I am sorry. I was going to tell you, really. But Schneidermann is really pissed at you because of that story you

ran about him being eased out to make room for Roxana. There was no way he would have agreed to have breakfast with you. And where is he?"

Najwa released his wrist. She put her fork down. Her voice was soft. "At Mount Sinai hospital, in the intensive care ward."

Sami was about to answer when his mobile phone beeped. He picked it up and read the header on the incoming e-mail: "A story for you."

Najwa looked at him, her eyes wide and querying. Sami turned the phone to face her. She quickly read the e-mail header. "Open it, habibi."

13

Yael sat on a bench at the entrance to Dag Hammarskjöld Plaza, waiting for Braithwaite. The plaza, named for the second UN secretary-general, covered a whole block of East Forty-Seventh Street, between First and Second Avenues. It was a tranquil oasis in one of the busiest sections of town. Rows of trees ran down either side, lush and newly green, their long branches reaching toward each other as though trying to make a canopy over the gray stone pavement. Hanging baskets filled with flowers were fixed under the art nouveau streetlights. In front of the trees were lines of park benches. A café in a greenhouse stood on the corner of First Avenue; half a dozen tables and chairs set outside in the chilly spring sunshine for hardy customers. The café was a popular spot for diplomats and UN officials to meet contacts without having them go through the hassle of security to get into the UN building.

Yael leaned back for a moment. Her shoulder pulsed, her back throbbed, and a headache was starting at the base of her neck. She closed her eyes and there he was again, lying on the floor of the restroom on the Staten Island Ferry, blood seeping from his nose, her foot raised above his head as the brown mist floated in front of her eyes. A downward strike, a twist of her hips to put her body weight into the blow, and he would never bother her, or anyone else, again. Yesterday, she had stopped herself in time. But barely. Something was slipping inside her, she knew. On top of that she felt guilty about going to Beaker's last night. She had carried out extensive anti-surveillance drills and was as sure as she could be that she had not been followed, or that if she had been, she had shaken them off. But it was impossible to be 100 percent certain. Merely knowing what was on the BlackBerry spyware put Beaker—and Lysette—in danger. On the other hand, she knew nobody else with Beaker's skill set. And he could have said no. Except, she knew, he could not have, not when she was asking. Plus, there were Jones's gun and silencer. Hidden safely away, she hoped.

Yael breathed deeply to stop her thoughts racing, and looked at the monument to Raoul Wallenberg on the island in the middle of First Avenue. Five black columns pointed to the sky, their edges ragged and twisted. At the base of one lay a briefcase, symbolizing unfinished business. When Yael was plagued with doubts about the deals she negotiated behind the scenes, she liked to come here and sit by the monument. It was stark, almost bleak, a reminder of the darkness and evil in which Wallenberg had worked. But it was also strangely calming, perhaps because without Wallenberg she would not be alive.

Wallenberg was a Swedish diplomat posted to Budapest during the Second World War. Like Yael, he had dealt with the devil, in his case the thugs and murderers of the Arrow Cross, the Hungarian Nazis whose bloodlust exceeded even that of the SS. Wallenberg had saved tens of thousands of Jews, including Yael's grandmother, Eva Weiss, whom he had plucked out of a line of Jews waiting to be deported or lined up on the banks of the Danube and shot, their bodies falling into the freezing waters. Wallenberg's reward for his courage was to be taken away by the Soviets in January 1945 and disappear into the maw of the gulag. Mystery still surrounded his fate—and that of his fellow Swede Dag Hammarskjöld, for whom the plaza was named.

Hammarskjöld had died in a plane crash in 1961, while mediating between the government of Congo and the secessionists in the province of Katanga. There had been three official inquiries into his death, but none had finally determined the chain of events. It was widely believed across Africa, and much of the UN, that Hammarskjöld had been murdered to prevent Congo's newly independent government from taking control of its rich resources, including coltan. The battle still raged, Yael thought, leaving a fresh trail of death and destruction. Coltan had made her into a killer, had almost triggered a new round of genocide in Africa, and should have brought down Fareed Hussein. A picture of Caroline Masters, sitting in the SG's chair, flashed through her mind. Maybe it had.

Yael glanced at the bronze briefcase. She too had her share of unfinished business. Sometimes whole weeks went by, especially when she was on mission, when she didn't think about him. And now he was back, embedded in her mind, as his genes were embedded in her body. The breakfast with Joe-Don yesterday at La Caridad had triggered the memories. Years had passed, but the anger, the sense of disillusionment, seemed as raw as ever. *How could you do those things?* she wanted to ask. *You raised us to be decent people, to have a moral compass, to do what was right. How?*

But beyond her anger was another voice, quieter but no less insistent.

*L*ook, Aba.

She braces herself, leans back, and kicks the driver in the back of the head. The car spins out of control, hits a BMW, whirls around, and crashes into a low wall by the sidewalk. She smashes the window and clambers out, dazed, bloody, and sprints toward Lake Geneva.

Look, Aba.

The hand rises out of water so cold it sears her skin. She locks the bald man between her thighs, forces his head underneath the surface. He thrashes underneath her, his eyes on hers, first furious then pleading, her legs a vise, until the water becomes still.

Look, Aba.

She raises the lighter to the corner of the photograph of the three smiling girls. The plastic covering turns black, melts, and starts to smoke. Hakizimani's face collapses as he pleas for her to stop.

Look, Aba, look, look, look. . . .

*W*ould she have burnt Hakizimani's last picture of his dead daughters? She desperately hoped not. But the truth was, she didn't know anymore.

Yael was so deep in her thoughts she barely noticed that someone had sat down next to her.

"Hey, stranger," said a friendly female voice.

Yael turned to see Isis Franklin. She snapped out of her

reverie, smiling with genuine pleasure at the sight of the American diplomat.

"You look like you were miles away. How *are* you? Full date update, please."

"Nothing to report. There was no date. You saw Al Jazeera?"

Isis nodded, her hand resting on Yael's arm. "Of course. A grade-A asshole."

Yael saw Isis looking hard at the powder on her right cheek, which covered the marks from her fight with Cyrus Jones. She resisted the surprisingly strong urge to touch her face and check that the scratches were still disguised.

Yael gave Isis a wry smile. "Is he? He is a journalist. He was just doing his job. My mistake was to think he might put me first. He didn't show for dinner. How could he, after that?"

Isis was indignant. "Sure, but no flowers, apology? Not even a call, or an e-mail?"

Yael shook her head. "Nope. No nothing. He is probably too embarrassed."

"There's no need for you to make excuses for him."

No, there is not, thought Yael. So why was she? She must really be a glutton for punishment. "And you? Any tall, dark, and handsome diplomats on the horizon?"

"Nope. Just Istanbul, Istanbul, and more Istanbul. A week until it starts, four days of complete craziness; then normal life can resume. I hope."

Born in Chicago, Isis was the daughter of an African American municipal official, a former radical who had been a founding member of the Black Panthers, and a Swiss violinist in the city's orchestra. She was petite, handsome rather than pretty, with tawny skin, a high forehead, and long curly black hair that she wore tied back. Her eyes were her most striking feature. Large and brown, brimming with curiosity, they made even the most jaded diplomats temporarily lose their bearings. Forty-four, divorced, childless, she had worked for the State Department since she graduated with a master's degree from Harvard.

Yael had heard the whispers, that Isis had been promoted to department head of the Public Diplomacy section because she was an old friend of President Freshwater. Both women had worked on the Rwanda desk at the State Department during the 1994 genocide. But to Yael Isis seemed smart and professional. Yael strongly sensed that there was much more to Isis beneath her bright and cordial exterior. She had seen Isis work a room, charged with a coiled energy, charming nuggets of information out of normally tight-lipped diplomats. During a reception for Turkey's national day, Yael had gone to the bathroom and seen Isis urgently tapping away at her BlackBerry, so absorbed in her task she did not even notice Yael slide into a cubicle.

Isis picked up Yael's hand and touched the ring on her second finger. "That's beautiful. Where did you get it?"

"From my brother, David."

Isis leaned forward, still holding Yael's hand. "You still miss him?"

Yael smiled sadly. "Of course. Every day."

It was curiously comforting to have Isis holding her hand. One of the worst things about her solitude was that nobody touched her. She was used to waking up alone, and going to sleep alone, even eating alone with only a newspaper or book for company. But sometimes she longed for the feel of another's skin against hers, no matter how briefly.

"How long is it now?" asked Isis. "Twenty years?"

Yael nodded. "Yes. It's incredible. He would be forty-three."

"What's incredible is that the peacekeepers weren't dispatched to save them. I knew one of them as well. Cornelius Roche. He was Swiss, a friend of my mother's." Isis looked directly at Yael. "That's why you stay, isn't it?"

"Stay where?"

"Here. There," said Isis, gesturing at the Secretariat headquarters, two blocks away. "You get sacked, sidelined, exposed on national television, you might get arrested by the NYPD or extradited to Switzerland, but you are still here. You want to know why David died and who was responsible."

Yael sat up straight, alert now that the conversation had taken such a personal turn. "It's not the only reason. But yes. I do want to know. Beyond Fareed Hussein's pusillanimity. He didn't take the decision himself. Someone told him what to do."

"Exactly." Isis hesitated for a moment, as though uncertain whether to speak. "Listen, honey. There may be some new information."

"What?" asked Yael. Her eyes really were remarkable, thought Yael; the irises seemed flecked with gold.

"I don't know exactly. Just bits and pieces I'm hearing. What Fareed and the P5 were really doing behind the scenes."

"And?" asked Yael, trying to keep the eagerness from her voice, her fingers tightening against Isis's hand. "Tell me. Please. Anything you have."

Yael had already trusted Isis with one of her darkest secrets—albeit only a part of the story. One night in a village in the Afghan mountains, cold, lonely, scared, Yael had slept with her interpreter, Sharif. He had immediately fallen in love with her and announced their forthcoming marriage. When Yael refused Sharif's proposal, he was consumed with shame. He joined the Taliban and offered himself for martyrdom. That much Yael had shared. Several days later Sharif, wired up with a suicide vest, was shot dead by an American sniper on his way to the Kandahar bazaar. Yael had not told Isis how the sniper knew what route Sharif would be taking. The guilt still gnawed at her: over Sharif's death, of course, but also for another life ended prematurely.

Isis frowned. "There may be some kind of French connection. A deal that went wrong. Something to do with the Bonnet Group. But I don't want to get your hopes up. It's all secondhand at this stage. Whispers and rumors. I will tell you when I have something definite. Promise." Isis squeezed Yael's hand, then let it go and picked up her purse.

"Thank you," said Yael, her mind racing. A deal that went wrong. That fitted with the whispers and rumors she had heard. But now, Yael knew, was not the time to push it. "And what's new with you?"

"Free at last," said Isis, a wry smile on her face. "The divorce is finalized."

Gerson, Isis's former husband, was also an American

diplomat, a highflyer who had just been posted to Paris as deputy chief of mission. They had met in Sarajevo six years ago, where Isis had been posted after Kandahar. A year later they were married and serving together in Montevideo. Until Isis walked into Gerson's office late one evening to find him entwined on the office sofa with the embassy's cultural attaché, a lissome Yale graduate fifteen years his junior. Gerson had confessed the affair had been going on for months. He moved in with his girlfriend the next day. Isis had confided in Yael that the marriage had been rocky for some time because they had been unable to have children. A battery of tests had revealed that her husband's sperm was fine—the problem was hers. A few months after the separation, Gerson's girlfriend gave birth to twins.

Isis had put a brave face on the breakup, blaming pressure of work and too much time apart. But Yael knew that she had been heartbroken. All her adult life Isis had hungered to create the kind of warm, stable family life she had missed in her own childhood. Like Yael, Isis had fractured relationships with her parents. Isis's father had been a serial philanderer, bedding a stream of colleagues in the Chicago municipal administration and even the mayor's sister-in-law. Her parents had divorced and Isis's mother returned to Switzerland, where she had suffered a series of strokes and now lived in a nursing home. Isis no longer spoke with her father. The last time Isis visited her mother she had not recognized her. Isis's inability to have children had sent her into a deep depression. After the separation, a year ago, she had taken six months' unpaid leave. She had done some pro bono work for a human rights organization and spent the rest of the time, she said, visiting all the places she wanted to see as a tourist. Isis was trying desperately to adopt a child, and Yael had heard rumors that Isis had even used her connections to UNICEF and other aid organizations to find a suitable girl or boy from somewhere in the developing world.

"I'm so sorry," said Yael.

"Don't be. It's better like this. We can both make a new life. At least Gerson's children can be legal," she said, a catch in her throat.

"The adoption?"

"It looked like it was moving ahead, but . . ." Isis's smile suddenly took on a frozen quality, her body language tense and stiff. "Bureaucracy, paperwork. You know how it is."

"I can imagine," said Yael sympathetically.

"Actually, you can't." Isis stared into the distance.

She sensed Yael looking at her and suddenly reverted back to her usual vivacious self. "Listen, I am in a hurry. But there are a bunch of new male diplomats in town. A couple seem to have some potential. We are heading downtown to a bar in the East Village tomorrow. There will be live music. It will be a fun evening. Why don't you come?"

Yael shook her head. "But everyone will have seen the Al Jazeera report. I'm kind of embarrassed. I don't think—"

Isis laughed, a deep, rolling sound. "Don't be coy, babe. You are a star. The whole building's talking about you. Everyone wants to meet you. Don't think. Just do. You are at Riverside and Eighty-First, right?"

"But really—"

"No arguments. Your lobby. Nine p.m. tomorrow, Friday. I will see you there," Isis said, standing up and blowing Yael a kiss.

Yael smiled as she watched Isis walk over to the greenhouse café. A night on the town could be just what she needed. And it would be certainly more fun than moping around her apartment. But something nagged at her about the encounter, welcome as it was.

The sight of Braithwaite—dressed in a green waxed-cotton jacket, check scarf, and a tweed cap—striding toward her pushed the thought from her mind. His ruddy cheeks shone with good health. He walked with a purposeful stride, as though he were about to saddle his mount and gallop across the English countryside in pursuit of a fox.

Quentin Braithwaite had been reassigned to the DPKO from the British Ministry of Defense in the early 1990s. Braithwaite's classic establishment background—born into an army family that reached back to the founding of the British Empire, Eton, Sandhurst army college, service in the Brigade of Guards—had brought him a warm welcome from Fareed Hussein, who was head of the DPKO at the time. Hussein assumed Braithwaite would follow the British government's line, emphasizing the UN's neutrality and opposing interventions.

Hussein was wrong, as he quickly learned. Braithwaite's first mission was to Bosnia in 1992, where he commanded a battalion of peacekeepers at the British base in Vitez. Hussein and many others believed that the UN mission in Bosnia needed the consent of the Bosnian Serbs to operate. It was not the UN's business to confront them as they organized their genocidal campaign of ethnic cleansing. Smoke curled skyward, columns of refugees trudged away from their burning houses, shells exploding around them, but still the peacekeepers watched and took no action. Braithwaite thought otherwise.

Soon after his arrival, Bosnian Serb troops had attempted to arrest Braithwaite and the British government minister he was escorting across the battlefield to besieged Sarajevo. The DPKO's recommendation in those circumstances was to open negotiations, which could last hours, if not days. Braithwaite simply closed the hatches on his armored personnel carrier and smashed his way through the checkpoint. The Bosnian Serb troops ran for cover as Braithwaite roared through no-man's-land to the Bosnian government's front lines, where he was met with cheers. Hussein was furious and called a special press conference in New York, where he described Braithwaite as "reckless, foolhardy, and setting a dangerous precedent that would draw peacekeepers into the conflicts they were supposedly defusing." Behind the scenes, Hussein had used every trick in his extensive armory to have Braithwaite recalled. But London, for once, stood firm. Braithwaite then further infuriated Hussein by inviting him to visit Sarajevo, offering to drive him through the front lines himself. Hussein had finally traveled to the Bosnian capital—in December 1995, when the war was over.

After Fareed Hussein had been appointed SG, Braithwaite had been promoted to run the DPKO. Hussein fought a ferocious battle to prevent his appointment, with the support of the Russians, French, and Chinese. But Britain and the United States had shifted position by then. NATO intervention had brought the Bosnian war to an end, not the UN's neutrality. London and Washington refused to back down. Eventually, after a week of back-room negotiating and diplomatic trade-offs, the Russians, French, and Chinese conceded. Hussein's objections were ignored. Nowadays, Braithwaite was the undeclared leader of the UN's interventionists. This was a shrinking band, especially after the fiasco over Syria's chemical weapons. But Braithwaite still argued that a fleet of attack helicopters and a battalion of properly armed peacekeepers had the edge on any Security Council resolution, no matter how strongly worded.

Yael both liked and trusted the Englishman. She stood up and fell into step beside him as he arrived. She was about to speak when her mobile phone beeped. She glanced at the screen. @najwaun had just tweeted to her thirty-six thousand followers, one of whom was Yael: "UN spokesman Schneidermann confirmed dead: medics say was massive heart attack, but he seemed healthy + was only 38."

Yael showed the phone to Braithwaite. "He's gone. I accessed Schneidermann's medical records this morning, as soon as I heard from Joe-Don that he was in the hospital. Schneidermann was paunchy and out of shape. But there was nothing wrong with his heart."

"I know. He had breakfast with Fareed this morning. I just spoke to him. He was very upset. He said Schneidermann seemed completely fine."

Yael was no fan of the UN spokesman. He embodied the willful obtuseness and irritating sense of self-righteousness that tainted the whole organization. He had done his best to end her UN career during the coltan conspiracy, brief-

ing the press corps—always off the record, of course—
that Yael had gone rogue, was a danger to the organization, and even to international security. But recently,
he seemed to have found his spine. Unlike many of the
officials on the thirty-eighth floor, he had stayed loyal to
Fareed Hussein. She knew Schneidermann had refused to
follow Caroline Masters's instructions to trash her at his
last press briefing. And he certainly did not deserve to die.
Had he been killed? This was a sad and very disturbing
development.

"Why was he meeting Fareed?" she asked.

"Fareed had decided it was time to release the information in the folder that I showed you when the three of us
met. Schneidermann was going to leak it."

"To whom?"

"To Sami Boustani. He was on his way to meet him for
breakfast."

"How cozy," said Yael, her voice barbed.

A teenage boy with a wild Afro hairstyle whizzed past
on a three-foot-long skateboard, rap music hissing out of his
oversized headphones.

Braithwaite waited until the skateboarder had passed before he spoke. "Now, now, Yael. Let's not allow personal feelings to intrude. Anyway, that plan is on hold now, obviously."

A thought struck her. She looked at Braithwaite. "Is
Sami in danger?"

"I don't think so. Not at the moment. It would be too
much of a coincidence. A dead UN official, followed by a
dead *New York Times* reporter with whom he was supposed
to meet? That would bring an awful lot of attention onto

people who would rather operate in the shadows. Or the toilet of the Staten Island Ferry."

Braithwaite turned to look at her. She blushed, to her surprise.

"You are right to be embarrassed. My dear Yael, you know I am one of your greatest admirers. But you are either very brave, or very stupid. Possibly both. Joe-Don told me what happened. He was very angry."

Yael slipped her phone into her pocket. "I know. He threatened to quit."

"Did he?"

"Of course not."

"Where is he?"

Yael gestured forward and sideways to the left with her head. A solidly built man of indeterminate age sat six benches ahead, bundled up in a black nylon winter jacket with his collar raised. He wore a woolen cap and Ray-Ban aviator sunglasses and was reading the *New York Post*. He slowly turned two pages as they walked nearer—the pre-arranged signal that the path was clear and they were not under surveillance.

"Schneidermann dead makes two," said Yael.

"How so?"

Yael told Braithwaite the full story of her encounter with Clarence Clairborne, about how she had provoked him so much he had slipped up, saying "we" in relation to the death of President Freshwater's husband. She described how she had been followed by two men on the train back to New York, stolen one of the men's mobile telephones, and how he had been found floating in the Potomac soon after.

"Who is 'we'?" asked Braithwaite, almost to himself. "What was on the phone?"

"The unlisted home numbers of Clarence Clairborne and several of his friends."

"I would like to have those. Anyone especially interesting?"

"William F. Stone."

Braithwaite furrowed his brow. "Founder of Stone and Partners, the most powerful law firm on K Street."

Yael nodded. "That's the one, among whose clients are Bank Bernard et Fils."

"Our favorite Swiss bank. I told Fareed that the BBF immunity arrangement was a mistake and would come back to haunt us. They are untouchable. But he wouldn't listen."

A middle-aged man in an ankle-length coat strode toward them, shouting at his secretary on his mobile telephone. Yael and Braithwaite both fell silent until he was far behind them.

"It was not a mistake. Fareed was right. Off-the-books money has to move somewhere, somehow. It's much easier for us to keep track of it if we know it goes through BBF. We have a line into that bank. It gives us ammunition. Clairborne could barely control his temper when I showed him the payment record."

"Maybe," said Braithwaite, unconvinced. He was silent for a few moments, his brow furrowed in thought. "Ten million dollars from Omega, the Prometheus Group's Swiss subsidiary, to Nuristan Holdings, one of the Revolutionary Guard's front companies in Tehran. So we have an American company, tied with the Pentagon, not just trading illegally with Tehran, but with the Revolutionary Guard."

"And arranging security at the Istanbul Summit," said Yael. "All thanks to Caroline Masters. Why do you think she agreed to that?"

Braithwaite stopped walking for a moment. He turned to look at Yael. "I don't know. I guess she doesn't know about the Nuristan Holdings connection. Why has Fareed surrendered without a fight? And what were you doing on the Staten Island Ferry anyway?"

Yael reached inside her jacket and took out a folded sheet of paper. She handed it to Braithwaite. There were three photographs on the paper: one of the Staten Island Ferry terminal and two of Cyrus Jones. The pictures of Jones, showing him full face and side-on, seemed to be taken from an identity card. The letters spelled out the previous day's date and 16:00. The letter *r* in *April* was missing its horizontal spar.

Braithwaite stared at the paper for several seconds before he handed it back to Yael. "So now he is calling himself Cyrus Jones."

Yael looked at Braithwaite, momentarily surprised. "You know him? How?"

"From Baghdad. He was smuggled out, over the border into Turkey, after he shot a family at a checkpoint near Samarra. But first, I think it's time you told me properly what happened in Istanbul."

14

S he is standing on the Eminönü waterfront, watching the police launch bounce across the waves. It is a perfect spring morning. The sun is warm on her face, the breeze scented with the smell of the sea. The V-shaped hull cuts through the water like a scythe at harvest time, pale spray fountaining in its wake.

The three policemen grimace as they drag the dead man into the boat. His back is crisscrossed by deep welts, their ruffled edges bleached white by the water. His arms and shoulders are dotted with semicircular rows of tiny puncture marks, each two or three inches long. The police commander shakes his head in disgust. He covers the body with a gray blanket, gently smoothing the fabric as though tucking a child into bed.

"We offered him a deal," says the man standing at Yael's side. He is wiry, muscled, in his midthirties. A long purple birthmark reaches from his left ear down the side of his neck.

"Which was?"

"Better than that," he replies, gesturing at the police launch.

"An orange jumpsuit?"

He laughs. "Any color he wanted."

Yael watches the paramedics maneuver the dead man into the body bag, his arms and legs lolling from side to side. His eyes are *wide open and the water drips off his straggly beard.* "Who was he?" *she asks.*

"Nobody important."

"Somebody thought he was, judging by his back."

"The important one is Abdullah Gul. Your friend. The one you are bringing in for us."

Your friend. Is Gul her friend? He certainly believes himself to be America's friend. Abdullah Gul has a PhD from Harvard in artificial intelligence, a Twitter feed with twenty-six thousand followers, and loathes the Taliban as much as they hate him. Gul believes women should be educated, that Sufism—a tolerant, spiritual Islam—offers a better future than the ascetic fanaticism of the Taliban. Gul has been courted by the United States and its allies, has visited the White House, spoken at the UN General Assembly, been touted as a future potential president. He is popular and, incredibly for an Afghan politician, not for sale.

In short, Gul is everything that the United States says Afghanistan needs: a pious but modern and progressive Muslim. Yael has enjoyed his company. Perhaps he is her friend. Lord knew, she didn't have many.

"Who was he?" *she asks insistently.*

The police launch docks at the waterfront. Two paramedics step out of an ambulance and wheel a stretcher forward.

"I don't know."

Yael knows he is lying. "You should. You killed him."

"I did not," *he snaps, his voice rising in anger.*

She turns to look at him. "But you were there. . . . You watched. You supervised."

He blinks twice before he speaks. She senses his body tense, despite his determined effort to stay relaxed, to give nothing away, which is itself the biggest giveaway of all.

"It was badly handled. He didn't know anything," he replies, a hard edge to his California accent. *The paramedics zip the body into a black bag, and the ambulance speeds away from the dock, maneuvering a path into the slow-moving traffic*

Yael pushes harder. "You watched him die. Who was he?"

He looks away. She feels anger, defensiveness, even a wisp of guilt. "He was Gul's cousin. If you are so concerned about his fate, take it up with the MİT." *The Turkish intelligence service is one of the United States' most reliable allies in the region—or had been, until recently.*

"Try again, Mr. Jones," *says Yael, remembering the rows of puncture marks. Dogs were anathema to Muslims.* "The MİT didn't do this. And I think they would much rather talk to you than me. Three drone strikes inside the Turkish border in a month. Twenty-seven civilians killed last week, including nineteen women and children who had gathered for a birthday party."

Jones is unmoved. "Very regrettable. Sure, the Turks shout a lot. They have to. But they understand. There is a war on. The border is porous. Jihadis are crossing back and forth from Syria. This whole region could go up in flames."

"Tell me why I should bring Gul in."

"He is the point man between the poppy growers and the Taliban and al-Qaeda. He runs the business end, takes care of the money and launders it. From Kandahar to Kabul, Kabul to Baku, and then on to Zurich."

"Really?" *says Yael, her voice disbelieving.* "Last time I met him, Gul was setting up a microloans bank in conjunction with USAID, which is a US government agency. So Gul is a colleague of yours."

"Gul conned us. It's a front. He controls the drug trade. He uses the microloans to move the money," says Jones, his voice insistent.

Yael watches his face. A small vein pulses at the side of his neck. Jones is lying. There is something else going on.

Yael says, "Fifty bucks doesn't buy a lot of heroin, even in Afghanistan. And why do you need me? Why don't you just kidnap him, wrap him in a giant nappy, and send him to Guantanamo?"

"We don't do that anymore," says Jones regretfully. "Gul needs to come over of his own free will. Everything has to be squeaky clean. Which is where you come in. We are offering Gul a deal."

Which was what?" asked Quentin Braithwaite.

Yael grimaced at the memory. "They were holding Gul at a villa on the island of Büyükada, an hour's boat ride from the mainland. He thought he had come to Istanbul for a back-channel meeting about Afghanistan to discuss policy options after the American pull out, this year. They detained him as soon as he arrived."

"Why?"

"The Americans are courting the Taliban. The Taliban wanted Gul out of the picture. Gul is their worst nightmare. Imagine, a patriotic Afghan Muslim leader who actually wanted girls to go to school. Gul was the price of the peace deal. The Americans refused at first, but halfheartedly. Then the Taliban shot down an Apache helicopter and killed seventeen marines. The Americans got the message. They dumped Gul like he was radioactive. They said he was laundering money for al-Qaeda."

"Was he?"

"The Americans gave Fareed a file on him, full of

e-mails that he had supposedly written, copies of bank transfers, photographs of Gul meeting al-Qaeda operatives. It certainly looked impressive. Fareed took it at face value. Or said he did."

"Which Americans?" asked Braithwaite. "State? Pentagon? Langley?"

Yael thought for a moment. "Good question. I don't know. It came via the USUN mission. I was not convinced. The whole thing didn't feel right to me."

"Why not?"

"It was all too pat. The e-mails were written in perfect idiomatic American English, from Gmail addresses. Nobody would use Gmail to talk to al-Qaeda. I checked with a friend who worked for Google. The Gmail addresses had never existed. One of the banks had gone out of business three years ago. The photographs had been photoshopped. Very skillfully, but still photoshopped. Joe-Don started asking around. There was something else going on. I told Fareed but he was not interested. Just go to Istanbul and bring Gul in, he told me."

"And Gul still surrendered, even though the evidence was fake?"

Yael nodded.

"Why?"

Jones takes out his smartphone from his pocket. The screen shows a young, pretty woman, with olive skin and dark eyes, chatting on Skype at an Internet café in Istanbul. She is dressed modestly in brown trousers and a long-sleeved beige top, her hair tucked away in a patterned hijab that reaches down to her shoulders.

She next appears sitting in the backseat of a car, jammed between two men whose faces are hidden in shadows. A hand is clamped over her mouth. She is wide-eyed with fear, a bright red mark down one side of her face, her head scarf askew. The third segment shows her lying on her back in a bare room with concrete walls, wearing a shapeless gray slip. Her eyes are closed and she appears to be unconscious. Her left foot twitches sporadically.

His wife?" asked Braithwaite.

"No," said Yael, frowning. "His daughter."

Braithwaite shook his head, his face tight with disgust. "My Lord. These people. And what did you do?"

"Jones said he worked for something called the DoD— the Department of Deniable. He could kidnap people. Make them disappear."

Yael softens her voice and edges closer. She smooths her auburn hair behind her head, subtly arching her back to show off her slim figure and the swell of her breasts.

She turns to look at him. "OK, Cyrus. Like you said, it's a war. And in a war there are casualties—not always the right ones. But if we can cut off Gul's money, we can stop the financing to the terrorists, and the attacks on American troops, defeat the Taliban, and bring democracy to Afghanistan."

"Yes. Exactly."

"The money men are the key to everything."

Jones nods, pleased that she seems to understand. "You said it."

He moves toward her, and she smiles, leaning back on the railing at the water's edge, raising her face to the sun. Her denim jacket falls open; she senses his eyes on her.

"We can talk about it some more at dinner tonight if you like," says Jones. *"I know a wonderful place overlooking the old city. No tourists. They have private dining rooms. It's quite isolated, at the end of a foot track. The view is incredible."*

Yael holds his gaze. "Count me in, Cyrus."

W hat about the Turks?" asked Braithwaite. "All this is going on in their territory."

"They were furious. They had no idea that the DoD had set up a black prison in a villa on the coast. You know how proud the Turks are. And that on top of the drone strikes and Big Oil making nice with the Kurds, handing them suitcases full of cash, which they gave in turn to their brothers inside Turkey to finance their independence movement. The Turks were really pissed with the Americans. That gave me an idea."

T *he ferry from Istanbul to Büyükada docks and Yael steps ashore. A policeman walks over and asks for her passport. She hands him her red UN laissez-passer. He leafs through it. A man in a leather jacket appears. He shows the policeman an identity card and holds his hand out. The policeman instantly hands Yael's passport to him, salutes, and leaves.*

The man is wearing a black leather jacket, unzipped, and is standing with his hand in the right-hand pocket, just as Yael had been told he would. He gestures for Yael to follow him. They walk through the crowds at the harbor, tourists chattering excitedly as they decided where to eat in the rows of seafood restaurants that overlooked the water. The smell of grilled fish makes Yael realize how hungry she is. All she has eaten that day is a banana for breakfast.

Yael's escort stops at a stand selling pide, *the Turkish version of pizza—a slab of crispy dough covered with minced lamb, tomato sauce, and peppers—and greets the owner. The food smells delicious. The owner immediately picks up two pide, rapidly slices them into sections, wraps them in greaseproof paper, and hands them over, together with two cartons of* ayran, *a sour yogurt drink. The man in the leather jacket offers to pay but the owner waves him away, already focused on the next customer. Yael and her escort walk away from the crowd toward Fayton Meydani, the central square. It is lined by pastel-colored houses, crowded with hansom cabs, tourists on bicycles, and locals chatting, drinking coffee, and smoking. There are no cars on Büyükada; the only means of transportation is by bicycle, horse, or foot.*

Yael and her escort sit on a bench. The breeze brings the scent of the sea, sharp and salty, making her even hungrier. He passes her one of the packets and a drink and she unwraps her lunch. The pide is delicious and they eat in comfortable silence.

"Thank you, that was excellent." Yael wipes her fingers on a napkin.

"You are most welcome, Ms. Azoulay," he says, his voice warm and genuine. "Shalom, Ms. Azoulay. Welcome to Istanbul."

"Thank you. And please, it's Yael. What's your name?"

"You can call me Yusuf." He smiles. It is an engaging grin and he knows it.

Yael watches Yusuf finish his pide. His fingers are long and slender, his dark eyes, somewhere between brown and black, warm and intelligent. A lock of hair, so black it almost shines, falls over his forehead. Yusuf is certainly different from the Turkish officials she has met so far. They have been polite, but distant and somewhat condescending, unused to dealing with assertive, even demanding, Western women.

To her great annoyance, Yael finds herself blushing. It has been a long time since a good-looking man has bought her lunch, or anything else, especially in such gorgeous surroundings. But she also has a job to do.

She sips her ayran, turns to look at Yusuf. "Gul was your guest."

Yusuf shifts on the bench and exhales sharply through his nose. His discomfort is plain to see. He takes out a packet of Camel Turkish Gold cigarettes and offers a cigarette to Yael. She places it in her mouth. Yusuf lights the cigarette with a shiny silver Zippo. The gesture is curiously intimate. The smoke is rich and smooth, the Turkish tobacco fragrant, scented with cloves. She breathes deeply, relishing the instant nicotine buzz.

"Abdullah Gul is still our guest," says Yusuf, his voice ironic.

"That's one word for it."

"He is being well treated."

"He is a prisoner."

"Like all of us. A prisoner of his time and place."

"Meaning?"

"He will be traded. Once you persuade him to agree."

"Traded for what?"

Two young German tourists approach on bicycles. Yusuf waits until they have passed. "American companies are investing heavily in Iraqi Kurdistan. Perhaps one of their oil pipelines will soon burst. A local partner will be found to be corrupt and will be arrested. Or a payment will go astray. Perceptions will change. In Washington they will start to whisper. . . . Perhaps the Kurds are not such reliable partners, after all."

Yael takes out her smartphone. She taps through the menu until she finds the right video clip. She presses play and hands the smartphone to Yusuf.

"Was she your guest as well?" she asks.

Yusuf's fingers grip the phone, his body rigid, his face dark.

Tell me more about this Yusuf," said Braithwaite, intrigued. "Family name?"

"Çelmiz."

"Did you check his ID card?"

"No."

Braithwaite looked doubtful. "Why not?"

Yael smiled at the memory of that afternoon. "I knew he worked for the MİT, and that was enough." *And because he was good-looking, bought me lunch, and I liked him*, she almost added.

Abdullah Gul rises to greet Yael as she walks up the path to the villa, accompanied by Yusuf. Gul is sitting on a terrace lined by rosebushes, shaded from the sun by a large walnut tree. A shiny brass coffeepot sits on a low table in front of him, steam rising from a filigreed china cup, next to a pitcher of iced lemonade. The sound of Sufi chanting carries through the garden, soft and hypnotic. Gul is as charismatic as ever: tall, athletically built, his manner welcoming, his gray beard neatly trimmed, gray eyes brimming with intelligence.

Gul gestures for Yael to sit in the adjoining chair. He nods at Yusuf, who sits a few yards away.

"They always send a friend for this," Gul says, his voice wry.

Yael smiles. "How are you, Abdullah?"

The answer is in front of her. His trademark black shalwar and kameez seem a size too large. The long shirt and baggy trousers, with embroidered cuffs and collar, were designed to be loose fitting, but his frame seems to have shrunk and his cheeks have sunk in on themselves.

Gul shrugs. "Alive. Bored. I would like to go home. Have you come to take me home?"

Yael feels sadness rise inside her. "I am so sorry, Abdullah."

The cicadas chirp in the greenery, an accompaniment to the chanting. There is no point delaying or pretending. Yael takes out her smartphone. She presses play and hands it to Gul.

He watches the video clip, his face twisted in anger and revulsion, before handing the phone back to Yael. "Truly, they know no limits."

"None. None at all."

"He was my cousin. He knew nothing. He had a family."

The weight in Yael's stomach becomes even heavier. "There is more," she says, scrolling quickly through the menu and returning the smartphone to him.

Gul looks down at the screen. His face is a stone mask. He watches for half a minute, then turns away. He places the phone on the table, its screen still glowing in the soft light of dusk. "Enough."

Gul stands up. One of the guards monitoring Gul's every step instantly spins on his heel, his Uzi in his hand. Gul walks across to the garden wall and looks out to sea. The sky is streaked with gold and purple, the sea turning black and silver.

"Is she alive?" Gul asks. His hand twists the fabric of his sleeve around and around.

Yael follows him to the edge of the garden. The breeze has turned cold. She watches him shiver. "Yes. She has been drugged, but she has not been harmed."

"You know why they are doing this?"

Yael shakes her head.

Gul fixes his gaze on her, his eyes like green lasers. He steps away from the garden wall. "Imagine, a modern, enlightened Is-

lam in Afghanistan, where children and women are educated and the people enjoy human rights. What do you think they will say in the Pentagon and in Langley when they learn that their budgets are to be slashed because peace and stability are coming to Afghanistan? They will not say, hurrah for Abdullah Gul, we do not need any more drone strikes or spies or satellites or safe houses or bombs or electric cattle prods or secret bases at Bagram air base to keep prisoners in dog kennels and send them across the border to Uzbekistan to be boiled alive. And even if the CIA and the Pentagon wanted peace in Afghanistan, their paymasters would never allow it."

"You are wrong," says Yael. "American politicians want the troops to come home."

Gul laughs. "The politicians. The politicians are irrelevant. What matters are the corporations, who pay for the politicians. The corporations want a deal. A deal on drugs. It is common knowledge that the war on drugs is lost. It is only a matter of time before they are legalized. Look at Uruguay and Colorado. Many more US states will follow, and then other countries. You cannot imagine how much money these companies will make. The corporations have been planning for this for decades. There is a German conglomerate, called KZX. A giant firm, with branches all over the world. Have you heard of it?"

Yael nods.

Gul continues, "KZX has excellent contacts with the Taliban. KZX managers and Taliban leaders regularly meet in Dubai. They were here, in Istanbul, last week, at the conference with the Taliban, the one organized by the Americans. There was a tall man, thin, with white-blond hair; he always wore a gray suit. German, or Austrian. He was in charge. KZX is negotiating to buy the poppy harvest. For now the drugs will be processed and sold illegally on the streets. But in the future, once they are legalized, KZX will be in prime position. Not this year, or next, but soon. KZX doesn't want our farmers growing wheat or apricots or forming cooperatives. Neither do Langley and the Pentagon. They want war. KZX wants heroin. Afghanistan can supply both, but not if I am there."

Yael processes what Gul has said. A tall, thin man with white-blond hair. German or Austrian. It all makes perfect sense. She says, "This is not over, Abdullah. Nothing is over as long as you are alive. But you know that even if the Turks let you go, the Americans will find you. She leans forward and searches Gul's face. She sees sadness and regret, but also determination. "And Samira?" he asks. "Can you guarantee her safety?"

"I cannot," says Yael. "But this can," she continues, holding her smartphone. "The footage of Samira and your cousin has been has been cut into hundreds of sections. Each section is backed up to a network of secure servers, with military-level encryption. Nobody can delete them. Not even Langley. I can splice the videos together and upload them to YouTube in a few seconds—with a commentary explaining exactly what happened." She pauses. "The blowback will last longer. Kabul will explode. No US embassy in the Muslim world will be safe if that film is released. Langley knows that. Samira is safe."

Gul drops his cigarette underfoot and twists the butt into the ground. He steps forward as if to walk to his room and start packing immediately. "OK."

"Abdullah, please, wait," says Yael. "There is something else."

She turns to look at Yusuf. He is slowly tapping his feet to the sound of the chanting floating through the garden. He catches her eye and inclines his head, almost imperceptibly.

Yael speaks quietly to Gul. He smiles, for the first time that day.

Braithwaite looked at Yael and nodded, as if seeing her for the first time. "Impressive. And the next thing we know is that Cyrus Jones is being held by the Syrian People's Armed Revolutionary Faction in Ayn al-Arab, just across from the Turkish border. All thanks to you and the mysterious Yusuf. I almost feel sorry for the fellow. He thought he was going on a dinner date and ends up getting kidnapped by jihadis."

"Actually he was kidnapped by some of Yusuf's friends. They handed him over to the Syrians. Only for a month."

Braithwaite stopped smiling. "You are very clever. You are also in grave danger, Yael. Eventually they will decide that Jones is a liability. They will throw him overboard. And then they will come for you. Again."

Yael stared ahead as Braithwaite spoke. They were almost at the end of the plaza. Second Avenue was fifty yards away, a familiar midmorning scene of honking taxis and bustling pedestrians. A cycle messenger flew past, his bright yellow jersey bobbing in and out of the traffic. Yael envied him his freedom and the fluid grace with which he maneuvered around obstacles. It was a bright spring Manhattan morning, the kind she usually enjoyed. But Yael knew Braithwaite was right. Her trick with Cyrus Jones had seemed just and smart at the time. It was both. But it came at a price, which was still to be paid. The video she had shot of Jones on the ferry would hold them off, but only for a while, while they considered their next move. In fact, she was not sure how to get out of this situation. She glanced behind her. At least Joe-Don was ten yards away, a reassuring presence.

"Baku?" Yael asked, although with no news of the courier, she already knew the answer.

"Your trip is off," said Braithwaite. He reached inside his coat pocket, took out a sheet of folded paper, and handed it to Yael.

She opened the paper to see a photocopy of a page of an Iranian passport, with the personal details and photograph of the holder. "Ramzan Hilawi. Is that the name he was using?"

Braithwaite nodded.

"And?"

"He was found dead yesterday morning on the road to Baku, twenty miles from Astara."

"What did he die of?"

"A heart attack, supposedly."

"Fuck," said Yael, closing her eyes and exhaling hard.

Braithwaite put his hand on Yael's arm. "He was very brave. He contacted us first. He knew the risks. We have to continue. Or he died for nothing."

Yael breathed deeply before she spoke. "The phone?"

"Gone. He had been stripped clean."

"Do we have any idea what was on the SIM card?"

Braithwaite shook his head. "Only that it was enough to get him killed. And there is more." Braithwaite took out his mobile telephone and swiped through the menus until he found the photograph he wanted. He showed the phone to Yael. "Does he look familiar?"

The screen showed an elegantly dressed man at South Ferry terminal. He was bald with a neatly trimmed salt-and-pepper beard. He wore a gray suit jacket and a crisp, spotless white collarless shirt.

Yael nodded. "Salim Massoud. The man in your folder. He's here? How?"

"He shouldn't be, but he is," said Braithwaite as they reached the end of the plaza. He gestured at a bench and they sat down. Joe-Don stopped walking and sat across from them. Braithwaite continued, "Massoud was seen at the Iranian-Azerbaijani border the day Ramzan crossed. He is on a watch list. It seems he is traveling on a Turk-ish diplomatic passport, which is especially worrying. We checked the CCTV for the subway at East Fifty-First Street where Schneidermann collapsed. Massoud was walking down the stairs and onto the 4, heading downtown. The cameras picked him up later at South Ferry. By then we had a team on him. He took a boat to Staten Island, and then a taxi to the botanical gardens on the island. Where he met—"

"Cyrus Jones?" interrupted Yael.

"Bingo," said Braithwaite.

"And then?"

Braithwaite looked annoyed. "He took an earlier boat back than Jones. They lost him at South Ferry."

Yael turned toward Braithwaite. "So the number two in the Revolutionary Guard, the money man who also car-ries out the occasional assassination on the side, despite be-ing on all kinds of watch lists, manages to sneak into the United States, possibly murder the UN spokesman in broad daylight on East Fifty-First Street, take a ferry ride to meet an operative from the US government's secret black-ops department, and we don't know where he is?"

"That's about the sum of it. He is very good."

"Evidently. I have Jones's telephone. It was encrypted, but a friend of mine managed to get in."

"And?"

Yael moved closer to Braithwaite and spoke in a low whisper for some time. By the time she had finished, the Englishman's face was no longer ruddy. He had turned pale.

15

Two hundred and fifty miles to the south, in a field in West Virginia, Clarence Clairborne stood to one side and watched Menachem Stein raise his shotgun to his shoulder. He pointed it to the sky, swiveled on the ball of his right foot, and swiftly pulled the trigger twice. The shots thundered across the field and the duck flew sideways. It tried in vain to correct itself, hung suspended in midair for a second, then nose-dived.

Stein cracked back the barrel as the vizsla sprinted across the field to his kill. The two empty shells popped out and fell to the ground. Stein strode forward, loaded, lifted his gun again, and fired. This time the duck spun around and plummeted straight down. The vizsla was beside itself with excitement, running back and forth between the two dead birds.

Clairborne whistled. "Nice shooting, Menachem," he said, pronouncing the last syllable with a "ch," as in "chew."

The vizsla, sleek muscles rippling under its luminous brown coat, raced back with the first duck hanging from its mouth. The dog dropped it at Stein's feet, bolted for the second duck, sprinted back, placed it next to the first one, sat still, and stared at Stein adoringly.

Stein crouched down on his knees, patting the dog. Clairborne watched, feeling absurdly jealous. The vizsla, a pedigree that he had imported from Hungary, had cost him $3,000. Highly intelligent and loyal, vizslas were bred to serve generations of the now almost-vanished Magyar aristocracy. Clairborne had owned the dog for six months. It had shown no interest in him, was willful, disobedient, and would only eat T-bone steaks from Clairborne's own supply.

"Thank you, Clarence. Actually, it's Mena-*chem*, with a 'ch' like 'Loch,' " said Stein. Clairborne flushed red. He knew that; he knew almost everything he needed to know about Menachem Stein. Samantha had prepared an extensive dossier, which even included the correct pronunciation of his name. And he still got it wrong.

"Here, Barack, come here, boy," Clairborne called. Stein bent down and patted the vizsla on his side.

The vizsla ignored Clairborne, rolled on the ground, and let Stein scratch its stomach. Clairborne damped down his rising sense of irritation. The two men were shooting on Clairborne's private estate, five hundred acres of prime farmland and forest, with a twelve-room hunting lodge at the north end. This was his land, as far as he could see, rich loamy fields that stretched almost to the horizon. The air was fresh and clean, the ground firm underfoot, although the sky was overcast. So why was he nervous? The contract was signed. The plan was worked out to the finest detail. All the pieces were in place.

But there were two large hogs snorting their way across his lawn. The first was the article in that day's *New York*

Times. He had read it so many times he had memorized the crucial first paragraphs.

UNITED NATIONS TO USE PRIVATE SECURITY FIRM AT ISTANBUL SUMMIT

Decision Sets Precedent, Seen as Blow to President Freshwater

By SAMI BOUSTANI

UNITED NATIONS—The United Nations has signed a $250 million contract with the Prometheus Group, a controversial lobbying firm, to provide security for an upcoming summit in Istanbul, according to an internal UN e-mail.

The rewarding of the Prometheus contract is a setback for President Renee Freshwater, who is a strong opponent of outsourcing military and intelligence duties to the private sector. Although she retains public support on this issue, her attempts to rein in private contractors have been sabotaged by rare bipartisan efforts in Congress. The Prometheus Group will have no role in protecting President Freshwater while she is in Istanbul, said a White House spokesman.

Prometheus, one of the most powerful lobbying and asset-management firms in Washington, DC, has extensive ties to the military and intelligence services and has recently set up a new corporate security division. Under the terms of the agreement, outlined in an e-mail obtained by the *New York Times*, Prometheus will provide high-level security at the summit next week, for all UN officials and several national leaders, in conjunction with the Turkish security services. The negotiations for the contract, which took place over four months, were carried out by Caroline Masters, the deputy secretary-general. Ms. Masters, an American diplomat who was formerly stationed in Berlin, was appointed acting secretary-general on Wednesday after Secretary-General Fareed Hussein went on sick leave. UN officials say he is suffering from fainting attacks.

The Prometheus Group contract will likely prove highly controversial, said Keir Rogerson, a former British diplomat who now runs Diplomacy Unbound, a research organization based in New York, and who is known for his wide range of contacts. "Masters is really pushing her own agenda here. President Freshwater is opposed, but her administration is being outmaneuvered by vested interests in DC. She is increasingly seen as a one-term wonder. The State Department and the Pentagon are going their own way. They want this deal with Prometheus and they are using Masters to force this through."

Caroline Masters, the deputy secretary-general, is known to be an enthusiastic advocate of expanding the role of the private sector in UN operations. Ms. Masters authored an influential memo calling for greater cooperation with industry while posted in Berlin, where she also served a three-month placement at the headquarters of the KZX Corporation, which is one of Germany's largest firms.

The rest of the article went over the plans for the summit, its agenda, and its historical significance. Clairborne did not care about that. But he did care that he had no idea how the hell Sami Boustani had obtained his e-mail correspondence with Caroline Masters. Ms.—as she insisted on calling herself—Masters had called to apologize that morning, promising a thorough investigation into the breach of confidentiality.

The other problem, and a much bigger one, was the girl. Jones had fucked up. Yet part of him was almost pleased. She was a feisty one, sitting in his office, those green eyes staring at him as she explained what he would be doing next. She reminded him of his wife, before the, the . . . accident. He couldn't remember the last time someone had told him what to do, not since the army, apart from Menachem Stein. She was attractive too. Kind of skinny for his taste. But nothing that couldn't be fixed with some good home cooking. *What am I thinking?* he suddenly asked himself. Must be last night's bourbon. He had drunk more than half a bottle. Clairborne breathed deeply to try and clear his head. He watched the vizsla follow Stein across the field. Fuck the stupid mutt. He would have it put down as soon as Stein was gone. He might even do the job himself. The Israeli was his guest. It was time he took control.

Clairborne strode toward Stein, his shotgun cradled in his hand, a cartridge ready in each barrel. He quickly looked around as he moved forward. Stein had come alone. There was no one else here. *Do a Cheney*, said a voice in his head. *You are on home territory. The cops are in your pocket. This is how you take control. Just do it.* The former vice president's shooting of his companion had been an accident. Clairborne could easily claim the same. All he needed to do was pretend to trip or stumble, and in the process pull the trigger. Even if he didn't kill the Israeli, he might take him down a peg or two. And he doubted very much that Mena-*chem* Stein would want to bring the attention of the authorities to any kind of incident, especially one involving guns.

Stein turned around to face him, holding his gun with his finger on the trigger, as if reading Clairborne's mind. The Israeli smiled, and Clairborne was amazed to see that this time the smile actually reached his eyes.

Stein bent down. "Go, Barack, go to your master."

The dog trotted off to Clairborne and stood in front of him, ready to receive instructions. Clairborne felt ridiculously pleased at the dog's obedience. Until he affectionately rubbed the dog's back. The vizsla stared at him with a cool curiosity, but otherwise did not respond.

Just as Stein was about to walk off in pursuit of more ducks, Clairborne called him back. "Mena-*chem*!" he shouted, rasping the last syllable so hard it sounded like he was coughing. "There is one more thing."

"What?"

Clairborne handed a sheet of paper to Stein. It showed a photograph, taken from an angle, of another photograph lying on a table. Clairborne watched Stein carefully as he looked at the printout. Beneath his bluff exterior, Clairborne was also an astute people watcher. His good ol' boy act was a useful camouflage for a subtle intelligence and instinct that had more than once saved his life.

"You know her?" asked Clairborne.

"I know who she is," said Stein carefully.

Clairborne saw something briefly pass across Stein's face,

and then vanish. "So do I. Ms. Azoulay came to see me earlier this week, on behalf of Fareed Hussein. She was trying to blackmail me into closing our connection with Tehran." He half-smiled at the memory.

Stein turned to Clairborne, fully alert. "Hussein is finished. How much does she know?"

"Enough to cause us a barrel load of trouble. They have copies of bank transfers from Omega, through Bank Bernard et Fils, to Nuristan Holdings."

Stein frowned. "First the *New York Times* story, now this. How the hell did she get them? You have a leak, Clarence."

Clairborne walked ahead, watching the sky and measuring the distance to a flock of ducks heading toward him. He rested his gun on his shoulder as he spoke. Thunder sounded in the distance and the clouds were turning dark and gray. "Menachem, I can guarantee you that if there is a leak, it's not from here. The only person here that has a copy of that correspondence is me, and I ain't telling. Maybe BBF is. What if Azoulay or someone else in the UN leaks the bank transfer to the press?"

Stein loaded again. "Don't worry about the media. We will stonewall. Claim it's a forgery. Anyone can manufacture a fake bank statement. We'll throw up a shitstorm about Fareed Hussein to distract attention. Our friends in Congress will launch a campaign to cut off America's contribution to the UN."

Clairborne fired. The ducks scattered and flew on, unharmed. Stein swiveled and fired. This time a duck suddenly flew leftward, wheeling around in ever-smaller circles, then plunged to the ground. Clairborne looked around for Barack. The dog was trotting alongside Stein. The Israeli patted its haunch, and it finally ran off to fetch Stein's duck.

Stein continued. "The campaign will continue until the UN apologizes for disseminating a forged document. The real question is what she knows about Istanbul."

Clairborne shook his head and walked forward, together with Stein. "Nothing. How can she? No printed copies exist. I'm not even sure that I know what I should. I don't like working like this. I like paper. Something I can read and hold in my hand."

"Like the BBF bank statement?" Stein snapped back.

"Bank statements can be locked away. Or destroyed if need be. But at least they exist."

"The Washington Stratagem also exists. But in hundreds of tiny parts, each encrypted and uploaded to a network of servers across the Internet. The people who need to can put the pieces together. They do not include Yael Azoulay," said Stein. The implication, that nor did they include Clarence Clairborne, was clear.

"We tried to take care of her."

Stein stopped. "*You—did—what?*" His was voice cold as he turned to stare at Clairborne.

Clairborne looked puzzled. "What's the problem? She was in the way. I put Cyrus Jones on it. He was raring to go. But he fucked up."

Stein's face darkened. "The terms are clear: any terminations have to be authorized by me. It's bad enough that there is now a murder inquiry into the death of Colin Duncan."

A flock of ducks approached. Clairborne raised his gun again and sighted on the birds.

Stein stood to the side, his hand resting on the barrel of Clairborne's gun. "Wait. Kill Yael Azoulay and you will have the media crawling all over the case. Eventually they will make the connection. She came to see you in your office." He pressed down on the barrel and slowly lowered Clairborne's weapon until it pointed at the ground. "Someone will get hold of the bank transfer and put two and two together."

Clairborne was incredulous. Now he was really ready to do a Cheney. Stein had actually prevented him from taking a shot. With his own gun. On his own land. Who was this guy? The last Clairborne knew, Menachem Stein had barely escaped an Interpol warrant after the coltan scandal. The whole thing had been reported in the *New York Times*. Clairborne was amazed that Stein was still walking around a free man. Just under a year ago, two of Stein's most senior lieutenants had been arrested in Congo for distributing arms to Hutu militants so they could launch a rerun of the 1994 genocide.

But Efrat Global Solutions was going from strength to strength. The firm was now the largest private military contractor in the world, with a fancy new headquarters in Washington, DC, five minutes' walk from Capitol Hill. Despite the Israeli connection, it had just landed a huge contract to train the army and new paramilitary police force of the Gulf Emirates, who were all terrified of their neighbor Iran—even more so now the rapprochement between the United States and Iran was flourishing.

Clairborne looked at Menachem Stein, about to tell him just what he thought of a guest who prevents his host from shooting his own ducks, when something in the man's face stopped him. His eyes, one brown and one blue, were like marbles.

"She did a great job for us in Istanbul. It was a textbook-perfect false-flag operation," said Stein. "She had no idea she was working for us. We got everything we wanted. Gul is out of the way. The Taliban are happy. The peace deal with the Americans will hold. The country will be stable and the opium will be harvested. Which means KZX is happy. We need that, because your guys and mine will be guarding those opium fields. But Afghanistan is a sideshow now. We need a new field of operations." Stein looked at his watch. "Which we will have, in less than a fortnight."

Stein's mood changed. He lifted his hand from the gun and slapped Clairborne on the back. "How about some of that Southern cooking you keep telling me about? I'm hungry."

Clairborne checked the time. It was five after noon. The barrel of his gun was spattered with raindrops and the sky was turning darker. It would take them twenty minutes to get back to the house. "Sure. We have a real feast waiting for us. But first we have some decisions to make. Cyrus Jones and Ms. Azoulay."

"Leave Jones to me," said Stein.

Clairborne gestured to Samantha. She unfurled the umbrella she was carrying and began to walk over to the two men. "And the girl?" he asked.

Something flickered in Stein's eyes for a moment before he answered. "Let her run. Watch her. Let's see where she leads us."

There had been three men in Yael's life who could trigger an emotional reaction strong enough to show on her face. The first, her brother David, was dead. The second was her father. The third was standing next to her by the bar in Zone, being introduced by Isis Franklin as the new chief of staff at the Israeli mission to the UN.

Yael could not disguise her shock. Her heart sped up. Her stomach flipped over. Her palms turned sweaty. She was sixteen years old again.

"Yael," said Eli Harrari, his arms wide open as if to hug her.

She froze. Eli, completely unfazed, moved forward instead to kiss her on her cheek. "*Motek*. You look as lovely as ever."

Isis watched, transfixed. "Wow, so you guys already know each other?" she exclaimed, her eyes sparkling at the promise of romantic intrigue.

Yael shut down the emotions surging through her. She fixed her brightest, warmest smile on her face and hugged Eli. He responded instantly, his arms around her. His back felt hard, toned, his hands on her warm and familiar.

Yael looked over Eli's shoulder at Joe-Don, three stools away at the end of the bar, suddenly alert, his vision locked on her and Eli. Joe-Don had not been happy about her coming out tonight. But they had agreed that he would accompany her, that she would ration herself to one glass of wine and be home by midnight. Yael caught his eye and mouthed Eli's name. Joe-Don relaxed, slowly inclined his craggy head, and sipped his Diet Coke.

Yael leaned back and glanced at Eli as they separated. The score so far: one–nil to Eli. Despite her quick recovery, he knew that he still provoked an emotional reaction in her. What on earth was he doing here? She had no idea that he was even in New York, let alone assigned to the Israeli mission to the UN. He had certainly aged well. Eli was tall for an Israeli, just under six feet, slim hipped, broad shouldered, wiry rather than beefy. His head was shaved, so closely it almost shone under the bar lights. He had large gray eyes, a wide mouth that was almost decadent, and a thin nose that had been broken and skillfully set. They had not seen each other for fifteen years, but Yael had followed his career progress: political attaché in Manila, more important than it sounded because of the vast Muslim populations across Southeast Asia; deputy chief of mission in São Paulo; posts in London, Paris, and Berlin; and a brief spell attached to the clandestine Israeli trade mission in the United Arab Emirates until it was closed down.

The diplomatic posts were fronts, providing Eli with a visa and diplomatic accreditation. His real work, Yael knew, was carried out in the shadows—where they had both been trained to operate. Behind the warmth of his greeting, and his charm, Eli had changed. His toughness, once the affect of a youth trying to impress his peers and elders, was now innate. This Eli, she sensed—no, knew— was capable of extreme and sudden violence. Yael had heard rumors that he had been recruited to the agency's most secret division of all. His eyes seemed to confirm the whispers: she could see them continually processing the bar and the people around, searching for any potential threat.

Isis must have felt the charged atmosphere. "Looks like you both have a lot of catching up to do. I'll see you later," she said, and walked over to a group of her colleagues.

"Thanks, Isis, we'll see you soon. Can I buy you a drink, motek?" asked Eli, his hand resting on Yael's arm.

She reached inside her purse, looking for nothing in particular, but causing his hand to fall away.

"No thanks, I have one," she said, picking up her glass of sauvignon blanc. "But there is something you can do for me."

"Anything."

Yael gave Eli her best smile. "Eli, it's really wonderful to see you. I want to hear all your news. But I'm not your sweetie. Please stop calling me motek."

The man in black stood on the dining table and swiftly extracted the tiny video camera from the lamp hanging over it. He wore latex gloves and a black nylon balaclava so he would not leave any hairs or DNA traces behind. He knew that the apartment was swept once a month for bugs and cameras. The last harvest had been extracted a week ago.

The camera, hidden in the ceiling lamp four days ago, had not yet been found and now it never would be. He slipped it into his pocket, stepped down, wiped the table surface clean, and double-checked the footage on his phone. The video showed her pulling up a loose plank of parquet flooring under the sofa, on the right-hand side. He knelt down and ran his hand over the wood until a piece moved. He took a coin from his pocket and levered up the slat.

16

E li blinked in surprise and stepped back. "Of course. Can I still call you Yael? Or do we have to be more formal?" He sipped his club soda.

"Yael is fine. How long have you been in town? Tell me about your new job."

"You heard our friend Isis. I'm chief of staff to the ambassador. I arrived two days ago. It's a mix, some policy advice and some boring admin and personnel stuff."

"Chief of staff? To the permanent representative?" asked Yael, amused.

"Why are you shaking your head?" Eli's face creased as he smiled.

"Let me count the ways," said Yael.

"I don't understand."

"Your reputation precedes you, Mr. Harrari."

"So does yours, Ms. Azoulay."

Yael inclined her glass toward him. "Touché. But yours, while less well known, is *much* more interesting."

"Meaning?" asked Eli, his smile fading.

She looked around before she continued. Nobody could overhear them. Yael moved closer and spoke softly. "Political attaché in Manila when Abu Yahya, the chief bomb maker for Islamic Jihad, in town to liaise with al-Qaeda's technical director, falls out of a window, forty stories up. Economic counselor in Paris when Khaled Aslan, director of Hamas's international bureau, slips under the Metro at the Gare du Nord; cultural attaché in London when Abas Fahani, number two in the Al-Quds brigade, is found floating face down in the boating lake on the Serpentine. The Foreign Office was very angry about that one. You took a long holiday in Tel Aviv afterward. Shall I continue?"

Eli stepped away and shook his head. "You have a very active imagination, *mo*—Yael. A series of coincidences, no more. But I am flattered you are keeping such a close eye on me." He peered at her face. "You are wearing makeup now? Why? You never used to."

Because I am thirty-six years old and the lines are showing and I would like to meet someone while I can still turn a few heads and have a child and maybe he will be here tonight, and because I was fighting for my life two days ago, Yael wanted to say. Instead she answered, "I scratched my face. I slipped in the bathroom. Really." She smiled to herself—her reply was technically true. It was clear from Eli's face that he did not believe her, but he did not press the point.

Yael let the conversation move on to safer ground. They exchanged gossip about mutual friends from their youth. Eli tried, not without success, to flirt with her. He was as charismatic as ever, and he knew it. His undercurrent of menace, an almost cruel sensuality, did not repel Yael. Quite the opposite—it was a dark magnet, pulling her closer to him, just as it always had. Which made him even more dangerous. The best thing to do, she decided, for this evening at least, was to put the past aside and concentrate on the here and now, which was really quite enjoyable. It was a treat for her to be out at night, somewhere buzzy, in male company. Yael rarely socialized and when she did, it was mostly near her apartment on the Upper West Side, a comfortable but not exactly cutting-edge part of Manhattan.

She liked this place, she decided. Zone was a microbrewery situated in a former sweatshop, on the corner of Avenue A and East Seventh Street. Most of the other customers were boho hipsters, with tattoos and multiple piercings. Much of the furniture, including the long zinc bar, had been salvaged from a former brothel in Paris. An enormous mirror hung on the wall behind it with a bullet hole in the middle, supposedly fired by a furious customer when he realized that the company he had booked for the evening was his wife.

A corner table was filled with the staff of *Sister*, a lesbian magazine, celebrating the editor's birthday. Isis and her UN crowd were overdressed but nobody seemed to care. The walls were rough brick, the furniture secondhand and refinished, the lighting soft, and African and Arabic music played softly in the background. There would be live music later, Isis had promised. Eli aside, Yael found herself actually relaxing. In any case, there was no need to stress too much about Eli—she was leaving for Istanbul tomorrow.

Eli went to the restroom and Yael walked over to Joe-Don, still perched on his stool, nursing his third Diet Coke. She could feel him almost aching for a bourbon to throw into it. Joe-Don knew all about Eli. He and Yael had spent many nights holed up in uncomfortable, often dangerous places, where sleep was out of the question so there was nothing to do except talk.

"Steer clear. He's dangerous," said Joe-Don.

"Not to me."

"Especially to you. He's not the boy you lived with all those years ago."

"Who is he, then?"

Joe-Don raised his glass and gave her a piercing look. "You know the answer to that."

Yael hugged Joe-Don, once, quickly, and went back to her spot at the bar. Eli returned and they talked some more about mutual friends and acquaintances. Israelis married young, and some were already divorced and on their second families. The atmosphere began to ease. Yael saw a spot of lint on Eli's shirt. She raised her right hand to brush it away. Eli instantly swerved left, as if to avoid a blow.

Yael sat back, amused. "Always on guard, I see." She pointed at the lint on his shirt. "That's all. I was going to take it off."

Eli blushed and looked down. "Thanks," he said as he picked off the scrap of fabric. "And you," asked Eli. "Don't you want to have a family?"

"It will happen. When I meet the right guy."

Eli's gray eyes bored into hers. "You have met the right guy. You already lived with him. In the right town, in the right country."

She held his gaze and shook her head. "No, Eli. I did not."

The talk of children produced the familiar pang in Yael

and she changed the subject, asking Eli where he lived. He hedged his answer, claiming that a bureaucratic mix-up meant he was still apartment hunting. She knew that was a lie. Israeli diplomats, especially those with a resume like Eli's, had their accommodation arranged far in advance of their arrival because of the security issues.

Eli paused for a moment, swirling the ice cubes in his glass with a gray plastic cocktail stirrer. "Yael, I want to be straight with you. I am very happy to see you again. But I am not only here tonight for social reasons. We have a proposition for you."

"We? Who is we?" she replied, suddenly totally focused. Now she understood what he was doing at Zone.

"I think you know the answer to that. Your former employers."

Yael raised her glass and sipped her wine. "Keyword: *former*."

"Yael, it doesn't work like that."

"How does it work? Please explain to me."

Eli leaned closer to her. "You signed up for life. We invested a lot of time, money, and resources in you. You were the best, by far, for many years. We have let you run for quite a while. You have had your adventures. Gained some useful experience. But now it's time to come home."

She could smell his cologne. After all these years, Eli still wore Issey Miyake. She had bought him his first bottle for his twenty-fourth birthday. She liked the smell so much she sometimes wore it herself. For an instant she was back in their apartment in Tel Aviv, frying eggs on a Sunday morning, Eli still asleep on their futon, the white sunlight streaming in through the windows. There were good memories as well as bad. But they were memories, of a time and a part of her life that had passed. Yael looked around the bar, enjoying the crowd, the hum of conversation, the Malian music playing in the background. "I am at home. I live here, in New York."

"Don't you miss Tel Aviv? Dizengoff at dawn, the sound of the waves, hummus in Jaffa?"

"Sometimes. But not enough. So thanks, but no thanks."

"Come back for just a couple of days. You have no obligations. Just to talk."

Yael was sorely tempted. She could see her school friends, her sister, her nephews and nieces, just be herself. Until she was sucked back into a world she had deliberately walked away from, one to which she had sworn to never return.

Yael shook her head. "We are talking now. The answer is no."

Eli looked thoughtful, his thumb resting on the top of the cocktail stirrer. "There are more than two hundred journalists accredited at the UN. I can see the headline now, 'The UN's Beautiful Spy: The Secret Past of the SG's Special Envoy.'"

She laughed out loud. "Do it, Eli. I don't have that job anymore. I'm running the Trusteeship Council. Do you think anyone cares? I am out of the loop and so is the SG. Anyway, you have a far more interesting CV than me. It would make a much more exciting article."

Eli's eyes narrowed as the plastic stick bowed in and out under the weight of his thumb. "Meaning?"

"Abu Yahya, Khaled Aslan, Abbas Fahani . . ." Yael

counted on her fingers as she stared straight at him. "I know some reporters. Any one of them could join the dots."

"I think that would be a very bad idea," said Eli coldly.

"Then don't threaten me. Motek."

"I apologize." He looked down at his club soda, swirling the ice cubes around. "There is something else," he continued, his voice serious. "You are not safe here. We can protect you."

Yael was alert now. "Protect me from what?"

Eli gently touched the side of her face, then looked at his finger, now coated with a smudge of makeup. "From slipping in the bathroom."

"I'll buy a mat."

He took out a business card from his pocket and handed it to her. "At least memorize my telephone number. You remember how to do that? Like they taught us? Ten numbers with a single glance. Call me anytime, from anywhere in the world, if you need help."

Yael looked down at the card. Blue letters on a thick white card said: "Eli Harrari: Chief of Staff." She couldn't help smiling when she saw the last five digits of the mobile number: 65232.

"Quite a coincidence, no?" said Eli, leaning toward her.

She moved back. "Sure. The last five digits are the same as our zip code when we lived together in Tel Aviv. About as much of a coincidence as you turning up here tonight."

Eli laughed, his arms open. "Yael, we go back such a long way. We don't have to have this discussion now. How about dinner sometime? Tomorrow? Or we could leave now. There's great Italian two blocks away. The truth is, I have a job offer for you. They want you back."

"Thanks, but I already have a job."

"Why don't we at least talk about it? That would be best."

"For who?"

Eli continued smiling, his thumb still bending the cock-tail stirrer, but now there was steel in his voice. "For both of us, I think."

Yael stared back at him, marveling at his confidence. Only Eli could threaten her at the same time as he was try-ing to seduce her. Part of her wanted dinner. Dinner and everything that would follow. Just touching his back when they briefly embraced made her realize that. They were perfectly matched in bed, their bodies flowing into each other, triggering rolling waves of pure pleasure that seemed to never end. Which is why she had to shut this conversa-tion down. For good.

She stands next to the boy, holding his hand, stroking his hair, calming him, as the bomb-disposal expert disconnects the vest. He places it to one side and orders the boy to undress. The boy looks at Yael; she nods, squeezes his hand.

The bomb-disposal expert swiftly checks the boy all over.

Sweat runs down her back and into her eyes. The previous month two soldiers had been killed here. The explosives had been inserted into the bomber's rectum. By the time they had stripped him and seen the wire, it was too late.

The bomb-disposal expert stands back. He signals to the second man in the Jeep: the boy is clear. The man in the Jeep turns to the passenger in the back, an Arab woman.

She jumps out of the vehicle and runs forward, her head scarf flapping in the breeze. Yael lets go of his hand. The boy sprints toward her. They embrace, crying and sobbing.

The second man climbs out of the vehicle.

Yael smiles at him, happy the mission is over. He smiles back and raises his hand in greeting, but walks toward the boy and his mother.

He says something to the boy and takes his arm. The boy starts sobbing again, shaking, saying no, over and over again, holding on to his mother. The mother keens.

Yael said, "How about if you write a letter to the family of the boy at the Gaza checkpoint, explaining what happened? He would be, what, in his late twenties now?"

Eli's smile vanished. The cocktail stirrer snapped, "Yael, it was lovely to see you. You know where to find me."

Eli took out the two pieces of plastic from his drink, dropped them on the floor, and walked into the throng.

Yael leaned against the bar, facing the crowd, and breathed out hard. Relief mingled with regret inside her. She watched Eli join Isis's group. He immediately started talking to a former Miss Chile, who Yael knew had just started work in the Department of Public Information. Miss Chile seemed very pleased by his attention. Yael ignored the pang of jealousy and drank her wine.

Isis walked over and stood next to her. "You let him go," she said, wagging her finger in mock admonition as she looked over at Miss Chile. "She won't."

Yael shook her head. "No, he let me go. A long time ago. I'll tell you, but not tonight."

Isis smiled, a warm grin of sisterly understanding. "Whenever you are ready."

Yael turned David's ring around on her finger. "Isis," she said, suddenly, absurdly, nervous, "You mentioned yesterday—"

Isis rested her hand on Yael's. "As soon as I know anything I will let you know. Promise."

The bar door opened and both women looked to see who walked in.

"Oh my," said Isis, clinking her glass against Yael's. "You are lining them up tonight."

Yael watched the new arrivals as they sat down at a table. She laughed. "Wow. I haven't had so much excitement for months."

Isis shot her a friendly but sharp look. "I find that hard to believe."

"Socially I mean. But now that I am exiled to the Trusteeship Council, I might have time to party."

"Good. It starts here," said Isis, beckoning Yael to come with her and join the group. "Don't worry. I'll protect you from Eli."

"Give me a few minutes. I'll be there."

Isis walked away and Yael turned around, resting on the bar with her back to the crowd. She continued looking at the new arrivals in the mirror, then briefly checked herself. She had spent an hour trying on different outfits before she left the apartment, trying to find the elusive formula of understated sexiness. She had eventually settled on a tight black scoop-neck top, skinny white jeans, and black Miz Mooz ankle boots, set off by her grandmother's onyx and silver necklace. Then she suddenly realized what had been nagging at her about her encounter with Isis yesterday morning. What was Isis doing in Dag Hammarskjöld Plaza at 9:15 in the morning? Yael knew that the US ambassador to the UN held a staff meeting every morning at 9:00 a.m. The counselor for public diplomacy was required to attend, to give a briefing on the day's news and issues affecting the United States and the United Nations. So why hadn't Isis been there? Yael's telephone vibrated in her pocket, signaling that an e-mail had arrived.

From: masters@un.org
To: azoulay@un.org
Cc: humanresources@un.org; staffprotocol@un.org

Dear Yael,
You will receive formal notification of this tomorrow, but as a courtesy I wanted to personally let you know that the decision has been made to temporarily revoke your UN laissez-passer while the Geneva and NYPD investigations continue, so please return it to the human resources department tomorrow morning. There should be no need to travel on UN business in your current position at the Trusteeship Council, but should such circumstances arise, we will discuss on a case by case basis. You will of course for the moment remain free to travel under any other passports you may own.
Sincerely,
Caroline

Masters's e-mail was a masterpiece of UN-speak, thought Yael. What it really meant was: *I am happy to ruin your evening with this news; you might still get arrested and I won't be sorry if you are; you aren't going anywhere under UN protection (but if you need to, you will have to beg) and I'm thinking about how to get your other passports revoked.* Yael pressed the forward button, inserted an e-mail address to be used only in case of emergency, added a new title—"help! ☹"—and pressed the send button. The game was in play. For now, there was nothing more to be done. And there was something much more interesting to watch.

Yael returned to watching the new arrivals in the mirror, checking their body language. There was certainly an easy rapport between them. But it was an almost familial kind of intimacy, not at all erotic. Yael waited until they ordered their drinks before she stepped into the throng and walked over to their table.

"*Masa' al-Khair*, good evening," said Yael. "May I join you?"

Sami looked very elegant, dressed in a clean white shirt and black linen jacket. Najwa nudged Sami as she replied. "*Masa al-Noor.* Sami, where are your manners?" Najwa gestured at the table. "Of course."

"Hi," said Sami, as Yael pulled out a chair and sat down. She was pleased to see him turn a satisfying shade of red. She looked around. "I wondered if you would be here tonight. I remember you telling me about this place. It's pretty cool. Just like you said."

Sami quickly recovered his poise. "It's great to see you. Can I get you a drink?"

"No thanks. I'm fine," said Yael.

Sami turned to Najwa. "Would you give us a moment, please?"

Najwa smiled, relishing the tension in the air. "Of course."

She stood up, ready to leave, when Yael's hand fell on her shoulder. Yael said, "There's really no need." Najwa sat back down, eyes wide as she watched Yael. Yael continued talking. "I don't want to take up your evening, so I will be quick. Don't worry—I'm not going to make a scene."

"You're not?" Najwa looked disappointed.

"No. Let's clear the air. I just wanted to say, no hard feelings. You have your job to do, and I have mine," she said, extending her hand across the table. "A different one now, of course. But still, a job."

Najwa's grip was firm, the look on her face friendly, with an undercurrent of interest, definitely not professional, that Yael could not quite read. Sami held her hand for longer than he needed to, which she allowed. She saw guilt, regret, and a powerful attraction. He really would be a terrible poker player. It was quite endearing, in a way. Yael squeezed Sami's palm twice before she let it go.

She got up.

"That's it?" he asked.

"That's it." Yael paused. "For now. Enjoy the rest of the evening," she said as she began to walk away. She turned around for a moment. Sami was still looking at her. "And *mabrouk*, congratulations, on your story in the *New York Times* today," Yael said.

Sami was still hooked, she thought, as she walked back

to the bar. The question was, was she? Either way, the evening's seed had been planted.

The man in black slipped the pistol and the silencer into his backpack. He slid the loose parquet slat back into place, and was about to put the coin back in his pocket when his telephone rang. He put the coin down on the floor and looked at the screen: a DC number. He silenced the call. It was nothing he could not deal with later. The rules said that once his mission was accomplished, he should leave immediately. Instead he walked over to the sideboard. An art deco mirror in a black and silver frame was mounted on the wall, above a display of family pictures. One showed a young girl with auburn hair, perhaps seven or eight years old, holding hands with her father in Central Park. The colors were faded, from the pre-digital age, and the picture was slightly out of focus. The child looked happy, her father proud. He reached for the photograph and looked at it for a long time before he carefully put it back in its place. He turned on his heel and started to walk out but suddenly stopped, and walked back to the sideboard. He picked up the photograph again and kissed it. He glanced at himself in the mirror—only his eyes were visible, one blue and one brown. Finally, he left.

17

The band stepped forward and started to play. Fus-tat, named for a city in Egypt, was a six-piece Arab African fusion group. The vocalist, a short, plump woman in her twenties, with wild curly black hair, had the most extraordinary voice Yael had ever heard. It soared, plunged, purred, and howled. By the end of the first song, conversation was fading away. By the end of the second nobody was talking anymore.

Yael looked at her arm. The soft hairs were standing erect. She looked around the room. Even Eli was tapping his feet. The vocalist launched into a funked-up version of "Baladi," an Arabic favorite that meant "my country" or "my city," and the audience started to sway in time with the music. Yael stepped forward and walked through the crowd.

Sami and Najwa watched Yael head over to their table.

"Let's dance," said Yael.

"Sure," said Sami, smiling with pleasure as he started to stand up.

Yael shook her head. "Not you." She turned to Najwa and extended her hand.

Najwa stood up and let Yael lead her onto the floor. The crowd made way for them, until they found a space in the center.

The music flowed through Yael's body. She lost herself in the beat, swayed and shimmered, her unbound hair flying behind her. Najwa was the perfect partner, sometimes following, at others leading. She felt Najwa's body heat, Najwa's legs sliding against hers, Najwa's breasts brushing against her chest, the grip of their entwined fingers, Najwa's eyes locked on hers. Najwa's scent rose in the heat, of musk and spices, perfume and wine.

The music sped up and the vocalist seemed to break the limits of the sounds a human could produce. Yael dissolved into the music, aware but completely uncaring that every eye in the room was on her and Najwa. The music stopped and Yael came back to earth. The air around them had turned thick, charged. So now she knew she could still turn heads, but she had drawn enough attention to herself. She saw Eli staring at her, felt the strength of his desire for her. She half-smiled at him and looked back at Najwa.

"*Shukran*," said Yael, letting go of Najwa's fingers.

Najwa stood close to Yael. She looked at her with a frank, appraising gaze, her fingers trailing against Yael's palm. "*Afwan*. I never knew you were such a sexy dancer. We should hang out more often."

"Thank you. It's up to you, *habibti*. You choose. Stories about me or dances with me."

"I'll think about that," said Najwa.

Yael glanced at Sami. He looked away but she knew he had been watching her. The hook was in.

Salim Massoud switched off the Canadian news channel on the television and picked up the black leather briefcase on his desk. He traced his fingers around the brass letters on the front flap. *H* and *S*. A gift, probably. Perhaps from a parent? He felt the familiar pang of guilt. The man's death was regrettable. Massoud did not enjoy taking a life, and it had caused a flurry of media interest, which was never welcome. But Iran was at war. This was not a military struggle, fought on front lines or battlefields. This war was waged in secret, a struggle for the soul of the revolution, and for the souls of those newly seduced by the Great Satan. And he would do whatever was necessary to win.

Massoud put the briefcase down and walked over to the window. The house was small, but comfortable enough, a two-room summer residence that looked out onto the edge of a small lake outside Montreal. He was safe here. The nearest neighbors were a mile away. A car with two of his men inside was parked at the end of the drive. Another man patrolled behind the house, where the garden stretched away into the forest. Massoud watched the water, shimmering in the moonlight. A heron hovered above. There was a sudden flash of silver, then another a few yards away. The heron dived, but the fish were too fast.

The drive from New York had gone smoothly. He had even slept some of the way. The border post, on a little-used dirt road, was unmanned, just as promised. But there had been a leak: in Geneva, in Tehran, in New York, or somewhere along the way. The problem was that once it was out, information took on a life of its own—especially in the digital age. He had headed off the threat from Schneidermann. The papers from the briefcase had long been burnt. But that still left several loose ends, most of all Fareed Hussein himself. How did he find out about Nuristan Holdings and the payment from Omega? What else did he know? What did Schneidermann tell the journalist? And who else had a copy of the payment record?

The journalist needed to be silenced and Hussein needed to be removed from the picture. The Americans had promised to take care of the journalist, which left Hussein. Perhaps his blackouts could become worse? Even permanent? Massoud shook his head to himself. Too obvious right after the death of his spokesman. The press would be all over the story. And what about the girl?

Massoud stared at the heron, waiting, patient. Its beak was a marvel, thin, curved, perfectly engineered. The water flashed silver again. The heron dived, flew up, the fish flapping uselessly. Massoud smiled. He knew what to do.

I'm kind of confused," said Sami as he and Yael walked down East Ninth Street toward his apartment. It was nearly midnight and the rows of brownstones stood dark and silent. The streetlamps glowed orange and a siren howled in the distance. Joe-Don followed a few paces behind them, not quite near enough to eavesdrop.

"Why?" asked Yael, her hand on his arm.

"I thought you didn't want to talk to me ever again. You wrecked my office."

"You deserved it."

Sami nodded, half to himself. "Maybe I did. Then you

act all cool and businesslike in Zone. And you dance with Najwa, not with me."

Yael squeezed Sami's arm lightly. "She's got great moves. She is very sexy. Why don't you date her?"

Sami laughed. "Why don't you? That dance was hot. She was really into it."

"So was I. But I like men better. And me and journalists don't seem to work."

"Are you sure about that?" Sami tried to keep his voice light.

Yael looked sideways at Sami. "Not completely. Maybe I could be persuaded."

Sami smiled. "I will see what I can do."

Yael glanced around. Beneath the flirtatious banter, she was completely focused. There was a reason she had invited herself back to Sami's apartment and it was not the one he had in mind.

They reached number 23. Sami turned to Yael. "Would you like to come in?"

"Sure. A coffee, but not for long."

Sami looked at Joe-Don. "Fine. But what about—"

"He'll see me safely inside. That's all."

Sami stepped forward and started walking down the stairs, Yael following. Sami reached the bottom and stood in front of the door of the basement-level apartment, hunting for his keys. He took them out of his trouser pocket and inserted one into the topmost of three heavy-duty locks. As soon as the key touched the lock, the door swung wide open.

Sami stepped inside. "*Shit*," he said, looking around. "Shit, shit, shit."

Joe-Don swiftly jumped in front of Yael, pushed her behind him, reached inside his jacket, and drew his gun, a nine-millimeter Glock. He stepped inside, his left arm up behind him, signaling that Sami and Yael should wait. Joe-Don walked through the apartment, checking the main room, bedroom, kitchen, and bathroom. All were empty.

He came out and stood by the front door. "It's clear. You can go in."

Yael entered total chaos. The boxes of papers, files, and old stories that Sami kept in the corner had been upended and spread all over the room, carpeting the floor in a sea of white paper. The furniture had been tipped upside down, the slashed cushions spilling dry crumbs of foam rubber. The coffee table had been turned over.

Sami was kneeling on the floor in the middle of the papers, trying to gather them up. Yael crouched down beside him and started to help. "Check your bedside cabinet, wherever you keep your valuables."

He got up and walked over to the corner. There was no bedside cabinet. But there was a cardboard box where he kept his passport, credit cards, and a couple hundred dollars in emergency cash. The box had been tipped over. He lifted it up. The passport, credit cards, and cash were all on the floor.

As soon as Sami was on the other side of the room, Yael quickly scanned the area around her until she saw Sami's shoulder bag that he used for work. It too had been shaken out, its contents half out on the brown nylon carpet.

"How about if I make us some coffee?" she said. "It looks like we will be here a while."

Salim Massoud sat down at the table and looked through the Canadian passport. It was two years old, used enough to lose its sheen but not so worn as to bring attention. Parvez Marwan was born in Toronto in 1968. There were entry stamps for Germany, South Africa, France, the United Kingdom, all countries Massoud had visited, in case he was ever questioned. Parvez Marwan was black haired and clean shaven, with brown eyes. Massoud touched the wig, then his chin. The fake hair felt strange, his now smooth, clean skin even more so, as though it belonged to someone else. He blinked slowly, several times, to settle his tinted contact lenses. The prospect of the flight home did not bother him. The passport was genuine, inasmuch as Parvez Marwan had once existed and lived in Toronto. The Canadian authorities were worried about Iranians coming in, not going out.

The real danger lay at home, in Tehran. The city was a snake pit. The nuclear deal and consequent easing of sanctions had turned the world upside down. Western companies were rushing into Iran, eager to get a foothold in a market of seventy-six million, more than half of whom were under thirty-five and connected to the Internet. Money was pouring in, loosening morals and tongues. Students were protesting daily, calling for freedom, democracy, the abolition of Sharia law. Facebook, Twitter, Western news websites were uncensored. A leader of the Revolutionary Guard had been arrested and more would soon follow him to Evin Prison. The Basij, the motorbike militia that crushed the protests of

2009, had been disbanded by the new government. Everyone was calculating, calibrating, trying to work out how to benefit from the sea change. Would the regime crack and collapse, or adapt and strengthen? Some former loyalists were now calling for faster change. Reformers, scared by what they had unleashed, were demanding a new crackdown.

Once forbidden questions were now asked openly. Why were they spending tens of millions of dollars supporting Hezbollah in Syria, when their own country needed roads, schools, hospitals? Some in Tehran even whispered—only to the most trusted of confidants—that they should consider making peace with Israel. The "Persians," an old word, once frowned on, which was now making a return, were not Arabs, they said. The Palestinian cause was not their cause. Everyone knew that Israel was secretly working with Saudi Arabia and the Gulf monarchies against Iran. Why let the Jews unite with the Sunni enemies, asked the heretics, when they could be on our side, as they used to be under the shah? We should explain to the Jews that the Wahhabi kingdoms were terminal cases. Be friends with the Jews, and America will ease sanctions even more. Then everyone can be rich. It was only a question of time.

It made Massoud sick, made him long for the return of President Ahmadinejad. Then, such talk would have brought the traitor a rope around his neck, dangling him from the end of a crane in a public square watched by thousands, his feet kicking against nothing. That was how things should be. How they will be again. Soon, very soon. He only needed to wait a little longer.

Massoud thought for a moment of his son, Farzad. Naive, innocent Farzad, completely uninterested in politics, who just wanted to do good. Who had disobeyed his father and had traveled to Afghanistan to teach mathematics in Kandahar five years ago. Now they were both paying the price. Farzad, only nineteen years old, had been picked up at a checkpoint one night by the Americans and never seen again. He was a prisoner of no value whatsoever—apart from his father. Massoud had traced his son's journey: Kandahar, Kabul, a week in a black prison in Romania, a plane to Warsaw, then . . . nothing.

Except the cards each year on August 21, on Massoud's birthday. "Happy Birthday, Dad," they said in English, with a picture of his son, thin, scared, holding that day's edition of the *New York Times*. Massoud had sent out feelers, of course, through the Germans, the Swiss; even his new friends in Washington, DC, had tried without success to get news, an offer, a demand, anything. What did the CIA want? What did he have to do? Nothing. *We are taunting you because we can*: the message unsaid, but clear enough. And then we will come for you.

Except Massoud had his own plan for his country and for the Middle East, one now shared by his new friends in the United States. A plan too, to get his son released. He leafed through the photographs in the folder. A young woman running along Riverside Park, her auburn hair blowing in the wind; entering her apartment building; walking through Dag Hammarskjöld Plaza with a tall Englishman. He closed the folder and tapped the cover, deep in thought.

PART 2

ISTANBUL

18

She points the gun at Jean-Pierre Hakizimani. He laughs, his eyes locked on hers like blue lasers.

She looks down at her hand.

The .22 Beretta is now a photograph of three smiling African girls. The picture is covered with cellophane and is singed in one corner.

She tries to give Hakizimani the photograph but he is no longer there.

Her hands are wet. She looks down again.

The photograph is covered in blood.

She wipes it on her clothes, frantically trying to clean it, but there is only more and more, a crimson tide pouring through her fingers. . . .

Yael jerked awake at the touch on her shoulder, her eyes wide, her body tense as she strained against her seat belt, instantly sweeping her surroundings. The stewardess, a matronly woman in her late forties, looked at her in alarm. "Madam, are you all right? We are landing soon. Please fold away your table and straighten your seat-back."

Yael nodded, slowing down her breathing. She pressed

the button on the side of her seat. The back sprung forward and she slid the tray table into place. The stewardess glanced at her again, not quite reassured, and moved on down the aisle.

Yael briefly closed her eyes and rested the side of her head against the cabin, feeling the steady vibration of the engines. Hakizimani was dead. She knew that, because she had killed him. His militiamen had killed David and, eventually, she had taken her revenge. Accidentally, or on purpose; the result was the same.

Still, Yael sensed the warlord's presence as though he were on board. Her nostrils filled with his scent: of sweat and tobacco, of blood and whisky. She shivered suddenly. She felt clammy: hot and sticky, then chilled and damp with sweat. She reached for the bottle of mineral water in the seat-back pocket and took a long drink. She looked up. The seat-belt light was already on. It was too late to go to the bathroom. She cupped her right hand, tipped some water into it, and splashed her face. She breathed slowly through her nose until her respiration fell into a natural rhythm and she felt centered again. This was reality, here and now. The water, cool and refreshing on her skin. The Mediterranean sunlight filling the cabin. Istanbul spread out below her like a tray of meze.

The Turkish Airlines jet banked leftward, its engines humming, flying low over the city. The Bosphorus shimmered in the spring sunshine, a sheet of azure dotted with turquoise and jade. Istanbul was built on three long fingers of land: two in Europe, divided by a narrow channel of sea known as the Golden Horn, and one in Asia. Ferries crossed back and forth, tiny dots leaving long white trails on the water. Two thin gray ribbons, the Galata and Atatürk Bridges, spanned the Golden Horn. All the coastlines were studded with cranes and building sites, the narrow, twisting alleys behind them dense warrens of houses topped with red tiles. Minarets of centuries-old Ottoman mosques pointed skyward, their tips needle sharp. Istanbul was booming, profiting handsomely from its newest incarnation as the crossing point between East and West. Money was pouring in: from Western companies scrabbling for a foothold in a thriving economy, and from Turkey's Arab neighbors, seeking a safe haven from jihadis and governments toppling from North Africa to the Gulf. A giant white roof emblazoned with a red crescent marked the new Osman Convention Center, on the edge of the historic Sultanahmet quarter by the Grand Bazaar, where the Istanbul Summit was scheduled to take place.

Yael watched a passenger ferry progress up the Golden Horn, remembering the many meetings she had held with Turkish officials at the country's UN mission on First Avenue. Helped by their friends in Congress and the firms they hired on K Street, they had lobbied hard to host the summit, beating off strong competition from Jerusalem, Doha, Amman, and Cairo. The Turkish officials argued that having the summit in Istanbul would send a message, to both East and West: Turkish Islam, a faith that engaged with the West instead of fighting a jihad against it, offered the best hope for the future. At a time of regional chaos, Turkey was a bastion of stability and moderation. That, and a promise to finally close the supply lines to al-Qaeda–sponsored rebels in Syria, had swung it for Istanbul, along with Fareed Hussein's support.

Yael had never seen him work so hard before. His habitual languor evaporated in a blaze of enthusiasm for the summit and all it could achieve, including, of course, a confirmation of his legacy as a peacemaker, one that would, he hoped, finally banish the ghosts of Rwanda and Srebrenica. And then, on the very eve of his triumph, the summit had been snatched away from him. Or perhaps not, Yael thought, as she took out Saturday's *New York Times* from the seat pocket and reread the story on the top of page 7.

GROWING FEARS OVER PREPARATION FOR ISTANBUL SUMMIT

US Officials Concerned about New Stewardship at United Nations

By SAMI BOUSTANI

UNITED NATIONS—Senior US officials are concerned that a UN-sponsored summit on the Middle East could be vulnerable to security lapses because of inadequate preparation by the new UN leadership, according to a confidential briefing note.

The briefing note, written by James Berger, the deputy chief of the US mission to the UN, highlights growing concern about the leadership abilities of Caroline Masters. Ms. Masters, a former US ambassador to the UN and deputy secretary-general, was appointed acting secretary-general on Wednesday. "Masters's appointment is bad news both for US policy and the UN in general. She is in thrall to the corporate world and has lost her sense of judgment," wrote Mr. Berger in the memo, dated Wednesday, obtained by the *New York Times*. "She has pushed to take over the Istanbul Summit for months and now she has done so; there is still no sign of a final agenda or delegate list." Neither Mr. Berger nor the spokesman for the US mission returned repeated calls and e-mailed requests for comment.

Fareed Hussein, the UN secretary-general, has been on sick leave since Wednesday and UN officials say privately he is suffering from fainting attacks. Mr. Hussein has notably failed to attend several high-level planning meetings for the summit in recent weeks. Ms. Masters is due to fly out to Istanbul on Sunday evening after finalizing a $250 million contract with prominent Washington firm the Prometheus Group to provide security services at the summit. The contract also includes a clause providing for a pilot scheme under which Prometheus will assist with security at UN buildings around the world, "supplementing" the role of the UN security department. Ms. Masters has long been one of the most outspoken advocates of a greater role for corporations in conjunction with the United Nations.

The summit, described by President Freshwater as the most ambitious diplomatic event in decades, will start in five days in Istanbul. It aims to solve the interlinked crises in Syria, Egypt, and Israel-Palestine. The rise of Islamic radicalism across the Middle East and the recent establishment of the self-declared Islamic Caliphate of Greater Syria by the al-Qaeda–sponsored Army of the Shaheeds (martyrs) in parts of Syria and Iraq have triggered a rare show of unity among the members of the UN Security Council as they attempt to bring all the warring parties to the negotiating table.

Mr. Berger's concerns are shared by a growing number of

Western and UN officials, according to Keir Rogerson. Mr. Rogerson, a former British diplomat stationed at the UN, now runs Diplomacy Unbound, a research organization based in New York. "The word in Washington, London, and Paris is that Masters is out of her depth. The summit is due to start next Thursday, in six days, and the planning is all over the show. Washington, London, Paris, Moscow, and Beijing are all getting increasingly nervous. There is too much at stake for the summit to fail."

In addition to the controversy surrounding the UN's agreement with Prometheus, there are increasing worries about security. The Istanbul Summit will be attended by the presidents of the Permanent Five members of the Security Council—the United States, China, Russia, Britain, and France—as well as the presidents of Israel, Egypt, Syria, Turkey (the host country), and leaders of other states, including Saudi Arabia, Jordan, and Iraq. The presence of so many leaders will be "a magnet for jihadis," said a US official with knowledge of security matters.

Two bombs recently exploded in downtown Istanbul, killing three German tourists and wounding several dozen. The Turkish authorities blame Kurdish separatists, and officials have launched a crackdown on the Kurdish community. Scores of Kurdish activists have been arrested, prompting claims from UN and Western officials that Turkey is flouting human rights. Ahmet Kirkuki, a spokesman for the banned Kurdistan Workers' Party (PKK), strongly denied that the PKK had any involvement in the bomb attacks. There have been daily protests at Taksim Square in downtown Istanbul against the detentions.

A new entente with Iran has opened a rare window of opportunity for regional stability, said a senior UN official who asked not to be named as he was not authorized to speak on the record.

"Tehran is open for business. It's ready to cut off aid to Hezbollah, its proxy militia in Syria and Lebanon. The Gulf monarchies are petrified of the Islamic Caliphate in Syria. The Israelis know they have to choose: peace with the Palestinians or another intifada. The Egyptians want a role for moderate Islamists. Everything is in place."

Roxana Voiculescu, Acting Secretary-General Masters's newly appointed spokeswoman, denied claims that the summit preparations are inadequate. "Months of hard work have gone into planning the summit. We are confident that everything will go ahead as planned."

Additional reporting by Najwa al-Sameera.

Yael smiled as she came to the end of the article, remembering her dance with Najwa. The mystery of Najwa's fiancé, often discussed, but never sighted, was now a little clearer. As for the man who might once have been Yael's fiancé—what, exactly, was Eli Harrari doing in New York? Yael did not for a moment believe his story about a job as chief of staff to the Israeli ambassador. Nor did she believe in coincidences, especially where Eli was concerned. Meanwhile, there was Fareed—down but certainly not out. The arch-conciliator had, over the years, built up a favor bank that reached around the globe. Now, it seemed, he was calling in some of his debts from his exile at Sutton Place and delivering the results to Sami. Masters, Yael was sure, would retaliate.

Thanks to Beaker's hacking of Cyrus Jones's telephone, Yael, Joe-Don, and Braithwaite knew the outline of the plan to attack the Istanbul Summit. The two bombs in Istanbul were just a foretaste of the carnage to come. The plan was to kill as many global leaders as possible. The attacks on the summit would destabilize the West, trigger massive retaliation against Muslims around the world, and tip the Middle East into bloody chaos. The question was, how were they going to stop it? They had discussed simply going to the US mission to the UN, asking for an appointment with the ambassador, and telling him everything. But the Prometheus Group had lines into every US government department, especially the Pentagon and the intelligence services. Even if the ambassador believed them and red-flagged their information, Prometheus's allies would surely dismiss it as fantasy. All they would achieve would be to draw more attention to themselves and drive the conspirators further underground with a new plan. Yael had agreed with Joe-Don that she would travel immediately to Istanbul. He and Braithwaite would follow the next day. It was not ideal, but Joe-Don wanted to visit a contact in Washington, DC, who, he said, had some useful information. And in Istanbul there was someone Yael could ask for help, someone with whom she had already worked. But could she trust him?

The Turkish Airlines flight had departed on time, on Saturday evening at nine o'clock. It was supposed to be a direct flight, a journey of eleven hours, due to land at three o'clock in the afternoon local time. At first Yael had had two seats to herself. She went to sleep, but eight hours in, the captain had announced that the plane would be making an unscheduled stop in Frankfurt, for "technical reasons." He assured the passengers there was nothing to worry about as a frisson of alarm ran through the cabin. Yael was an experienced traveler, attuned to the sequence of engine noises that marked an airplane journey. There had been no bumps, lurches, or grinding sounds. Nothing was on fire. The cabin staff, the best barometer of any danger, seemed completely relaxed, so she fell back to sleep. She woke up somewhere over Serbia to find she had a neighbor. A young woman had boarded in Frankfurt. She was in her early twenties, plump with olive skin, short-cropped brown hair, glasses, and a snub nose. Yael had glanced at her, wondering how a passenger was allowed to board during an unscheduled stop, but she was exhausted, still sore from her fight with Cyrus Jones, and soon fell back sleep.

Yael had folded away the newspaper and was jamming it into the seat-back pocket, when she sensed movement on her right. Her neighbor was peering through the window, leaning so close that Yael could smell her almond-scented shampoo.

"It's so beautiful, isn't it?" the young woman said, her voice full of enthusiasm.

Yael stifled a yawn. "Very."

She turned to look at Yael. "First time in Istanbul?" She spoke English with an American accent, overlaid with the long, harmonious vowels of Turkish.

"Yes."

"Lucky you. You have a treat awaiting," she said, her right hand touching and smoothing her hair.

"If we ever get off this plane," said Yael, noting her nervous gesture.

"I'm so sorry about that; it's partly my fault," said

the young woman, before launching into a long, detailed explanation of how she had been traveling back
to Istanbul from Hamburg in Germany, with a layover
in Frankfurt, but her original flight was canceled, and
then it turned out there were seats on this one, even
though it was not supposed to stop at Frankfurt and was
only there to get something checked in the engine and
so on and so forth.

She looked at Yael. Yael nodded, not especially sympathetically, and did not say anything as the young woman
continued talking. She was not picking up Yael's signals
that she did not want to chat. Maybe she was a nervous
flyer. Maybe she was just trying to be friendly. But Yael
did not feel very friendly. After fourteen hours sitting in
seat 8A she wanted to be left in peace, until she could get
off the plane.

"Do you mind?" her neighbor suddenly asked, leaning
toward Yael, her iPhone in her hand.

Before Yael had a chance to answer, the young woman
moved sideways again, holding her phone against the cabin
window. "It's such a stunning view. I want to grab a quick
video."

"Quick is fine," said Yael, leaning back in her seat to
make room.

The young woman held her phone in three different po-
sitions against the window for about a minute, then stopped
filming. She thanked Yael, apologized for the inconvenience, and placed it in her purse. She sat back and closed
her eyes.

Yael looked out the window once more. The plane began its direct approach to the airport and she felt the wings clunk as the landing gear came down. She checked her watch. It was now six o'clock. She could see the fishermen standing on the quay, tiny figures with their rods leaning against the rail, and the boat-restaurant bobbing in the tide that sold only one dish: fried mackerel sandwiches with salad and onions, the most delicious fish she had ever tasted. Just the thought of them made her hungry. Until she remembered a darker harvest.

The policemen grimace as they drag the dead man into the boat. His back is crisscrossed by deep welts, their ruffled edges bleached white by the water.

Yael picked up her newspaper again and found the item in the Metro section.

MAN FOUND DEAD IN CAR IN MANHATTAN

A man was found dead in a car yesterday on the Lower East Side, police said. Officers responded to a call at 4:20 a.m. and found the man dead apparently from a single gunshot wound to the head. The car, a blue Volkswagen Touareg, was parked under the Williamsburg Bridge by East River Park. The police said the victim appears to be in his thirties and may have committed suicide. He was holding a .22 Beretta fitted with a heavily scratched silencer. He was carrying no identification documents or credit cards. However, he had a distinguishing purple birthmark on the right-hand side of his neck. There was no sign of a struggle. Police have appealed for anyone with possible information to come forward.

Yael felt no regret at the death of Cyrus Jones. Neither the news of his demise nor its manner was a surprise. But the murder weapon was. Yael slipped her hand inside her jeans pocket and took out a silver earring. It was a half loop, with a small turquoise stone set underneath, one of a pair her father had bought in the Jaffa flea market when she was a teenager. She had not worn the earrings for many years, and as far as she could remember, they were jumbled in a pile in her jewelry box. Since she'd found it she had searched for the other half of the pair, but it had disappeared. More to the point, why had the earring been on the floor of her apartment, next to the space where she had hidden Cyrus Jones's gun? A space, she had discovered, that was now empty.

Joe-Don sat back in the polished leather armchair and sipped his bourbon. It was too sweet for his taste, especially at eleven o'clock in the morning.

"Does she know you are here?" asked the man sitting next to him in a matching armchair.

"Of course not."

He picked up the bottle and offered it to Joe-Don, who declined. He topped up his own drink and swirled it around his glass, staring at the amber liquid as though it held the very secret of existence. He looked up before he spoke. "JD, we go back a long way."

Joe-Don returned his stare. The man's eyes were red rimmed, the collar of his hand-tailored shirt stained with grime. He appeared to have been up all night. "Yes, we do." Joe-Don gestured with his glass at the pictures on the wall. "And now look what impressive friends you have."

The man laughed, the sound catching in his throat and turning into a cough. "They aren't my friends. They don't know the first thing about me, except what they read in the newspaper and the number of zeros on the checks I write for their campaign funds. You are my friend. I owe you. If you hadn't seen that sniper and taken him out, I wouldn't be sitting here."

Joe-Don smiled. "You would have done the same. We looked out for each other."

"Yes, sir, I would have. Remember Cambodia?" A grin spread across his wide, doughy face. "The raid, when we busted out that colonel? The one held by the Khmer Rouge? They were one bunch of crazy motherfuckers. Shoot one down and three more little yellow men pop up out of nowhere, running at you, screaming and shouting. How old were you?"

"Twenty. I was a kid. We weren't even at war with the Khmer Rouge," said Joe-Don. He raised his glass in tribute. "To Cambodia. And to Laos. Those Hmong camps, rows and rows of tents. They fought with us, believed in us, and we sold them down the river. But you got our guys out. Every last one." He took a sip and put the bourbon down. "Could I get some coffee as well?"

Clarence Clairborne stood up and walked over to his desk. "Sure." He leaned over and pressed a button by his telephone. "Samantha, we need some coffee here. Can you rustle up a pot for us?"

"Yes, sir," said a bright female voice.

Clairborne picked up his bourbon. He stood up and walked over to the photograph of him shaking hands with Eugene Packard on the wall, swaying slightly. "The Lord has taken away, JD. From both of us. But the Lord also giveth," he said softly, almost to himself. "Rapture is coming, JD. Rapture. It just needs a little help."

Clairborne suddenly swiveled around to Joe-Don. "So, my friend, I guess you didn't travel all the way to DC on a Sunday morning just for a social call. What can I do for you?" he asked, with the fierce concentration of someone who has drunk a little too much but has just remembered something vitally important.

Joe-Don put his glass down. "You can save a lot of lives."

"Well now, that's always a fine thing. And how would I do that, JD?"

"Stop it."

Clairborne tipped his glass back and swallowed the rest of his bourbon. He walked back to his chair and sat down. "Stop what?" he said, his glass rattling on the table as he put it down.

"Your plan to hit the Istanbul Summit."

Clairborne furrowed his brow. "And why in God's good name would I want to blow up the world's best chance for peace in decades?"

"Chaos, Clarence. Chaos is good for your business. Chaos means profits. The more the Iranians destabilize the Middle East, the more we'll need Prometheus to pick up the pieces."

Clairborne drummed his fingers on his glass. He picked up the bottle of bourbon, then put it back, exhaling loudly.

A gust of rye fumes floated across the room. "That's a theory, JD. An interesting one. But nothing more."

"It's more than a theory and you know it. There are over two hundred journalists based in the UN headquarters in New York, Clarence, including almost every major American news organization. If this gets out, that Prometheus is planning to attack the summit to profit from the ensuing chaos, you are finished. However much you deny it, you will be all over the front page, the networks, and the Internet. Just the suspicion will be enough. Your share price will plunge. Your board will convene an emergency meeting and find a way to get rid of you. Your friends in Langley and the Pentagon will drop you straight into the waiting arms of the Justice Department and the district attorney's office. Who are already interested in Prometheus."

Clairborne shrugged. "What's new? Prometheus, the source of all evil. I can read that on a dozen blogs any day of the week. To make anything stick, the press needs evidence. There is no evidence because there is no plot by Prometheus to blow up the Istanbul Summit."

"We have evidence."

"Which is?"

"The architectural blueprints of the Osman Convention Center; a schedule and diagrams of where the first wave of suicide bombers will hit; the names of the Prometheus personnel who will let the bombers through; blast wave and casualty projections; estimated response times of the Turkish emergency services; the plans for the second wave, to take out the first responders. It's all there. Hidden on the darknet and encrypted but traceable back to an IP address in your office."

"Nice try, JD. I don't know what that fantasy of yours is, but it's certainly not evidence and you know it. Any fool can come up with diagrams and a schedule and stick our name on it. It means nothing. And every newspaper, website, and TV station in the land knows that if they threaten to link our name to a planned terrorist attack, our lawyers will sue their ass from here to kingdom come."

A knock at the door sounded. "Come in, honey!" shouted Clairborne.

Samantha opened the door, carrying a tray with a pot of coffee, sugar, cream, and chocolate-chip cookies. She was perfectly made up, wearing pristine white Nike running shoes, a pale blue Armani AX jogging suit, her blond hair tied back with a navy band. Samantha looked at Clairborne, taking in his disheveled state. She shook her head, a tight, precise gesture of disapproval. She picked up the bottle of bourbon, three-quarters empty, and put it on the tray. Clairborne turned, about to protest, but then thought better of it. Samantha put the tray down poured two coffees, and handed one each to Joe-Don and Clairborne.

"Samantha, you are a lifesaver," said Clairborne.

"Enjoy your coffee, sir. Perhaps it would be a good idea to eat something as well." She gestured at the cookies. "I baked these myself."

"You see, JD," said Clairborne, "I found the perfect woman. It's too late for me, but she is going to make a lucky man very happy one day."

"Thank you, sir," said Samantha, smiling. She picked up the tray and left the room.

Clairborne bit into a cookie. "Mmm, these are good," he said, demolishing it in two bites and reaching for another one. "OK, JD. I'm not gonna BS you anymore. Like I said, I owe you. But no can do, JD. It's out of my hands now. It's gone way beyond my pay grade." Clairborne looked over at the photographs of his children on his desk, suddenly thoughtful. "Way beyond. Which leaves us, my friend, at an impasse. And me with a problem. Operational security says you should not be allowed to leave this room."

Joe-Don opened his jacket to show his shoulder holster, which held a Glock 30 pistol. "Are you gonna shoot me, Clarence?"

Clairborne smiled. "I don't think so, JD. Not today. Apart from not shooting you, anything else I can do for you?"

"The Jews have a saying. *He who saves one life saves the world.*"

"The world is beyond my means. But I made some calls as soon as I heard you were coming. It took some hard bargaining. I had to call in serious favors."

He paused and leaned forward, reaching for his glass of bourbon. He looked at the inch of amber liquid inside for a second, sighed, then put it down and picked up his coffee. "If she's not in the way, they won't come after her again. That's the best I can do. Send her on vacation, somewhere far away, preferably to another continent. Just keep her out of Istanbul. It's nothing personal. And certainly not from me. She's a firecracker. I offered her a job, you know."

"Did you? And what did she say?"

"'No thank you, Mr. Clairborne.' Or words to that effect," he said, briefly smiling at the memory. His voice turned serious. "JD, you need to understand this. The moment she steps foot in Istanbul, she becomes a target. They will find her, they will take her, and it won't be pretty."

Clairborne paused as he reached inside the drawer of his desk. He took out a heavy, well-worn US Army .45 Colt pistol and placed it on the green leather surface.

"And one more thing." He looked straight at Joe-Don as he spoke, his eyes cold and flat. "Our account is clear now."

19

Large banners draped across the airport terminal proclaimed "Welcome to Istanbul, City of Peace" in English and Turkish. But the reality, Yael immediately noticed as she clambered down the staircase onto the tarmac, was less hospitable. Security was much heavier than it had been on her last visit, just a few weeks before. Police commandos wearing bulletproof vests stood on the runway and at the door to the terminal, trigger fingers resting on the Heckler & Koch submachine guns strapped against their chests. Signs in a dozen languages, from Arabic to Swahili, exhorted passengers to be alert and report anything suspicious. More security personnel patrolled inside the building, holding German shepherds on short, double leashes, scanning the passengers with cold, hard stares.

Yael made sure to fall back as the travelers disembarked from their bus and entered the terminal. The young woman who had sat next to her strode ahead and was soon separated from Yael by half a dozen others. Transit through immigration was also slower, with every arrival, including Turkish citizens, being questioned. After standing in line for thirty-five minutes, Yael eventually presented her passport at the immigration control. The policewoman in the glass booth had shoulder-length brown hair, thin pursed lips, and a severe expression. A sign on the glass announced that photography was forbidden and all conversations would be recorded.

"Julia Albihari?" asked the policewoman, as she slipped the identification page of Yael's passport into an electronic reader.

Yael nodded. The recording was a new feature added since her last time through. It must have been introduced as part of the heightened security measures for the summit.

"Please answer me, Ms. Albihari."

"Yes, that's me," said Yael. She was not traveling on her UN laissez-passer, but on an American passport.

"The purpose of your visit?"

"Tourism."

"What do you plan to see?"

"The Blue Mosque, the Grand Bazaar, maybe take a ferry to the Asian side. Is there anything you would recommend personally?"

The policewoman ignored the question. She stared hard at Yael, looked at her passport, then at the computer screen in front of her. She entered a series of numbers and waited.

Yael began to feel uneasy. The passport was real, issued by the State Department. It would survive the most rigorous background checks, as would the credit cards and driving license, all in the name of Julia Albihari, that Yael was carrying. Julia Albihari had black hair, as did Yael now, having dyed it on Saturday morning. Tradecraft rules were that aliases should be reasonably similar to the operative's actual name, to make them easier to remember. Nevertheless, Yael was not Julia Albihari. She was traveling under a fake identity, a serious crime under any legal system. Her UN immunity, already fraying, would easily unravel if the Turkish authorities probed further.

The policewoman handed Yael her passport back. "Enjoy your stay in Istanbul," she said.

Süleyman Mevsim perched on the entrance of his home in Üsküdar, playing with his toy car, sweeping it back and forth across the front step. The car was his favorite, a red Porsche, although the back left wheel was hanging off and he didn't know how to fix it. A crippled car, for a crippled boy, he thought. Süleyman was used to playing on his own. He was only nine, but he had to be strong, like his hero and namesake, Süleyman the Magnificent, the most powerful Ottoman sultan in history, the scourge of Budapest, the conqueror of Baghdad. Süleyman had a withered right leg, a legacy of childhood polio. He could not keep up with the other children's games and so they didn't invite him to play. It wasn't too bad during school time, but he didn't like the holidays because he was on his own all day, apart from his mom and two younger sisters, whom he loved, of course, but they weren't much good as playmates. Sometimes one or two of the neighborhood boys were nice to him for a while, but they always changed. They said things like he wasn't a "good Muslim," even though his family prayed several times a day, went to the mosque at least on Fridays, and kept Ramadan. Still, Süleyman loved living in Üsküdar. This part of Istanbul, on the Asian side of the Bosphorus, was quieter and more traditional than the European side. He could see the sea at the end of the street; there was a synagogue, an Armenian and a Greek Orthodox church all just a few minutes' walk away. The shopkeepers were always friendly to him, giving him fruit, sweets, and chocolate.

Süleyman looked like he was absorbed in his game, but he was not. He was on a mission. He was watching what he had named the "target house." Süleyman knew there was something strange about that place. The house next door was smart and clean, painted dark green. But the target house looked old and dirty. The paint was peeling; big flakes of dirty white hung from the gray woodwork. Two plants stood outside the front door, but both were turning brown from lack of water. Every morning, the local women opened their windows and sometimes brought the rugs down to beat on the street, sending puffs of dust into the air. But nobody ever opened a window in the target house. It always looked dark and gloomy inside. The curtains were always drawn, brown grubby things that looked as if they had not been washed for years. The only new thing was the giant satellite dish on the roof, bigger than all the neighbors'.

A car pulled up and parked nearby. Süleyman quickly dropped his head down and swept his Porsche back and forth across the step, apparently completely absorbed in his task, but secretly still watching. The car, a brown Fiat sedan, was nothing exciting, not like his Porsche. Three men got out. He had seen the driver and one of the other men before, many times—they were thin, and dark, darker than most Turks, especially the Istanbulis. They spoke Turkish with an unusual accent. The third man must be important, Süleyman thought, because the driver had got out of the car first and opened the door for him, and the second one carried his bag. The new arrival had thick black hair, Süleyman noticed. And then something strange happened. The driver turned around, yawned, and stretched his arms out. The driver didn't see that the new man was next to him, and his right arm brushed against the new man's head. His hair moved. All of it.

Süleyman moved the Porsche faster back and forth, pretending to look down at the step but secretly watching even harder. He had never seen anything like that before. Now he really had a lot to report when his cousin came over tonight for dinner. His cousin had an important job. He worked for the government, "catching the bad guys," he said. Süleyman had told him about the target house. His cousin said he should keep an eye on it, but carefully, so the bad guys inside did not notice. Although he knew his cousin was joking, Süleyman had followed his instructions. There was something not right about the place. And now this. His cousin had given him a mobile telephone. It was an old model, but he didn't care. It had a camera with a zoom lens.

The smell of the sea coming up the street was making him hungry. Süleyman picked up his car and went inside. His mother had promised to make his favorite lunch today: lamb *köfte* with french fries. He would eat and then perch himself on his favorite place, by the window of the wooden balcony, watch the house some more, and take some pictures. Then his cousin would really be impressed. Perhaps they would sit and read Süleyman's favorite books together, the old ones with the Greek and Spanish writing, which the family had kept for hundreds of years.

Kemal Burhan sat motionless, wreathed in smoke, cigarette in hand, as he calculated the likely consequences of the operation: for Turkey, for his service, and, most of all, for himself. His basilisk face was a mask, his angular features so sharp they seemed to have been chiseled from granite. In theory, the plan was a clever one. The bungled kidnapping would be blamed on Kurdish terrorists seeking a high-profile target while the eyes of the world were on Istanbul. But still, the death of a foreigner, especially one with connections, would bring trouble. Embassies would be involved, journalists would arrive, foreign journalists. A plane load of reporters, traveling with the United Nations secretary-general, was due in the next day. Unlike the troublesome domestic variety, they could not simply be thrown in jail and forgotten about. But orders were orders, and these were his. As was the $500,000 sitting in his numbered Swiss bank account. His mind started to wander to Natalya, his twenty-two-year-old Russian mistress, and how grateful she would be after a shopping trip in Paris. And how she would show her gratitude. He banished that delicious vision and stubbed out his cigarette. The decision was made.

Burhan looked around the table. There were just two others there. His most trusted operative and this young woman, a new recruit, just three weeks out of her training. He had been doubtful about using her so soon on an operation as important as this one. The target's psychological profile indicated that she would be least suspicious of another female, but judging from the young operative's initial debriefing, her attempts at bonding did not seem to have been especially successful.

A crystal bowl sat in the center of the table, overflowing with candies wrapped in shiny paper, the tray next to it heaped with nougats and pieces of *lokum*, Turkish delight. Apart from his mistress, sweets were Burhan's greatest weakness. He reached for a chunk of lokum studded with pistachios. He chewed it slowly, savoring the contrast of the crunchy nuts and the sticky sweetness. He looked at the young woman. "Show me the film again."

She swallowed, touched her short brown hair, clearly nervous, but her chubby face showed her pride at being chosen for such a sensitive mission. "Yes, sir. The second segment is the clearest."

Burhan wiped his fingers on a blue silk handkerchief, carefully chosen to be a shade darker than his hand-tailored Italian suit. "Play all of them."

The sound of airplane engines filled the room. The computer monitor showed Yael's profile from the left side. Her face was clear, but the screen was pixilated and vibrating slightly. After twenty seconds or so, the picture moved to show her from a slightly different angle, and then did the same again.

"The front-facing camera is considerably lower resolution than the rear one," said the young woman, apologetically, as the film finished, the last frame frozen on Yael's face.

"It's fine. And the sound file?"

She pressed several keys. Yael's face vanished, replaced

by a graphic that looked like a cardiogram, with a straight line running through the middle. She pressed play.

The sound of an airport terminal: the murmur of nearby conversations, announcements about flight delays. The straight line moved up and down, in time with the sounds. A female voiced asked "Julia Albihari?"

There was no answer. The voice said, "Please answer me, Ms. Albihari."

"Yes, that's me."

"The purpose of your visit?"

"Tourism."

"What do you plan to see?"

"The Blue Mosque, the Grand Bazaar, maybe take a ferry to the Asian side. Is there anything you would recommend personally?"

The first female voice did not reply. The click of her fingers on a keyboard cut through the background hum. After several seconds she said, "Enjoy your stay in Istanbul."

Burhan drummed his fingers on the top of the desk, thinking. He turned to the man sitting at the table.

"You can confirm her identity?" Burhan asked.

Yusuf Çelmiz nodded. "Yes. Visual and audio confirmed. That is Yael Azoulay."

"Good, Melita, if you could go over the chronology again, please."

Melita checked her notes. "Yael Azoulay arrived just over four hours ago. The plane landed at 5:32 p.m., about two and a half hours late. She was through immigration by 6:38. She was not questioned at customs. She took a taxi into the city. She had a reservation, prepaid, at a budget hotel in Sultanahmet. We had it covered. The room was prepared. We had a team outside in a car and in the building across the street." Melita paused and bit her lip.

"Carry on," said Burhan.

"I'm sorry, sir. She didn't go there. She went to the Hotel Fatima. It's women only. We followed her but I couldn't get too close. She would have recognized me immediately. I found a café nearby and watched from there. She checked into her hotel at seven thirty p.m. She ate in the hotel dining room and went back to her room. We are trying to get inside her mobile but the security and encryption are NSA standard. We have set up an operation in an apartment across the street. We have a laser directed at her window to pick up any sound vibrations if she speaks. We are inside the hotel switchboard if she uses a landline. So far she has not made any calls. There is no Wi-Fi at the hotel. She is still there now. We think she is asleep. We will keep trying her phone."

Burhan nodded. "Good." He reached for the bowl of candies and offered it to the young woman. "You may leave us now. Well done on your good work."

Melita shook her head, flushing pink at his praise. Burhan waited until she had picked up her purse and left, before he turned to Yusuf. He opened a packet of Camel Turkish Gold cigarettes, offered it to Yusuf, took one himself, and lit both their cigarettes with a silver Zippo lighter.

Burhan was silent for several moments, smoke trailing from his nostrils. He looked at his agent as though seeing him for the first time, appraising his strengths and weaknesses. A lot was riding on this judgment, Burhan knew. A mistake could be fatal, perhaps for more than his career. Burhan had not survived thirty years of service in the MİT by making errors. His nickname was "the Hawk." He knew when to ride the thermals and when to strike. Born in a slum in Fatih, Istanbul's most religious quarter, Burhan had quickly learned to use his fists to survive. His father died when he was six, leaving his mother to raise four children on her own. Burhan had left school at sixteen, trained as an amateur boxer for two years, then joined the MİT. He had started out as a foot soldier, doing the rough work the state deemed necessary for its survival. Burhan remained a loyal functionary of whichever regime was in power, well aware that, just as in Ottoman times, the higher he rose, the more danger he was in. Sometimes he awoke in the night, drenched in sweat, dreaming of a cushion on top of which lay a silken cord: a sultan's message to a troublesome vizier that suicide would be the best of options.

Despite his taste for hand-tailored shirts and suits purchased on London's Savile Row, Burhan's downtown office was modest: a plain room in a nondescript sixth-floor apartment, one of many owned by the MİT. The walls were a pale cream fading to gray, the furniture drab and functional. A single sheet of paper, a fax of a newspaper article, sat on the desk. The only hint of luxury was the tray of lokum and the crystal bowl of sweets. Kemal Atatürk, the founder of modern Turkey, resplendent in a cream suit stared out from a framed portrait on the wall. The view, over the Sultanahmet quarter, the heart of old Istanbul, was spectacular.

Burhan had served under army generals, secular democrats, and several shades of Islamists. These were, he liked to tell his subordinates, *challenging* times in a rough neighborhood. Syria and Iraq had collapsed into a patchwork of warring statelets. Iran was on the edge of . . . what exactly? Worst of all, the regional chaos had emboldened the Kurds to push for autonomy, which everyone knew was just a code word for secession and the eventual breakup of the Turkish state. The Kurds had to be derailed. And, if all went well, this operation would help do that. If . . .

"Yusuf, there is some . . . concern about your involvement in this operation."

"Why, *patron?*" Yusuf used the slang term for boss, a rare privilege.

The Hawk stared at Yusuf. "Because of your personal connection."

"I have no personal connection. I cleared the operation with you; you cleared it with your superiors. Everything was authorized. It all went well," said Yusuf confidently.

The Hawk inclined his head in agreement. "Yes, it did. At that time our interests and those of Yael Azoulay coincided. We will not let the Americans use our country for their dirtiest work. We both wanted to get rid of Cyrus Jones. A message was sent, and received. It will not happen again. Still, there is a feeling that you let your emotions become involved."

"I did not, patron. Nor were there any loose ends."

"None at all. Especially not now," he said, passing the fax of the *New York Times* newspaper article to Yusuf. The headline proclaimed, "Man Found Dead in Car in Manhattan."

Yusuf quickly read through the text. He looked up at Burhan, his eyes wide in surprise. "Did we . . . ?"

The Hawk reached for the bowl of candies. He took out a bonbon wrapped in gold foil, unwrapped it, and inserted it into his mouth. He shook his head as he slowly chewed the sweet. "No. Which makes me wonder who did. But what is done is done."

He turned to Yusuf, his face impassive. "And what needs to be done?"

"Will be," said Yusuf.

20

Najwa held the top of page 7 of Saturday's edition of the *New York Times* in her left hand and flicked the lead article with a manicured fingernail. The sharp crack resounded across the aircraft cabin. Jonathan Beaufort, sitting in the neighboring row, jerked awake and turned around in alarm.

Najwa waved at Jonathan, then folded up the newspaper and handed it to Sami. "Additional reporting by Najwa al-Sameera," she said scornfully. "You promised me a joint byline. You would never have got half those quotes from the dips without me."

Beaufort groggily watched the scene, decided it was not worth staying awake for, and instantly went back to sleep.

"Could be worse," said Sami. "You could have got an 'additional research by. . . . '"

Najwa pointed at the page, her expression severe. "This makes me sound like an intern."

Sami laughed. "Najwa, I don't think *anyone* would ever mistake you for an intern. And I made sure that you get a proper byline in tomorrow's newspaper. It's being printed as we speak. You are getting so many bylines, maybe they will give you my job."

Najwa picked up her glass of champagne and looked ahead, as if properly considering the matter. "I'd have to keep my own office." She turned to her side. "You could be my intern."

"Ha-ha," said Sami. His voice turned serious. "You know he's dead in the water now. We've finished him off."

"Not necessarily," said Najwa, as she drank some of her champagne. "This is the UN we are dealing with."

"Don't you ever feel kind of used? Like we are just one big channel for leaks?"

"No, I don't. They use us. We use them. It's a win-win. Speaking of which, here comes our new best friend."

Sami looked up and watched Roxana Voiculescu walk down the left-hand aisle of the airplane, smiling and chatting to the journalists. Tall and slim with long chestnut hair and pale blue eyes, she was as attractive as she was ambitious. The daughter of the Romanian finance minister, Roxana had a degree in journalism from Bucharest University and a postgraduate diploma in development studies from Oxford. Now that Schneidermann was gone, she finally had the job she wanted. Every time Sami saw her he remembered taking her for drinks at Grad, an upscale vodka bar, and the envelope he had stolen from her handbag containing Fareed Hussein's itinerary of his journey to Geneva on the KZX Corporation executive jet. Sami ran his fingers over the fabric of the seat-back in front of him. The letters *KZX* were embossed in a tasteful shade of gray on a black background. Now it was his turn to accept a ride from the German media conglomerate.

Roxana stopped at every seat, working the airplane

like a presidential candidate, checking on the journalists and exchanging a few pleasantries with those who were awake.

"Sami, Najwa," she gushed when she reached their aisle, as though they were long-lost relatives she had not seen for years. "I'm *so* glad you could join us. Are you enjoying the flight?" Roxana looked at her watch, which Sami noted was a Patek Philippe. "I'm very impressed you are still awake." She leaned forward and spoke more softly. "Do you have everything, all the information you need?" she asked, her voice injected with an extra layer of meaning.

Najwa replied, "We're fine, thanks. Congratulations on your promotion. And I love your jacket. Where did you get it?"

Roxana smiled, a dazzling display of perfect dentistry. "Thank you. It's MaxMara, the new spring collection. You know, I'm really looking forward to working together on this trip."

"Thanks. How about Caroline? Is she going to take a stroll down the aisle to say hello to the press?"

"We certainly hope so, her schedule permitting. She's deep in some paperwork at the moment."

"Where's Quentin Braithwaite?" asked Sami. "Shouldn't he be here? He is the special envoy for the Istanbul Summit."

Roxana smiled beatifically. "Quentin was delayed. We found such a backlog of things that still needed doing before Caroline could take over, so it was thought best that he stay behind to sort them out."

"You must miss Henrik," said Sami.

Roxana looked puzzled for a moment, then quickly recovered. Her face turned grave. "Yes, yes, of course. A terrible loss to the UN," she said, slowly shaking her head.

"Will there be a memorial service for him?" asked Sami.

The airplane suddenly lurched, hitting mild turbulence. Roxana grabbed the seat-back to steady herself. "Not as far as I know. When do you need me to get back to you on that?"

Sami stared at her, momentarily nonplussed. "Uh, it's not for a story. It's just if there is some kind of service, we would like to go."

"I'll let you know once I find out. Do let me know if you need anything else," Roxana said, before moving down the aisle.

Najwa waited until Roxana was several rows away before she burst out laughing. "When do you need me to get back to you on that, *Sami*?" Najwa dropped her voice a key to imitate Roxana's husky tone. "Maybe you could take Roxana for some more cocktails, once we get to Istanbul. See what else she has in her handbag."

"Or maybe you could take her dancing."

Najwa drank some more champagne, her expression thoughtful. "That's a very good idea. Shall we have another glass?"

"Not for me. It's two o'clock in the morning New York time. We will have to work tomorrow. I'm not sure I should be here, let alone be drinking champagne."

Najwa looked puzzled. "Why not? Everyone else is. You have traveled with the SG lots of times."

"Yes, but I didn't know what a corporate jamboree this would be. I thought the Turkish government would provide the plane. I'm not allowed to accept gifts from companies."

Sami took out the menu for the in-flight meals and began reading. "The KZX Corporation welcomes the UN press corps on board and is happy to provide hospitality for the flight from New York to Istanbul . . . a five-course dinner, with a different wine for each course, as well as champagne and cognacs. New American cuisine, French, or Turkish." He slid the menu back into the seat-back pocket and picked up the black and silver leather messenger bag on the floor in front of him. "Look at this, you wouldn't even know it was a corporate freebie," he said, pointing at the lower right-hand corner, where the letters *KZX* were subtly embossed in the leather. Sami opened the bag. "An iPad Air, an iPhone 6, a leather portfolio with artisan writing paper and a Montblanc pen with a ten-gigabyte USB stick. All engraved with our names. There's at least three thousand dollars' worth of stuff here." Sami took out the Montblanc pen and turned it around in his hand, enjoying its perfect balance and symmetry. The black lacquer coating gleamed under the cabin lights. Sami checked the end. "They even spelled my name right. It's beautiful."

"Thank you, I am glad you like our gifts," said a voice overhead. Sami and Najwa looked up to see a tall, rake-thin man standing by their seats, his shoulders slightly stooped.

Even five hours into a transatlantic flight Reinhardt Daintner displayed his customary elegance. The communications director of the KZX Corporation was wearing his trademark gray silk suit, white shirt, and slim black knitted tie. So pale he was a near-albino, Daintner had a widow's peak of white hair with equally white eyebrows and near translucent lips. Perhaps because of his unusual looks, Daintner had a powerful charisma, which he usually deployed to good effect.

Daintner leaned forward. "We hope they will help you to do your job even better. Especially after our recent misunderstandings."

"Good morning, Mr. Daintner," said Sami. "What misunderstandings?"

Najwa turned to watch as Sami spoke, relishing the coming exchange.

A faint trace of a frown flitted across Daintner's face. "Good morning to both of you. The misunderstandings in your reports on the planned KZX–Bonnet Group Goma Development Zone. A series of articles and a documentary film, if I recall. But that's all in the past now. Let bygones be bygones."

Sami put the pen back in its box and the box into the messenger bag. "Mr. Daintner, I am in an uncomfortable position here, because it seems we are traveling on your ticket. But we didn't misunderstand anything. Our reporting was accurate and fair."

Daintner inclined his head. "Let's agree to differ, Mr. Boustani, on the definition of 'fair.' But this is neither the time nor the place to rehash last year's news. You and Ms. al-Sameera, all the UN press corps, are our most welcome guests."

Sami nodded. "Thank you. Please don't think me churlish but my newspaper will be requesting a bill for this journey, Mr. Daintner."

Daintner shook his head. "It will not be forthcoming."

"In that case we will make an equivalent donation to charity."

"As you wish," said Daintner.

Sami was immune to Daintner's smooth talk. Tired from the flight, and irritated at being bounced into a freebie—which he knew could have been avoided if he had bothered to check—he went on the attack. "Child coltan miners are a worthy cause, don't you think? Children working in slave-labor conditions so that we may enjoy the latest smartphones and tablets. Which reminds me," said Sami as he reached for the messenger bag. "Again, don't think me rude, but my newspaper's policy strictly forbids me from accepting gifts. I am sure you can find a good home for these," he continued, handing the bag to Daintner.

"Do they really need to know?" asked Daintner, his smile taking on a somewhat fixed quality. "I won't tell if you don't."

"They do."

Sami gently nudged Najwa with his elbow. She gave him a beseeching look. Sami stared at her, unblinking. Najwa opened her eyes even wider. Sami continued staring. Najwa sighed, reached down for her messenger bag, and handed it to Daintner. "Thank you, Reinhardt, but Al Jazeera has the same policy."

Najwa looked up to see Caroline Masters walking down the aisle. She looked tired, almost disheveled, as though she had just woken up. Her blouse was crumpled, there were dark circles around her eyes, and her skin looked dry and puffy. She stood close to Daintner as Najwa finished talking and greeted the two journalists.

"What policy, Najwa?" Masters asked.

"Freebies," said Sami. "We are not allowed to accept them."

Masters glanced at Daintner, who was now holding the two messenger bags.

Daintner said, "It's really not a problem, Caroline. The *New York Times* and Al Jazeera don't accept free gifts. We should have checked first."

"Really? Then why are you on this plane?" Masters asked, her irritation plain.

"Because you didn't tell us that it was going to be sponsored by a corporation. Otherwise we would have made our own way to Istanbul," said Sami.

"You didn't ask."

Daintner shot Masters a look of alarm. Arguments with prominent journalists were not part of the KZX PR strategy for the summit.

"Why would I?" said Sami. "It's never happened before."

Masters registered Daintner's look and lapsed back into cordial UN-speak. "Well, Sami, we will be making a number of changes over the next few months, many of them in conjunction with KZX, which is one of the UN's most valued partners. And we look forward to a productive working relationship with you, with all the media, as the UN evolves to meet new challenges."

Daintner smiled at Sami and Najwa as he placed his hand on the small of Masters's back. "We hope to be discussing those with you both at a later date. Enjoy the rest of the flight. We have an exciting week ahead, and now, if you will excuse us . . ." He turned around and gently guided Masters back up the aisle.

Najwa waited for several seconds till Daintner and Masters were out of earshot, then turned to Sami. "You owe me, habibi. An iPad, an iPhone 6, a Montblanc pen, and a leather messenger bag," she said, counting on her fingers, her voice mock angry. "With my name engraved on each. This time in English and Arabic."

Sami reached over and tipped the last of her miniature bottle of champagne into his glass and swallowed it in one gulp. "Yeah, yeah. Did you see that body language? She looked at him before she spoke, like she was seeking permission. Daintner had his hand on her back. He ended the conversation when he wanted to."

"Welcome aboard KZX Airways."

"Do you really think they are an item?"

"Yup. Speaking of loving couples . . . I hope you aren't still jealous of my dance," said Najwa, leaning closer to Sami, her full breast pressing against his arm.

Sami smiled. "Hey, I got to walk her home."

"So you did. You abandoned me. I ended up dancing with that handsome Israeli guy. But all he wanted to talk about was Yael. What happened? Did you ditch the bodyguard?"

"I was burgled. We spent the next two hours cleaning up the apartment."

"Burgled? I'm sorry. That sucks. What did they take?"

"The only thing missing was the copy of the DVD that you made for me of the film clip of Yael in the Millennium Hotel."

Najwa frowned. "That's weird."

"So is this," said Sami. He opened Saturday's newspaper and went through the pages to the Metro section and the story about Cyrus Jones. He folded the newspaper over and handed it to Najwa. "Read this."

Najwa looked up when she finished the story, frowning in concentration. "A long purple birthmark on his neck. I remember something—"

"Jones. Cyrus Jones. The American who was held by the jihadis in Syria. We watched the video on YouTube."

"And why are we interested in him?"

"Jones came to see me, just before I got burgled. He and another guy. They said they were from the Immigration and Naturalization Service. But they weren't."

"What did they want?"

"Information about Yael."

"What did you tell them?"

"Only things that were already public. What she used to do for the SG. The Trusteeship Council. Then he threatened to have my citizenship revoked."

Najwa looked at Sami, her eyes wide. "He did what? How?"

Sami reached inside his jacket pocket and took out an envelope. "With these," he said, handing her half a dozen photographs of himself and his mother in Gaza.

The beggar was barely in her teens, still chubby from baby fat.

Yael watched her from her window seat in Café Markiz, steam rising from her tea. The girl sat on the sidewalk in front of a trendy household-goods shop, her legs twisted, useless, underneath her body. Every few minutes she crawled back and forth along İstiklal Caddesi, holding a gray plastic bowl. Most of the shoppers ignored her. Occasionally a passerby dropped a coin in the bowl. Then the girl would look up, one milky eye swiveling sightlessly, as she mouthed her thanks.

İstiklal Caddesi, Republic Avenue, was a wide pedestrianized street at the heart of the old European quarter of Beyoğlu, once home to Greeks and Jews, Italians and Armenians. Most had now vanished, but their former homes and businesses remained. A century-old, mile-long eclectic architectural cocktail of nineteenth-century Ottoman, Oriental-tinged art nouveau, and modern buildings, the avenue was now the modern shopping center of Istanbul, home to Western-brand boutiques, modern cafés and restaurants, and several old-fashioned book and record shops. The narrow alleys running from the side led to hidden art nouveau apartment blocks and warrens of tiny shops and bars. The Tünel, the underground cable car leading to the Galata Bridge, marked one end of the avenue; Taksim Square, the favorite site for Istanbul's protestors to battle the riot police, the other. A single-carriage old-fashioned wooden tram, painted red and white, trundled up the center of the thoroughfare.

Yael reached inside her purse and took out a twenty-lira note, worth around ten dollars, to give to the girl when she left. She looked at her watch. It was ten o'clock on Monday morning. She had lost a day traveling because of the seven-hour time difference between Istanbul and New York. But now she felt refreshed, certainly more alert than when she had finally arrived in the city last night. Yael had stumbled into bed at eight o'clock and slept for twelve hours. She felt safe at the Hotel Fatima—no male planning to make life difficult for her would ever make it past the fearsome owner and manageress, who guarded the reception like a eunuch watching over a sultan's harem.

She sat back and adjusted her hijab, using her reflection in the café window. Yael wore hers tied around her head and knotted underneath, with the crown of her head showing. She had chosen a black and gold scarf, to coordinate with her new black hair and gold-rimmed glasses with plain lenses. She wore slim-cut black jeans, a white T-shirt, and a fitted cream safari-style jacket she had picked up on her previous trip here. If anything, she thought, she was dressed too modestly for this part of town. She was the only woman wearing a head scarf in Café Markiz. Markiz was an Istanbul landmark, an elegant, old-fashioned Parisian-style café. The wooden entrance and dark furniture set off the two giant art-nouveau-tiled murals on the main wall: each showed a creamy-skinned woman, her shoulders daringly exposed, surrounded by flowers and greenery, representing autumn and spring. Most of the other female customers were indistinguishable from their fashionable peers in London or New York, with their hair free and a hint or more of cleavage, gossiping excitedly or hunched over their smartphones.

Her mission aside, Yael was happy to be back in Istanbul, a place where she always felt at home. Like her, Istanbul was a crossbreed, carrying the genes of both East and West, including, perhaps, some of hers. The Azoulays, she knew, had fled Spain in 1492, one among tens of thousands of Sephardic Jewish families expelled by the Catholic king Philip. She still remembered the history lesson about the expulsion, and the teacher telling her how Philip's decision had been greeted with incredulity in the Ottoman court. "Do they call this man a wise king, who impoverishes his country so?" asked Sultan Bayezid II, who promptly dispatched a fleet of boats to bring the Jews to the Ottoman Empire. The Azoulays had sailed from Grenada, finally settling in Baghdad. Yael liked to imagine her forefathers passing through Istanbul on the way, standing on the deck of the ship, watching the shore as it came into view, its harbor jammed with boats, its wharves echoing to a babel of languages, wondering how they would make a new life in a new land. Perhaps she should make a new life here too, far from the UN. She might meet someone, settle down, have a family, live normally. How hard could it be to learn Turkish, she thought, smiling to herself.

Yael watches Yusuf finish his pide. His fingers are long and slender, his dark eyes, somewhere between brown and black, warm and intelligent. A lock of hair, so black it almost shines, falls over his forehead.

Yusuf Çelmiz, senior operative in the Milli İstihbarat Teşkilatı. Her accomplice in the rendition of Cyrus Jones. But could she trust Yusuf with what she now knew? The CIA, Mossad, MI6, even France's DGSE had all reduced their information exchange with the MİT, judging its new director to be too close to the Iranians. The truth was, whether or not she could trust Yusuf Çelmiz, she wanted to. In fact, she had to. Her other contacts had all been mysteriously busy, unavailable, or unreachable. But where was he? They were supposed to meet at Café Markiz at 9:30. Her new mobile telephone beeped—a text message had arrived. The phone was one of three cheap pay-as-you-go phones Yael had purchased that morning from a tiny shop in a back street of Sulta-nahmet. According to Turkish law, even pay-as-you-go mobile telephones must be officially registered in some-one's name, with proof of address. But an extra $200, in cash, had persuaded the owner that this time, the law could be ignored. In any case, she would only use each burner for a few hours, then dispose of it. The obso-lete Nokia candy-bar model felt tiny in her hand. She could close her fingers around it. The sender's number was blocked, but apart from Yusuf, only one person had this number.

Your disc is a master copy

Yael smiled as she read the text. Beaker's code was not very subtle. But then it didn't need to be.

She picked up the tulip-shaped glass and sipped her tea. It was strong and delicious, scented with cinnamon. Once she got home on Friday night, Yael had played the DVD she had stolen from Sami on her computer and watched herself at the Millennium Hotel. Like Sami and Najwa, Yael had looked for the metadata. Yael too found nothing. She had met Beaker on Saturday morning and handed him the DVD with a request to see if he could find out where the video file had been created. "A master copy," she read again. And now she knew who had sent the DVD to Sami and Najwa.

Sami and Najwa. Yael did a quick mental calculation: it was 10:00 a.m. in Istanbul, which meant it was 3:00 a.m. in New York. The Monday edition of the *New York Times* must be online by now. She rummaged in her bag for her iPhone and clicked on the newspaper's app.

FAREED HUSSEIN "ORDERED BOSNIANS FROM UN COMPOUND AT SREBRENICA," INTERNAL DOCUMENTS REVEAL

Many Killed Soon After, Hussein Return to Post Now Judged Unlikely

By SAMI BOUSTANI, NAJWA AL-SAMEERA, Special to the *New York Times*

UNITED NATIONS—Fareed Hussein, the secretary-general of the United Nations, personally ordered the handover of three hundred Bosnian Muslims who had taken refuge in the United Nations base at Srebrenica in July 1995 to the Bosnian Serbs, according to internal UN documents obtained by the *New York Times*. The women were put on trucks and sent across the front lines. The men, including several teenage boys, were shot soon after, their hands tied behind their backs.

At the time, Mr. Hussein was serving as the head of the Department of Peacekeeping Operations. The leaked documents reveal that Dutch troops panicked and retreated to the UN base when promised air strikes failed to materialize. A group of some two hundred Bosnian Muslims, some of whom worked for the UN as translators and drivers, managed to flee to the UN base with their families. But they were forced out under Fareed Hussein's orders, for fear that their presence would compromise the UN's neutrality. Srebrenica was a UN-declared "safe haven." About eight thousand Bosnian Muslim men and boys, taken prisoner by the Bosnian Serbs, were ultimately killed over several days in early July 1995.

Mr. Hussein is currently on medical leave. His deputy, Caroline Masters, has been appointed acting secretary-general. The revelations about the massacre at Srebrenica have caused shock across the United Nations headquarters. They come just three days before the start of the Istanbul Summit, the UN-sponsored Middle East peace conference. There is concern among Western officials that Ms. Masters lacks the necessary leadership skills to oversee the conference. In a memorandum obtained by the *New York Times*, James Berger, the deputy chief of the US mission to the UN, accused Ms. Masters of having lost "her sense of judgment."

Many Western officials would prefer to see Mr. Hussein in charge of the summit, said Keir Rogerson, a former British diplomat stationed at the UN. Mr. Rogerson now runs Diplomacy Unbound, a research institute based in New York. "The people I have spoken to, in Washington and London, say they wanted Fareed Hussein to take charge of the summit and, once he is recovered, return to run the United Nations." But this is now seen as unlikely. "I cannot see any way back for Fareed after this. The Srebrenica documents are explosive. They link him personally to the death of several hundred people," said Mr. Rogerson.

Ms. Masters planned to leave for Istanbul late on Sunday night. Roxana Voiculescu, her spokeswoman, said that the contents of the documents would need to be verified before the UN could comment, but that they appeared to be "very disturbing," especially if they did implicate Mr. Hussein in the deaths of those forced from the base. Mr. Hussein could not be reached for comment. His former spokesman, Henrik Schneidermann, died earlier this month, reportedly from a heart attack. No replacement has yet been named.

Page 3: The leaked memo in full; the long shadow of Srebrenica

Page 4: What future now for Fareed Hussein?

Page 12: Op-Ed: A Survivor Remembers

Yael sat back and breathed out hard, processing what she had just read. Fareed Hussein's whispering campaign against Caroline Masters had just been vaporized. Yael had heard the rumors, of course, about Hussein and Srebrenica, but nothing had ever been confirmed. Until now. She ran through the likely sequence of events in her head. Sami's story on Masters had run on Saturday morning. Masters must have arranged for the documents to get to him as soon as the newspaper hit the newsstands. Sami would have needed a day to confirm and verify the material. He must have filed this second story on Sunday evening, to make Monday's edition. And now Masters and the UN press corps were on their way to Istanbul. Even by UN standards, the contents, the speed, and the ferocity of Masters's response were breathtaking.

Clairborne slid the end of the cigar into the cutter. "Are you familiar with the word krysha?" he asked.

"It's Russian for roof."

Hers, Yael knew, was gone. But far more importantly, so was her best chance of finding out the truth about David's death. Unless Isis could deliver on her promise.

21

Yael's Nokia mobile beeped again. Another SMS message.

Sorry for lateness and delay. Meet you taxi stand NW corner Taksim. Y.

Yael picked up her purse and rummaged inside, looking for her wallet, buried somewhere under her extra Nokia phones, cigarettes, lighter, tissues, crumpled receipts, miniature makeup palette, chewing gum, antiseptic wipes, Swiss Army knife, emergency tampons, and assorted lipsticks. She pulled out a folded square of glossy paper and opened it up: it was a page torn from last month's *Vogue*, showcasing a black, off-the-shoulder cocktail dress by Versace. She smiled to herself, folded the paper up again, and slipped it back inside. Her fingers brushed against a piece of thick cloth, trapped in the bottom right-hand corner. Curious as to what it could be, she took it out. It was a napkin, heavy and white. Yael opened it up, her smile vanishing at what she saw. Silver stitching spelled out "Millennium Hotel, Manhattan." A small shiny square with serrated edges sat in the center of the cloth. The blue lettering said "Durex: Perfomax."

It had taken Yael several afternoons to teach Mahesh Kapoor to learn to control his excitement and extend his—and her—pleasure. The condoms had helped. Her affair with Fareed Hussein's former chief of staff, seven years earlier, had lasted for several months. It had been a fine example of what the French referred to as a *cinq à sept*—a liaison conducted between five and seven, in the hours after a gentleman's work for the day is completed, before he is obliged to return home or attend an evening engagement. But Kapoor had tried to kill her in Geneva and was now serving a life sentence for the murder of Olivia de Souza. And the hotel held even darker memories for her: of Jean-Pierre Hakizimani, lying still on the floor of his suite, his eyes unseeing, his skin turning gray.

Yael banished the vision. She suddenly realized that she was sitting in a café in Istanbul, dressed as a moderately observant Muslim woman, staring at a silver and blue condom wrapper, nicely framed on a clean white napkin. She scrunched the condom back into the napkin, put it in her purse, and finally found her wallet. She looked around for her waitress, who was deep in conversation with two young women on the other side of the café, by the coffee machine. Yael pulled out a ten-lira note and left it under the saucer. It was more than enough to cover the bill, with a generous tip.

Yael looked out the window once more. The beggar girl was still crawling back and forth along the sidewalk. A jazz trio—saxophonist, drummer, and double bass player—were setting up nearby.

Yael left the café and stepped into the hubbub, enjoying the buzz of the street. The sky was a deep, bright blue and the Mediterranean sunlight, softer than Manhattan's harsh glare, cast a golden tint on the buildings. A cool breeze blew down the avenue, bringing the smell of freshly roasted coffee. Three teenage Turkish schoolgirls in white blouses and blue skirts walked by eating ice cream, totally engrossed in their conversation. Two tall, thin African men, Sudanese or Ethiopian, Yael thought, stood in front of a computer showroom, pointing at various tablets and discussing their merits. A gaggle of Arabic women, each dressed from head to toe in a black abaya with a gold trim, sat on a nearby terrace, eating large sticky slabs of baklava. Yael had barely taken a few steps before she heard American and Australian English; Gulf and Levantine Arabic; French, German, and Hebrew. The workday had hardly started, but İstiklal's passeggiata was in full swing.

Amid the crowd, Yael did not notice a tall, bald man in a gray hooded sweatshirt step out of an apartment building doorway twenty-five yards to her right. He wore a Bluetooth earpiece in his right ear and followed her.

Yael walked across İstiklal toward the beggar girl to give her the twenty lira. She was still now, crouching in front of the household-goods shop. Black metal flowers studded with colored glass flowed in and out of each other's stems across the art nouveau façade. The girl was reflected in a large horizontal mirror on display in the window. A siren howled in the distance.

Two hundred and fifty yards away, the old-fashioned tram set off from the terminal at Tünel and began its steady trundle toward Taksim Square.

Ten yards to the left of the household-goods shop a short, fat man, wearing a brown leather jacket, stood in the entrance of a bookshop. He had a moustache like a black caterpillar and also wore a Bluetooth earpiece. He looked at the man in the gray sweatshirt, nodded, and watched Yael cross İstiklal. He touched his earpiece and started walking toward Yael.

The band started playing, a jazzy version of "Night and Day," the long clear notes of the tenor saxophone carrying over the bustle of the tourists.

Yael stopped after a few steps, smiling as a young woman in a loose white slip and baggy pink trousers began to dance in front of the group, her eyes closed as she swayed in time to the music. Yael suddenly remembered her dance with Najwa, the feel of Najwa's fingers entwined with hers. She had never believed herself to be interested in women. Just the touch of Eli's hand on her back still triggered a desire she had thought long dormant. Eli was a no-go, but Sami, despite his betrayals, was a much safer option. He was smarter and funnier, and he touched her in different ways. Or he would have, she guessed, if their dinner date had worked out. And then there was Yusuf. Tall, dark, handsome, enigmatic—and late. Or maybe she should just forget about men completely for now. Her dance with Najwa had left them both quite breathless, and not just from the exertion. What was that term she had read the other day . . . *bi-curious*.

Yael was so absorbed in her thoughts that she failed to pick up the first signals from her sixth sense. She bent down in front of the beggar girl, the twenty-lira note in her hand, her back to İstiklal Caddesi.

The tram slowly rattled down İstiklal, crowded with excited tourists, street kids hanging off the bumpers, its bell ringing merrily.

The bald man walked swiftly toward Yael from the right. The fat man with the moustache approached from the left. An ambulance appeared by the Tünel funicular station and drove down İstiklal, scattering tourists and pedestrians, siren wailing.

Yael dropped the banknote in the bowl.

"*Teşekkür ederim*, thank you," said the girl.

"Excuse me, miss," said the bald man.

Yael was still looking at the beggar girl when the bald man spoke. Yael glanced up, into the mirror of the household-goods shop, and all thoughts of Eli, Sami, and Najwa vanished.

She saw the bald man bending down toward her from her right side, a small blue aerosol can in his hand. The fat man with the moustache was almost at her left side. He wore brass knuckles on his right hand with a small pointed blade.

"Excuse me, miss," the bald man said again, pointing the can at Yael's face.

Yael's sixth sense was screaming now, sending alarm signals down both sides of her body. She had, she knew, a fraction of a second at the most.

She was vulnerable, already halfway to the ground, and outnumbered. There was no time to turn around and face her attackers—she could only use the mirror.

The ambulance was just a few yards away now.

The bald man slowly pressed down on the nozzle, a yard from Yael's face.

Just as the first puff of gas escaped, Yael yanked her hijab down from her forehead with her right hand and pulled it over her mouth. She turned her head sharply rightward, down into her shoulder away from the gas, holding her breath.

Still holding her head scarf over her mouth, she jammed her foot against the bald man's leg. She grabbed his sleeve with her left hand, using the momentum of his body weight to pull him toward her. He stumbled forward, unable to escape.

As Yael dropped back on her right foot, the fat man's fist flew toward her, a flash of skin and metal. She released her head scarf and blocked his hand with her right arm, simultaneously kicking out with her left leg at the tall man.

She aimed for the side of his knee, coughing. Most of the gas had dissipated but the fumes still caught in her throat, sapping her concentration. The move should have disabled him, but her foot slipped and hit his upper thigh instead. The blow was still enough to floor him. He collapsed onto the ground, grunting and swearing.

Yael jumped backward into a fighting stance, left leg forward, her hands up, now five yards away from the fat man.

The beggar girl scurried away to the corner of the doorway, crying in fear.

Yael's vision narrowed.

The fat man jumped forward, lunging at Yael and slashing his fist through the air, as though trying to slice her open from shoulder to hip.

Yael jumped back, her head dropped down, shoulders raised, her forearms in front of her neck to protect herself.

Each time the fat man stepped toward her, Yael leapt away and kicked out at his groin, again and again. But despite his bulk, the fat man was surprisingly agile and dodged her blows.

The ambulance stopped by the side of the shop with the art nouveau façade, its siren still howling.

Yael bumped into two elderly French tourists. They scurried away as fast as they could. Yael righted herself instantly but the collision gave the fat man a half-second advantage.

He jumped aside, wheeled around, and hit Yael's left shoulder with a left hook. The blow sent her reeling, shooting bolts of pain down her left side.

Yael staggered back. A crowd was forming around the fight. Several tourists were filming the scene on their smartphones. The tram had stopped a few yards away. A middle-aged Danish couple, oblivious to the chaos around them, were standing in front of the red and white wooden carriage, taking selfies. Two street urchins, boys around ten or eleven, wearing Arsenal soccer shirts, leapt off the tram and stood watching excitedly.

Yael barged past them and jumped onto the tram's metal step.

"Hey," said the Danish man, "you barged into my wife and now you are in my picture."

The fat man walked toward Yael.

She willed the carriage to move.

Nothing happened.

"I'm talking to you," said the Danish tourist, advancing on her. He was tall, nudging sixty, his blond hair now almost gray.

The fat man touched his earpiece. "Look over there," he said to Yael.

The tram began to pull away.

Yael did as he bade.

The bald man had one of the street kids by the neck, the blade of a knife in his hand.

The fat man reached into his pocket and scattered several leaflets around.

He walked up to the ambulance and opened the door, still wearing the pointed brass knuckles. The Danish tourist saw the blade, quickly grabbed his wife, and walked away as fast as they could.

The fat man turned to Yael. "Coming?"

Yael stepped off the tram as it gathered speed. "Let him go and I will."

Yael heard the fat man say something in Turkish.

The tall man looked up. He lifted his knife from the boy's neck. He sprinted away as fast as he could.

The ambulance door opened.

Yael looked inside.

A man sat on the ambulance gurney, pointing a gun at her with one hand.

"Get in," said Yusuf.

Clairborne sits at the café table, sipping a warm Coca-Cola, watching lines of Iraqi prisoners trudge toward the trucks taking them to the Kuwaiti border.

The air is thick, stinking of burning gasoline, so hot it is almost unbreathable. A long plume of black smoke rises over the horizon. The soldiers' fatigues are filthy, their faces exhausted, covered with grime.

A young woman walks up to the prisoners and spits on the ground. The Iraqis turn away in shame. Clairborne looks up as a slim man with a neatly trimmed beard walks over, greets him, and sits down.

S*obh bekheir*, good morning, Salim. Sorry I can't be there with you. How's the house?" asked Clairborne, peering at the computer monitor on his desk.

Salim Massoud was sitting at a Formica-covered table in a small, dark room, a tulip-shaped glass of tea in front of him.

"Sobh bekheir. Not as comfortable as Montreal. But we will manage."

"Good. How long has it been since we last met? Six, seven years?"

"Baghdad seven years ago, and Kabul five years," said Massoud.

Clairborne steepled his hands and rested his chin on his fingertips. It was three o'clock in the morning but he was wide awake and completely sober. He looked briefly at the photograph of his daughter on his desk, wondered what she was doing at midnight in San Francisco, forced himself to concentrate on his conversation.

He needed to focus. Without Salim Massoud there would be no Prometheus Group. Their relationship reached back more than thirty years. After the United States had pulled out of Vietnam, Clairborne had joined the CIA to train as a spy. His experience in the Phoenix program put him far ahead of the other recruits. He graduated from the Farm, the agency training school, at the top of his class and was sent to Tehran, undercover as the cultural attaché. Salim Massoud had been his liaison with SAVAK, the brutal Iranian secret police. Massoud penetrated the Islamic revolutionaries and passed on vital intelligence to Clairborne. In return Clairborne supplied Massoud with detailed satellite intelligence about the Iraqi military, which was preparing for war with Iran. Clairborne also opened a numbered Swiss bank account for Massoud where he made regular, substantial deposits.

In early 1979 Clairborne wrote a series of long, detailed reports to Langley, outlining what he had learned from Massoud: that the shah was doomed and would soon be replaced by Islamic fundamentalists. Cooperation and subtle support now for the revolutionaries would pay substantial dividends later when they took power. Clairborne, who had been present at the capture of the US embassy in Saigon four years earlier by the Vietcong, also recommended that the US embassy staff in Tehran be reduced to a bare minimum, including himself, with the rest evacuated immediately. All of Clairborne's reports and recommendations were ignored.

Just as Massoud had predicted, Ayatollah Khomeini returned to Tehran in February 1979. In April the revolution erupted and the Islamic Republic was declared. On November 4, revolutionaries attacked the US embassy, taking fifty-two Americans hostage. Clairborne had stayed away from work that day. He fled overland to Turkey, on a route mapped out for him by Massoud, his guilt about abandoning his colleagues competing with an even stronger sense of self-preservation.

Clairborne's connection to Massoud survived the embassy crisis. Despite all the Iranian denunciations of the "Great Satan," back-channel links between Tehran and Washington were soon reestablished. Massoud, like many of his colleagues, made a seamless switch from SAVAK to the new Ministry of Intelligence and National Security, known as VEVAK, which was even more brutal than its predecessor. In 1980, the year after the revolution, Iran went to war with Iraq. The conflict lasted eight years and cost hundreds of thousands of lives. Throughout that time Clairborne continued to supply Massoud with satellite intelligence. In exchange Massoud gave Clairborne information on the inner workings and vicious power struggles inside the Islamic regime.

The two men met again in Kuwait City during the first Gulf War, in 1991, when the United States had liberated Kuwait from Saddam's army. Massoud was in charge of VEVAK's covert liaison with the CIA, and the Iranians had been happy to help the Americans and their Arab allies strike a blow against their greatest enemy. Since then Clairborne and Massoud had remained in contact, continuing to exchange information. A decade later, on September 12, 2001, Massoud reached out to Clairborne with an offer. Iran would help depose the Taliban in Afghanistan, in exchange for a resumption of diplomatic relations. Clairborne's recommendation, that Massoud's offer be seriously considered, was ignored. The following month, weary of the bureaucratic infighting that had helped open his homeland to attack in the first place, Clairborne left the CIA and set up the Prometheus Group.

"Just three days to go, my old friend," said Clairborne. Three days until Thursday, the start of the process that would lead to the rapture, a thought he did not articulate.

"Please update me as to where we are," said Massoud.

"Pabst came to see me on Saturday morning. The plan worked perfectly, just as you said."

Massoud smiled with pleasure. "What did he do?"

"Played on our shared history, then made a crude attempt at blackmail with a threat to go to the press with what he thinks he knows."

"Which is?"

"Just what we loaded onto Jones's mobile phone. Architectural details of the Osman Convention Center, the first and second wave of suicide bombers, timings, response protocols of the Turkish security forces—it's all there, leading back to Prometheus. They had to work hard to get it, so they believe it."

"So you are sure that he has no idea of the actual plan?"

Clairborne nodded. "Sure as a cat can climb up a tree."

"However, he could still go public with what he has. Clarence, I know this man is an old comrade of yours, but—"

"Don't worry, Salim. He won't. Not yet. He and the girl will want more details, to find out what's going on at the Turkish end, how it's all been put together. They will keep digging for something that does not exist. Everything is under control."

September 11, 2001, had been good for business. Clairborne had used his network of contacts across the US military and intelligence services to make the Prometheus

Group the gateway to Kabul. Any American or foreign corporation wishing to supply services to the US government in Afghanistan, local governments, or even the legion of charities and nongovernmental organizations operating there, had to go through Prometheus. The firm's clients included banks, corporations, oil and energy companies, and, of course, private military contractors. From Kabul to K Street, the equation was clear: the greater the chaos, the greater the profits. The Iraq War had brought the greatest rewards. When the Bush administration needed "evidence" of weapons of mass destruction to make the case for invading, Prometheus had helped provide—or manufacture—it. The hard part had been Clairborne's years of work building up his network of contacts. Once in place, it was simple to use. A leak to a friendly European intelligence service that was soon rippling over the Atlantic; a quiet dinner in Georgetown with an influential journalist; a few carefully doctored intelligence reports; subtle nudges, nods, and winks at Langley and the Pentagon, and hey presto, shock and awe over Baghdad.

Prometheus's turnover quickly reached seven figures a year, then eight and nine. The more Americans—and Iraqis and Afghans—that died, the more demand there was for the United States to prop up the shaky local bureaucracies, train their militaries and police forces, and supply the darker services needed to deal with the myriad of domestic militias and terrorist groups.

Within a few months, the Iraqi bonanza far outstripped that to be earned in Kabul. It was then that Clairborne crossed the line, one he had pledged to himself that he would never breach. Forewarned by Massoud of a terrorist attack on the UN complex in Baghdad—the same headquarters that Joe-Don demanded be properly secured, to no avail—Clairborne had kept quiet. Twenty-two UN staffers died.

The Prometheus Group's takings soared even higher. Salim Massoud knew about the attack on the UN complex because he had helped organize it. By then Massoud was in charge of the Iranian military campaign in Iraq, providing arms, logistics, and training for the Shia fighters battling their Sunni enemies. After the Baghdad bombing it was a comparatively small step for Clairborne to suggest American and Western targets for Massoud's militia. Each outrage brought more contracts for Prometheus's clients and more profits for the firm. Massoud had encouraged taking this course of action to its logical conclusion. He had proposed that Prometheus set up a special black-operations unit to carry out joint attacks with Iranian Shia militants against US forces and installations in Iraq and Afghanistan. Even Clairborne had balked at this—in part because it would give Massoud unwelcome leverage over him.

But Massoud's proposal had planted a dark seed in Clairborne's mind. Meanwhile, Clairborne's payments to Massoud's private account at Bank Bernard et Fils, and the one in the name of Nuristan Holdings, had made Massoud a very rich man.

"*Kheili khoob,* very good. Clarence . . . ," said Massoud, his voice suddenly hesitant. "Is there any news . . . ?"

Clairborne shook his head. "I'm working on it, Salim, doing my best. I have lines out everywhere. But still nothing so far."

Massoud's face briefly twisted. "Clarence, isn't there anything? Anything at all? With all your connections, there must be a way to find out."

Clairborne looked somber. "I'm sorry, Salim. Since Snowden everything's locked down tighter than a nun's—" He quickly stopped himself. "There are new government agencies, so deep and so dark, even I have never heard of them. But I'm on the case, and once I hear anything, which should be soon, I will let you know."

"And the girl?"

"The operation is under way, even as we speak."

"Thank you, Clarence," said Massoud.

Clairborne bade Massoud good-bye and closed the screen.

He pressed a series of keys. A new window opened on the monitor. It showed Farzad Massoud sitting on a bed in a gray-walled cell, staring blankly into space.

22

Yael blinked several times trying to open her sticky, gritty eyes. Her mouth tasted sour and metallic. Her throat was so dry it felt as if it had been vacuum cleaned.

She looked around, her head heavy, her movements slow. The light-green walls wobbled and shook, and a wave of nausea rose inside her. She breathed deeply until the room stilled and her stomach calmed. She was lying on a gray blanket, her right wrist handcuffed to a narrow metal bed. The room was about twelve feet square. The ceiling was a grubby off-white, and the floor was covered with cracked red linoleum. There were no windows, but an air conditioner hummed quietly in the background. The air smelled musty, but pleasant, of old books and paper. The door was closed.

Yael tried to sit up. The room began to spin again. Her limbs would not respond properly to her brain's commands. She flopped back down again, more enraged at her weakness than at Yusuf's betrayal.

She looked up when the door opened.

Yusuf walked over to her. He placed a brown paper bag at the end of the bed and took Yael's arm to help her sit up.

Yael pushed his hand away and forced herself upright. The room shook. She closed her eyes before she spoke. "Don't touch me, *orospu çocuğu*, son of a bitch." Her voice was raspy.

Yusuf looked shocked. "Where did you learn such bad words?"

Yael raised her left arm to punch Yusuf. He easily batted away her feeble blow.

"In another life," said Yael. She glared at him, her eyes full of fury. "The one where I trusted you."

"You can still trust me, Yael. I saved your life."

"It doesn't feel like it. It feels like you have kidnapped me. What's next? A little trip over the Syrian border to your jihadi friends, like Cyrus Jones got?"

Yusuf unlocked the handcuff attaching her wrist to the bedframe. "That was your idea. Which makes them your jihadi friends as well."

Yael did not reply. She rubbed her wrist where the handcuff had chafed the skin.

Yusuf continued speaking. "You are quite free to leave. But I don't recommend it."

Yael slowly moved her hands, her arms, her legs, and her feet. Everything still worked. Her left shoulder ached from the roundhouse punch she had taken. But her right shoulder was even more stiff and sore. She touched the skin where it met her neck. It felt tender, as if bruised deep under the skin.

"You shot me. *Piç*, bastard."

Yusuf laughed. "Your Turkish is really improving."

Yael took a deep breath, gathered her strength, and tried

to hit Yusuf. He caught her right hand and placed it on the bed. He passed her a large green bottle of mineral water.

"Enough. Drink. You are weak and dehydrated from the knockout dart."

Yael opened the bottle, smelled it, then took a tentative sip.

Yusuf smiled. "If I wanted to poison you, I would have."

Yael drank the water in long, steady gulps. Once she had finished, she held the bottle in her hand. She glanced at the metal bed stand with its sharp edges, at the glass bottle, and then at Yusuf.

As though reading her mind, Yusuf reached over and took the bottle from her hand. He reached for the brown paper bag and took out a carton of ayran. He passed it to Yael. "Drink this too; it will settle your stomach. But slowly."

Yael did as he said and felt her strength begin to return. Whether or not she was in danger, she still needed to eat and drink. For the moment at least, she was in no condition to try and overcome Yusuf and make a break for it. More importantly, her sixth sense told her that despite appearances, she was in no danger. His body language was relaxed and confident; his concern for her seemed genuine.

"How long have I been here? And how did I get here?"

"I kidnapped you," said Yusuf. "Or, better to say, I stopped you from being kidnapped. My boss ordered me to arrange your abduction, which was to be blamed on the Kurds. Everything that goes wrong in Turkey is the fault of the Kurds. Or the Jews. So I did as instructed—I didn't know about the knife, by the way; that was a late addition, or I would have changed the plan. You did very well," he said admiringly. Yusuf looked at his watch. "I should have handed you over about five hours ago."

"To who?" demanded Yael.

"To my boss. And he would have handed you on."

"Where? And what happened to the other guys?"

"I will explain. It's five o'clock in the afternoon. Time for the news."

Yusuf took his mobile telephone from his pocket, swiped through the menu, and pressed the screen. He handed it to Yael. It showed Al Jazeera's New York studio. The anchor, a portly Pakistani man, was interviewing Najwa.

Najwa was standing on İstiklal Caddesi, outside the household-goods shop. Najwa was a fast worker, thought Yael, impressed. She must have gone straight to İstiklal after the UN airplane landed at Istanbul airport.

"Who are Yael Azoulay and Julia Albihari, Najwa? And what are they doing in Turkey?" asked the anchor.

"Riz, they are the same person. Yael Azoulay works for the United Nations, often undercover, as a covert negotiator. It seems she was traveling on a false passport. The Turkish authorities very much want to talk to her about that."

Two photographs flashed up on the screen: one of Yael how she usually looked, and another of her with her dyed black hair, wearing her head scarf.

"Where is she now?"

"We don't know. She was last seen around ten thirty this morning, fighting two men here, on Istanbul's main shopping street. It seems they were attempting to kidnap her. Then she suddenly surrendered and got into an ambulance."

"Who was trying to kidnap her?"

"Well, Riz, the Turkish authorities blame an organization called the Kurdish People's Liberation Army. Turkish officials are saying that KPLA leaflets, claiming responsibility for the most recent bombings, were found here this morning. You can imagine how tight security is now for the upcoming Istanbul Summit. The whole city is going into lockdown mode. The merest hint of trouble, let alone any alleged terrorist activity, will bring down the wrath of the police and the security services."

"What do the Kurds say?"

"What they have been saying for weeks, which is that they had nothing to do with the bombs in Sultanahmet, and now that they had nothing to do with the kidnapping of Yael Azoulay. In fact she may not even have been abducted. Some sources are saying that the whole thing was staged. The two men with whom she was seen fighting were found this afternoon. They had been shot with a knockout dart and dumped under the Galata Bridge. They are now recovering in the hospital and police are waiting to question them."

Riz frowned. "It's all very mysterious. If Yael Azoulay works for the UN, doesn't she have immunity? She could just take the next plane home, and with her the truth about what happened today on İstiklal Caddesi."

Najwa shook her head. "Not anymore. Interpol has just issued a warrant for her arrest on two charges of murder, for the death of Rwandan warlord Jean-Pierre Hakizimani and American Bradley DeWayne. Both men were killed last October. Hakizimani was found dead in New York, and DeWayne was drowned in Lake Geneva."

Riz nodded slowly. "Tell us more, Najwa."

"Jean-Pierre Hakizimani was wanted by the International Tribunal for his role in the Rwanda genocide. He had been on the run for almost twenty years but, rumor has it, came to New York to broker a peace deal in Congo with the knowledge and blessing of the UN. And we have some intriguing footage of his last visitor, Riz."

The screen showed the now-familiar CCTV footage of Yael dressed in the raincoat, showing a fake ID to the two security guards outside Hakizimani's door.

"Is that Yael Azoulay?" asked Riz.

"Yes, it is. She is posing as an escort in the name of Sharon Mantello. The next thing we know Jean-Pierre Hakizimani is found dead on the floor, dressed only in a white hotel bathrobe, and Ms. Azoulay—or Mantello—has vanished."

"Intriguing stuff. Tell us about Bradley DeWayne, Najwa."

"DeWayne may not be his real name. All we know is that he was American. It seems he tried to kill Yael, but she ended up drowning him in Lake Geneva, just a few days after the death of Hakizimani. Caroline Masters, the acting secretary-general, has said through her spokeswoman that all of Yael Azoulay's immunities and privileges have been revoked. The UN leadership urges her to turn herself in to the Turkish authorities."

Yael laughed and put the phone down on the bed. She held her hands up to Yusuf. "Here I am. I surrender to the Turkish authorities."

"I accept. Come," he said, offering Yael his arm.

This time she took it. They walked through into the next room. Yael looked around. It was double the size of the other space. Three walls were lined from floor to ceiling with books, their dark leather bindings split and torn, the letters on their spines faded. Six old-fashioned wooden filing cabinets stood in front of the fourth wall, each secured by a heavy brass lock.

A single wooden desk stood in the center, its varnish chipped and worn. Every square inch of the desktop was covered with more books, towering unsteadily, many coated with dust. Yael picked up a book from the top of the tallest pile.

She turned to Yusuf. "May I?"

He nodded.

Yael carefully opened the thick black cover. The frontispiece, she saw, recorded that the book had been printed in Salonika, now Thessaloniki, in Greece, in 1898. The paper was thin, turned yellow with age. She suddenly felt a powerful presence in the room, of generations of the books' owners, watching her to make sure she took care of their legacy.

The book seemed to be a Jewish liturgy, written in Hebrew. Yael began to read, puzzled at first, as the letters did not form words that made sense. And then she realized that she was reading Judeo-Spanish; the words were medieval Spanish, transcribed in Hebrew script. The language was also known as Ladino. The language of her ancestors who boarded the boat from Grenada and sailed to the Ottoman Empire. The language still spoken today by the scattered descendants of Sephardic Jewry.

The hair stood up on her arms.

Yael stared at Yusuf, her eyes wide open. "Where are we?"

Good evening, Mr. Utley. President Freshwater is expecting me," said Isis Franklin as she walked toward the Air Force One conference room.

Aldrich Utley, the presidential chief of staff, stepped out in front of her, his pale blue eyes instantly assessing her like the maître d' of a Michelin-starred restaurant judging a questionably dressed diner. "The president is busy preparing for the Istanbul Summit. And she is likely to be for some time." His Boston Brahmin accent was so dry he sounded almost English. Utley gestured down the airplane cabin. "We have a full kitchen service, Ms. Franklin. They can make you whatever you would like. I recommend the rib of beef. Why don't you get some dinner, have a glass of wine? I will speak to the president and see if she might have a few minutes for you later."

President Freshwater's chief of staff did not hide his unease at Isis Franklin's presence on the presidential airplane. Franklin was neither a White House official nor an elected officeholder, which meant he could not control her, and control was very important to Aldrich Utley.

A tall man in his early sixties, Utley wore a cream-colored linen-cotton blend suit and handmade British shoes. He had thick, swept-back silver hair of which he was immensely proud and an imperial manner that had been hard-wired into him by centuries of good breeding passed down by ancestors who had landed in North America a hundred years before the United States came into existence.

His predecessor, a former State Department colleague of President Freshwater's, had been sacked three months earlier after failing to prevent a series of bipartisan filibusters wrecking Freshwater's attempts to rein in private security contractors in the military and intelligence services. Utley was nominally a Democrat, but one so far on the right of the party many believed him to be a Republican mole. His appointment had caused consternation across Freshwater's administration. But so far, Utley had lived up to his reputation as Washington, DC's best-dressed political bruiser. Restless senators and House representatives were steadily being brought back into line, and he was steadily building support for Freshwater's next campaign on the issue.

Utley knew all about Isis Franklin. She and Renee Freshwater had known each other for more than twenty years, since Freshwater was a junior official on the State Department's Rwanda desk during the genocide, writing memos calling for intervention that nobody read. The two women had stayed in touch through the years, sometimes closely and at others not for months on end. Their common bond now was the United Nations. Isis Franklin worked at the US mission while Renee Freshwater had served as US ambassador to the UN. From there Freshwater had been appointed secretary of state, her stepping-stone to the presidency. Utley did not like the United Nations. He could not understand why the United States spent millions of dollars of taxpayers' money funding a rolling hate-fest against America and the West in the heart of Manhattan and gave its members diplomatic immunity. Nor could he understand what Isis

Franklin was doing on this airplane. She was not part of the official delegation for the summit.

Isis stood her ground. Two small sprouts of silver hair poked out of each of Utley's nostrils, she noticed. "Mr. Utley, I have been cleared by the Secret Service to travel on this airplane and I am doing so at the president's personal request. So I would be grateful if you would step aside and let me through."

They both knew that Isis had the advantage. The White House, with its endless locked doors, security codes, biometric access, Secret Service agents, legions of flunkies and presidential gatekeepers, was Utley's kingdom. But onboard Air Force One, at thirty-five thousand feet somewhere over the Atlantic Ocean, there was nowhere else for Isis to go other than another part of the airplane. And she could wander back whenever she liked.

Utley was about to refuse, just to make a point, when President Freshwater's voice sounded from the conference room. "Aldrich, it's fine. Let her in."

He reluctantly stood aside to let Isis walk into the conference room. A long table of polished wood ran down the middle, flanked on both sides by rows of beige leather executive chairs. Two bowls of fresh flowers stood in the center of the table, together with jugs of fresh orange juice, a flask of coffee, and bottles of mineral water. The area had been partitioned off from the rest of the airplane by artificial walls and soundproofed, the hum of the engines just a distant background noise. Television screens on the rear walls showed all the US domestic networks, CNN's American and international channels, the BBC, and Al Jazeera's United States channel.

President Freshwater sat at the center of the table, her papers in front of her, next to a satellite telephone console and airplane intercom. The most powerful woman in the world was striking, in her early fifties, with a full mouth and strong chin. Her sharp cheekbones, sleek, shoulder-length black hair—now pulled back in a ponytail—and dark eyes were a gift from her Native American forbearers. She was dressed in jeans, loafers, and a white shirt. She wore no jewelry except for her wedding ring and two plain silver earrings.

The president stood and walked over to Isis, and the two women greeted each other with a kiss on the cheek. She gestured for Isis to sit next to her and picked up the thick document on top of the pile of papers on the desk.

"Look at this." She rifled through the sheets. "In four days we are going to fix Syria, Egypt, Israel, and Palestine. I make that a day for each. Bilaterals, trilaterals, multilaterals, plenaries, backgrounds, statements of intent, position, plans, projections. The most ambitious diplomatic summit in the twenty-first century. In all of history, I would say," she said, laughing. She reached for the next document, filled with lines of type. "And this is my schedule, just for tomorrow, before the conference even starts. I'm sorry, I'm so rude, Isis, unloading on you like this. Coffee or something stronger?"

"It's fine. I'm glad you could make some time for me. I'll have whatever you are having. So why are you going if the summit is not going to work?" asked Isis.

Freshwater leaned forward and pressed a button on her telephone console. "Henry, can you please bring us two of your gin and tonics. Tanqueray, but not too strong. With a slice of cucumber."

"Yes, ma'am," replied a tinny voice. "Coming right up."

Freshwater put her schedule down on top of the papers. She looked at Isis. "To answer your question, I'm going because all the P5 presidents and prime ministers, plus everyone else that counts, will be there. Who knows what might come of it. It can't be worse than being in DC. Diplomacy is like that. Nothing happens for months or years, then all of a sudden the pieces look like they are falling into place. We can thank the Islamic Caliphate of Greater Syria, I guess. That and the prospect of even more millions of Syrian refugees pouring out of what remains of the country. Suddenly it's in everyone's interest to sort out the Middle East. Frankly, I don't think peace and stability will suddenly break out this weekend. But as Winston Churchill said, jaw-jaw is better than war-war. And if not, then at least I get to see Istanbul in the spring," she said, smiling.

A light cough interrupted her. The two women looked around. A thin man with red hair and pale skin stood at the entrance to the conference room, holding a silver tray with two glasses.

President Freshwater nodded. "Thank you, Henry." She turned to Isis. "Henry makes the best gin and tonic you have ever tasted."

"Thank you, ma'am. But there's not much competition at thirty-five thousand feet," said Henry, as he handed the two women their drinks.

"Even if there was, you would still beat it," said Freshwater.

Henry smiled with pleasure. "Thank you, ma'am," he said as he left.

Freshwater raised her drink to Isis and the two women clinked glasses. Freshwater took a sip of her cocktail. "Eric used to make these for us." She smiled wanly. "He was a hopeless barman. It was either too strong or too weak and never enough ice. What I wouldn't give for one of his drinks now, though."

"You must miss him so much. How long has it been?"

"Ten months." President Freshwater looked down into her drink, swirling the ice cubes. "It's been really tough on the kids. They put a brave face on, but they're teenagers. A fourteen-year-old boy and a twelve-year-old girl need their dad."

"I know, I'm so sorry. What's up with the investigation? I read a story in the *Times* that they thought his ski bindings might have been tampered with."

Freshwater exhaled, sat back, and put her feet up on the conference table. "When you are president of the United States, you think you are the most powerful person in the free world, and certainly in the United States. You think that if you want something to happen it will. Especially when it's an investigation into how your husband died. But it doesn't happen. Or rather, it does, but it doesn't get anywhere. It gets stuck in the quagmire between the Secret Service, the FBI, the cops in Aspen, the local coroner, the National Security Agency, the CIA looking for possible international connections, and at least one other organization I am not supposed to talk about. All of whom hate each other's guts and are far more interested in fighting turf wars and empire building than finding out why my husband hit a tree at fifty miles an hour." Freshwater took out the slice of cucumber from her drink and chewed it thoughtfully. "You know what they call me? At first it was just inside the Beltway. But it's caught on quick."

Isis said, "It's not true."

Freshwater turned to Isis, her face suddenly full of anguish. "A woman wrote to me after Congress sabotaged the Syria intervention plan, after Assad gassed all those people. She was eighty-eight years old. It was a short letter. I remember every word. 'Dear Madam President, please don't go to any more Holocaust memorial events and say "never again," when you let it happen again. Yours sincerely, Sadie Greenberg. Auschwitz inmate 28765.' Maybe I am dead in the water." Freshwater turned her wedding wing, a plain white-gold band, around on her finger. "God, I miss him."

Isis looked at her. "You are the first female president of the United States. You will go down in history."

Freshwater sipped her drink. "Thanks. Speaking of which," she said, her voice businesslike now, "I received your memo about the drone strike in Kandahar."

"And?"

Freshwater shook her head. "Isis, I can't bring criminal charges against the commander of that operation."

"Why not? A crime was committed."

"It was not a crime. It was a tragic accident. There was no intent to kill civilians."

Isis put her glass down. "That Hellfire missile didn't hit the car by accident. It was guided every step of the way from a control room under the command of the US military, whose commander in chief you are. A child was killed.

A two-year-old boy. There was nothing left for his family to bury."

"I know, Isis, and I am so sorry. But I have seen the internal report. The strike was based on faulty intelligence. This is a war. These things happen, unfortunately."

"Can I see that report?"

Freshwater shook her head.

"What about the Black File—the records of all the drone strikes?"

"If—*if*—such a file existed, it would only be available to those with the highest level of security clearance."

Isis reached into her purse and pulled out a sheet of paper. "Can I read you something?"

Freshwater shrugged. "Sure."

"The United States has a clear moral duty to intervene in Rwanda. If our commitment to human rights means anything, we need to take action. Many thousands of people are being slaughtered every day, most of them by hand. Comparisons with the debacle in Somalia are inaccurate. The 101st Airborne Division could swiftly deal with the genocidaires, most of whom are armed with nothing more than machetes, in a few days if not a few hours. . . ." Isis looked at Freshwater. "Shall I continue?"

"No need. I remember what I wrote."

"A clear moral duty. Don't we have a clear moral duty in Afghanistan? People died because of our negligence. They should be called to account."

Freshwater frowned. "Isis, why are you so excited about this case? It's awful, horrible, but it was an *accident*. There is no way I can bring charges of criminal negligence. Everyone involved has to live with the consequences. That's punishment enough."

"Yes, it is," said Isis, a faraway look in her eyes.

Freshwater smiled. "Hey, come on, cheer up. Now tell me all the gossip at the State Department and the UN mission. And what's up with Fareed? Did you see the piece in the *New York Times* this morning about Srebrenica? That was pretty shocking, even by UN standards."

The two women talked for another few minutes, until Utley appeared at the entrance, a stern look on his face. Freshwater turned to Isis. "Duty calls," she said apologetically. "But hold on a moment." She pressed a button on the telephone console on her desk. "Henry?"

"Yes, ma'am? Another round?"

"No thanks, not tonight. Can you bring you-know-what for Isis?"

"Yes, ma'am."

Utley walked away and Henry appeared a few seconds later, holding a new black flying jacket on a wooden hanger. It was made of heavy nylon, with a padded lining. The Air Force One logo was emblazoned on the top left-hand corner. He handed the jacket to Isis.

Her eyes opened wide with pleasure. "Thank you, Renee. Thanks so much."

"Try it on," said Freshwater. "Everyone who flies on Air Force One gets one."

The jacket fit Isis perfectly. She turned around, trying to catch her reflection in the window of the cabin.

Henry left and Utley reappeared. He glanced at Isis as if to say, *Are you still here?*

"On my way out now, Mr. Utley," said Isis. "Just one last thing."

She picked up her purse, took out her iPhone, and stood next to President Freshwater, behind the pile of papers on the conference table. Isis handed the telephone to Utley. "A photo please. It's not every day that a girl gets to travel with the president on Air Force One. Just press the button on the screen."

Utley took the photograph. He handed the telephone back to Isis. She checked the photograph and handed the telephone back to him.

"Just one more, please. Then I promise I'm out of here."

Isis stood next to President Freshwater, ushering her closer to the table edge.

Utley accepted the telephone and took three more shots. "That should do it," he said as he gave the phone back to Isis. "And now, if you don't mind . . ."

Isis and President Freshwater kissed each other on the cheek. The president stood up as Isis left. "Enjoy your jacket—and Istanbul. I'll see you somewhere soon."

"You got it," said Isis as she left.

23

Yael followed Yusuf up a steep, narrow path of in-
terlocking gray paving stones, happy to be out
in the fresh air, feeling her limbs move and her muscles
stretch. The breeze was fresh and cool, light with the
smell of the sea. The sun blazed red against a purple sky
and the tombs and headstones glowed in the soft light of
dusk. The sound of the muezzin calling the faithful to
Akşam, the evening prayer, flowed through the trees and
over the graves. "*Allāhu Akbar*, God is great," the muezzin intoned four times, his rich baritone seeming to echo
not just across the streets and down the city's hills, but
through the centuries. "*Ash-hadu an-lā ilāha illā alla*, I
bear witness that there is no god but God."

Yusuf took Yael's arm as the path rose steadily through
two rows of trees. The walkways were swept clean. No
weeds sprouted in the cracks between the paving stones.
The graves were raised, framed by walls of gray marble
a foot or so above the ground, covered with a layer of
earth from which plants, bushes, and flowers sprouted.
Yael and Yusuf walked for another hundred yards, higher
and higher, until they reached a small, raised plaza in a

far reach of the cemetery. A rusty park bench stood at the edge, its green paint peeling. The flagstones were larger and older here, their edges chipped, and the gravestones weather beaten.

Yael sat down gratefully, slightly out of breath. She had slept for another two hours, and drunk more water than ever before in her life, to flush the toxins out of her system. She felt almost back to normal, although her left shoulder throbbed, the right side of her neck ached, and she was still not completely steady on her feet.

Yusuf passed her another carton of ayran and a banana.

"Thanks. No pide today?" she asked, remembering the delicious, greasy Turkish version of pizza Yusuf had bought for her on the island of Büyükada. It was just a few weeks ago, but it already felt like a scene from another life.

Yusuf shook his head. "Tomorrow. When your stomach is settled."

She drank half the ayran, relishing its sour tang. "Will I be here tomorrow?"

"I think so. Unless you plan to escape."

Yael looked around, remembering Najwa's report. She was wanted by Interpol and the Turkish authorities. She had been stripped of her immunity. Yusuf's boss had tried to kidnap her. But she felt oddly calm. The cemetery was a profoundly peaceful place. The muezzin's chant faded away, and the birds chirped merrily, happy to have no more competition. A canopy of trees reached overhead, their branches twisting into each other. She watched a squirrel scamper up a tree. No, she didn't feel like running anywhere.

A memory flashed into her mind, of the last time she sat on a park bench, in Dag Hammarskjöld plaza, waiting for Quentin Braithwaite. Was that really just four days ago—last Thursday? Yael began to sort through the events of the last few days, hoping that the chronology might bring some kind of clarity.

She glanced at her watch. It was now almost eight o'clock on Monday evening. Exactly a week ago, she was sitting on the train from DC to New York after her confrontation with Clarence Clairborne. The next day she had made dinner for Sami and been exposed on Al Jazeera. On Wednesday she had met Caroline Masters, been demoted to the Trusteeship Council, and fought for her life on the Staten Island Ferry. She'd met Quentin Braithwaite on Dag Hammarskjöld on Thursday and on Friday night she had danced with Najwa, met Eli Harrari, and stolen a DVD from Sami. She had flown to Turkey on Saturday, lost a day to the time difference, and been attacked and rescued this morning. A busy week, she thought, smiling to herself. But where was Braithwaite? The summit was due to start in three days and the P5 presidents were already on their way. More to the point, where was Joe-Don? She had called, sent text and e-mail messages, but no reply. This had never happened before and it made her very uneasy.

Yael peeled her banana and took a bite. "Now please tell me where we are."

"In Üsküdar, on the Asian side. This is the Bülbüldere, the Nightingale cemetery."

Yael frowned. "Cemetery for who? There are pictures

on the graves, so it's not a Muslim one. There are no crosses so it's not Christian. I can't see any Stars of David, but you have a room full of books in Ladino."

Yusuf took out a brown paper bag of pistachio nuts from his jacket pocket. He offered the bag to Yael. She shook her head. "In 1666 a Jewish man was born in Salonika. He was a famous Kabbalist, an expert in Jewish mysticism," he said as he cracked a shell and took out the nut. "This man said he was the Messiah."

Distant memories of school history lessons stirred in Yael's mind. "And was he?"

"His followers thought so," replied Yusuf, his voice wry. "They still do."

"Shabbetai Zevi," said Yael as the story came back to her.

"You have heard of him?"

"Of course. We studied him at school, in Israel. Thousands of people believed in him, gave up everything to follow him. Shabbetai was causing a lot of trouble, disrupting the empire. The sultan summoned him to Istanbul to explain himself. The sultan gave him a choice: Islam or the axe. He converted."

Yusuf took out another pistachio nut and held it between two fingers, examining it. "Shabbetai Zevi *said* he converted to Islam. So did many of his followers. But they didn't. They still kept Jewish rituals, like the Marranos, the Jews in Spain who pretended to convert to Catholicism. After a while Shabbetai's followers invented a new kind of religion, mixing Judaism, Islam, Sufism—they called it Sabbateanism. They kept their liturgy secret. Very secret. They had their own mosques, schools, communities across the Balkans and the Ottoman Empire. They only married within their community, but they kept very detailed records of every birth, death, and marriage. They were very careful to keep the bloodlines separate."

"Is that what those books and ledgers are, in the basement, records of births and deaths?"

Yusuf nodded. "That's about all that's left, those books, a few dozen families in Istanbul and İzmir, and this cemetery." He continued to talk, staring ahead. "We helped build this country, modernized it. We brought commerce, education, industry, newspapers. But we were never accepted. The Jews thought we were Muslims. The Muslims thought we were Jews. They called us 'ships with two rudders' or Dönme. It means turncoats. We call ourselves Ma'aminim, believers."

Yael looked at Yusuf. "What do you believe in, Yusuf?"

Yusuf was silent for several seconds. "Come," he said, standing up. "I want to show you something."

Yusuf walked with Yael across the small plaza to a large grave, about fifteen feet by fifteen feet. It was two feet high, contained within four gray marble walls. Each wall was topped by a flat marble shelf about a foot wide. The center was filled with earth, from which half a dozen well-tended rosebushes grew. There were nine names on the large, flat, marble headstones, engraved in plain lettering, with a small photograph set into the tombstone next to each. All the names ended in "Çelmiz."

"Parents, grandparents. All here," said Yusuf, a sad smile

on his face. He pointed to a circular black-and-white photograph in the center of the headstone. The picture showed a proud, upright man, dressed in an old-fashioned high collar, wearing a fez. Faded letters spelled out "Yakup Çelmiz D: 1920 O: 1997." "My grandfather. He was three years old when they arrived from Salonika in 1923 in the great population exchanges, when the Turks were expelled from Greece and vice-versa."

Yael bent down and touched a photograph of a young woman on the headstone. She was pretty, with long curly hair. The lettering said "Rahel Çelmiz D: 1986 O: 2012."

Yael looked at Yusuf. "My wife," he said, brushing some earth from the marble shelf around the grave. "Killed in a car crash. She was twenty-six."

Yusuf's sadness was almost tangible. "I'm so sorry," Yael said.

"So am I. She was three months pregnant," he replied. Yusuf stared at the grave for several moments, lost in memories, then brought himself back. "I have some more news for you. It's not good."

Yael looked at him, waiting.

"Your colleagues Quentin Braithwaite and Joe-Don Pabst. They were arrested at JFK airport this morning, just before they boarded their plane to Istanbul."

P ut that down and stop admiring yourself," said Sami as he sat next to Najwa.

Najwa was staring at her mobile telephone, watching the video of herself reporting from İstiklal Caddesi. She ignored Sami and played the clip again. She shook her head, frowning, as her tinny voice came out of the tiny speaker. "I'm not happy," said Najwa.

"Why not? It's a great story. You were the first one there. You beat CNN and the BBC."

The two journalists were sitting on a backless leather couch in a quiet corner of the Osman Convention Center foyer. The center, two hundred yards from the Grand Bazaar, was a brand new addition to the historic quarter of Bayezid. Built in the shape of a crescent, on the grounds of Istanbul University, it overlooked the main faculty building. The hypermodern edifice—a glass-fronted smart building with biometric security and a self-regulating air-conditioning, heating, and humidity system—was completely out of character with its surroundings.

The foyer was crowded with government officials, diplomats, and journalists rushing hither and thither, their credentials swinging from colored lanyards, and jabbering into their mobile telephones. The security was intense: concrete barricades manned by Turkish police commandos had been erected all around the building to prevent car bombs. Every visitor had to present two forms of photographic identity, pass through a scatter X-ray machine similar to those used at US airports, be frisked, and answer a series of questions from unsmiling security guards supplied by the Prometheus Group and the Turkish police. Tall, well-built men in suits with wires leading from their ears patrolled back and forth, muttering into their lapels.

The reporters were heading to the state-of-the-art

pressroom that had been set up in one wing of the building. Sponsored by the KZX Corporation, it boasted free,
superfast Wi-Fi, translating and interpreting services,
hundreds of computer terminals and printers, and nonstop
complimentary soft drinks, snacks, and meals served by
attractive, multilingual young hostesses. Reinhardt Daintner's plan, approved by the organizers, was to provide
everything for the press corps so that there was no need for
them to ever leave the building. It seemed to be working.
By now, Monday evening, the press center was packed.
Journalists had arrived from all over the world in time for
the start of the summit on Thursday morning, together
with a legion of local Turkish reporters and freelancers,
known as stringers, who worked for the major foreign
news outlets. Whether full-timers or freelancers, all the
journalists were gossiping, trading information, and trying to eavesdrop on each other. Which was why Sami and
Najwa, once they had been accredited, had not set foot
inside the press center.

Najwa put her phone down. "I'm not worried about my
story." She turned to Sami, reached for something in her
pocket, deftly gathered her thick black hair in her hands,
slipped it into a hairband, and made a ponytail. "I think I
look better like this than having my hair loose." She turned
her head from side to side, her ponytail swinging. "It's much
more professional, don't you think?"

"Absolutely," said Sami, laughing. "It will make all the
difference."

A pair of thick plastic folders lay on the leather bench
next to Najwa, their covers emblazoned with the Turkish

flag and the emblem of the United Nations. She handed one to Sami. "I picked up your press pack. Your complete guide to the Istanbul Summit and world peace that will break out by the end of the week."

Sami thanked Najwa and flicked through the folder. It was jammed with schedules and timetables, thick background briefing papers on the three crises—Syria, Egypt, and Israel-Palestine—biographies of the presidents and prime ministers in attendance, a list of useful telephone numbers, including local hotels and restaurants offering a 50 percent discount for accredited journalists.

Sami pulled out a credit card–sized piece of plastic from the folder pocket, which was branded with the logo of the Sultannet mobile telephone network. He snapped out the SIM card at one end and held it between his thumb and forefinger. "Look at that. Eighty-four hours of free unlimited calls, including international, and unlimited data usage. That's worth hundreds of dollars."

Najwa reached for the SIM card and took it from Sami's fingers. "We could use that. Or we could just post hourly updates on YouTube, saying where we are and who we are talking to."

Sami put the folder down. "I just had a coffee with our stringer."

"And was he pissed that you are bigfooting him?"

"She, actually. Her name is Alma. And no. Well, maybe. But she covered it up well."

"*Wa heya jameela?* Is she pretty?"

Sami laughed. "Are you asking for me or for you? She's pretty good at her job."

"And Alma told you what?" asked Najwa, serious now.

"The two men who tried to kidnap Yael this morning, that they found under Galata Bridge, are being held under armed guard at the hospital."

Najwa shrugged. "Of course they would be. The authorities say they are Kurdish terrorists. Although the Kurds deny it."

"The Kurds are right. There were lots of tourists around. One of them put some footage on YouTube. Our stringer recognized one of the men—he used to be married to her second cousin, until he started beating her."

"Is he a Kurd?"

"No. He works for the Turkish intelligence service."

Najwa looked at Sami, her eyes narrowing in concentration. "The MİT wants Yael out of the way, so they set up a kidnapping and then blame the Kurds." She thought some more. "That part makes sense. But why do they want her out of the way?" Najwa flipped the SIM card into a nearby trash can.

"Good question," said an English voice behind them.

Najwa and Sami stood up to greet the new arrival. "Jonathan, *marhaba*, welcome," she said as the two journalists kissed each other on the cheek, before he shook hands with Sami.

"May I?" asked Beaufort, sitting down next to them on the leather bench before they had a chance to answer.

"Be our guest," said Najwa, smiling, as she wondered how much of her conversation with Sami he had overheard. The competition between journalists at the summit was even more intense than usual, with hundreds of reporters prowling the corridors, hanging around outside conference rooms, lurking in the cafés and restaurants desperately seeking any snippet of insider information upon which they could construct a story.

Jonathan picked up one of the press packs on the bench and idly leafed through it.

"Well, isn't this exciting? Here we all are in Istanbul. And you know what they like to do in Istanbul?"

"Business?" said Najwa, knowing that Jonathan was not making a social call.

He put down the press pack. "Precisely. Which is why I have a cast-iron investment opportunity for you, one that will pay dividends within just a few hours *and* keep your editors happy. With a money-back guarantee if you are not satisfied."

Najwa smiled. "It sounds irresistible. How much?"

"I have personally staked fifty dollars," said Jonathan.

Najwa reached inside her purse, took out a fifty-dollar bill, and placed it in Jonathan's hand. Sami did the same.

"Thanks. One fifty should do the trick."

"When does this investment pay off?" asked Sami.

"Tomorrow morning," said Jonathan as he slipped the money into his pocket. He looked thoughtful. "I was also thinking of a little trade. Seeing as how we are in Istanbul and all . . ."

"And the deal is?" asked Sami.

"Your contacts that gave you the scoop on Yael and the Kurdish kidnapping attempt. If it really was the Kurds."

"It wasn't." Sami paused for a few seconds. "And we get?"

"The name of the very, very, very important person who is going on an unannounced shopping trip tomorrow to the Grand Bazaar."

24

Yael shivered and rubbed her arms. The sun had set and the cemetery was becoming dark and cold. "Joe-Don and Quentin have been arrested on charges of what?"

"Terrorism."

Her eyes opened wide. "That's so absurd. What's the evidence?"

"They were both carrying information about a detailed plan for an attack on the summit. They had the architectural plans of the Osman Convention Center, the places where the bombs would be planted, damages estimates, the timings for first responders, the plan for the second wave. It was all there, apparently, hidden in encrypted files on their telephones. Everything has been sent to us. Security is being raised to the highest level, for an imminent attack."

This was her fault. They had, all three of them—she, Joe-Don, and Quentin—been set up. She had passed on the information—or rather, the disinformation—from Jones's phone to them. Part of her was enraged, another part almost admiring. Clairborne had made her work so hard, first to get Cyrus

Jones's telephone and then to decrypt the information on it, that it had never occurred to her that she was being used.

All Clairborne had needed to do was tip off the Secret Service or his friends in the agency for the two men to be detained. It would come out eventually, of course, that Joe-Don and Quentin were innocent, trying to prevent an attack on the summit, not carry out one. But by then it would be too late. The more Yael thought about it, the more diabolical Clairborne's gambit was. She could imagine them both, claiming immunity, denouncing Clairborne, trying to explain the provenance of the information on their mobile telephones—to no avail.

The more they protested and demanded to be freed, the longer they would be held. Clairborne would deny everything, proclaim he was the one being set up, call on his network of contacts within the United States' deep state. Thinking back, Yael realized she had meant to check the names of the Prometheus Group staff on the plan. They had set an alarm bell ringing. Why would Clairborne ever use real names? It was a security risk. Now she understood. The names were fakes. Joe-Don and Quentin would ask the Secret Service to check the names, but Clairborne would be able to say, truthfully, that nobody by those names worked for Prometheus. Clairborne's argument, that he was being set up, would be even further strengthened. Once discovered, the plan would be sent to the Turkish authorities, as Yusuf had confirmed. Security would be tightened further, everything triple-checked in anticipation of an attack from the outside. It was a brilliant maneuver. Clairborne was hiding something in plain sight. But what?

Yael shivered again. "Can we go back now?"

Yusuf nodded. He led her down the way they had come. They soon reached a small iron door set into a wall, under an incline where the cemetery grounds rose steeply upward. Yusuf opened the door and led Yael down a narrow corridor, back to the archive room.

Yusuf busied himself making tea. Yael sat down at the table and rested for a moment. She felt strangely at home here, among the dusty, musty old books and ledgers of the Dönme, a small tile in the dazzling mosaic of Mediterranean history.

Yusuf put an aluminum teapot on the table, together with two small tulip-shaped glasses. For a moment Yael was back in her window seat in Café Markiz.

"The girl," she asked. "The beggar girl on İstiklal Caddesi?"

"She is fine. I alerted a friend of mine who runs a charity. They will help her." Yusuf poured tea for both of them. "And now, I think it's your turn to talk."

Yael reached for her tea. She looked at Yusuf, his dark, expressive eyes, his obsidian-black hair, his long slender fingers, the look on his face as he brushed the earth from his wife's grave. Her instincts had never let her down. She told him everything she knew: about Clarence Clairborne, Cyrus Jones, the Prometheus Group, the plan to attack the summit, which she now knew was disinformation, and Prometheus's links with Nuristan Holdings through Bank Bernard et Fils.

Yusuf stared at Yael. "Which bank did you say?"

"Bernard et Fils, in Geneva."

"Nuristan Holdings," Yusuf said, thoughtfully. "We know who runs Nuristan Holdings." He reached inside the desk drawer and took out a folder. He passed a photograph to Yael. "Does he look familiar?"

Yael peered at the picture, frowning. The image was quite poor quality and pixilated after being enlarged. It showed a clean-shaven man in his late forties, with dark hair, getting out of a car, with two other men in front of a rundown house at the end of a street of wooden-fronted houses, each with an enclosed balcony on the first floor.

Yael frowned. "Yes, but I'm not sure. Is he Turkish? Persian?"

Yusuf passed her another photograph. It showed the same man, but bald now with a neatly trimmed beard, in a collarless shirt.

"Salim Massoud," said Yael. "Is he here, in Istanbul? Where?"

"About a mile from here." Yusuf took out another photograph, much sharper, showing Massoud entering the rundown house. "I agree with you, Yael. There is no plan by jihadis to bomb the summit. Nor by the Kurds. We have people inside every radical, Islamist, Kurdish, far-left, far-right, Syrian-refugee, and jihadi group. There is no increase in activity—no chatter, no surge in telephone calls. We would know if there was."

"Then why is Massoud here, in disguise, if nothing is planned?" asked Yael. An idea began to form in her mind, a train of thought that could perhaps explain events so far and answer her question, when her UN mobile beeped. She checked the screen. An SMS message from Isis:

V. worried to see TV reports. You OK? Can you meet me 11am Mercan kapisi grand bazaar tomorrow. Have David info.

Yael put the phone down, her hand shaking, her heart pounding, all thoughts of Clarence Clairborne, the summit, terrorist attacks: gone.

She pushed the phone across the table.

Yusuf read the message. "Your brother?"

"Yes. How did you know?"

"We like to keep an eye on our VIP visitors. You understand that meeting Isis is out of the question."

Yael said nothing, her head tilted to one side as she looked at Yusuf.

"You are wanted by Interpol. There is a warrant out for your arrest," he said.

Yael merely held his gaze.

"There is a terrorist alert. The whole city is on lockdown."

Yael continued looking.

Yusuf refilled their tea, smiling despite himself. "You are a *very* difficult woman."

Yael picked up her glass. "I hope so," she said brightly.

Yusuf sighed with exasperation. "Every policeman in Istanbul is looking for you."

"But what if they cannot see me?"

President Freshwater looked her security chief straight in the eye. "I. Want. To. Go. Shopping."

Dave Reardon looked at the ceiling for a moment,

gathering his thoughts. "Madam President, we have talked about this. Istanbul is under a complete lockdown. We've had two bombs in the heart of the tourist quarter. An attempted kidnapping of a senior UN staffer, apparently by Kurdish terrorists, who has now disappeared. The P5 presidents and their entourages will all soon be gathered in one place, in a building helpfully made of glass. The Istanbul Summit is *the* number one target for every kind of crazy from here to Baghdad."

President Freshwater smiled. "Baghdad is just next door."

"Precisely."

It was nine o'clock on Monday evening. The president, Aldrich Utley, and several staffers were sitting in the lounge of the Marmara Suite at the Four Seasons Hotel in Sultanahmet. The room was tastefully decorated, the polished hardwood floor covered with pastel kilims, traditional woven Turkish rugs, the curved wooden sofa dotted with richly brocaded cushions. The hotel, a thick-walled former prison, was used to hosting VIPs. But the Secret Service advance security team had been deeply unhappy about the president's choice of accommodation. The surrounding area was a jumble of narrow alleys and hidden courtyards, jammed with tourists from all over the world. The three balconies, each ablaze with flowers, had spectacular views over the Bosphorus and Sultanahmet. However, if the president could look out, others could look in, which was why thick curtains now blocked the windows. Secret Service agents were posted on each balcony, with a further contingent inside the suite, by the door, in the corridor, and in the lobby of the hotel. The presidential armored Cadillac, known as "the Beast," was parked nearby. The Beast weighed a ton and a half, and its ceramic and titanium armor could withstand bullets, RPGs, and bomb blasts. Its doors were as heavy as those on a Boeing 757, and the tires were reinforced with Kevlar, able to run while flat. A supply of presidential blood, type O, was kept refrigerated in the trunk.

"Dave," said Freshwater as she picked up her thimble-sized cup of Turkish coffee, "you already have me sitting here in the dark. I can't move three feet without bumping into one of my Secret Service contingent."

Reardon, a black, Bronx-born, stocky five-foot-eight ex-marine, veteran of Iraq and Afghanistan, smiled. "We are in a near lockdown situation, ma'am."

Freshwater sipped her coffee appreciatively. "This is good. We should have this in the White House." Her voice turned serious. "We are in a flying-the-Stars-and-Stripes situation, Dave. The leader of the free world cannot be seen to be hiding in her hotel room. I want to go shopping. I want to bargain in the bazaar. I want to see where they shot *From Russia with Love*. We talked about this. It's in the schedule."

Reardon frowned. "That was a contingency plan, Madam President. Drawn up some time ago, before the bombs went off and before we got here. I walked over to the bazaar this morning. The place is a maze. Tiny narrow streets shooting off in all directions. Thousands, tens of thousands of people wandering around. I strongly recommend that we drop it."

"And that is the plan I agreed to and want to stick to. I know how hard you are looking out for me, Dave, and I really don't want to pull rank, but Zincirli Han is on the edge of the bazaar. It's not like we would be stuck in the middle." The han was a small, covered courtyard. Once a resting place for travelers and their horses, its living quarters had been converted to small artisan shops. Freshwater picked up her schedule from the table in front of her. "There it is. Grand Bazaar. Tuesday 11:10 a.m. to 11:30 a.m. Shopping for jewelry in the Zincirli Han. Aldrich, what do you think?" she asked, turning to her chief of staff.

Utley, like everyone else in the room, had come straight from the airport after a twelve-hour flight, but it didn't show. He had changed into a fresh suit and looked as immaculate as ever. "I agree with Madam President. We can't hide here and in the convention center all week. The Russians, the Chinese, the Brits, they will all be out and about, having photo ops, taking—what do you call those photographs— selfies. We need to show a presence."

Reardon leaned back and thought for several seconds before he spoke. "Two helicopters. Two advance and two chase cars. Six plainclothes motorcycle outriders, three in front and three behind. Once we are inside the bazaar, twelve Secret Service agents, three in front, three behind, and three on either side. You wear a vest and we travel in the Beast."

President Freshwater cradled her chin in her hands as she considered her reply. "I was thinking about walking."

"I was thinking about resigning," said Reardon.

"OK, we drive," said Freshwater, laughing. "But no

helicopters. One advance, one chase car. No motorcycle outriders, four Secret Service agents, two in front and two behind."

"Two cars, two outriders, eight Secret Service agents, two in front, two on each side, and two behind, and you wear a vest. Ten minutes, maximum, once we are inside."

"This is not Walmart, Dave. What can I do in ten minutes? I have to bargain with these guys. Drink a tea. Haggle."

"Twelve. And no teas. Unless we bring our own," rejoined Reardon, proffering his hand.

"Deal." President Freshwater shook his hand. "Welcome to Istanbul."

Yael leaned against the ship's railing, pulled off her niqab, the black veil that covered her face, and stuffed it into her purse.

Yusuf's eyes opened wide in alarm. "Yael! Please, you must keep covered up."

"I will, I promise. Just give me a minute," she said, grinning as she tried in vain to gather and tie up her windblown hair. There were few other passengers on the ferry from Üsküdar to Eminönü at this time of night, and none at all on the open top deck.

For a few moments she was a tourist, savoring the city. The Bosphorus rippled black and silver, and the breeze blew hard over the water, heavy with the smell of the sea. The coastline was studded with seafront cafés and restaurants, their colored lights a rainbow against the night. The Şemsi Pasha Mosque, a few yards from Üsküdar port, shone white and yellow, its wide dome and stubby minaret shimmering on the water. It was 9:15, time for *Yatsi*, the nighttime prayer, and a legion of muezzins sounded up, one after another, their calls carrying so loud and clear over the water, they could surely be heard all the way to Galata.

As well as her niqab, Yael was dressed in the full-length, plain black robe, or abaya, of an observant Islamic woman from the Gulf. She sensed Yusuf watching the wind blow her robe back and forth, framing her body within the flapping fabric. Yusuf gave her a few seconds, then gently took her arm and guided her back inside. A white metal wall and large windows enclosed the front half of the top deck. New wooden benches stood in horizontal rows, their seats back to back, facing both the prow and the hull. Steel railings marked the staircases down to the lower decks—one in the front, one in the middle, and one at the back.

Yael sat next to Yusuf and put her niqab back on. To her surprise, she enjoyed wearing the coverall. The head scarf she previously wore had barely mattered—her vision was unencumbered, her face exposed. The niqab was very different. Nothing of her was visible except her eyes, which were already disguised by brown contact lenses. A separate piece of black cloth covered her mouth, loosely enough for her to breathe. Behind the fabric, she felt invisible. In an Islamic society, she was virtually untouchable.

She watched a tourist boat pass by, its lights bright in the darkness, tiny figures visible on deck—laughing, drinking, chatting. She turned David's ring around on her finger. What information did Isis have?

Yael knew, as much as she knew anything, that there was

a reason why peacekeepers had not been dispatched from the UN base at Kigali to save her brother and his colleagues. Fareed Hussein held the key to the answer, of that she was certain. She could still see the way his body stiffened whenever she pressed him on the subject, hear his voice become brittle. He was lying. There was a cover-up, one that reached back twenty years. But Hussein could not be the only one who knew the truth. There were files, she knew, files buried deep in Paris and London, Kigali and New York. As an American diplomat Isis might be able to access them. *But why now?* asked a small voice in Yael's head. Wasn't this strange timing, in the middle of the world's most important diplomatic summit? *Maybe it was,* Yael answered herself, *but Isis is my friend and she understands my determination to find out what happened to my brother.* For now, there is no point worrying. She would meet Isis tomorrow, find out what she knew, and continue her quest.

The ferry ride from Üsküdar to Eminönü took around fifteen minutes. From there they would take the tram to Sultanahmet, the heart of the old city. Yusuf's plan was for them to spend the night in an apartment there owned by one of his many cousins. The narrow streets and alleys of Sultanahmet were crowded with shops, bars, and restaurants, home to a legion of tourists from across the world. Even the nosiest neighbors would take no notice of new arrivals coming and going.

Yael glanced ahead. The shore at Eminönü came into view, the fried-fish restaurant, now closed, bobbing on the waves like a seesaw. A cruise ship was docked nearby, seven stories high. Perhaps, once all this was over, she might stay in Istanbul for a couple of days, go shopping, finally get to see the sights. There was a vintage clothes shop, a giant emporium, just off İstiklal Caddesi, that she had read about. She looked at Yusuf. Maybe he would come shopping with her. She felt relaxed in his company. Yusuf was an attractive man, and unlike Sami and Eli, she had no history with him. Apart from his shooting her in the neck with a knockout dart, she thought, and started laughing.

Yusuf turned to her, smiling. "What's so . . . ," he started to say, when two heavyset men in black leather jackets came up the staircase at the front of the deck and walked toward them.

Two more men came up the center staircase and a further two appeared at the top of the third staircase at the back of the deck. All six advanced on Yael and Yusuf. One sat next to Yael, another next to Yusuf; two sat on the facing bench, and the last pair split, one man standing at either end of the bench.

A seventh man, potbellied, with a wide face and dark brown hair, came up the staircase by the prow of the boat. He stood in front of Yael and Yusuf. A pistol was jammed in his belt.

"Funny," finished Yusuf, completely unfazed.

Yael looked around, her heart racing, processing their situation, calculating potential angles of attack. All the men were armed. Four were carrying Uzi submachine guns; the remainder had pistols. She had nothing except her hands and feet. Yusuf had a pistol.

They would be mown down in seconds. Their best chance was to try and make a break for it when they disembarked at Eminönü. There would be a vehicle waiting there, she was sure. Getting the target into the vehicle was always the hardest point of any abduction. Once inside, it was virtually game over. If she and Yusuf created enough of a furor, if they could somehow involve passersby, *if . . .* Yael looked at Yusuf, wondering how to communicate this to him.

Yusuf glanced at her and smiled reassuringly. He stood up and shook hands with the potbellied man, then turned to Yael. "This is Mehmed. A colleague."

Mehmed nodded at Yael in greeting. She frowned as she tried to process what was happening. Were she and Yusuf being arrested, or was this their security escort?

Mehmed reached into his pocket and took out two pairs of handcuffs. Yael sensed the six men with him tense. Her question, she realized, was answered.

Yusuf glanced at Mehmed. "In a minute," he said. "Can I have a cigarette first?"

Mehmed gestured to one of his subordinates, who handed Yusuf a cigarette and lit it.

Yael watched Yusuf standing by the men, lazily blowing smoke rings.

Mehmed's mobile rang. He pressed a button and spoke rapidly into the phone. "Yes, we have them. Both of them. Is the transport ready when we dock?"

He listened, nodded, and passed the phone to Yusuf. "It's for you."

"Good evening, *patron*," said Yusuf. "How is Natalya?"

25

The instructor is a legend. Her black hair is shot through with silver, but she is still beautiful—her posture erect, her eyes clear and shining.

The other students speak about her in whispers, that she was used as bait, three times, to lure the architects of the Munich Olympics massacre. Once everything was in place, she was to leave and let others take over. But on each mission she finished the job herself.

"There are three rules when meeting a contact. What are they?" she asks the class.

Yael raises her hand. "One: be early."

"Yes. And two?"

"Carry out anti-surveillance drills on the way and reconnaissance once you arrive. Check it's not a trap. Work out contingency plans, map escape routes."

"Good. And if your contact changes the plan at the last minute, wants to meet somewhere else?"

"Don't go. You choose another location. Always make them come to you."

The instructor nods and turns to the whiteboard. She writes, "Make Them Come to You."

The Mercan Kapısı, the Coral Gate, had a dilapidated charm. A lesser-used entrance to the Grand Bazaar on its northern side, the gate was framed by two gray marble columns and a portico. The gate stood at the top of Tiğcilar, a crowded, narrow alley flanked with shops that sloped down toward the waterfront at Eminönü and the Galata Bridge.

Yael leaned against the right-hand marble column while she checked her watch. It was 10:45 a.m. The weather had changed overnight, for the worse. The sky was dark and overcast; a light rain had fallen all morning, in fact was still falling, making the sidewalks slippery and greasy. The wind blew in hard, funneled along the alley. The rain spattered on Yael's black baseball cap and wraparound Ray-Ban sunglasses. She shivered, suddenly cold in her thin cream jacket, as she ran though the events of the previous evening in her head.

Yusuf had handed the telephone back to Mehmed after saying the name Natalya. Mehmed had listened for some time, then put the handcuffs away and apologized to Yusuf. He and his men walked to the other end of the deck, out of earshot.

Yusuf then talked some more on the telephone. His voice was confident, as though he were explaining something. Among the torrent of Turkish, Yael picked out the words "Bank" and "Bernard." Mehmed and his men returned as the boat docked. A white van was waiting for them, parked on the pavement a few yards from where passengers disembarked from the ferries. Mehmed had ushered them inside. Yael remained tense, despite the obvious change in atmosphere.

The van took them to the MİT office in Sultanahmet. There, a man with a face carved from stone had introduced himself as Kemal Burhan and apologized profusely to Yael. A young woman, whom Yael recognized from the airplane, had brought endless trays of teas, coffees, plates of kebabs, rice, and salads, blushing fiercely every time she entered the room. Ravenous, Yael ate everything on offer.

Yusuf and Burhan had gone into another room. There had been a lot more talking, even some shouting, with more mentions of Bank Bernard, Geneva, Natalya, and Galata. Then the racket stopped suddenly. There were several seconds of silence. Yael was alert, until she heard loud laughter. The two men emerged, and Yusuf explained that his boss was going to call the Ministry of the Interior to have the arrest warrant for Yael lifted. In addition, all police officers were to aid her if she so requested. Burhan had ceremoniously presented her with an MİT identity card, assuring her that it would extricate her from what he called "even the most delicate situation."

They had spent the night in the apartment, Yael sleeping on the sofa bed and Yusuf on the floor in the room next door. In the morning Yusuf had gone back to work, and Yael had insisted on meeting Isis, ignoring the ever-louder question nagging inside her: *Why had the information about David suddenly come up now?*

Yael arrived at the Coral Gate just before nine o'clock. She had walked from the safe house in Sultanahmet. The journey would normally take fifteen minutes. Yael had spent almost two hours scouting out the area around the gate, doubling back on herself, taking last-minute turns, proceeding slowly through choke points—narrow alleys, underpasses, and gateways—always alert for the same face twice, or a familiar car. Members of a surveillance team could change their jackets, hats, glasses, sunglasses, even wigs. The best professionals even brought different shoes, but they still could not alter their faces in a hurry. There were two key giveaways that someone was watching: multiple sightings of the same person or people in the vicinity, and suspicious behavior. Talking when no mobile telephone was visible could mean a radio earpiece; a hand always in a pocket could indicate a pressel—a small switch connected to a radio that an operative could use to tap out signals about the target's movements, according to a prearranged code. So far, everything seemed clear, yet Yael's unease was growing.

Yael took her UN mobile telephone from her purse and swiped through the menus until a plain gray icon appeared. She tapped on the image. A 3-D computerized image of the bazaar appeared. It revealed aspects of the complex that tourists never saw, the secret tunnels that dated back to the bazaar's construction in the fifteenth century after the Ottomans conquered Constantinople, as the city was then known, from the Byzantines; long-abandoned storerooms, bricked-over doors; a network of narrow passageways that ran under the roof; and a map of passageways along the roof. Yusuf had given Yael the app, which was highly classified. He had been strongly opposed to Yael meeting Isis. If it all goes wrong, Yusuf had said, get up on the roof and we will come and find you. Yael was tracing a virtual path through the hidden passageways when her phone beeped.

It was a message from Isis.

On my way. Was stuck at work with summit BS.
Good news about the Interpol warrant being lifted.
Xxxx.

How did Isis already know that? Because she clearly had
excellent contacts—*the type of contacts that might know something about David,* Yael told herself. Again. She stepped aside
to let a young French couple pass by. The man had a goatee
and a large mole on the side of his nose, the woman thin lips
and short blond hair. They were both well dressed in stylish black woolen coats, holding hands and laughing. Yael
instinctively checked the woman's shoes: she wore a pair of
black and pink Geox loafers.

Yael waited a few more minutes, but there were no more
messages from Isis. She turned around. She had waited
enough and decided to carry out another anti-surveillance
drill. Mercan Kapısı was a good choke point, a narrow fun-
nel through which anyone following her would have to
pass. Assuming, that is, that they were on the Tiğcilar side of
the entrance. Once inside the maze of the bazaar, it would
be far more difficult to know if she was being followed.

She stepped through the gate into another world. The
bazaar was a city within a city, with four thousand shops,
many just a few feet square, jammed into sixty-six streets
and alleys through which flowed tens of thousands of people
a day. Rich with the smell of coffee and leather, spices and
dusty carpets, the air crackled with the promise of commerce. Owners stood outside their emporiums, instantly

switching between a babel of languages. Turkish flags and powerful electric lights hung from the vaulted ceiling. The edges of the yellow stone arches had been painted red, a delicate floral pattern. Hordes of tourists examined trays of gold and silver jewelry, bright woven kilims, tea sets, fake Louis Vuitton handbags, leather jackets, sacks of dried fruit, and painted ceramic plates and dishes. Within a few steps Yael heard English, Russian, German, French, Hebrew, and Hungarian. A sign pointed the way to Zincirli Han.

She stopped to look in the window of a jewelry shop, apparently admiring the rows of fine gold chains on display, but in reality using the glass to check who was walking through the gate behind her. It seemed clear. She walked a few yards farther into the bazaar and stopped to look at a backpack, one of many neatly piled outside a shop. The top half of the backpack was made out of a kilim with a bold blue and red geometric motif, the bottom of brown leather. Instantly sensing her interest, the shopkeeper, a gray-haired man in his sixties, put down his glass of tea, poured another one, placed both on a small tray, and stepped outside, ready to start his sales pitch. He offered the tea to Yael. She was about to accept when her telephone rang. She looked at the screen. It was Isis.

"Hey, I'm so sorry. I'm still on my way."

"Where are you?"

"On the Galata Bridge. I'm stuck in a car. The traffic is horrendous. It's worse than New York. The whole city is gridlocked because of the summit."

Yael looked at the shopkeeper, smiled, pointed at her telephone, and raised two fingers. He nodded and went back inside.

"How long will you be, do you think?" asked Yael.

"At this pace, at least another twenty minutes."

"Why don't you get out and walk? It would be quicker."

"Sorry, babe, US diplomats aren't allowed to walk anywhere at the moment. Do some shopping. You are a free woman now. I will be there soon." Isis paused. "Unless . . ."

"Unless what?"

"I'm in a blue Ford van, tinted windows, registration. . . ." Her voice faded slightly. "Can I tell her the registration?"

"No," Yael heard a man in the background say.

"Walk toward me. I'll meet you on the corner, where Tiğcilar turns onto Mercan Caddesi. We can talk in the van."

Yael walked out of the bazaar, wearing her new backpack, her other purse jammed inside. She headed down Tiğcilar, toward the turning where Isis had suggested that they meet. The wind was blowing harder now, its damp spray covering her face, the T-shirts and blouses hanging on display outside the shops flapping back and forth.

Yael briskly wove a path through the crowd, her senses on high alert. The shops on Tiğcilar sold more practical goods than those inside the bazaar: pots, pans, groceries, bolts of fabric. Many of the customers were local women, observant Muslims wearing ankle-length dresses and head scarves with brightly colored patterns. Yael almost slipped on the wet stones, barely avoiding a statuesque Turkish matron with four young children in tow. They watched in awe as their mother haggled with a shop owner, relentlessly driving down the price of a cast-iron saucepan. There were police officers everywhere, stopping passersby, checking their identity papers, calling their details in on their radios. A helicopter roared by overhead, "Polis" painted on its underside, the downdraft so strong that Yael's hair flew every which way.

Her mobile telephone buzzed. She checked the screen. Another message from Isis.

Don't tell anyone I told you: 34 DF 1987.

Yael memorized the registration number and carried on walking. The blue van, she saw, was parked on the corner where Tiğcilar met Mercan Caddesi, a wide, busy street crowded with midmorning traffic.

She walked past a vendor selling roasted corn on the cob, each seared chunk wrapped in paper. Her sixth sense was an almost physical force inside her, trying to turn her around. She was breaking every rule in the tradecraft book. Why *had* Isis appeared at Dag Hammarskjöld Plaza last Thursday at 9:15 a.m., when the US mission held a compulsory staff meeting every morning at nine o'clock? Had Isis known she was there? If so, *how* had she found out? And *why*, in the middle of the world's most important summit, did Isis need to share new information about the death of her brother, inside a van with tinted windows? *Why* wouldn't she come out and meet her? Yael twisted David's ring around her finger. If there was any chance that Isis knew something about David—any chance at all—she would be there.

The hairs on the back of her neck prickled. Yael looked

around. Ten yards to her right stood a young man in his twenties, wearing sunglasses, a woolen hat, a denim jacket, and jeans, looking in the window of a grocery shop. He was clean shaven but had a large mole by the side of his nose. A woman of similar age, also wearing sunglasses, stood on the other side of the street examining a selection of T-shirts. She had long brown hair and noticeably thin lips. She wore a navy down jacket, and black and pink Geox loafers.

Two policemen watched the crowds a few yards away. Yael walked up to the older officer. He had short gray hair and a pudgy face. He looked at Yael suspiciously, but she showed him her MİT card and his demeanor changed instantly. She pointed at the man in the woolen hat and the woman with thin lips. The policeman barked out an order at his colleague. They split up, one running toward the man, the other toward the woman.

Yael's heart was racing now. She knew she was heading into a trap. But she had no choice. And she was not completely unprepared. She continued walking, holding the small, round weight in her right hand inside her jacket pocket, feeling the pressure of the spring against her fingers.

She was fifty yards from the van when she slowed down. The sidewalk was crowded, the traffic almost stationary, despite the cacophony of horns blaring. A street seller stood nearby, rapidly scooping sugared nuts into brown paper bags. He caught her eye and proffered a bag.

Yael shook her head and kept moving forward, slowly, toward the van.

She knocked on the door.

Nothing happened.

She knocked again.

She stepped forward to check the front of the vehicle when a sharp pain shot down her back.

"Nice work," said a familiar voice.

Yael froze, wincing as the barrel of the pistol pushed hard against her spine.

"But not nice enough, motek."

Roxana Voiculescu leaned forward, her hands resting on the polished wood podium as she looked out at the rows of journalists. Salon three of the Osman Convention Center was jammed with hundreds of reporters and television and radio crews, from Albania to Zimbabwe, all scribbling furiously, taping or filming her every word. She was on a high, lapping up the attention. She had just finished a fifteen-minute talk about the summit, its schedule and agenda, and then fielded several dozen questions. She had ignored the New York–based UN press corps, who, she could see, were becoming increasingly irritated.

As satisfying as that was, Roxana knew she would have to work with them again once the summit was over and everyone was back in Turtle Bay. An official complaint from the UN Correspondents Association would make her life difficult. Murat Yilmaz, the correspondent for the Turkish news agency Anadolu, and the association's president, had been trying to get her attention for some time. Finally, Roxana directed the hostess to hand Murat the microphone.

Murat frowned. "Roxana, I have looked through your schedule, but there are no press conferences planned with any of the delegations or their leaders. Will we have a chance to speak to any of the P5 presidents?"

She smiled broadly as she shook her head. "I'm sorry, Murat, but there will be no press conferences with any of the P5 presidents during the summit. We—and they—agreed that it is best if they are left alone to concentrate on the extremely valuable work they will be doing in the next few days. But I will be available to assist you, and as you can see, I will be hosting a daily press conference."

Murat looked puzzled. "And Caroline Masters? Will the acting secretary-general be available?"

"Again, I'm sorry, Murat. But the acting SG will not be available."

Murat continued, holding on to the microphone. "Then why have we come all the way to Istanbul, Roxana, if nobody will talk to us?"

The other journalists looked around and nodded to each other, their indignation almost tangible. Murat had said what everyone was thinking. Roxana sensed her control of the room starting to slip away.

She straightened her back, keeping her voice calm and well modulated. "As I said, all of you are welcome to talk to me, whenever you need or like. But the main reason to be here is to report on the most important diplomatic summit in recent history, Murat. Your voices, your reporting, will help ensure the summit's success. My press team will do all they can to assist you. I should have mentioned that we will be supplying a steady stream of remarks that you can attribute to the various delegations, reflecting their views as the summit continues. Some of the remarks will be kept to within around a hundred characters so they will be ready for Twitter, with your own additions of course. The remarks will be available in all the official languages of the UN as well as Turkish. Please include the hashtag 'UNIstanbul.' "

Murat shook his head, sat down, and passed the microphone back to one of the hostesses. Jonathan Beaufort jumped up and waved his hand. Roxana ignored him, looking out over the assembled journalists. But apart from the British reporter, there were no other journalists with further questions.

"Thank you all for your attention," said Roxana as Jonathan walked over to one of the hostesses and politely asked for the microphone. "If that is all, I wish you all a very productive summit."

"Actually, it's not all," said a loud British voice, suddenly booming through the speaker system. "I have some questions, questions shared by my colleagues from the *New York Times* and Al Jazeera."

Roxana suddenly seemed discomfited. She gestured at the technicians, signaling that they should switch off the microphone. The technicians shrugged, pressed some buttons, and aimlessly moved a slider up and down. It only made Jonathan's voice even louder.

"Where is Yael Azoulay, what is she doing in Istanbul when she is supposed to be running the Trusteeship Council, who tried to kidnap her, and why has the Interpol warrant for her arrest been rescinded?" he demanded.

Hello, Eli," said Yael. "Can I turn around?"

"Slowly." He was standing so close she could feel

his breath warm on her neck. He smelled of soap. "Hands out of your pockets and no sudden movements."

"OK, I am taking my hands out of my pockets now, slowly, just as you asked." She removed her right hand, feeling the weight in it, the spring pushing against her fingers. "But can you stop twisting the gun into my back, please?"

The door of the van opened. There were two more men inside, both in their twenties, dark and tough looking. "Shalom, Yael," said one. "It's time to come home."

Eli stepped back and eased the pressure of the gun barrel a fraction. It was all she needed.

She stepped forward, dropped her head, and slammed the back of her skull into Eli's face.

At the same time she threw the weight in her hand into the van.

The stun grenade exploded with a deafening roar. The two men inside pitched forward, facedown and unconscious.

Salon 3 was completely silent, waiting for Roxana's reply. "Thank you, Jonathan, for your question. But if you could please check your schedule, you will see that this is a briefing about the agenda of the Istanbul Summit, not about the whereabouts of a single former UN official," she said, her smile fading.

Jonathan drew himself up to his full six feet two inches. "This briefing," he announced, like a professor beginning a lecture on a subject he knew inside out, "is about spoon-feeding us preprepared tidbits of information that you then expect us to tweet so that your hashtag trends. I've been to plenty of UN pressers in my time, but this is the first one where the spokesperson has actually asked us to actively spread Turtle Bay's propaganda."

The rows of journalists turned to each other, muttering and nodding. Roxana looked back and forth at the technicians, her face increasingly anxious. One raised his hands in supplication, mouthing his apologies.

Jonathan surveyed the room, sensing the rising wave of dissatisfaction and indignation rippling through his colleagues. He put the microphone down and turned to Sami and Najwa, his head close to theirs as he spoke softly and quickly. Their conversation was brief, only lasting a few seconds. Sami nodded, reluctantly. So did Najwa, but with much more enthusiasm.

Jonathan stood up again. "If anyone wants some nice color for their coverage of the summit instead of retweeting the UN's handouts, President Freshwater will be shopping somewhere in the Grand Bazaar, five minutes' walk from here"—he paused and looked at his watch—"in about ten minutes."

Yael spun around on her right foot and ducked down under Eli's gun arm. She slid her left arm under his right elbow, hooking his arm into a lock. With Eli trapped, she used his body weight to stabilize herself, pivoted leftward, and smashed her right elbow into his face. She grabbed the barrel of the pistol, twisted it, and pushed it outward, making sure she was out of the line of fire. She yanked the gun around, using her hips to put the full force of her body into the twist until Eli let go.

Yael slammed the gun barrel into Eli's face. He staggered back, blood pouring from his nose.

She stepped backward, making sure to keep a distance, but keeping the gun trained on him.

He wiped his face, coughed, spat a long spout of blood, and advanced toward her.

"Stand back, Eli. I will shoot you."

Eli laughed as he walked toward her. "I'm waiting, motek."

Yael moved away, still pointing the gun at Eli, her finger on the trigger, aiming at his chest.

Eli continued walking. "You won't shoot me. You can't. Now give me the pistol. We can still get you out of here."

Yael glanced behind her and backed into the door of a shop. It was a dark, narrow space, packed with bolts of brightly colored cloth piled up against brown walls.

The owner, a wizened old man in his seventies, took one look at her and scurried out.

Yael retreated farther until she stood in front of the counter, her gun still trained on the entrance.

Eli was framed in the doorway. "This is it, Yael. There is nowhere else to run. Come with me now. We can still get you out of here."

"Get out, Eli. *Get out!*" Yael's finger tightened on the trigger, trying to control the tremor in her hand.

Eli laughed and stepped toward her.

The underground shooting range is cold, noisy, and stinks of cordite.

"Happy sixteenth birthday," her father says, as he hands her the Glock 17.

The weapon feels heavy in her hands, almost unreal.

He shows her how to hold the gun. "Stand with your legs apart. Breathe steadily, aim at the heart, and squeeze the trigger slowly."

She does as he says, points the gun at the paper target, and nervously presses the trigger. The Glock jumps in her hand.

The shot goes wide and high, clipping the target's shoulder.

He gently guides the pistol down a fraction of an inch.

She fires again. This time her shot hits the edge of the bull's-eye.

"Look, Aba!" she exclaims, her nervousness turning to excitement.

She fires again and hits the center of the target.

"Look, Aba!"

He nods, and his approval courses through her veins, a drug that she craves.

She holds the gun steadily now. Her finger tightens and eases, tightens and eases.

The shots start to bunch up in the center of the bull's-eye.

Look Aba, look, look, look.

26

The back door of the fabric shop opened onto a large courtyard surrounded by three high walls. Offcuts of cloth were scattered across the ground, the bright yellows, reds, and blues a sodden mess after the morning rain. Wooden pallets were piled up in one corner; a colony of cats had taken over another. They meowed indignantly as Yael sprinted across their space.

Three Dumpsters stood against the far wall. The gap between the top of the Dumpster and the wall was about eight feet, she estimated. Yael jumped up on top of the center Dumpster, stood astride the lid to spread her weight, launched herself upward, and grabbed the top of the wall. The bricks had been covered with rough concrete, which scraped her fingers as she clambered upward.

Her shoulder muscles howled in protest as she dragged herself onto the ledge, swinging her body up behind her. She rolled over the top onto a large flat roof. Yael lay on her back for a moment, gasping for breath, ignoring the daggers shooting down from her neck, when a shadow fell across her.

"You should have fired at me, not at the wall," said Eli, standing on the edge of the roof.

Yael sat up and reached around for the pistol. The weapon, now empty, was jammed into the waistband of her jeans, pressing against her spine.

She arched her back and yanked the gun out.

"None left. I counted." Eli stepped toward her.

"Who needs bullets?" replied Yael, holding the gun like a hammer. She hurled it just to the side of Eli's head. Just as she had anticipated, he swerved left. The gun hit him full in the face.

"*Ben zonah!* Son of a bitch," he shouted as he toppled backward, landing with a crash.

Yael walked over to the edge and looked down. Eli was lying on the top of the Dumpster, unmoving.

Even now she had a strong urge to climb down and check that he was all right. But he had fallen straight. No blood seeped from his head, and his neck was not twisted. None of his limbs appeared to be broken or dislocated. He would live.

And in any case, she knew there would soon be a backup team on the spot, especially after her stun grenade.

The gunman quickly set up the sniper rifle on the roof of the apartment building. The call had come five minutes before: "The target is on the roof of the bazaar."

The Dragunov was accurate to a range of about three-quarters of a mile. It fired a steel-jacketed bullet with an air pocket, steel core, and lead base, for what was known as "maximum terminal effect." The target was about five hundred yards away but would soon be moving—and swiftly. It was going to be a difficult shot, but he felt confident.

The Dragunov's barrel rested on a small bipod. The gunman felt the weight of the weapon, adjusted the sight, compensated for distance, wind shear, bullet-drop, the rifle's idiosyncrasies. The trigger felt taut under his finger, coiled, ready. A breeze blew through the window, cold and damp. He could smell the the sea, a whiff of cigarette smoke, grilled meat.

It made him hungry. A single shot, he hoped, then lunch. Some fish, grilled, and a carafe of chilled wine. A reward.

He peered through the telescopic sight and turned a dial. She came into focus, the pattern on her blue kilim backpack clear and sharp.

Yael walked away from the edge, looked ahead, and took her bearings. The sky was gray, the clouds the color of dirty water, the air damp and chilly. But this was Istanbul as she had never seen it before.

A sea of red-tiled roofs, dotted with air conditioners and satellite dishes, stretched into the distance. Narrow pathways, their edges cracked and crumbling, snaked across the top of the buildings. Rickety windows and tiny wooden doors marked long-abandoned rooms and passages. An ornate gateway, its arch inscribed with Ottoman Turkish script, written in Arabic characters, was bricked up, its secrets sealed forever. A hundred yards away was the roof of the Iç Bedesten, the oldest section of the bazaar. Over it all loomed the dome of the Hagia Sophia, the seventh-century Byzantine church that was now a mosque, its four minarets aiming skyward, like rockets about to launch into space.

Yael walked forward. A pigeon coop, twelve small cages in two rows, six high, behind a mesh fence, stood halfway across. The birds rustled their wings as she walked past, cooing excitedly.

She reached the end of the flat roof and looked out over the top of the bazaar, mapping an escape route. The ledge was worn and dilapidated. There was a gap between it and the roofs of the bazaar about two yards wide.

Could she make it? The jump was not the problem. Landing on the other side, and not sliding off, would be. Yael flexed her legs. She leapt back as a piece of concrete gave way underneath her, shattering when it hit the ground, two stories below.

One part of her was furious with herself, another oddly vindicated. Of course she should have listened to her sixth sense. It had never been wrong, and certainly had not been today. She had been set up. Tel Aviv wanted her back. She understood why Tel Aviv was ready to kidnap her if necessary. Her former employer had a long memory, even longer arms, and she had invaluable intelligence about the inner workings of the world of secret diplomacy. She was only surprised that they had taken so long to make their approach, first through Eli at the bar, and then more forcefully. Still, she had also proved, if only to herself, that she would go to any lengths, confront any danger, to find out what had happened to her brother.

But why had Isis betrayed her? Why did she want her out of the way? That was a mystery. Yael thought back over what she had learned and about Clarence Clairborne's disinformation plan. It had worked. Security was now at the maximum possible level in anticipation of an attack from the outside.

She looked into the distance. She could just see the farthest edge of the bazaar on the other side of the complex. There was a small parking lot on the side of Tiğcilar, not far from the Mercan Kapısı and the Zincirli Han. A long limousine was parked there, together with two large black SUVs. Two American flags flew from either side of the limousine's hood. The han would be her choice too if she were president and wanted to visit the bazaar: somewhere near the entrance, enclosed, easy to reach, a place where the crowd could be controlled.

Isis Franklin and President Freshwater.

An old friend, in the same city as the president. An old friend with security clearance.

Yael suddenly understood what was going to happen.

Ten yards behind her, the pigeons erupted.

President Freshwater held the necklace up to the light, marveling at the way the black opals, each encased in thick white gold, appeared to glow. "Look at this, Isis," she said, her voice full of admiration. "Isn't it beautiful?"

Isis nodded, smiling widely. "It's stunning, Renee. Try it on."

They were standing outside a jewelry shop in the Zincirli Han. The han was a narrow oblong courtyard, about fifteen yards wide and four times as long. The walls were reddish brown, and each door and window frame was painted white. A large chestnut tree stood in the middle. The lower floor, once used for accommodation for the animals of visiting travelers, hosted silver- and goldsmiths and their workshops. Gray sidewalks extended a yard or so from the shop fronts into the central stone floor, which now glistened in the rain. The merchants and their families were gathered outside their doors, watching intently, chattering and snapping endless photographs of the president with their mobile telephones.

Yaşar Izmiri, whose necklace President Freshwater was examining, was doing his best to control his excitement—and that of his six-year-old son, who kept peeking out from behind his father's legs. Izmiri, a jolly middle-aged man with lively brown eyes, had already received two visits from the Secret Service advance teams. Until this morning, he had not really believed that the president of America would actually come and buy something from him. But here she was, and with so many bodyguards. There were at least six out here, two more inside his workshop, one on each side of the doorway, and a dozen more patrolling the covered walkway above the shops.

Izmiri looked at Isis for a moment. *I am right*, he told himself, *I have seen her before*. "Did you find what you were looking for, madam?" he asked politely.

Isis frowned. "I'm not sure what you mean."

"Yesterday, when you were here, you dropped something, by the tree," said Izmiri, gesturing at the roots of the chestnut. "I saw you looking on the ground there."

Isis blushed. "Oh, yes, yes. I did. Thanks for asking."

Dave Reardon stood close by, not listening to the exchange, his eyes continually scanning their surroundings.

He had not factored in Isis's appearance, but the two women had met by chance—Isis had just been leaving the bazaar at the Mercan Kapısı when the president and her entourage arrived. Reardon had watched, almost amused despite his state of high alert, as Isis showed the president her new black leather gloves, insisting that the president touch them to see how soft they were. The president, impressed with Isis's eye for a bargain, invited her to come shopping. Isis had readily agreed.

Izmiri looked at Reardon and pointed at the necklace in the president's hands. "May I?"

Reardon nodded. He was focused on the entrance to the han. There were at least a hundred reporters gathered there. He had agreed to let three come to the front. They would operate a pool and share their material with their colleagues. Murat Yilmaz, from the Turkish news agency, would supply the print news wire services such as Reuters and Associated Press, Sami Boustani would share his material with the newspapers, and Najwa al-Sameera would feed her sound and video footage to radio and television stations. Najwa was already in prime position, standing at the front of the crowd, directing her cameraman.

Izmiri picked up the necklace from Freshwater's hand and stood behind her, fastening it around her neck. He handed her a small mirror.

Freshwater regarded herself, pleased with her purchase. The black stones went perfectly with her dark complexion and strong features.

"What do you think?"

"It's perfect," said Isis.

Freshwater smiled, for a moment relaxed and happy. She walked over to Najwa and her camera crew. Najwa moved forward, but a Secret Service agent blocked her path.

"It's OK," said Freshwater, "I want to talk to her."

The agent stepped aside. Freshwater started to speak to Najwa but the words would not come out properly.

She made a strange gargling noise, stared at Najwa, and collapsed.

The pigeons fluttered.

Yael launched herself over the gap.

She landed on the edge, dropped down on all fours to stabilize herself. She scrabbled forward to grab the peak of the roof.

Her feet slid on the wet surface. She grabbed the rooftop. The tiles began to crack and give way.

Eli leapt after her.

Pandemonium erupted.

The Secret Service agents instantly formed a cordon around the president's supine form.

She groaned, a thin trickle of saliva leaking from the side of her mouth. Her eyes rolled backward.

A female agent in her late thirties, red haired and freckled, kneeled next to Freshwater. Trained as a paramedic, she quickly removed the necklace, checked Freshwater's airways, pulse, respiration, all the while muttering furiously into her radio earpiece.

The reporters surged forward, all thought of pool agreements now gone. Four Secret Service agents instantly formed a cordon across the gateway to the han, but they could not hold back a hundred people.

Dave Reardon was speaking rapidly into his radio. "Mermaid is down, Mermaid is down," he said, using the code name for the president. "Need reinforcements and urgent medevac."

Isis watched the spectacle for several seconds, then walked up to Reardon. "She's been poisoned."

Reardon wheeled around. "How do you know?"

The roar of helicopter blades sounded in the distance.

"Because I did it."

The gunman kept his scope on Yael as she hauled herself up onto the point of the roof, shards of roof tiles falling behind her.

She sprinted down the rooftop pathway toward Zincirli Han, Eli running after her.

Reardon picked up Isis by her arms and slammed her against the wall of the han.

Isis grunted in pain. "You have ten minutes before her heart stops."

"Antidote? Where's the fucking antidote?" demanded Reardon, his face twisted in fury.

"Near. Very near. But you won't find it in time."

"*What. Do. You. Want?*"

"Do you know why I joined the State Department? Chose a life of public service?"

"I don't give a shit."

"You should, Dave. You and the rest of this administration should give a shit. Because I believed that America stood for something. Something good: progress, democracy, human rights. And then I saw the reality. . . ."

Reardon pushed Isis harder against the wall. "The reality is that unless you tell us where the antidote is you will spend the rest of your life in a supermax prison. In a tiny concrete cell, twenty-four hours a day with no visitors. Ever."

Isis laughed. "Sure, Dave. You know all about that stuff."

Reardon frowned. "What the fuck are you talking about?"

"I'm talking about a seventeen-year-old boy locked in a dog kennel at Bagram air base for two weeks until he was strapped to a gurney with a towel over his head. And a thickset black American guy"—Isis paused and looked at him—"maybe five-eight, tipping water over his face. Not a mercenary or a contractor. A US government employee, acting with the full knowledge and support of his superiors. A torturer. But the boy didn't tell you much, did he? Because he died."

Reardon shook his head, several times. "I don't know anything about that."

"You are a bad liar, Dave. Or let's talk about the video I saw last week. In the US mission on First Avenue."

"Fuck your video. *Where's the antidote?*"

"It's your video too, Dave. I watched a teenage boy crawl across a field in Afghanistan after a drone strike. He was dragging himself forward on his elbows. His legs were stumps. They left a black trail behind him. He was trying to reach his house. I saw his mother and father run out, trying to help him. His sister ran back and picked up the stumps of his legs. It was quite a sight. A little girl holding her brother's legs. It was too late. He—what is the technical term—bled out."

"Tragic. *What do you want?*" shouted Reardon, pushing her harder against the wall.

"The Black File," said Isis calmly.

"The what?"

"You know full well what it is. The secret record of all the drone strikes. The intel, the chain of command, the poststrike debriefings. The casualty count. Of the women and children that the United States has killed. And never taken responsibility for."

Reardon's grip eased slightly. "I may be able to get you sight of that."

Isis laughed. "Not for me. On the net. Unredacted."

He called over two Secret Service agents. "Cuff her and search her. Everywhere."

The agents yanked Isis's arms behind her back and handcuffed her wrists together.

"You are wasting your time," Isis said.

Isis turned to watch Freshwater moan, semiconscious, as the Secret Service agents began to hustle her away. "Make those calls, Dave," Isis said, her voice confident. "You have eight minutes."

The pathway between the roofs was made of concrete slabs barely more than a foot wide. Now wet and shiny from the rain, it was designed for slow, careful negotiation. There was no safety barrier to prevent anyone on the path slipping and plunging down the side of the roofs.

Yael ran forward. Her left foot slid out from under her. She landed on her right side as she slammed onto the path, gasping in pain, gripping the edge of the roof tiles to prevent herself from sliding off.

She glanced around. Eli was still behind her, his Glock in his hand.

She crawled ahead as fast as she could, almost gagging from the ammoniacal stink of encrusted pigeon droppings.

She was just a few yards from the edge now and could see down into Zincirli Han. A woman was lying on the ground, a circle of men in blue suits standing around her. A helicopter swooped low over the bazaar, its side emblazoned with a red crescent.

She felt a pressure on the back of her neck. The hairs rose again, not just from danger, but also from a strange sense that someone was watching her.

Eli was just a few yards away now.

"Yael," he shouted, "don't make me do this!"

The gunman watched the two figures through his scope. Eli stopped, raised his pistol, and pointed it at Yael's leg.

The gunman gently squeezed the trigger.

Yael froze at the sound of the rifle shot. There was nowhere to go.

She was lying on the edge of the roof. If she stood up and ran, she would make herself a bigger target. She forced herself down as flat as she could, bracing herself for the exploding tiles, for the searing agony of the bullet, the plunge to earth, the moment of impact.

She looked down.

It was a twenty-foot drop into the han. With luck and a good landing she would live, but she would almost certainly break at least one limb, maybe more.

She slid forward, preparing to make the drop.

She glanced behind her, one last time.

Eli was gone.

The gunman began to dismantle his Dragunov.

It had been a tricky shot, hitting a moving target at five hundred yards. He had earned his lunch.

The gunman unscrewed the barrel; removed the stock, magazine, and telescopic sight; and placed all the pieces in a long aluminum case lined with dense foam rubber. He checked all around him, ensuring that he had not left anything behind in the dusty attic.

Just before departing, he pulled out a small leather pouch from his trouser pocket. He opened the pouch and tipped it over his hand.

A small silver and turquoise earring fell into his palm.

He stared at it for several seconds, then nodded, a smile on his face. He slipped the earring back into the case and left.

Yael lifted her head and looked down. The hairs on the back of her neck slowly settled.

President Freshwater lay on the ground, semiconscious, surrounded by Secret Service agents. Isis was handcuffed, her arms behind her. A line of agents, now backed up by Turkish plainclothes policemen, stood at the entrance to the han, blocking the crowd of journalists, who were pushing forward.

Najwa was standing with her back to the han, giving a running commentary.

Yael slowly raised her hands to show she was not a threat. "Isis!" she shouted. "It's me."

Four Secret Service agents instantly spun around, their guns trained on Yael.

Isis stared up at the roof.

"I know about Babur," said Yael. "I know how it feels. Isis, let's talk about Babur. We can work this out. Isis, please."

Reardon looked at Isis. Her face trembled.

The decision, he knew, was his alone, and had to be taken now.

"Help her down," he told the Secret Service agents, directing them toward Yael.

Isis was standing against the wall of the jewelry shop, a female Secret Service agent on either side of her. Yael saw fear, anger, but most of all, longing, grief, and regret.

"I need some time alone with her," she said to Reardon.

"We don't have time." He glanced at his watch. "Six minutes at the most."

"That should be enough," replied Yael as she walked forward. "You guarantee my authority? That anything I agree with her on will be acted on?"

"Yes, yes," said Reardon. "Just get the antidote."

"*In writing!*" shouted Isis, her face set and determined again. "I want it in writing."

"There's no time for this bullshit!" yelled Reardon.

Isis turned to Freshwater, now unconscious. "Five minutes."

Reardon gestured at the Secret Service agents. "Someone give me a pen and paper."

The paper and pen were thrust into Reardon's hand.

He quickly wrote:

By the power vested in me as the ranking US official I hereby authorize Yael Azoulay to negotiate with Isis Franklin for the antidote—any agreement reached will be honored.

Dave Reardon

He handed the paper to Isis. She read it and handed it back. "Date and place."

He scrawled the date and "Istanbul," then pushed the paper at Isis, his face murderous.

Isis nodded. "OK."

"Undo her handcuffs," said Yael.

Reardon gestured for the two agents to stand aside. One freed Isis, barely able to control her anger.

Yael sat down on the bench and beckoned for Isis to sit next to her. Reardon moved forward.

Yael shook her head. He stepped away, his fury almost tangible.

Yael held Isis's hand, their heads almost touching.

Isis shook her head, protested.

Yael looked at her, and took her other hand. Yael continued speaking for a long minute.

Isis began to cry softly. Yael nodded.

Isis stood up, walked over to the tree in the courtyard, and pointed at a spot in its base, her whole body shaking.

"*Go, go, go!*" shouted Reardon, as the Secret Service agents leapt forward.

27

TURMOIL CONTINUES AT UNITED NATIONS

Fareed Hussein Returns, Deputy Resigns, Detained US Diplomat "Used UN Connections" to Adopt Afghan Child

---

By SAMI BOUSTANI

UNITED NATIONS—Fareed Hussein, the secretary-general of the United Nations, returned to his post Monday after being absent for almost two weeks on medical leave. Mr. Hussein, who had been suffering from fainting fits, declared himself "fully recovered."

At the same time Caroline Masters, the deputy secretary-general, resigned. As acting secretary-general in Mr. Hussein's absence, Ms. Masters had taken charge of the Istanbul Summit, the global gathering last week aimed at resolving the crises in Syria, Egypt, and between Israel and the Palestinians. The summit was postponed after Isis Franklin, the head of public diplomacy at the US mission to the UN, was arrested by Turkish authorities a week ago. She is currently being held on charges of attempted murder. She is accused of trying to poison President Freshwater. Secret Service agents were able to administer the antidote for the poison in time, after a dramatic intervention by senior UN official Yael Azoulay, who persuaded Ms. Franklin to reveal the location of the antidote.

Ms. Azoulay narrowly escaped serious injury herself after a rooftop chase at Istanbul's Grand Bazaar, during which Eli Harrari, the new chief of staff at the Israeli mission to the UN, was shot in the hand. Ms. Azoulay, a former covert negotiator for Fareed Hussein, was demoted by Ms. Masters and placed in charge of the Trusteeship Council, a largely defunct arm of the organization. It is unclear why Ms. Azoulay was in Istanbul. Neither Ms. Azoulay nor the Israeli mission to the UN responded to requests for comment by telephone and e-mail.

Internal UN documents obtained by the *New York Times* show that Ms. Franklin used her UN connections to try and adopt a two-year-old orphan from Afghanistan. Ms. Franklin, an ambitious career diplomat, had previously worked for USAID in Kandahar, Afghanistan, running literacy programs and had also served in Sarajevo and Montevideo. She is divorced and has no children. Babur Hamid, the child whom Ms. Franklin planned to adopt, was killed earlier this year, along with three of his relatives, in a US drone strike. The family was en route to the UN headquarters in Kandahar, where Ms. Franklin was serving; she had planned to take charge of the child. The drone strike has been described by US officials as a "tragic mistake," but no investigation has taken place and no officials have been held to account.

Negotiations with Turkey over Ms. Franklin's extradition are continuing, said a senior US official who was not authorized to speak on the record to journalists. President Freshwater is recovering well, and is expected to be back at work next week, said a spokesman for the White House. Both Republican and Democrat leaders have pledged to speed a new bill through Congress allowing fast-track adoptions for five thousand orphans from conflict zones, including Afghanistan and Syria, by American families.

Ms. Masters's resignation will raise questions about the push by some UN officials for closer cooperation with corporations. Ms. Masters is widely seen as the architect of a controversial policy by which the UN will increasingly outsource services to the private sector. Confidential UN e-mails newly obtained by the *New York Times* reveal that as early as a year ago, Ms. Masters was negotiating a pilot scheme with Clarence Clairborne, chairman and owner of the Prometheus Group, to supply security services for the Istanbul Summit. The e-mails detail how, behind the scenes, Prometheus was working with Efrat Global Solutions (EGS), the world's largest private military contractor, which is owned by Menachem Stein.

If successful, the scheme, referred to in the e-mails as the "Washington Stratagem," would pave the way for a wholesale privatization of UN security and potentially, international peacekeeping, a market worth billions of dollars annually. Mr. Stein was named by German prosecutors as a potential co-conspirator in last year's coltan scandal. EGS, the KZX Corporation, and the Bonnet Group attempted to take control of global supplies of the mineral, which is vital for the manufacture of mobile telephones and computers.

KZX supplied the transport and accommodation for members of the New York–based UN press corps, who traveled to Istanbul for the ill-fated summit, including the *New York Times* (the *New*

York Times has made a donation to charity equivalent to the estimated cost of the flight). Earlier this month German authorities dropped all charges against three senior KZX executives and Mr. Stein. All charges have also been dropped against Joe-Don Pabst and Quentin Braithwaite, two senior UN officials who were arrested on their way to the Istanbul Summit.

Roxana Voiculescu, the newly appointed spokeswoman for Fareed Hussein, declined to answer a series of questions submitted by the *New York Times* on the relationship between Ms. Masters, the Prometheus Group, Efrat Global Solutions, and the KZX Corporation, and the reasons for the arrest of Mr. Pabst and Mr. Braithwaite. In a written statement Ms. Voiculescu said that all these matters were under investigation, as was the death of her predecessor, Henrik Schneidermann. Spokesmen for all three companies declined to return repeated telephone calls or reply to written questions by e-mail.

Mr. Hussein is likely to survive the revelations about his role in the collapse of Srebrenica and the death of three hundred civilians who were forced from the UN base there, reportedly under his direct orders, said a US official who asked not to be named as he was not authorized to speak on the record. "Nothing has been proved and Bosnia was twenty years ago. The P5 need Fareed as much as he needs them."

Yael stepped out of Saint Ignatius Loyola Church and into the warmth of a sunny April afternoon. The sky was a pale blue, studded with fluffy white clouds. The air smelled of exhaust fumes, and the road was filled with the surging tide of Manhattan's lunchtime traffic. Police officers stood on every corner, their radios crackling. More than two hundred of Henrik Schneidermann's colleagues had attended his memorial service, as well as several dozen diplomats and most of the press corps, including Sami Boustani, Najwa al-Sameera, and Jonathan Beaufort. The service had been poignant and moving. Fareed Hussein had spoken eloquently and movingly about Schneidermann's commitment to the ideals of the United Nations and the tragic loss of a life cut short. Roxana Voiculescu had also paid a touching tribute to her former colleague. The most notable absence was that of Caroline Masters.

The SG and his new spokeswoman were now standing in front of the church, on the corner of East Eighty-Fourth Street and Park Avenue, in the bright sunshine. There was a queue in front of Yael, and she waited as Hussein and Roxana greeted the mourners one by one. They both worked the crowd with impressive professionalism, shaking hands, making eye contact for several seconds, occasionally hugging the person in front of them before moving on to the next in line. Hussein looked imposing in his black Nehru jacket, black silk collarless shirt, and trousers. Roxana had splashed out, Yael saw, on a new Prada two-piece trouser suit, which she wore with a plain gray blouse and matching black and gray Christian Louboutin shoes. Her hugs, Yael noted with amusement, seemed to be confined to those of the rank of assistant secretary-general and above.

Yael's turn came and she greeted Fareed. Hussein hugged her, holding her surprisingly tightly. His belly pressed against her and she smelled his coconut hair lotion. The familiar aroma was curiously comforting, a rare constant in her chaotic life. The SG stood back and looked at her, his hands warm on her forearms.

"Welcome back, Yael. And well done. You saved the president's life. That's something to tell your grandchildren."

Yael smiled. "Thank you."

The SG looked like his old self again, confident, clear skinned, straight backed, loving being the center of attention, albeit at such a sad occasion. They exchanged a few words about Schneidermann. Beneath Hussein's public front, Yael felt his guilt and regret. They both knew that Schneidermann had been murdered—murdered because the SG had wanted to pass the Prometheus file, with the details of the connection to Salim Massoud, to Sami. However, neither of them wanted to discuss that in public, or in front of Roxana. Yael sensed Roxana watching her interaction with Hussein with intense interest, weighing and analyzing every word of the conversation and watching their body language to try and gauge the extent of their relationship.

Yael turned to Roxana. For a second she froze, unsure how to behave. Then she stepped toward Yael. The two women hugged for a second before Roxana stepped away, her body stiff and unresponsive. Yael felt the turbulence of Roxana's emotions. Irritation at Yael's obvious closeness to the SG. Confusion—why was Yael so indestructible and how come she kept bouncing back? And nervousness— what kind of threat did she represent?

The two women stepped apart. Roxana was staring at Yael, her realization that she would have to get rid of her written clearly on her face—until she suddenly remembered where she was. She gave Yael a broad smile.

Good luck with that plan, Yael thought. She smiled back until she saw Roxana looking at the jacket of her Zara trouser suit, where the button was still missing.

Roxana touched Yael's cuff, her face the very picture of guileless assistance. "I know a wonderful seamstress if you need one. She could fix that in a couple of minutes. She has the buttons from all the chain stores."

"Thanks. I can do it myself," Yael said, suddenly back in the foyer of the Prometheus Group. *Chain stores*. Now war was really declared. And she would definitely be asking for a wardrobe allowance.

Yael turned to Hussein. "I'll see you later in the office," she said, and walked around the corner of the church to wait for Joe-Don and Quentin Braithwaite. She pulled out her iPhone and flicked through Sami's story again. At least something good had come out of Istanbul. New homes for five thousand orphans. An impressive result for a few minutes' work. And Sami was doing well, she thought. He had not yet made the Iranian connection, that Prometheus was sending millions of dollars to Nuristan Holdings, a company owned by the Revolutionary Guard, or perhaps did not have enough information to go into print, but that, she was sure, would come. She could certainly speed up the process, and tell him much more about Iran, Efrat Global Solutions, and Menachem Stein—if she chose to. For now, she would think about it.

Joe-Don and Quentin Braithwaite emerged from inside the church, blinking in the sunlight. They shook hands and exchanged a few words with Hussein and Roxana and walked over to Yael.

"Drink? Lunch? Both?" asked Joe-Don.

"Both, I think," said Yael, straightening the lapel of Joe-Don's creased suit, which had been the height of fashion in 1979.

Yael looked at Roxana, her facial expression solemn but cordial as she shook hands with the French chief of mission to the UN. "That girl's going places."

"She certainly is. Forty-four blocks south and four avenues east," said Braithwaite dryly. He glanced at his watch. "In about twenty minutes, once the last mourner has been glad-handed."

Yael thought for a moment, calculating the location. "Are you sure?" Her voice was disbelieving. "He's got almost forty years on her."

"Trust me. When was the last time you saw Zeinab?" asked Braithwaite. "Hussein's wife hasn't been around for months, since the scandal about her coltan shares. The SG's booked an executive suite at the Millennium Hotel, in the name of Mr. Patel."

Absurdly, part of her felt jealous. Not because she wanted to have sex with the SG. She certainly did not. But she knew, from personal experience, that an office romance in the hothouse claustrophobic atmosphere of the UN brought a rapid, almost dizzying intimacy. Fareed was always attracted to pretty things. She knew he was lonely, with his wife away and his daughter estranged. Roxana was a more dangerous adversary than Yael had realized. Which did not bode well for Yael's quest to find out more about the death of her brother.

"We can check ourselves, if you want," said Joe-Don. He turned to Yael. "I believe you know your way around that place," he said. His voice was deadpan, but his eyes were smiling.

Yael blushed. Did Joe-Don mean her mission posing as Sharon Mantello, or her affair a few years ago with Mahesh Kapoor? Best not to ask, she decided.

"Hack alert at five o'clock," said Braithwaite, looking over Yael's shoulder.

Yael turned to see Sami walk toward her.

Sami nodded at Joe-Don and Quentin, then looked at Yael. "Can I have a minute?" he asked.

"One," said Yael.

"Please excuse us," Sami said to Joe-Don and Quentin as he guided Yael to a quieter spot, around the corner, at the side of the church.

Yael leaned against the wall, her arms folded across her chest. "What do you want?"

"You need to see this," said Sami as he passed Yael a photocopied sheet of plain paper, with that day's date.

Dear Fareed,

It is with great regret that I hereby announce my resignation from the United Nations. It has been an honor and a privilege to serve and I wish the organization every success in the future.

Yours sincerely,

Caroline Masters

Yael quickly read the letter. "So what? She's gone. Good riddance. I already read your story. I don't have any comment or insight for you. Is there anything else?"

Sami handed her another photocopied sheet.

Yael glanced down. Two words were written on it: "More follows."

"What's this?" she asked.

"It arrived with the DVD of you in the Millennium Hotel," said Sami.

Something about the letters looked familiar to Yael. Then she realized—in both printouts the letter *r* was missing its horizontal spar.

She reached inside her purse. The envelope was still there. She opened it and took out a sheet of paper. It showed three photographs: one of the Staten Island Ferry terminal and two of Cyrus Jones. The letters spelled out a date in April and a time. The letter *r* in *April* was missing its horizontal spar.

Sami looked at Yael and at the paper she was holding. "I shared," he said.

She handed Sami the paper. "Same printer."

Sami nodded. His eyes opened wide when he saw the photographs. "You know this guy?"

"You could say that," said Yael. "Do you?"

Sami did not answer. He took out his mobile telephone and scrolled through the menu until he found the video clip he was looking for. "This is strictly between us. I need your word on that," said Sami.

"Sure. Scout's honor," said Yael, her voice sarcastic.

Sami shook his head and made to put his phone away. "Forget it."

"OK, OK. You have my word."

"I'm serious," said Sami, his voice tight. "I need to trust you on this."

Yael unfolded her arms. "You can."

Sami pressed play. The video showed Cyrus Jones and another man inside Sami's apartment. It appeared to have been shot by a stationary camera, a few yards away. Yael watched Jones threaten to expose Sami as having lied on his immigration forms, accuse him of having terrorist connections through his family, and produce a series of photographs that could not be clearly seen.

"Cyrus Jones," said Yael. "He's dead."

"I know. But his friend isn't. Neither are the people who sent him, or took the photographs."

"Photographs of what?" asked Yael.

Sami looked at her for a long moment. He made his decision. "Gaza. I went to Gaza with my mother. We have relatives there."

She stares at Eli. "How about if you write a letter to the family of the boy at the Gaza checkpoint, explaining what happened? He would be, what, in his late twenties now?"

How did you film Jones and the other guy?" Yael asked, careful not reveal that she already knew about Sami's connection to Gaza.

Sami said, "I made them wait outside before they came into my apartment. I set up my laptop on the other side of the room and used the camera."

"Is there a terrorist connection?" she asked, although she already knew the answer.

"No. There is not."

Yael looked at Sami. He was wearing a well-cut black

suit, white shirt, and black silk tie. His hair was trimmed and he was clean shaven. His black eyes held her gaze. He was a bastard, she told herself, who had burned her twice. A bastard who looked stylish, cool, and confident, the *New York Times* reporter who knows there is much more to report, who is going to get the scoop. And he was a good liar.

Joe-Don appeared by the corner of the church. He looked at Yael. She smiled at him, to say that everything was under control. Joe-Don nodded and returned to wait with Braithwaite.

"Can I get a copy of this?" said Yael as she handed Sami his mobile telephone back.

"I'll think about that."

"Please do. So what's next?" Yael asked. She also had a video clip of Cyrus Jones, filmed after their fight on the Staten Island Ferry, uploaded via Shredbox to a secure, encrypted server, although she was not about to share that with Sami. At least not now.

Sami slipped his phone into his trouser pocket. "Keep on digging, I guess. Meanwhile, I'm relocating."

"Is Yuri finally giving you a bigger office? Or are you moving in with Najwa?"

Sami smiled. "Yes and no. I've been promoted. I'm heading up a new investigative unit."

"Oh," said Yael. "So you will be leaving. . . ."

Sami shook his head. "No. We will still be based in the Secretariat Building. There's too much at the UN now for me to cover on my own. KZX, Prometheus, Isis Franklin, the attempt on President Freshwater, Schneidermann. There will be another reporter working with me. She's also a Columbia graduate. She has just joined the newspaper. She knows you."

She.

"Who?" asked Yael.

"Colette Moreau. Do you remember her?"

Yael did. Chic, petite, Parisian, a line of male students queuing up to help with her assignments.

"It was nice to see you," Sami said, turning to go. "Please keep the Cyrus Jones stuff between us."

"I will, but . . ."

"But what?"

The words were out of Yael's mouth before she could stop them. "You owe me dinner."

Yael slid into the taxi, switched off the small television screen mounted on the partition behind the driver's compartment, and pulled her new dress—not quite Versace, but black and short enough—back down over her legs. The driver, a voluble Sikh in a purple turban who talked non-stop on his hands-free telephone, seemed to think he was in a rally, weaving and dodging through the traffic as he drove up Eighty-First Street. He turned right onto Broadway, tires squealing. Yael was about to tap on the window and ask him to slow down, but instead she decided to enjoy the ride.

Manhattan shone in the early-evening light, the granite façades of Upper West Side apartment blocks still varnished by the afternoon's spring showers. The taxi stopped at a traffic light at Seventy-Ninth Street. Yael opened the window. A bearded white Rastafarian was standing on the corner, playing a funked-up saxophone version of "All Blues," his dreadlocks flying. Two elderly Jewish ladies, both dressed in smart two-piece suits, their silver hair immaculately coiffed, stood gossiping outside a new pastry shop, exchanging pictures of their grandchildren. Yael looked at the window of La Caridad. The diner was already filling up for supper. The elderly Cuban man was still sitting in the corner, reading *El Diario la Prensa*, as though he had not moved since she had last had breakfast there with Joe-Don. It was hard to believe that had been barely a fortnight ago.

Yael took out a small compact from her purse and checked her makeup in the mirror: hair up, a dusting of blusher, medium-thick mascara, and bright red lipstick. A little more femme fatale than usual, she thought, turning her head from side to side, and why not?

Pleased with her new look, excited to be heading downtown on a date, she did not notice the black Mitsubishi SUV with tinted windows pull in behind the taxi, six cars away. She slipped the compact back into her purse and took out a postcard. It had arrived that morning and was blank, apart from her address and a Turkish stamp. The front was a picture of a catamaran doing a racing turn on the sea, one rudder almost out of the water, the top of the other still visible.

Yael smiled, put the card back inside her purse, and checked her watch. It was 6:30 p.m. It would take at least forty minutes to get downtown and cross over to the Lower East Side, but she was on time, even allowing for rush-hour traffic. The lights changed and the taxi driver roared down Broadway.

She suddenly looked around the taxi. Where was the

wine—a forty-dollar bottle of Puligny-Montrachet? She definitely had it when she left the apartment. She had stopped to say hello to the new doorman, she remembered. She must have put it down and left it in the lobby.

As if on cue her mobile telephone rang. Yael looked at the number—it was the lobby of her building.

"Ms. Azoulay, excuse me for bothering you," said a voice with a soft Southern Californian accent, "but I have your wine here. I'm sorry. My bad. I should have checked when I called the taxi for you. Will you come back for it? I can come out to the corner at Riverside and meet you."

"Hey, thanks, Michael; it's no problem and not your fault. I'm on my way now." Yael finished the call and leaned forward. "Can you turn around please, driver; I left something behind."

"Whatever you say, lady." The driver checked his mirror, switching lanes and turning sharp right at Seventy-Second Street, in front of a bus, triggering outraged hooting from the driver. The Mitsubishi followed the taxi, always staying at least three cars behind.

Yael was pleased that Michael had called. Raymondo, his predecessor in the lobby, had been a fixture of the building for decades. But his sudden death from a heart attack had left a vacancy. There had been a long discussion at the co-op board about Michael. Some of the residents had been opposed to giving the job to a homeless person, but Yael's impassioned plea in his favor had swung it.

Michael had just moved into the apartment building's service apartment. It was a tiny studio that looked onto a courtyard. Despite being cramped, everyone agreed it was still incomparably better than his previous lodgings—under the Soldiers' and Sailors' Memorial Monument at Eighty-Ninth Street.

The taxi driver turned onto Riverside Drive and sped up toward the corner of West Eighty-First. Yael took out her mobile telephone. She wrote a quick text message.

On my way. Forgot the wine. This time let's drink it. ☺

With the message sent, she checked the video folder. That afternoon, she had downloaded the clip of Cyrus Jones lying on the floor of the washroom of the Staten Island Ferry from the secure server. The clip was there, safely encrypted. Would she share it with her dinner date? Perhaps. It mainly depended on how the evening went.

Her phone rang, showing a 510 area code. She took the call.

"You sound excited," said Barbara.

"I'm going on a date, Mom."

"About time. You'll tell me all about him on the weekend. I land at LaGuardia on Friday at six p.m. It's been too long."

"It has." Yael looked out the window. "I'll pick you up at the airport." The Mitsubishi SUV four cars behind looked familiar. Or was she just being paranoid? "What did you want to talk to me about?"

"Not now. When I see you. But it involves your father."

The mention of her father broke Yael's mood. She

turned around and glanced at the Mitsubishi again. Tinted windows. Her sixth sense was howling. There was definitely something wrong here.

"OK, Mom," she said. "Can't wait to see you. Gotta go."

The taxi started to slow down as they approached the corner of Eighty-First Street. Yael could see Michael the doorman standing under the dark-green awning, holding her wine. She ended her call, leaned forward, and spoke to the driver. The wine, and dinner, would have to wait. Again. The driver smiled and nodded. Yael sat back and braced herself.

Two hundred and thirty miles away, Clarence Clairborne sat back in his office chair, a glass of bourbon in his hand, a cigar smoldering gently in the nearby ashtray. His computer screen showed Yael's taxi doing a sudden and illegal U-turn on Riverside Drive, sailing past the Mitsubishi SUV that was now on the other side of the road. Clairborne frowned, reached over to his telephone, and punched in a number.

AUTHOR'S NOTE

M y interest in the United Nations began in the early 1990s, when I covered the Yugoslav wars. That experience led to my nonfiction book *Complicity with Evil: The United Nations in the Age of Modern Genocide*, which examines the UN's failures in Bosnia, Rwanda, and Darfur. I welcome feedback from readers and reply to every e-mail. Contact me at aleborwork@gmail.com or follow me on Facebook or Twitter: @adamlebor.

ACKNOWLEDGMENTS

Every writer should be blessed with an editor as talented and dedicated as Hannah Wood at HarperCollins US. Her scrupulous attention to plot, character, and narrative drive helped turn a first draft into a book. Thanks also to Claire Wachtel, who launched the Yael Azoulay series, and to Matthew Patin and Julie Hersh for their eagle-eyed copyediting. A big shout-out goes to the team at William Morris Endeavor: in London, Elizabeth Sheinkman, Jo Rogers, Annemarie Blumenhagen, and Amy Fitzgerald; in Los Angeles, Anna DeRoy and Erin Conroy; in New York, Suzanne Gluck and Samantha Frank gave me valuable editorial feedback, and thanks also to Eve Atterman. On the television front, working with Lynda Obst, Rachel Abarbanell, and Stephen Schiff has been both a pleasure and an education.

I am grateful to my friends Clive Rumbold and Paulina Bren, who read early drafts of this book and provided much-appreciated feedback and advice. Many thanks to Dan Bilefsky, who edited Sami Boustani's articles, excised Britishisms, and ensured that Sami's copy kept to the rules of the *New York Times* stylebook. Once again, "Z" proved a most valuable guide to the dark side of American politics. Ruth Gruber gave me some useful pointers about Israelis and Palestinians. In Britain, Peter Jenkins kindly invited me to join a course on surveillance run by his company, ISS Training Ltd. (www .intelsecurity.co.uk), where I learned much about this most subtle of arts. Peter also gave me a copy of his excellent book, *Surveillance Tradecraft*. In Istanbul, Andrew Finkel, author of *Turkey: What Everyone Needs to Know*, read the manuscript, generously shared his insight, and corrected minor errors. Andrew also introduced me to Monica Fritz, who took me on an insider's tour of Istanbul's Grand Bazaar, including a memorable stroll on the roof. *Teşekkür ederim!* Thanks also to Lt. Joseph Leal of the UN Security and Safety Service, and to Special Agents Anne C. Beagan and Robert L. Moore at the New York Field Office of the Federal Bureau of Investigation.

Val McDermid and Andrew Taylor were inspiring tutors at an Arvon Foundation course on crime writing. Peter Savodnik's article on Astara in *The Atlantic* was a small masterpiece. Carne Ross, of Independent Diplomat, was always insightful. Matthew Thomas, a sharp-eyed reader, gave me some welcome feedback. My fellow thriller writer Matthew Dunn has been generous with his praise. Joshua Freeman kept me company on a day trip to Staten Island. *The Dönme: Jewish Converts, Muslim Revolutionaries, and Secular Turks*, by Marc David Baer, was both fascinating and informative. Thanks, as ever, to my hosts in New York: Peter Green, Bob Green, and Babette Audant. In Budapest, Csaba Szikra introduced me to Krav Maga and Marton Pinter honed my rudimentary skills. Leora Seboek corrected my Hebrew grammar. Justin Leighton, Roger Boyes, Annika Savill, Sam Loewenberg, and Lutz Kleveman were always encouraging. Thanks most of all, of course, to my family.

ABOUT THE AUTHOR

ADAM LEBOR lives in Budapest and writes for *The Economist*, the *New York Times*, *Monocle*, *Newsweek*, the *Daily Beast*, and numerous other publications. He is the author of a number of nonfiction books, including *Tower of Basel*, the first investigative history of the secretive Bank for International Settlements; the groundbreaking work *Hitler's Secret Bankers* (short-listed for the Orwell Prize), which revealed the extent of Swiss complicity with the Third Reich; *City of Oranges* (short-listed for the Jewish Quarterly Literary Prize); and *Complicity with Evil*, an investigation into the United Nations' failure to stop genocide.

www.adamlebor.com
@adamlebor

BOOKS BY ADAM LEBOR

THE WASHINGTON STRATAGEM
A Yael Azoulay Novel

Available in Paperback and eBook

In this action-packed, suspenseful sequel to the international thriller *The Geneva Option*, UN covert negotiator Yael Azoulay is drawn into a web of betrayal and intrigue that leads from deep within America's military-industrial complex to the Middle East and beyond.

THE GENEVA OPTION
A Yael Azoulay Novel

Available in Paperback and eBook

A gripping thriller of international espionage, *The Geneva Option* pits a young, smart UN staffer against a brutal conspiracy to control Africa's natural resources.

THE ISTANBUL EXCHANGE
A Yael Azoulay Short Story

Available in eBook

Yael Azoulay, the brilliant and beautiful negotiator for the United Nations, is tasked with persuading an Afghan warlord to surrender to the Americans. The high-stakes game soon turns deadly as Yael finds herself up against a shadowy agency of the US government.

THE BUDAPEST PROTOCOL
A Novel

Available in eBook

Inspired by the 1944 "Red House" meeting of Nazi industrialists to plan for Germany's post-war recovery, this riveting thriller spins a web of conspiracy linking Central Europe's Nazi past to the fascist renaissance shadowing its present-day politics, revealing a hidden heart of darkness . . .